Brenna Lyons

Paranormal Paramours

FIREBORN
PUBLISHING

All characters and events in this book are fictitious. Any resemblance to actual persons, living or dead, is strictly coincidental.

This book is written in US English.

PUBLISHER

FIREBORN
PUBLISHING

PO Box 5216
Haverhill, MA 01835

Nevermore

Dedicated to...

Tamer, who hasn't quite tamed me yet.

Nevermore

Traia sat before the fire, fuming that she'd been reduced to this. She was a witch. A witch! She was supposed to be smart. At the very least, she was supposed to be more powerful than her adversaries were, than the pathetic creatures that skulked in the darkness.

How a pointed-eared, shape-shifting mutt had tricked her in the first place was a mystery. His getting a hook in her soul was unbelievable. Traia was hardly a dabbler or even a journeywoman. Far from it.

She was *Mistress* Traia, strong in the natural magicks and learned in spells of protection and healing. People traveled days to barter for her aid. Those who were in great need paid modestly for what they sought. Those who asked for the frivolous or foolish paid more than they could afford as a lesson.

If she failed tonight, those days were over. All she had to do was keep the stinking werewolf away from her...or kill him.

For some reason she couldn't name, the thought of killing him sent a completely unwarranted pain through her. It wasn't right to feel this way. If he reached her again, her wards were useless.

"He'll rip my throat out." Traia pressed a hand to it, abruptly nauseated. Losing her livelihood would be bad enough. Losing her life was decidedly worse.

And what werewolf wouldn't kill a witch who knew what he was? None that she'd heard of.

* * * *

Galen watched the cottage from the tree line, his palms sweating at what he was about to attempt. Of all the women to set off his mating instincts, the *usually* fair and kind Goddess had cursed him with a witch.

What did I do to deserve this one? He tried to live a good life, despite his cursed birth. Galen wasn't a nomad like most of his kind. He didn't kill farmers' stock and deprive the innocent of their livelihood. But he'd obviously gone wrong somehow.

"Badly wrong," he muttered.

His shoulder ached in a stark reminder that Traia would doubtless try to kill him again, given the chance to. It had taken several weeks to heal the wound that would have killed any human man.

Had he been any slower, or Traia's aim been true, Galen wouldn't have needed the reminder. Instead, he would be the occupant of a shallow grave, laden with monkshood and witches' potions to guarantee his descent into hell. Still, he couldn't help wondering if Traia's aim was so bad or if her heart hadn't been in the attack.

There was only one way to solve this. He would have to go to her. Either the night would end with Traia as his mate, or Galen would be dead by her hand. With his instincts raging, Galen couldn't walk away. Nor could he harm her.

He could, however, seduce her again, if she gave him the chance to do so. Just the thought of it had him hard in anticipation. It was a certain wager that Traia wouldn't submit without a fight, and a buck in the mating cycle loved nothing more than a challenge.

The tickle of the near-full moon on his neck reminded Galen that it was time to claim his mate. "Or die trying," he reminded himself. That was a disheartening thought, but it was accurate. There was a good reason bucks avoided the chance of scenting a mate.

Galen ambled to the border of her circle of power, shivering at the tingle of her wards and shields against his skin. They were stronger now, but by the decree of the Goddess Herself, they could not keep him from what was his own.

Traia's scent had drawn him in, but the invitation of her protective spells had confirmed what she was to him. Only someone who meant Traia no harm would be welcomed in, and his mate was the only person in the world Galen wasn't in danger of harming.

Smiling at the irony of the situation, he stepped across the line of power. He couldn't harm Traia— didn't want to harm her—but she was about to do her best to kill him. Though her magick was useless against him, her blade wasn't.

"Yet." A smile twisted his lips at the thought of the truth she would have to face, then disappeared at his mind's rebuke. She would only have to face it *if* he succeeded.

Caution firmly in mind, Galen took the final steps and knocked smartly on her door. He bit back a laugh at her muttered curses.

* * * *

Traia didn't question who knocked at her door. With vampires, weres, and zombies hunting the night, no human came to her door after sundown, late enough that he couldn't complete his business with her and return to the safety of his own shields before the sky darkened. She rarely saw visitors after mid-afternoon.

He knocked again, a jaunty little children's song backbeat. Traia crossed one leg over the other, making a conscious effort at ignoring him. Though it probably wouldn't discourage him, Traia was hardly about to invite him in.

He's not a vampire, she reminded herself. Refusing to invite him in would make little difference.

Vampire or not, I am not welcoming a foul creature into my home.

He knocked a third time, a more impatient cadence, heavier than the previous inquiries. "Traia." His voice was soft, taunting, and all too familiar.

Traia bristled. "I've been nice so far, mutt. Push me much farther and I'll make cuffs of your hide."

He laughed at the warning. "Now, Traia. The fact that I'm knocking on your door should tell you something."

"That you're persistent and stupid?" she ventured rudely. *He deserves no better.*

"That your shields and traps won't work against me," he countered.

"They are simple magick. I have stronger." As if to reassure herself, Traia picked up the items she would use to drive him off. Her gaze strayed to the final weapon in her arsenal, and she shuddered at the thought of using it.

"Perhaps." The truth didn't seem to concern him. "Probably so."

"If you enter my home, you will be carried out." Memories of his tall, strong body prompted a silent addition to that statement. *By a very strong man or two of lesser strength.*

"Would you care to open the door and be proven wrong? I would hate to have to break it down to do so."

The presumption! He really is a dog.

"Traiaaaa..."

She shivered in arousal. Her thighs dampened, and her nipples tightened. It didn't make sense. She knew what he was. Why was he still able to affect her this way?

Traia forced her mouth to unglue. "The door is not bolted."

He hesitated. "You're inviting me in?"

"You wish."

His dark chuckle set off another round of shivers and several warning bells. Traia wished she could claim a sense of dread caused them, but nothing about his approach made her feel it. It was only her mind screaming warnings. It made no sense. Her senses had never failed her so completely before. Then again, neither had her magick.

The door opened, and Traia's mind rioted. She'd invited him in the first time—had she nullified her defenses in the process?

No. He's not a vampire. Vampires were the only ones who nullified the magick with an invitation. Not to mention, the vampire had to be invited in at each visit, and she certainly hadn't done so. Not at the shield line and not at her door.

He stepped into her line of sight, and for a moment, Traia forgot how to breathe. *Galen!* Goddess, but the man was beautiful. And he knew how to use that cock to keep her in bliss.

Too bad he means to rip my throat out.

As if in agreement, he licked his lips. Traia raised the silver amulet in warning, belatedly musing that she should have simply tied it around her throat.

Galen arched an eyebrow at the move. The door swung shut behind his hand, and he added the bolt for good measure.

Traia stared at him in disbelief. He was cutting off his means of escape. In her moment of indecision, Galen stripped off his shirt and started toward her.

* * * *

Galen inhaled her scent, an intoxicating mix of adrenaline and ready woman. His cock and fangs lengthened in response to the challenge. There was no question Traia wanted him, but she would fight herself and him to deny them both what they needed. It was a witch's way.

Traia scrambled to her feet, gathering up her trinkets of power in a vain attempt to kill him. If she were any other witch, he'd be a mile away and still running. But she was his mate.

Luckily for him, Traia had never studied the wolf tomes. She was the typical superior witch; there was nothing a lowly mutt book could teach her. His lip curled in wry amusement and disgust mixed.

No, there is nothing the wolf tomes can teach you. Nothing except that you are powerless as a human against me...and I am as safe as a puppy with you.

Traia thrust the monkshood stake at his heart.

Galen snatched it from her hand, smiled, and pitched it over his shoulder. Ordinarily he would be in agony, but not with his mate handling the weapon. "I do prefer the flowers," he teased. It was a lie, of course. While they would have no effect on him—if Traia carried them—the smell of the flowers was abhorrent to him, in general.

Her eyes went wide, and she held up a woven twig doll decorated with the usual strings, candle wax, and other effects, anointed in oils and rubbed with potent herbs.

He snapped it in two and let his half fall to the floor. "We have better things to play with, Traia." Her attempts excited him past reason. He'd known she would fight him. He'd dreamed of it for weeks.

She dropped her half of the doll and pressed the silver amulet to his bare chest, to the lupine mark she'd tried to spear their first morning together. Galen hummed in pleasure at her touch, and his cock jerked in anticipation of the bedding to come.

"I don't...don't understand," she stuttered. Her deep blue eyes pleaded with him. Her eyes were a gift, the color of the eastern sky late in a sunset.

Galen turned his head, nipping her wrist playfully.

"No," she gasped.

Traia released the amulet, and it landed in his hand. Galen settled it carefully around her neck. It might hold no power against him, but it would protect her from other weres. She dragged it off and threw it. He watched it fly, noting its path. Traia *would* wear the amulet.

She turned to run, and Galen wrapped his arms around her. No doubt she meant to make it to the dagger on her worktable or some other weapon she could still strike him down with. As long as Traia didn't do that, there was a chance for them.

She fought him, twisting in Galen's arms. His cock thickened fully at the challenge...at the struggle with his mate. A strong woman was every buck's dream come true.

Traia's teeth pressed to his forearm.

Galen smiled at the move. *You should have read the wolf tomes.* She didn't know what biting him would do, and that would work in his favor.

He groaned at her breaking skin, at the trickle of blood escaping his body and coursing into her mouth. Traia didn't know it, but she'd played right into his hands. He would have had to find a way to make her drink from him; the bite was a dream come true. Perhaps the Goddess wasn't quite as put out with him as he'd thought. His arms tightened, a silent urging for her to continue, to bite down harder and speed the process.

The change came over her at a painful pace not unlike the moments when the last of the moon's glow surrounded the far hilltops and taunted him with the return to humanity. Traia's struggles weakened, then ceased. Her teeth eased away, but her mouth remained. His cock bucked at the first weak suckling motions.

"That's right," he crooned.

Traia collapsed in his arms, her breathing harsh. She turned to him, opened his trousers with shaking fingers, and stroked a hand up and down his cock.

It was what he'd been waiting for: the mindless need. Galen captured her lips, growling at his blood in her mouth and staining her face. Traia tangled her tongue with his, her hand working him more eagerly.

Just when Galen would have broken off the kiss to proceed to something more involved, Traia went to her knees. Her mouth engulfed his cock, and she worked him in and out.

He tangled his hand in her hair, every muscle strung tight. Galen didn't worry that she'd bite down and attempt to emasculate him. In the fervor, she wouldn't consider hurting him. Even if she did, his blood would still the urge and make her more fevered for his loving, and his accelerated healing would take care of the damage.

She sucked hard, moaning around his length, causing an alien tremor in his hand. Traia had started the process of bonding by biting him. Before the night was over, she'd finish it.

She became more avid. One hand worked his sac while she sucked. The other opened fasteners on her clothing.

The combination of sights and scents, coupled with her ardent sucking, was too much for him. Galen climaxed into her mouth with a roar of possession.

Traia rocked back on her heels, cum dotting her deep red lips as his blood had moments earlier. He pulled her to her feet, stripping her clothing away. She shook her head slowly, speaking bits of words that made no sense. Galen took his time, pushing his trousers to his ankles and stepping out of them.

He lifted Traia over his shoulder and carried her to the bed they'd shared, grabbing bright-colored scarves from her worktable as he walked past. Halfway there, she started struggling again. Her fists pounded against him ineffectually, and her nails dug furrows in his back.

Galen stopped, gasping for breath. "If you keep challenging me, I will be hard all night."

Traia went still. At first, he thought he'd shocked her into the response. Then her mouth pressed to one of the cuts. Galen groaned, then again as she sucked at him. Now that she'd had a taste, the smell of his blood drew her.

At the limits of endurance, Galen deposited Traia on the mattress. The sight of her hair fanned over the pillows, as dark and glossy as raven wings, stole his breath.

Her tensing muscles spurred him to motion. His blood wouldn't keep her enraptured for long. Galen had to have Traia tied down before she recovered her senses enough to attack him...and before he was the one incapacitated by the bonding.

* * * *

Traia's head cleared minutely, enough to curse the mixed flavors in her mouth. What was his blood doing to her?

She reassured herself that it wasn't turning her into a werewolf. Blood exchanges were for vampires. Bites were for zombies.

Despite the old human myths, werewolves didn't turn others. They mauled, maimed. Murdered. But they couldn't curse another with their bites.

"You're going to rip my throat out," she murmured. It should have concerned her more than it did, but her mind was still muddled. Galen had overpowered her senses with some magick that was foreign to her.

His dark laughter sent curls of awareness through her body. It was all she could do to swallow down pleas for his cock.

Galen paused in the process of binding her left ankle, his golden gaze panning up her body from between her wide-spread legs. "There are parts of you I'd much rather eat than your delicate throat."

It took a moment for his meaning to sink in. When it did, she moaned at the mindless response of her body.

He sank a long finger into her, baring his fangs in a wide smile. Traia gasped, pushing her hips up as far as the scarves allowed.

"That's right," he crooned. "Invite me in."

Traia shook her head in a negative response. The old magick claimed you should never invite an enemy in, vampire or not.

Was that where I went wrong? When she'd first seen Galen standing on her stoop, she'd been fooled by his fine clothing and grooming. The foul were reported to always show signs of what they were. Why didn't Galen?

She'd been charmed by his height, his red-brown hair and golden eyes, and by his persistence and attention to her pleasure. Overall, she'd been lulled into a false security by his ability to pass through her shields.

"No. I won't invite you in." It was one line she wouldn't cross.

The hair on his chest and arms bristled in warning, and his eyes narrowed. Slowly, deliberately, Galen started pumping his finger in and out of her.

"You do invite me," he reminded her, no doubt referring to her traitor body's ready state. "And still you challenge me." He added a second finger, wringing a gasp from her.

His earlier words echoed in her mind. "If I was no challenge, you'd lose interest?"

Galen added a third finger, teasing her with the length and girth they both knew she wanted. "You're inviting me in then?"

Traia cursed silently at the position he'd maneuvered her into. If she didn't invite him in, she was a challenge the wolf lived for, the hunt he thrived on. If she did, she was surrendering to him.

She shook her head. "Nevermore," she forced out.

"Then you will always be a challenge," he concluded.

Her heart stuttered at that. *Always?* Whether he killed her or screwed her, she'd thought the challenge was for the night.

Werewolves were nomads. They constantly moved on to further kills, new hunting grounds...fresh meat to sate the palate.

Except with a mate. The nomad beast established a range around a mate's home, enchanting her with his own brand of magick, protecting her, moving if she moved. *Planting his were sons and human daughters.*

Is that what this is? Is that the spell he's woven over me?

But how could he?

Humans had only the magick they purchased from witches to fight with. Those spells could have been set by the inexperienced. Those who bought them might have skimped on the price. Maybe they couldn't afford spells at all.

None of that was true of Traia.

Galen's fingers moved more insistently, reminding her of the challenge he'd set.

"I do not intend to bear your puppies," she ground out from between teeth clenched in pleasure instead of fury.

A crooked smile pulled up one side of his mouth. "They will be babies, Traia." He twisted inside her, seeking out the deep pleasure spot he'd found countless times their first night together. "And you will beg me to plant each one."

The denial stuck in her throat. He had her at the edges of climax. If he'd just touch her clit, she would shatter. *And he knows it.*

Confirming that, he passed his thumb close enough to fire her nerves with radiant heat. "Shall it be my thumb that finishes you off?" he offered.

Traia forced herself into a shake of her head. Her legs tensed and trembled with need. Her breathing went harsh. It was sweet agony. With her legs and arms tied down, she couldn't finish herself. Galen could keep her at the edges all night.

"My mouth?" he suggested.

She whimpered. Her turncoat hips cycled up and down in a parody of a nod.

Galen was ruthless. His sucking mouth was bruising in its intensity, just the added stimulus she needed to climax hard.

His fingers retreated, and his tongue thrust inside her spasming body. Traia grasped at the scarves, her cries echoing off the stone walls.

He growled, the vibrations sending her into a stronger climax. His fangs scratched at the tender folds of her sex, mixing sweet pleasure with pain.

Traia wondered vaguely if he'd drawn blood. As if in answer, Galen withdrew and started sucking at her body, greedily drinking down her mixed flavors much like she'd done with him. At the thought, aftershocks wracked her, and Galen groaned.

He didn't hesitate. In the next moment, Galen was feasting on her, inside and out. Climaxes overlapped, soaking her already muddled mind in rapture.

Words exploded from her throat. Traia didn't care what they were. Most likely, she was begging for his talented cock. She might even be begging to carry young weres, for all she knew.

She must have offered something Galen wanted to hear. The cock thrusting deep into her attested that she'd said something right.

Right?

Oh yes, this felt right. Nothing—not even her first night with Galen—compared with how right this felt.

The guilt she'd expect to accompany such a shocking thought didn't emerge. Who could feel guilt while experiencing such pleasure?

Memories of the delightful pleasure-pain he'd gifted her with had Traia biting her lower lip, trying to recreate it. Galen went still, half-sheathed in her, urging her mouth open for a searing kiss. Then he was sucking at her lower lip, her chin...her throat.

Just when she would have tensed, he laid a gentle kiss at her pulse point. It was a completely disconcerting thing for a marauding werewolf to do.

He started thrusting again, hard and fast, staking a claim she was at a loss to fully comprehend. And she didn't care. Goddess, but she wanted this!

"Bind yourself to me." Galen didn't order her. It was a request, nearly a plea.

Traia stared up at him, waiting for some instruction in how to accomplish such a thing.

"Surrender to me."

His cock working her as it was, Traia couldn't imagine anything she'd want more than that. Visions of Galen binding her in countless positions made her dizzy.

That simply, climax loomed over her. "Yes!" No man had made her come like Galen did.

He pushed to the hilt in her and halted, stretching Traia to the limits of endurance and beyond. A litany of pleas for more left her lips.

Galen extended one wicked-looking claw and slashed the lupine birthmark that lay off-center on his broad chest. Traia watched the blood bead up, shoving away memories of her attempts to pierce the mark the morning she'd woken with him and realized what manner of creature he was.

"Surrender to me."

She knew what Galen wanted. Her mouth watered at the chance to taste him again, loathsome as she would have found the thought an hour ago.

"Traia."

She extended her tongue, swiping off the beads of powerful lifeblood.

Galen's cock bucked against the walls of her sheath, and he moaned. "Don't tease," he admonished.

Traia raised her head, suckling hard at the cut, heat radiating through her body until she felt faint in it. Galen roared, his cock erupting with wave after wave of cum.

He moved, nestling his mouth to the base of her throat. Traia sobbed, tensing in preparation for the expecting tearing.

It didn't come. Galen laid a line of gentle kisses from her throat to her collarbone. He nipped with his fangs just enough to fire her nerves and draw blood. He sucked, leaving a love bite that encompassed the marks left by his teeth.

In the aftermath, they lay together, Galen drawing scent from her hair, his cock softening within her.

"You haven't surrendered to me," he whispered. "Not fully. You won't just invite me inside again." The thought didn't seem to bother him.

Traia darkened in impotent fury at the truth that it was just another challenge to him. "Nevermore," she vowed.

His eyes glittered, and his renewed cock eased out of her. Galen took his time, raking a gaze up and down her body that heated her blood and made her heart race. "We shall see."

* * * *

Traia opened her eyes to the gray of predawn, staring at Galen in the semidarkness of her home. Her entire body ached pleasantly from the excesses of the night before.

16

She had no memory of Galen untying her arms. On some level, she was glad she didn't remember; Traia hoped he'd unbound them after she'd slid into sleep. The memories of him unbinding her legs were embarrassing enough. She hadn't kicked at him or pushed him away with them. Instead, she'd wrapped them tight around Galen while she'd begged for more of his cock.

Why Galen had chosen to leave her unrestrained was a mystery. He'd said it often enough: Traia hadn't surrendered herself to him. She had no intention of being his mate, despite the quality of the sex.

That in mind, she started to rise. Something indefinable stopped her.

Traia worked at it, at a loss. True, Galen was as physically stunning as he'd always been. True, he played at her body as a master musician would his instrument.

But that doesn't mean I'll bind myself to a murdering mutt.

She slid from the mattress, careful not to wake him, and padded across the stone floor to her worktable.

The spell lay in readiness, only awaiting the final incantation. It had taken her thirteen days to prepare it. The other four she'd cast had only added to its potency. Though she'd believed the lesser magick would repel Galen and hurt him, in some cases, she'd prepared this last to kill him.

She'd planned to touch the bowl and speak the words when she'd bolted from him the night before. His restraining arms had prevented her from doing it then.

And his blood on her tongue had caused some change she didn't fully comprehend.

Again, that alien pain sliced in the vicinity of her heart at the thought of doing him harm. Traia swallowed down a growl of frustration. Whatever this magick was, it would die with him. All magick did. A witch would never suffer being bound without seeking retribution.

Resolved, Traia settled her left hand on the edge of the bowl and picked up the dagger in her right. The words tripped off her tongue in a rush.

She looked up at Galen, steeling herself for his anguished cries, his inhuman howls. There was nothing. No response to the magick she'd unleashed at him. He sighed in his sleep, rubbing his whiskered cheek on the pillow as if intent on leaving his scent behind.

I must have misspoken the words. It was the only possible answer.

Traia opened the ancient text to the spell and then placed her hand back on the bowl. She forced herself to slow, to annunciate each phoneme of the incantation.

The silence in the wake of her efforts was mind numbing. The answer brought her rage to a full boil. He'd stolen her magick; somehow, Galen had done the impossible. He'd rendered her powerless. *He's made me human.*

Her hand tightened around the hilt of the dagger, and she sprung at him. Her left hand had clenched as well, and her movement sent the bowl crashing to the floor. She ignored the discordant sound and added a bellow of fury.   ı

The sound woke him, and Galen turned her way, his eyes widening as they had the last time she'd come at him with a blade. This time, he didn't swing to intercept or deflect the weapon.

Instead, he rolled to his back and spread his arms. It was an irreverent challenge, she guessed, based on his mocking smile.

* * * *

Though he knew her limitations, Galen's heart pounded in fear at the sight of Traia hurtling toward him with a blade in hand. Her arm arced down toward his lupine mark, just to the left of his heart. Of the two, it was the one guaranteed to kill him.

It stopped a whisper from his skin. Galen sighed in relief, then swallowed down a laugh. Traia would certainly mistake it for a taunt if it escaped him.

She growled, trying to force the dagger down with two shaking hands. Galen watched her with mounting pride. Every buck dreamed of having a woman this strong beside him.

The blade tip pricked his chest, and Galen shivered in delight. Traia was the strongest woman he'd ever known. Even now, the terror that she was more powerful than the mating magick persisted, giving him a healthy fear of the woman he loved.

Then the blade was gone, pitched across the room to clatter in the cold hearth. Traia dropped to the floor, burying her face in her hands. Sobs wracked her body.

The sound ripped at him. Traia was his mate. Galen rolled off the mattress and landed in a crouch behind her. He hesitated and then wrapped his arms around her. She fought him, and Galen found himself praying to the Goddess that she wouldn't bite him again.

It wasn't that he feared injury. Her bites and scratches of the previous night had already healed to broken pink lines and would be gone entirely in another few hours.

Rather, Galen didn't want Traia to launch them both into another mating frenzy. Nothing would be resolved that way. She would simply emerge more confused and upset at the end of their romp.

The only way to solve this was to forge on. "Why are you crying?" he asked. He had his suspicions, of course, but it was best not to make assumptions.

"Why? Why!" she screeched. Traia turned on him, trying to lay punches that Galen blocked.

"Tell me why, Traia."

She growled at him. "You've stolen my magick, and you dare ask—"

"No!" he denied.

Traia made another attempt to strike him. When she failed, she glared at him.

"Your magick isn't gone," he soothed her. "And the changes are the work of the Goddess, not me."

"I've tried," she snapped. "I cannot—"

"You cannot harm *me*," Galen corrected. "You can cast no spell or craft no amulet or ward that will keep me away or harm *me*."

Her brow furrowed, and Traia worked at words that didn't come readily to her tongue.

"Try it," he invited.

Her face darkened to crimson, and she averted her eyes. It was a sure sign that she'd attempted to harm him with magick before attacking him with the dagger.

"Try to light the fire, Traia. Use your magick to draw something to you. But not your dagger," he hastened to add. "If you intend to harm me with it, your magick may fail." He wasn't certain it was true, but it couldn't hurt to discourage her.

Traia swallowed hard. She extended a trembling hand toward the hearth. With a gesture and a series of whispered words, it roared to life. She pressed her hands to her chest, paused, then nodded.

"And...the dagger?" she gasped out.

Galen tipped her chin up. "We are mated, Traia. By the Goddess's decree, you cannot harm me. Nor can I harm you."

* * * *

Traia worked at that, her head spinning. They couldn't harm each other? Her heart sank with the realization that it wasn't so.

"What is it?" There was something tender and completely at odds with what she knew Galen to be in that question.

"Your presence here harms me," she blurted out. Another part of her screamed that his leaving would harm her as much or more.

"How?"

"How?" Her voice went shrill again. How blind was he?

"How?" he repeated patiently. Galen dipped his head and inhaled her scent. His cock rose between them in response.

"Stop that!" Sex did not erase the very real problems they faced.

He offered a wicked smile. "How do I harm you by being here?"

Traia rolled her eyes. "A werewolf in the village I personally protect?" she hinted. "Stock going missing? My wards and shields failing, because it is *you* testing them?"

He chuckled. Then he laughed...great whooping laughs.

She slapped him, wincing that she was still able to do it. Traia had fully expected her hand to rebound, but perhaps—with his werewolf healing—a slap wasn't seen as more than an annoyance.

Galen seemed unfazed by her reaction. "I have a farm, Traia. I raise my own meals."

Traia considered his clothing and appearance. If he was careful to hide his birthmark... If he was careful in his dealings, it would be possible to hide his curse from neighboring farmers. Her mouth went dry at the implications. "You're not a nomad," she guessed. She'd heard wild tales of tame weres, but she hadn't believed them.

He shook his head. "My farm is one village over. I could construct a shop like this one on the outskirts of my lands. It wouldn't be a far move for you." His fingers tunneled in her feminine curls, as if his decree was enough to solve their difficulties.

She smacked at his hand. "You're taking an awful lot for granted. Aren't you?"

Galen leaned toward her, his cock bobbing in excitement, most likely at her challenge of his decision. "The choice is yours, Traia. Here, where a werewolf is ruining your reputation, or at my farm, where I'm not." One brow went up to punctuate the choice.

"Are you going to make every interaction a loaded choice?" she countered, already resigned that he'd prevailed again.

"It seems to be working so far," he taunted.

Traia crossed her arms under her breasts. She knew full well that her next move would incite him, but that held a power and magick all its own. By challenging him, she would get what she wanted, when she wanted. "Nevermore."

Black Sail

Dedication

Ms. Harrigan, who assigned Edith Hamilton's *Mythology* to her Sophomore class and fed my love for mythology.

Ms. B, who taught me careful research and cross-checking facts.

All the people at the Mystic Moon, who will understand this story better than anyone else who knows me.

Author's Note

All my facts come from Edith Hamilton's *Mythology*. Initial readers challenged the facts I used to weave the web of this story, but careful examination showed that cross-referencing the facts does tie the basic premise of *Black Sail* together. I hope you enjoy the story, and rest assured, there are more like this to come.

NOTE for those who don't know the story of Theseus intimately: Theseus was killed at the home of his friend King Lycomedes. I will leave it to the reader's imagination to decide exactly how that happened after reading this tale.

Happy reading!

Brenna

Black Sail

The birds were loud that morning. Ariadne opened one eye a slit, viewing the lush vegetation of Naxos. Did the blasted birds have to celebrate the day so early? Apparently so.

She rolled over with a sigh and pushed the woven blanket off. It was a warm, sunny day with a brisk breeze—a good day to hang the blanket to air and wash the meager clothing she had created for herself in the last year.

Naxos was a beautiful place, a fitting exile for a princess, she supposed. Ariadne laughed at the pampered life she'd once had. *A daughter of Minos! A princess of Crete!* "Ha," she barked at the clear, blue sky, startling a family of birds into hasty flight.

"*A* princess!" Of course, that had always been her problem. Ariadne was simply *a* princess, not *the* princess. She had never been *the* princess.

When Theseus had come to her father's kingdom, Ariadne had not known he was the prince of Athens. She saw a wealthy man, a beautiful and fearless man, a man unlike any she was like to have on Crete.

With her sister Phaedra around, no man was interested in Ariadne. If only the pampered toy had married, perhaps one of her lovesick throng might have glanced Ariadne's way. Phaedra, however, would not deign to simply choose a husband. She was like to taunt the men endlessly, raising the stakes of her affections until some fool set the stars at her feet in homage. By then, Ariadne would be an old woman.

When beautiful Theseus boldly offered himself as a sacrifice to the Minotaur's labyrinth, Ariadne saw her chance. She sent for Daedelus and bribed him for a way to allow Theseus to escape the deadly maze. That her actions were treason affected her not. Anything was worth escaping Crete and having a life away from Phaedra.

Hiding herself in the rough cloak of a commoner, Ariadne approached the prisoners with food. The guards looked through her, as they usually did with commoners who came to care for the offerings to the Minotaur. She found her golden man in private rooms and offered him a simple trade, the secret of the labyrinth for his promise to take her back to Athens as his wife.

"Who are you that you have such knowledge?" he asked her in hushed tones.

"I am the younger daughter of Minos. Do you accept my bargain?"

His eyes glittered in the near-darkness of the room. "You have my vow. Hide yourself away on my ship and do not show your face until we are away. We set sail immediately after I best the trap. What is the secret?"

Ariadne explained the string Theseus must tie at the entrance and play out behind him as he moved.

His fingers brushed hers as she gave him the ball of string to hide within his clothing.

Theseus touched her face and drew Ariadne to his body to kiss her. With words of thanks and love, he took her maidenhead in his darkened room. Theseus was a gentle lover, erasing her pain with wave upon wave of pure bliss. As Ariadne left him, he gave her a momento off his person, his embroidered sash, to prove to his men that she was coming aboard under his protection.

Ariadne went to the docks with a small pack of her belongings and the sash before Theseus even set foot in the labyrinth. She knew her father would not miss her presence with his jewel at his side.

For almost a day, Ariadne paced his quarters, afraid that Daedelus' plan had failed and she would be denied her promised husband, her gentle lover. When the cry went up that Theseus had boarded, Ariadne longed to run to him, but she had to remain hidden as he ordered.

At last, she heard his voice in the corridor. "...the princess of Athens...all the wealth you could imagine..."

Ariadne threw open the door but stopped short of throwing herself at him. She stood frozen in shock.

Phaedra was on his arm.

For a moment, no one spoke, though Phaedra's face was set in a smug smile that announced her perceived victory. Ariadne raised the sash to him wordlessly. It was a plea, a question, perhaps of his honor. Surely, Phaedra could not take this from her, too. Theseus had given his word. He took her maidenhead.

Theseus looked from one sister to the other with a pained expression. Ariadne knew then. He was weighing his vow to her against his longing for her sister.

"I will go," she decided, reaching for her pack.

At least with Phaedra gone, Ariadne might still have a happy marriage with one of the broken- hearted men her sister left behind. Better that than holding an unwilling man to a vow he made to the wrong sister in a dark room.

"It is too late," Theseus breathed. "We have already cast off."

Ariadne nodded. "I will expect to be returned to my home as soon as we safely reach Athens. In the meantime, I will remove my belongings from your quarters if you would direct me to ones of my own."

Theseus looked at her in surprise and bowed his head. Apparently, he'd expected Ariadne to be more like Phaedra. Would that he knew what he was asking for behind that golden visage he desired.

"As you wish. I have suitable quarters for you."

Ariadne sighed. The quarters had been small but comfortable. She should have been suspicious after Phaedra's visit, but Ariadne had been ill from the rough seas and sick from the enormity of her error. And so, the subtle intimidation her sister had used had escaped her notice entirely—until later.

In retrospect, it made perfect sense to Ariadne. Phaedra had not wanted her to return home to Crete. If their father ever learned the truth of her shame, Minos would use the incident as an excuse to speed his armies to Athens. His real reason would have been the death of his Minotaur and the loss of his jewel, but his younger daughter's disgrace would have been a reason that the people of Crete would have appreciated and rallied behind.

Ariadne had not seen it at the time. Such was her folly. When Phaedra had approached her with promises of a marriage to one of Theseus's male relatives for the heartbreak she'd endured, all Ariadne could think of was the laughing stock she would be if she stayed in Phaedra's shadow. Her sister would see to it.

When the ship pulled in to Naxos to change the black sail for the white that would announce Theseus's survival to his father, Ariadne had leapt at the chance to set foot on shore and escape the endless rocking of the decks beneath her feet. The sweet wine Phaedra gave her had soothed Ariadne and lulled her to a deep sleep.

She'd awakened with a head she would have begged a swordsman to separate from her body and her new life on Naxos. *Drugged!* The wine had been drugged, and the ship had been long gone before she'd woken from it.

Ariadne had found crocks of wine and oil, a sack of grain, two knives, and a bit of meat. Her own belongings had been stowed in the pack she'd taken to the ship with her—including the hateful sash Theseus had given her in return for her innocence.

She still wondered if the supplies were gifts to ease Theseus's conscience or the pity of one of his men for the wrong done her. Surely, Phaedra had not begged for the kindness shown her discarded sister.

Ariadne had wondered at the time—why had they had not left her the foul black sail, for all that Phaedra had cursed what it would have meant for it to sail home to Athens? Ariadne supposed that its value had simply outweighed her own in the end.

Surviving on Naxos was not difficult, once Ariadne taught herself the skills she needed to survive. Her play at learning to weave tapestries when she was a child was a good beginning to learning to weave loose nets of wool thread from the spinning top she carved— though it took more than her share of cut fingers to learn the skill of carving. She had seen servants set snares in her life. In truth, Ariadne had spent more time with servants than her equals. It took her only a few weeks to discover the correct way to construct and arm a trap. It was amazing what a few weeks without meat could accomplish in teaching a person to overcome obstacles.

The fish she caught in her woven nets were plentiful. Fruits grew wild. Rabbits were often caught in her traps, and a herd of wild sheep grazed the slopes of the central mountain and provided easy meat on occasion and a fine source of wool. There was a cool stream of fresh water below a waterfall and pool that seemed designed by the gods themselves. The weather was typically fair and the seas calm.

Despite her lack of companionship—or perhaps because of it, Ariadne's time on Naxos had been the happiest time of her life. No other inhabitants meant no sour looks for her dark features, so different than Phaedra's golden presence. It meant no comparisons between them and no pained looks like the one Theseus had cast at her when he realized she was not his imagined prize.

Ariadne wiped away a bitter tear and laughed aloud as she made her way to the waterfall to bathe. "He traded a vain, useless flower for the strength of the oak that saved him," she murmured, not for the first time. Ariadne often wondered if Theseus knew how foolish she found his choice.

* * * *

Dionysus stepped ashore, rising from the sea with a sigh. He could have willed himself to Naxos, but he enjoyed the feel of cool water on his skin, and so he glided on the back of a great fish instead. Once on shore, he could have dried his clothing easily, but the wind felt so wonderful as it skated over his wet skin and through the delicate material of his robes to his body beneath that he decided to enjoy the sensation of it.

His visit to Proteus in the depths had been a long one, and Proteus was stranger than usual this past visit. He bade Dionysus to come here to Naxos for an end to his wanderings.

Dionysus shook his head as he surveyed the island. It was a treat to escape to a place so beautiful, but even a god could go mad with no company.

He sighed. If only Proteus had not been so secretive, perhaps Dionysus would understand what dratted quest was here and fulfill it so he could be on his way.

The smell of brine assaulted him, as the sun dried his robes and his purple cloak. It had been many years since Dionysus had been to Naxos, but he remembered a cool waterfall that would wash away the smell of the sea and feel refreshing on his body.

At the edge of the meadow that stretched around the small pool, Dionysus stared in disbelief. A woman stood bathing in the waterfall, just as he had come to do. The water ran in glistening sheets over her sun-touched skin and splashed away from her erect nipples. It pulled at the dark hair that all but covered the curve of her bottom and flattened the matching curls at the apex of her long legs. She was perfection.

Dionysus barely noted that he was moving toward her while he watched, so enthralled with her presence that his mind scarcely seemed to work.

He considered the situation carefully. Was this what Proteus sent him to see? What was his purpose here? Was Dionysus to take this woman back to her people? Her presence on the isle must be some misfortune such as the wreck of a seagoing vessel. People did not live on Naxos. No mortal had ever lived on Naxos. Such was the gods' decree.

Her eyes opened, then widened in shock. Dionysus felt a smile touch his lips. She was enchanting in her naiveté. He reached a hand out to her, and she retreated from him with a squawk.

Her robe was suddenly held to her perfect breasts by one shaking hand. The other held a knife, just as unsteadily. She moved nervously from foot to foot, and her wide, brown eyes completed the image of a doe about to bolt.

She found her voice. It was strong despite her obvious fright. "Who are you? How came you to my island? Have you a ship?"

Dionysus stifled a laugh at her audacity. "*Your* island? Are you queen here then?"

She blushed. "No. There is no royalty here. No peasantry either." She was not a peasant, he knew. She had a lady's speech and bearing.

"A goddess then?" Dionysus bowed his head, hiding his amusement. "By what name should I call you, wondrous one?"

Her laugh was harsh. "I will grant that the gods blessed this place once, but they have long since gone from here. No gods will answer your prayers on Naxos."

"Really? What prayers of yours have gone unanswered?"

She shrugged. "Does it matter? I provide well enough for myself here."

"You wish to leave then?" If she did, he would provide.

"Where would I go?" There was a cynical note in her voice.

"To your people, of course."

"I have no people."

"Nonsense! Everyone comes from somewhere."

"But is there always a place to return to?" she answered cryptically.

Dionysus shook his head. She was fascinating—a most unusual mortal. "So, you wish to stay here?"

"I have done worse." She glanced at her robe. "Do you mind?"

"Of course not. I came here to bathe, anyway." Dionysus turned from her and stripped off his cloak. He could hear her pulling her robe on and smiled as he stripped off his own and stepped under the rush of water.

He turned to her as he grabbed his robe and cloak to rinse them under the spray. She was riveted, staring at him as the water ran down his chest. When her breathing hitched, Dionysus knew its cause. Her examination of him had stirred his half-awake member to full readiness.

Dionysus rinsed his clothing slowly, gauging the effect of his movements on her color and breathing. Just as he threw the robe over his shoulder, she dragged her gaze to his face, and her color deepened to scarlet. Was she virginal, then? Or perhaps simply sheltered or shy?

"What is your name, woman?" His voice was low and gravelly. Gods, if he thought for an instant that she would not bolt from him—

She hesitated. "Ari."

Her quiet answer was not the truth. He could tell that much. Why would she be afraid to tell him the truth?

"And yours?" she inquired simply, her eyes still flicking between his face and the length of him aching for her.

Now, *that* was a difficult question. Dionysus thought of what the peoples of the North called him, but 'Ari' might be familiar with the name Bacchus, though her voice held not the inflection of a Northcomber. "My name is Baccs."

She nodded. "Are there others with you, Baccs? Have you a ship?"

"You do not wish to leave, but you ask if I have a ship."

"I only wonder if you are stranded here or if you will soon leave."

He bit back a smile. "I fear I am not leaving for quite some time."

"Are there others with you?" Ari asked nervously, her hands clasped tightly before her.

"No. I am the only person other than yourself, unless you know of another I do not."

Ari let out a breath that announced her relief clearly. "Are you wrecked or somehow lost here?"

"Wrecked on the rocks. And you?"

She hesitated again. "My ship left without me."

Dionysus stared at her in disbelief, but it was the truth she told him. "Without you? You must be joking. How could someone misplace such a jewel?"

Her eyes were suddenly sad. "I thank you for your kindness, but I am aware that I am no jewel. I have seen jewels. I should hope never to be so useless, and I know I am not so beautiful."

Again, she believed she spoke the truth. Had the woman never seen her own reflection? "How could you be missed?"

Ari dropped her gaze from his. "It was not by accident that I was left here, Baccs. It was...a misunderstanding about a wedding that caused this."

A half-truth. "You have no one here?"

"Now I have you, I suppose." A wry sort of smile half-lit her beautiful eyes.

"How long have you been here?"

"Yours is the first face I have seen in a year."

By my father's name, that was the truth! His heart ached for her.

* * * *

Ariadne reminded herself to move a step away from Baccs as her shoulder brushed his. It had been so long since she had company that she could scarce believe he was real and not some dream or the imaginings of a fevered mind.

Proving that was only part of her drive to touch him, though. Seeing his blatant arousal caused a tingling deep inside her. It was not a sensation she had encountered with Theseus, though she was sure that her body was craving the simple pleasures lovemaking unleashed in her.

She surveyed him out of the corner of her eye. Baccs was much younger than Theseus—perhaps six or eight years her senior, unlike Theseus, who was almost twice her age and with a son as old as she.

Baccs was a simple man, though obviously of a good family, as his speech and dress attested.

Where Theseus was a golden, god-like man, Baccs was a man of the earth with dark curls that brushed his shoulders and intense black eyes. While not a soldier—or so he attested—Baccs was taller and broader of chest than Theseus was.

As if reading her thoughts, Baccs turned his face to her and smiled. "I am real, Ari."

"I know you are." She flicked her attention to the still-visible erection beneath his robes and suppressed a shiver. Oh, how real she wanted him to be. "What is your business, Baccs?"

"I am a merchant of sorts. I deal in wines."

Ariadne sighed. "That is one thing I do miss."

"Well, that is one wish I can grant you."

"What do you mean?"

"I have pulled several small casks of wine from the sea and hidden them on the other side of the island while I investigated the best place to settle."

"You had a shipment of wine with you when you wrecked?"

"I did. I do not know how many will wash up, but I already have three casks in my possession."

Her heart tripped in excitement. "Would you share one with me? Such a thing is more precious than gold, here."

Baccs laughed lightly. "Would you share your food and shelter with me? It seems we each have something to trade of almost infinite value."

Her heart took up a choppy rhythm. He wanted to share her shelter? "Yes. I think we can reach an agreement."

* * * *

Dionysus watched Ari, as she waded in the water, netting fish for their meal. The garment she wore barely covered her upper thighs and was sleeveless. As if the memory of her naked in the waterfall were not bad enough, the sight of her in the tunic robbed him of sanity.

He rubbed at his erection impatiently, trying to ease the tension he felt. Dionysus was a creature of comfort. Tension was not something he enjoyed overmuch.

In frustration, he hiked his robes and took the problem in hand. He watched Ari move in the water as he stroked himself, and his mind formed a fantasy for him.

He waded out to her, stripped of his robes, and pulled Ari into his arms. She was sweet and responsive, her lips parting to allow him to taste her.

His hands strayed down her spine to her firm bottom, drawing her up his body to tease his aching member at the heat of her. Ari arched to him, and he drew the offending tunic off and tossed it toward the shore. She looked after it, not in embarrassment for her nude body, but in concern of losing what little possessions she had.

Dionysus cupped her face back to him. "If it washes out to sea, I will fetch it from Poseidon's depths for you," he promised.

Ari smiled, and her eyes glittered as she shifted her body, playing the tip of him in her warmth. "Can you do

*that? Are you a god, then? What name should I call you,
wondrous one?"*

*"Yes, I am, and you shall have your fondest wishes,
for I am Dionysus. Tell me what you wish, Ari."*

*He leaned to take her mouth again, but she pushed
him away nervously. There was fear in Ari's eyes.*

Dionysus's head snapped up. "What in the name of
Olympus?" he cursed. After all, how does a *fantasy* go
wrong? He grumbled in frustration. "Aphrodite," he
warned, putting his power into it to send his complaint
to her, "I am not a mortal to be played with thus. If this
is your doing, end your treacherous games."

His sibling did not answer him directly, but
Dionysus was sure that he heard her lilting laughter
carried in on the waves. He cursed soundly at yet
another interference in his life.

Still, his anger had solved one problem. He had no
need to relieve his arousal at the moment.

Dionysus straightened his robes and looked back
to Ari.

Was there a message in this? Would revealing
himself to her bring only disaster? Certainly, his father
had bad enough luck revealing himself to women.
Dionysus was the perfect example of that.

* * * *

Ariadne watched Baccs over the fire he'd built up.
He had been helpful and not afraid of a little hard
work, fetching water from the stream and firewood
from the tree line. Still, he seemed distracted.

She sighed. Perhaps he was pining for his home
and dealings. A man accustomed to gatherings and the

challenge of barter would be expected to miss the loss. Would Baccs try to leave her, then? Would he fashion a raft and brave the sea back to his home?

Ariadne met his eyes over her plate of wild fruits and fish brushed with herbs. "Where are you from, Baccs?"

"Thebes. And you?"

"Crete. Have you family there?"

"Not there, but I have family—a father and many brothers and sisters."

"Your mother?"

"She—died when I was born."

Baccs seemed pained, and she felt for him. Ariadne's own mother had died when she was but an infant.

"I apologize for my prying," she mumbled. "I am sorry for your loss."

"No need to be. I took her home long ago. She is at peace now." A smile curved his lips.

"I suppose you will want to return to your family. You must miss them." She fought to hide her fear that he would do just that.

He laughed lightly. "No. I miss my father, but I do not often see him. As for my brothers and sisters—as the youngest, they tend to meddle in my life too much."

"Why do you not see your father more often?"

His jaw tightened. "His wife does not care for me."

"Then she is a fool." Ariadne said it confidently. It was too much like the reasons her own family had not prized her. "But, you will try to return to them, will you not?" she persisted, praying all along that his answer would be no.

Baccs shook his head. "I am no shipbuilder, and I know nothing of sailing. I simply ride the winds with others at the till. I am your mate for some time. People rarely pull in here, as you have seen."

Ariadne sucked in her breath at his use of the word *mate*. Gods, but she wished Baccs meant that in the intimate sense of the word.

If she were as worldly as Phaedra, Ariadne would know how to make her wishes known to a man, but in Phaedra's shadow there had been no men to ply such games on, and games of that sort had been her sister's life, not Ariadne's.

"Does that distress you, Ari?" His voice was low and rough again, and his eyes were like smooth seawater on a still, dark night.

"Not at all. I enjoy your company."

His smile was slow and dangerous. Ariadne had never seen such a smile, and it took her breath away. "Good. I am glad I do not unsettle you."

Unsettle? Baccs rattled her. He made her feel empty and needy. "What of you? Do you have family somewhere?" he asked.

She sobered. "No. No one will miss me. There is no one for me to miss." That much was true. Phaedra's treachery was proof of her heart, and her father seemed to forget he had a second daughter most days.

Baccs eyed her suspiciously, as if he did not believe her, but he nodded and questioned her no more on the subject.

Ariadne felt the sudden need to move the focus from herself. "Where were you traveling from when your ship wrecked?"

* * * *

Dionysus hesitated. Proteus's watery realm would go too far. "Athens." It was the last mortal place he had been.

Ari stiffened. She spoke the truth when she said she was from Crete. Why would Athens rattle her? "I have heard it is very beautiful," she whispered.

"No more so than Crete or Thebes. It is but a place," he dismissed her belief.

"I met the prince of Athens once—when he visited Crete." Her smile was slightly strained.

"Really? I was not aware that Hippolytus had ever traveled to Crete."

"Not Hippolytus. I met the other prince—Theseus."

Dionysus nodded in understanding. "You have been here more than a year. I forgot." He took in her look of surprise. "Theseus is king now."

Ari blinked away tears and seemed to be hiding some deep emotion. "I thought Aegeus was vital. I heard as much. Did he die of some mishap or a sudden illness?"

"Ah. That is a sad tale. Aegeus and his son had arranged a signal—one that could be seen even when his ship was still far out to sea—"

Her eyes widened. "Good gods! The sail. They were supposed to change the sail. They never did, did they? Did his heart fail in his grief?" she asked urgently, her words tumbling one over the next.

Dionysus stared at her in shock. Her color was high, her eyes full of tears for a foreign king she had never known, which stunned him, but it was more than that.

"How did you know about the sail?"

A deep blush touched her cheeks. "I told you. I met Theseus when he was in Crete."

"In what fashion?"

"I brought him food."

It was another half-truth. "He confided such a thing to a servant?"

Her spine stiffened, and Ari raised her chin proudly. For a moment—an instant in time, Dionysus could have sworn he knew her. Then the haughty expression was gone and the sense of familiarity with it.

She looked into the fire with sad eyes. "I— overheard it while I was nearby."

That part was a lie. Ari confused him. Why was she so intent on hiding her true self from him? She was hiding on Naxos in more ways than one.

"Did his heart fail him in his grief?" she repeated.

"No. He threw himself from the cliffs near the Acropolis." Dionysus cringed, remembering the cry from the gods at his loss. Aegeus had been a most loved son of many of Dionysus's siblings and his father alike.

Her face hardened. "What a foolish thing to do," she stormed. "Losing someone does not mean you give up on life."

The determination on her face solidified the image, and Dionysus knew why he thought he knew her. Still, he had no idea what the resemblance meant. Ari had not been lying about her lack of family, though the fact brought her great sadness.

"Aegeus acted on a moment of grief and weakness."

43

Her eyes softened at the thought of it. Ari obviously understood moments of pain.

"Theseus was distracted," he continued.

"One should hope so!" The bitterness was back in her voice.

"No. He felt guilt and grief, of course. He was distracted and forgot to change the sail. It was not his intention to do harm. Something unsettled his mind."

"Good. At least he pays for his sins like everyone else."

"You know, I met Theseus's queen when he returned to Athens. She was from Crete as well. Did you know her?"

"Of course. How does one not know one's princess?" There was a bite of sarcasm in that question.

"You look quite a bit like her," Dionysus noted, laying bait for a glimmer of truth he knew was eluding his grasp.

Ari's eyes went wide in surprise, and then they hardened and reminded him again of the resemblance between the two women. "We are both women of Crete. 'Tis nothing more than that." She looked away to her shelter, while he reeled from the outright lie she'd told him. "I am fatigued. I will bid you good night now."

The sadness in her voice touched him, and Dionysus found it difficult to be angry with her for the lie. "I admit to being worn by the day as well. I will join you."

She looked at him in confusion. "Join?"

"Our deal? If you do not feel comfortable with my company, I will sleep elsewhere," he offered.

"No. Of course not. Please, you are most welcome here." Ari retreated into the structure with a look of—

By his father, Dionysus prayed he was right. Her look seemed to be one of anticipation.

Dionysus gave her a few moments to collect herself before he followed her in. Ari was wearing her fishing tunic and was in the bed box under a woven blanket.

She looked at him shyly. "There is only one bed, I am afraid, and the blanket was not really designed for two."

A smile touched his lips. "'Tis a chilly night. You share your bed. I will share my cloak. It is large enough to cover both of us."

She nodded and moved to the far side of the bed box. Her eyes widened, as Dionysus stripped off his robes, and her eyes traveled the length of him slowly in the firelight filtering through the doorway. He settled into the bed with her and fanned the cloak over them.

Ari seemed frozen in fear, and he softened. Taking her would not be easy, but he had all the time in the world to put her at ease with him. Dionysus wrapped his arms around her and eased Ari into the shelter of his body. She did not protest the move, and he stifled a groan of pleasure at that.

"It is all right, Ari. You do not have to fear me." His voice was hoarse in his need, but unlike some gods, Dionysus was not in the habit of taking an unwilling woman, no matter how much he might desire her.

"I do not fear you," she whispered, her breath teasing at his chest. It was the truth. Ari was quaking, but it was not him she feared.

"You do not need to fear anything. Nothing will touch you unless you wish it. You have my vow on that."

She raised her face to him and looked as if she wanted to say something, but she held back. "Thank you," she said instead.

He held her for hours, as the fire burned down to embers, but she did not sleep. Ari did not even relax in his arms. Finally, Dionysus feigned sleep, hoping to put her at ease.

Ari relaxed against his body. She ran her fingertips over his jawline. Her voice was a whisper in the darkness that touched the spark of his arousal like the caress of a breeze on kindling, stirring the fire for her in his blood.

"Did the gods send you to me, Baccs? Perhaps they did. Do you think they will show me how to be happy as well?"

Dionysus moved in the darkness, turning to wrap his body around her and striving to make it seem a random act done in sleep.

Ari sighed as she pressed her lips to his chest. "Surely, only the gods could craft a man like you. Would that others were so honorable. I hope you are not another who is lovesick for Phaedra. It would be a gift to meet a man who is not so short-sighted. If only the gods would give me a sign—"

She fell asleep shortly after that wish. Dionysus lay for a long time, considering her words. Ari had been hurt by a man—or by men in her past. Was Phaedra responsible for it, or was that unconnected?

Dionysus shivered, as his mind connected what little he knew of her. Ari met Theseus in Crete, but

Theseus took Phaedra as his queen. Was Theseus the man who'd hurt her? It would not surprise Dionysus to learn that he was. Theseus had been unwise in many ways in his life, up to and including the oversight that had cost Aegeus his life.

But why did the two women bear such a striking resemblance when Ari had no family? And, why was Ari hiding on Naxos? Or was it her choice to come here at all? She only said that it was not by accident that she was left on the island. Did Phaedra exile Ari here to win Theseus for herself?

Dionysus sighed and kissed her brow. Ari was an intriguing mystery, and he would not rest until he unraveled every one of her secrets. Then he would make her his alone. Dionysus smiled. He had promised her wine. This would work out well.

* * * *

Ariadne looked to the horizon for the hundredth time that afternoon. "He is coming back," she assured herself. "He has simply gone to bring back a cask of wine." Still, she looked to the tree line, fearful that Baccs would not return. Ariadne shook her head in disbelief that she had come to depend on his presence so completely in so short a time.

She shivered at the memory of waking in Baccs's arms. Ariadne had opened her eyes slowly, her heart beating rapidly as her position became clear to her. She was stretched against Baccs, held to him by his hands on the curve of her buttocks, her fishing tunic pushed up almost to her waist.

As Ariadne came fully awake, his hand stroked across the skin of her bottom. Breathing suddenly seemed difficult, and when his touch came again, she moved her hips to him, needing to feel Baccs pressed to her.

Feel him, she did. The length of his shaft, resting on her thigh, hardened as she moved. Ariadne gasped, as his hands pressed her closer and the rigid heat of him brushed into the liquid gathering between her thighs.

Baccs's eyes opened. His gaze was intense. He searched her face for an answer, though he asked no question. No, he did ask a question with his body, but Ariadne knew not what answer he was looking for.

His mouth covered hers, tasting her slowly. This question, Ariadne knew how to answer. When his tongue touched the seam of her lips, she opened for him. Baccs groaned as he explored her mouth, and the feeling of it sent a wave of heat to her already aroused core.

He was not gentle in his discovery. Perhaps gleaning her knowledge of the art in her reactions, Baccs's tongue moved in quick strokes that mimicked a man's possession. Ariadne moaned into him, her hands seeking the dark locks tangled around his cheeks.

Baccs turned until his body pressed down on her and drew his length against her, moving his hips in a rhythm that made her ache for his possession. His mouth kept time with his hips, in mute promise of the loving to come, a fierce mating of their bodies that she longed for.

His mouth traced her ear, nipping at the lobe. Ariadne cried out and arched to him.

"Baccs, please." She was begging for his touch now. She would do anything to feel his body inside her, his passion unleashed.

"Who are you, Ari? Who are you that I burn for you this way?" Baccs's tongue played at a spot behind her ear that scattered her thoughts. *"Please tell me. I must know you."*

"You do know me. I want you to know me." She wanted him to know every finger-width of her body, inside and out.

"Your name, Ari—tell me your name that I might call to you as I climax in you."

Ariadne stilled in Baccs's arms, the force of his request burning through the haze that gripped her mind. He knew she lied about her name. What else did he know?

"Who are you, Baccs? Did they *send you to me?"*

She ached that she suspected him, but her past experiences proved that her judge of a man was not sound. Would Phaedra stoop to this? Would she send Baccs to Ariadne to win her love and quell some unease between Athens and Crete?

"Who? The gods?" he asked in confusion.

Ariadne hoped it was truly confusion. *"If* they *sent you, you know who I mean. There is no need for me to speak their names."*

Baccs hesitated. *"No one sent me, Ari. No one. Trust me."*

She nodded. *"There is nothing, Baccs. I am no one. I have no home or family or past. My existence here is all I am."* It was all Ariadne wanted to be—all she wanted to remember.

His gaze hardened slightly. "I want you, Ari, but I will not take a woman who does not trust me—or who deceives me." Baccs rose and pulled on his robes, facing the doorway angrily.

Terror rose up in her at his withdrawl. "Baccs, where are you going?"

"To collect one of the casks of wine. I will gather fruit as I walk, so you need not worry about a fire for me this morn. If you wish, we will still share the wine this evening over a meal?"

"Of course. I will arrange it."

"And share your shelter?"

"Yes. Of course...if you still wish my company." Ariadne clasped her hands tight under her woven blanket, praying to the silent gods that he still wanted that.

He nodded. "I only want to know you, Ari. Please, do not deny me this."

And so, he had walked away, leaving her in the bed aching for him. Ariadne had not seen him in all the hours since then.

As she prepared the rabbit she found in her snare, Ariadne fingered the packet of herbs she'd taken from her pack. Arol, one of the keepers assigned to her when she was a child, had told her of the uses for various herbs. Arol had given Ariadne the packet when she was fifteen and the old woman saw her struggle to attract any man away from the brilliance of Phaedra. The herbs were an ancient mix designed to fire a man's lust, Arol had explained. Ariadne had never considered using them—until Baccs. She'd kept them all these years out of love for Arol, the one woman who would care enough to give Ariadne such a gift.

Ariadne wavered. Was such a thing right? She sighed. Could she do this to him?

"Not a full dose," Ariadne decided aloud. If she used half a dose and it was split between them, it would only be the barest nudge.

* * * *

Dionysus watched Ari from the tree line. He had not gone to get a cask of wine. There was no wine to collect. Being a god had its advantages. Producing a cask of wine out of thin air was a simple matter. Dionysus could have done so the previous night, but he was presenting the appearance of a mortal for Ari.

He had watched her all day. Ari checked her traps and gathered herbs and fruit. She cooked and collected water. Better, she preened for him—and she thought.

Thinking was the important part. She wanted to trust him. Dionysus could feel it. Ari had to be willing to open up to him for his plan to work. The magic he would place on the wine would only magnify her willingness to comply to his wishes, not instill it in her.

It was a push, a simple push to help her trust him. Dionysus sighed, wishing there were other alternatives. No, there was no other way. Then, why did he feel so guilty for doing it? Dionysus hefted the cask, creating it as he rose. He had to go to her before he could talk himself out of the deception.

Ari smiled at him as Dionysus entered the open area around her fire. Her eyes glittered, and a comely blush stained her cheeks.

"The food will be ready shortly," she informed him.

"Good. Let us enjoy a cup of wine while we wait."

She nodded and turned the rabbit on the spit before collecting two cups from the shelter, the newer made only the day before, when she realized the need for more than her solitary setting. Ari had carved the piece in earnest while they talked, a rough but functional cup, which she used herself, granting him the better of the two. He remembered her nervousness, as she hid the scars announcing her dedication to her own survival, handing him a drink of water and pulling her hand back almost before he saw those scars clearly. His urge to uncover the truth had only grown.

Dionysus knocked the end cap of the cask free and dipped the cups. "To love?" he asked.

Ari's eyes were suddenly sad again. "I do not believe the gods grant such frivolous wishes."

Dionysus nodded. The gods rarely did. *Would that all mortals were so wise.* "What then?"

"To a comfortable life on this beautiful island, with our thanks."

"Agreed." He watched as she drank the first quarter of her cup, then sampled his own.

Ari beamed at him like a child with a favored gift in hand. "Oh, Baccs. This is wonderful."

"My own vines." A half-truth, but not a bad tale to spin for her. "Drink. We should drink as much of this as we can, so we do not waste it."

She was halfway through her second cup before Dionysus started seeing the evidence that his magic was at work, and it was more than simply the wine affecting her. As he refilled her cup a second time, Dionysus sat close beside Ari and fed her fruits from the platter she'd filled. It would not be long before she was ready to tell him the truth of herself.

Near the end of the third cup, she started to sit forward to tend to the meal.

Dionysus eased her back with a slow, sweet kiss, knowing that Ari was more unsteady than she realized. "Let me take the rabbit from the fire," he offered. In the condition he had placed her in, it was dangerous to let her attempt it.

Ari smiled a lazy smile and touched his cheek, as he moved away. She was ready for his questions.

"Where did you get the name Ari?" he inquired as he cut a slice of meat and tested it. The herbs she used were unusual but tasty. He cut another slice immediately and ate it, too.

She hesitated. Perhaps Ari was not ready to answer, after all.

"It was a pet name one of my keepers used for me," she admitted, her voice slow and measured.

Dionysus turned with the spit in hand. Very soon, Ari would be ready to tell him what he really wanted to know.

He offered her meat, but she declined in favor of another slice of fruit. Dionysus asked her about her keeper, a woman named Arol who was more a mother to Ari than anyone had ever been. He ate ravenously, plying her with the magic-laced wine all the while and watching her resistance to answering fade with every sip.

When her fourth cup had disappeared, Ari laughingly took a slice of the meat from his fingers. Dionysus hardened as her lips closed around his fingers. He shook his head as he tried to clear the visions of her from his mind, then looked at the cask suspiciously. His own magic would not work on him this way. Was this Aphrodite's doing, then? He decided to forego more wine and took another bite of the succulent meat.

At any rate, Ari was ready for his questions. "Ari is a pet name. What name is it short for?"

"Ariadne." There was no hesitation that time. "My father named me."

Dionysus smiled widely, leaning close to her and rewarding her openness with another slow kiss. "Who is your father?"

Ariadne adopted a stern look that was no doubt one her father often used. When she spoke, her voice had a gruff edge to it. "Minos, King of Crete." Her face crumpled as she thought about him. "Dread ruler of his people," she whispered miserably.

"Was he dread to you?"

"Dish-interested," she slurred. "His jewel was all he saw. I might never have existed."

For a moment, Dionysus was certain he'd heard her wrong, but as he replayed the statement over and over, his anger claimed him. "He cared more for his treasure than his daughter?" If Minos had, he would lose that treasure. Dionysus would see to it.

Ariadne shook her head and took a drink from her cup. "Not his treasure. Just a single jewel."

He leaned close to her. "What jewel could be fairer than you?" He wondered at that, but he did not wonder at the sudden urge to kiss her again. She was so beautiful and trusting.

She scowled. "You have met her. Phaedra. My elder sister. Nay! She is *not* my sister. What sister treats another thus?" Ariadne waved her hand at their surroundings, then shook her head, the anger fading from her as abruptly as it had come. "I would rather be here than in her shadow, so I suppose I should give thanks for this fate."

He did kiss her then, a less restrained kiss than the last few had been. Dionysus would not allow Ariadne to doubt herself. "Yes, I have met Phaedra. Do you know what I saw?"

Ariadne shook her head and ran her fingertips down the folds of his robe over his chest.

"I saw a spoiled child who pouted and fussed to get her way. I saw a woman unfit to wear a crown, so interested in her own whims that she ignored the needs of her people."

Ariadne nodded and kissed him. Dionysus cupped her head to him, eager to consummate. She wanted him. The magic could not create a want. It could only intensify an existing want. He would not use any other type of magic.

Some measure of sanity broke in and reminded him that he had many questions still to ask while she was under his magic, and making love to Ariadne could well take all that time and more. Questions first. "Ariadne, you must tell me. Was Theseus yours? Did Phaedra take him from you?"

A tear spilled down her cheek. "No. He was supposed to be mine, but it was all a dream. I saved his life to make him mine, but he never was—not really. All along, he thought he was making his vow to Phaedra. She was the only one he saw. Phaedra was the only daughter of Minos any man saw." She looked at him hopelessly. "What good would holding such a man to his vow be when he would be dreaming of my sister all the time?"

"None," he agreed, aching for her. Dionysus furrowed his brow. "How could Theseus make such a mistake? You bear a resemblance, but not so much that he would not know the difference."

Ariadne blushed. "It was dark, and I was wearing a hood. Had he seen my accursed hair, Theseus would have realized I was not the woman he believed."

"He vowed to marry you?"

She nodded, but a pained expression crossed her face.

There was more. "How did he come to have Phaedra instead?"

"He sent me to his ship with orders to hide and wait his arrival. When he came out of the labyrinth, Theseus saw her and brought her along, believing Phaedra too lovesick to wait as he ordered.

"For his part, Theseus did not realize his mistake until he was faced with me holding his sash. Phaedra knew, but she also knew a smitten fool when she saw one. She hoped Theseus would break his vow for the woman he thought would be—that he wanted to be his queen. By that time, we had already cast off. I released him from his vow, asked for quarters away from him, and demanded to be delivered home once he and Phaedra had reached Athens safely."

His head spun. "Quarters away? Of course. Why would he think—"

Ariadne blushed and looked away.

"It was dark, and he took you thinking you were Phaedra." Dionysus did not question that it was the truth.

She nodded.

"Were you a maiden?"

Her voice was a choked whisper. "Yes, I was. I thought—but, what does that matter? All his sweet words and gentle touches were for Phaedra. When he saw me in the light, the look of dismay—what woman would want him?"

Dionysus pulled her to his chest, wavering between the pure fury at Theseus and Phaedra and the torment for Ariadne warring in his soul. "How came you to Naxos?" He had to know. How guilty were her persecutors?

Ariadne laughed a hearty laugh with an edge of hysteria. "We came to change that fateful sail—or so I was told. Phaedra and I came ashore with some of the sailors while they got fresh water. She fed me drugged wine."

Dionysus cringed inwardly at his offering of wine. How he had wronged her.

"I woke to find myself stranded with a minimum of supplies and the rest of that horrible wine. I wonder sometimes if Phaedra thought I might use it to finish myself off." Ariadne barked a short laugh that showed how close she came to giving in to that very thought. "So, you see, Baccs. Were it not for poor Aegeus, I could almost find the whole story of the black sail very funny."

Dionysus found his anger blooming into something of a living thing. "Theseus allowed this? He knew?"

"When he left Naxos? I know not. Phaedra could have lied to him for a day or even two. By the time they made harbor in Athens, he had to know. In that, Theseus allowed it. Had he wanted to send someone for me, he has had ample time to do so.

"You said he was disturbed when he reached Athens. I can only hope that means he had just learned that I was left behind—or that he saw Phaedra as she really was when she convinced him not to come for me. That is all it is—a vain hope. I know that."

"What did they leave you with?"

"Enough to support me until I learned to support myself. A few crocks of wine and one of oil. A bit of meat and grain. Two knives and my pack from the ship." She laughed that heartbreaking laugh again.

"What is it?"

"Phaedra did not check the pack before she left it with me. The sash was still in it. I do not remember putting it there. I must have been so upset that I left his quarters with it still in my hand—"

A crooked smile touched Dionysus's lips. "You still have it?"

She nodded in confusion.

"Get it for me." It was more than a request, less than an order. His mind was set on a course, and he would not be turned from it.

"So we can burn it together?" Her eyes glittered at the prospect of it.

"No. So I can wear it."

Ariadne shuddered. "Baccs, no. Why would you want such a thing?"

He kissed her, not gently now but with a fierce need. "After tonight, you will only remember me when you see the sash. You have my word. Get the sash, Ariadne."

Her eyes widened, but she did not voice a complaint. Ariadne disappeared into the shelter and came back with the offending sash in her hands. It was black as Theseus's sail with ships embroidered in gold on its ends.

Dionysus smiled as he took it from her. He led Ariadne to a young tree and swept off his cloak to lay it on the ground. He kissed her, demanding all of her passion and reveling when she gave it freely.

For a single moment, he wondered if Aphrodite had a hand in this affair. Then, Ariadne's hands began to trace the muscles of his chest, and Dionysus decided to thank his sister for this moment, if it were her doing.

He stripped her robe from her and watched her in the firelight. Ariadne blushed, but she raised her chin proudly and met his eyes.

Dionysus sucked in his breath at the sight of her. "You are so lovely." He smiled as he silently called on the elements to aid him in his plan for her.

"Why will I remember the sash, Baccs?" There was a teasing tone to her voice now.

"Do you trust me?"

She nodded.

"Then I will show you."

Ariadne watched in confusion as he bound her hands with the hateful sash, but she did not balk the move. Dionysus lowered her to his cloak and bound her hands to the trunk of the young tree by her head.

That accomplished, he stripped off his own robe. Ariadne surveyed the length of his body. The stark hunger in her eyes drew him, and he captured her mouth. She arched beneath him. Dionysus groaned as he felt her wiggle toward his erection, trying to capture him within her.

"Too fast," he chided her, nipping at her lower lip. He pushed to his feet. "Baccs?" She was concerned but not frightened.

He smiled to reassure her. "I simply need a few things. I will be quick."

Dionysus brought the tray of fruit and a cup of wine to the edge of the cloak. Before she could question him further, he lowered a slice of fruit to her lips. He pulled it back so Ariadne could only take a small bite. She met his eyes and smiled as she chewed the offered treat.

Just as she swallowed, Dionysus rubbed the bit edge of the slice over her nipples. The cool breeze he called stirred over her body, caressing her skin and teasing her nipples, sensitized by the fruit, to rigid peaks. Ariadne cried out as his mouth closed on one taut nipple. He sucked them clean then played at them, warming them and allowing his breeze to tantalize them before he returned to warm them again.

She writhed beneath him, trying to find purchase. Ariadne bit her lip as she watched the motions of his mouth. "Baccs, please."

"I am far from done, my love."

Dionysus reached for the cup of wine next, cradling her head to offer her a drink. He kissed her, reveling in the taste of the libation mixed with Ariadne's personal flavor. Her feminine musk was rich and drugging.

He raised the cup to his own lips and drank from it. "It tastes sweeter when I drink it from you."

Dionysus poured a bit over each nipple, ordering his wind to caress her again. He started at the hollow between her breasts, laving the drops that raced over her body, while Ariadne stifled another cry.

Dionysus met her eyes. "Still," he instructed her. "You must be still, now."

The wind was slightly colder now, bringing the rain he wanted, but Dionysus still had time to play. He poured a bit of wine into her navel. Ariadne stilled and her head came up to watch what he was doing, just as he'd hoped she would.

She was still until his tongue started to trace the edges of the dip filled with wine. Her muscles tightened, and wine skittered over her body. Dionysus cast her a look of mock censure before he started chasing the droplets over her stomach and hips.

Ariadne gasped as his tongue played at her dark curls, stealing droplets that carried a hint of her musk to his starved senses. She shivered, spilling more of the burgundy liquid over her creamy skin.

He laughed lightly at her groan. "If you are not still, it will take me all night to finish," he teased her.

A blush touched her cheeks, and she arched her body to spill most of the wine left toward her curls. It was a blatant invitation that Dionysus could not ignore. He cleaned her stomach first, swirling his tongue in her navel, while Ariadne moved against him and pulled at her bound hands.

She grumbled in frustration. "Baccs, please untie me."

"You will have your chance, Ariadne. I will use this sash in so many ways that you will not remember it has any purpose but allowing me to make love to you."

"My chance?" she panted as he returned to capturing the wine from her curls.

Dionysus smiled as he ran his tongue over her core, giving her one jolt of intense pleasure that caused her to jerk against her bonds.

"My chance?" Her voice was a gasp of delight, uttered as she shifted toward his tongue again.

He favored her with another slow lick, smiling as Ariadne shivered in response. "After I have shown you the many ways to please a man, I will let you return this favor." His voice was raw in his need for such a thing.

"Show me. Please show me how to please you."

"Next time. This time, I intend to pleasure you." Still, his erection jerked at what he wanted from her.

"It would please me to scatter you as you scatter me—if only for a moment."

Dionysus smiled. "I admit to a certain—hunger." That was an understatement, and he knew it very well. The urge to have her mouth and hands on him was almost all consuming.

"Show me." Her voice was silk seduction.

"Would you like a drink of wine?" he offered.

Ariadne smiled in understanding. "It would taste sweeter from your body."

Dionysus shivered at the invitation in that simple statement. He moved further up her side and immersed as much of his member as he could fit into the cup of wine. He set it aside and played the tip of his erection over her soft lips.

Ariadne's tongue darted out, cleaning the wine from him in long strokes that had him aching to take her. "Like that?" she asked shyly.

"Do you want to make me forget all control?" His breathing was already ragged in the last of that control.

She nodded. "Very much."

"Take me in your mouth as I do your breasts."

"Will you feed me some wine?" Her eyes glittered in the knowledge of what she was doing to him.

Dionysus groaned as he complied with her request. Ariadne took his length in her mouth, sucking at him and running her tongue around the head until he felt he might go mad from the sensation.

When he started moving his hips to slide in and out of the moist heat, her eyes widened. Then they fluttered shut and Ariadne groaned. The vibration surrounded the length of him in her mouth and rode through his body as a rumbling that touched his soul.

As the fine mist of rain began, Dionysus laid down beside her, returning himself to her torture while he spread her legs. He smiled as the rain gathered on the broad leaf over her, just as he'd planned. When the first drop fell, Dionysus watched its progress. It slid down the folds of her sex slowly. He met Ariadne's eyes, as she released him and gasped. She trembled in his hands.

"Relax," he soothed her as he spread the folds to bare her sensitive inner self to the next drop. The drop fell, finding her tender self waiting for it.

She uttered a cry that was somewhere between shock and longing. Her eyes were heavy lidded. "Baccs, what are you doing to me?"

Another drop fell and made its way down her core, and Ariadne squeezed her eyes shut, working her kiss-swollen lip through her teeth. Dionysus smiled. The magic made her so receptive to him—so responsive.

"I am making you mine, Ariadne."

Another drop fell. She moaned and turned her head away, trying to close her legs against his insistent hold. The fine mist of rain mixed with the sheen of sweat on her skin and made her dark hair appear nearly black in the firelight. Ariadne cried out harshly as the next drop fell on her heated body.

"Do you want to be mine?" he asked.

Her eyes opened and she nodded slowly. "How do I make you mine, Baccs?"

He lowered his mouth to her as another drop fell, following its path over her, then darting inside her to taste her musk better. Ariadne cried out, pulling against her bonds again. She was so sweet, so ready for him. Dionysus set out to drive her to the edges of climax, turning her body slightly to position her to the ravishing of his mouth.

Dionysus groaned into her body, as she captured his shaft between her lips and sucked at him as if she might die without him. For a few moments, his mind ceased to function. It had been decades since a woman had wanted him this desperately.

Ariadne did want him. There was no question of that. The magic could not make her feel something that was not already there, and even in larger doses than this, Dionysus had never seen a woman, even one who all but threw herself at him before the magic, react so intensely to him.

Dionysus pulled away. Ariadne was confused by his withdrawl, but she was also in need of him. It showed in her eyes. She started to speak, but he covered her mouth with his fingers while he turned beside her.

He kissed her in slow, thorough movements while he covered her with his body. Dionysus met her eyes. Under the influence of his magic, she could not lie to him. He would need to know her true mind.

"Ariadne, I am going to make you mine, now." He brushed her hair from her cheek. "A woman, when she climaxes, is fully open—her heart and mind as well as her body." He seated himself fully in her and sighed as she arched against him. "Come for me, Ariadne."

Dionysus anchored her hips to his and took her in hard, hot strokes. He prayed to Aphrodite for stamina, for the ability to hold off for her. Never before had he felt the burn to climax before the women he bedded. Always, it was a given that Dionysus would bring them to ecstasy before finding his own release. Now, when it was so important, he felt himself slipping. The edges of the void sucked at him as he fought to hold back the rising tide sweeping him away.

Ariadne's shattering climax was a joy to him. *One more moment—one more thing before I follow* her.

"Ariadne, if you feel anything for me, tell me now." His voice was a plea. Never had he wanted something so much and so feared losing it.

"Oh, Baccs. I love you. Tell me you will be mine forever."

His heart soared, and he flew off into the abyss of color and sensation. Recovery was slow coming. Dionysus lay his face on the rapid heartbeat at her throat, as the sky gave up its load in a torrent of warm, cleansing rain.

"I am yours, Ari. You have my word that for every moment you draw breath, you will have me by your side." *And Aphrodite help me, would that I was mortal to follow after her!*

* * * *

The first days after Ariadne took him as her love were little more than a blur to Dionysus. He took her again and again, just as he'd promised he would. After every time, he would cause her to say that accursed mortal's name before teasing her that his job was unfinished. Ari still remembered the name of Theseus.

It became a game of sorts. Ari would smile sweetly as she said it, knowing he was about to tease her body to joy again. At times, she would saunter up to Dionysus with the sash in her hands and ask him to remove a stubborn memory. It never failed to make him want to do just that.

Every time, he asked her if she felt for him, and she would cry out his name or profess her love. Ari begged him to be truly hers and to tell her he loved her as he claimed her. It was never a lie for either of them.

Dionysus educated her in countless positions and techniques. He used the sash as a blindfold as he made love to her with down and fruits, the soft feathers and chill juice almost more than she could stand. He bound her to himself as he took her beneath the waterfall. He bound Ari's hands behind her as she rode him, and he teased her with the soft material as he took her from behind. Every new experience was accompanied by the sash, as he'd promised.

He let Ari bind him more than once. Dionysus smiled at the memory of the first time. She brought him to climax with her mouth. Then she brought her sweet, wet body to him for his attentions. He hardened again for her, as she cried out her pleasure to his handling, and she pulled him back to her mouth. At the moment she felt her release coming, Ari straddled him and let her body's milking draw Dionysus over again.

When he found the packet of love herbs, Ari tearfully admitted using them on him the night he gave her the laced wine. She begged his forgiveness, unknowing that he had done the same to her. Dionysus shivered at the knowledge of how desperately she'd wanted him, even before his wine.

He closed on her, stripping off her robe so that Ari stood naked before him. His fingers teased at her, bringing her quickly to readiness. Dionysus pulled back the tunic that he had produced and claimed washed up from his wreck and settled Ari on his length. He rode up into her with a fierce need.

Dionysus cupped her face to him as his body tightened to spill in her. "I am not drugged now, Ari. See how I crave you?" He held her to him as he climaxed, feeling his seed set off her own release.

Then, there was the wine—he coaxed fine vines on the mountainside and pretended to find them by chance on a walk with Ari. As a tribute to their first joining, she loved to tease Dionysus with wine, pouring some on herself and laying out in invitation or pouring some on him and sinking to remove it without a word.

They seldom wore clothing. The first morning, Dionysus convinced Ari to fish with him unclothed.

Over time, they were unclothed more than clothed, casting appreciative looks at each other and enjoying the union of their bodies at barely a moment's notice.

Ari asked him once if Dionysus missed the things he lost when he was stranded on their island. He laughed as he admitted that he was hard-pressed to see anything as lost when he'd gained so much.

* * * *

Dionysus smiled at Ari as she cooked at the fire in the home he'd built for her. She got to her feet awkwardly, the formidable mound of his son pulling her off balance as she worked.

They had almost given up hope of this blessing, but Hera had put her dislike of him aside in favor of Ari's pure and simple prayers. For four years, Ari had prayed for his child, while his esteemed step-mother ignored her pleas. Ari never gave up. She never showed bitterness in her prayers. She simply continued asking for Hera's blessings, day after day and year after year, until the coldest of the gods could not help but be moved by Ari's sincere love for her husband.

He started, as Ari looked at him strangely. "What is it?" Dionysus inquired, rising from his place on the floor.

"I do not know. I am—tired of a sudden." She wavered on her feet.

He scooped Ari into his arms and headed to their bed. Her eyes closed as he walked, and she did not answer when he spoke. Dionysus lay her on the bed, afraid of what illness would take her from him. His fevered mind did not note the approach of his favored siblings, until Apollo's hand touched his shoulder and he spoke.

"Come, brother. Artemis has seen to her safety, and I have seen to her sleep, so your woman will not miss you."

Dionysus turned on him in anger. "What have you done? Release her," he demanded.

Athena touched his face, her gray eyes wide in concern. "Calm, brother. Dress quickly. We would protect her from those who would harm you both."

Dionysus looked to her uncertainly. If Ari was in danger, he could not leave her.

Apollo's voice was rough and commanding. "She is safe here. She will not know you have gone. You have my word on both."

He nodded and waved his hand to clothe himself, a bit of magic Dionysus had not used since Ariadne came into his life. As an afterthought, he tied on the sash and added his purple cloak. He kissed Ari's brow and tucked a blanket around her, laying his hand over his son fondly. "I will return, my love. You have my solemn vow. I will return."

Dionysus turned to his siblings and waved a hand theatrically, indicating that they should lead the way. He followed them through the doorway, sucking in his breath as he felt himself transported through space in the way of the gods. He stepped through the other doorway—and into his father's throne room. Dionysus peered about at the full council of all of his closest siblings warily.

Zeus looked up at the congregation before him in concern. "My children, why have you come here?"

Apollo bowed. "We ask for your mercy in granting Dionysus his woman for all time, Father."

Aurora stepped forward in obvious agitation. "Forever young, Father—not as I made my poor Tithonus."

Zeus touched her cheek and nodded his understanding. "Tell me the tale," he commanded. "I would know of her importance."

Dionysus began to speak, but Aphrodite cut him off. "Theseus played with this woman's heart for want of her sister. Ariadne released him from his vow. Still, that was not enough. To avoid punishment for his crimes against her heart, Theseus allowed his wife to banish her sister to the isle of Naxos with little more than her will to live to sustain her. It was an affront to me and to love. It could not go unpunished."

"Punished? Daughter, you know how the Fates feel about interfering in mortal futures. Has the ire of the Fates taught you nothing?"

Athena approached Zeus next, knowing their father could never be angry with her. "He and his wife were an insult to my great city, father. Their crimes had to be punished."

Zeus nodded and smiled indulgently. "Continue, Daughters."

Aphrodite continued her story. "Love for love, Father. Theseus sought to possess Phaedra, but she was a self-serving and inconstant woman. She took her own life when her bid to lure Theseus's son, Hippolytus, failed her."

Artemis stepped forward. "Theseus blamed and banished my dear huntsman, Hippolytus, his own son.

He sent away my pride for the word of a devious, lying wench that showed him not even faithfulness."

Zeus nodded. "We must set things right for Hippolytus."

Apollo met his eyes. "My son, Aesculapius, waits my orders to do what needs be."

"Aesculapius," Zeus roared, his face darkened in rage. "You killed him? Hippolytus was innocent. You said so yourselves."

Aphrodite raised her chin in challenge. "It was necessary—is necessary. Theseus will affect his own banishment to win his son's reprieve. He must do so now that he knows his own guilt."

"Explain why this is necessary." Zeus' eyes fanned over his children suspiciously.

Aphrodite sighed, shooting a pained look at Dionysus. "With the loss of Phaedra, Theseus thinks to force Ariadne to the vow she released him of."

Apollo locked a grip on his arm as Dionysus tried to bolt back to protect her. He stilled as Aphrodite continued speaking.

"Her maiden's blood on him means nothing," she decided hotly. "I requested Proteus to name him who should be Ariadne's true mate, and his vision showed Proteus our brother, Dionysus. Ariadne is a most loving and accepting woman, and their love is the strongest I have seen in all my years. Dionysus cannot lose her, Father."

Zeus caught his youngest son in his gaze. "Tell me, Dionysus. Tell me of the things that draw you to this woman."

Dionysus nodded. "Ari knows not who I am. She thought me a simple merchant, washed up from a shipwreck. Still, she shared her food and fire, her shelter and bed. Ari, a princess born and raised, took me to her heart—a merchant in her eyes. She asks no finery and no pomp.

"She mourns Aegeus, a man she never met, for Theseus's inattention due to his dealings with her caused the man's death. I never once heard her wish ill on Theseus and Phaedra, those who abandoned her thus. Ari is a most rare jewel, Father."

Zeus nodded sadly. "Your mother was such a jewel. If I grant this, will you bring her here?"

Apollo answered for him, a fortuitous circumstance since Dionysus had no idea of the answer to that question. The thought of bringing Ari to Olympus made his head swim. She would not care for it, he was certain.

"With your permission, Father—Poseidon has agreed to create unfavorable currents, and Aeolus has agreed to cause winds to spirit any ship away from the island."

"You mean to inhabit Naxos?" Zeus asked in sincere interest.

Dionysus nodded. "I believe Ari would like that."

Zeus sighed and steepled his fingers. "If Ariadne agrees, I give her the gift of eternal youth and health with my son, Dionysus."

"Thank you, Father."

"What will you do, now?" the king of the gods asked, a knowing smile curving his dark lips.

Athena laughed. "Now we go to Athens to seal Theseus's fate."

"No," Dionysus decided. "He is mine alone."

He sent his siblings off to the tasks they must attend to: Aphrodite and Artemis to Hippolytus, Apollo to his son to call the young prince back from death, Athena to speak to her high priests and demand that Theseus never again set foot in Athens, and Aurora to hold off the sun so that Dionysus might greet the dawn in Ari's arms. After a goodbye to his father, Dionysus visualized his route and walked out of Zeus' throne room and into Theseus's quarters on board his ship.

Theseus did not see him arrive. The old king was deeply engrossed in his amusements with a young servant. Dionysus screwed up his face in disgust and placed his hand out for the cup of wine that appeared at his thought.

"No wonder Ariadne was so affected," Dionysus announced. "If that was the extent of your performance, any man would have seemed an improvement."

Theseus rolled off his servant, grabbing for his sword. "Who are you? How did you come to my quarters?"

Dionysus looked at the frightened serving girl sadly. "Go, child." He called her child, but surely she was at least seventeen. *So very young,* he mused.

She looked to Theseus fearfully.

"Go," the old king ordered her, "but do not go far."

The girl left, clutching her tunic to her chest.

Dionysus sighed as she left. "You thought to go to Ariadne with the slick of another woman on you," he spat. "Of course, you went to Phaedra with her sister's maiden's blood staining you."

"Who are you?" Theseus demanded again.

"Put your clothing on, Theseus. You disgust me."

Theseus looked at the intruder in stunned silence, but he lay his sword near him warily and pulled on his robes.

"Come have a cup of wine, and we will speak." Dionysus placed his hand up to grasp the cup as it appeared.

Theseus's eyes widened. "By Zeus," he swore.

"Ah, yes. My beloved father. I should warn you that he is no happier with you than my siblings and I are."

"The gods are angry with me? How have I injured them? What can I do to make right my misdeeds?" he asked urgently, his ruddy face paling in the knowledge that he had crossed the gods.

"To appease Athena, you will banish yourself for all time from Athens. To appease Apollo and save Hippolytus, you will deliver up the whole of your library to Aesculapius at Mount Pelion."

"Hippolytus will be returned to me?" His face lit in savage glee.

"No. Hippolytus will be returned to Athens. To appease Artemis, you will not attempt to contact him."

"I lose my son?" Theseus raged.

"You have already lost your son. Do you wish him to continue his long walk in the underworld?" Dionysus asked pointedly.

His anger disappeared. "No. Of course not. It is a small price to pay for his life."

"In retribution for your crimes, Apollo withdraws his healing. No more should you seek danger. He no longer backs you. Aphrodite has seen her revenge in your wife's own treachery, and Aurora—" Dionysus paused, as his sister's plea filled his mind. "Aurora would have you go to your friend King Lycomedes. I know not why, but it will appease her."

"And you? Tell me, mighty Dionysus, what was my crime against the gods?"

"Ariadne was your crime," he growled. "The root of your many crimes."

"I go to make it right. It is all I wish."

He lied, as Dionysus knew he would. The surety of that fact burned in Dionysus.

"You go to bury your cock in the body of the woman who should have been your queen," he shouted. "You go to lay with the true jewel of Minos's loins."

"It is my right. I gave my vow. Her maiden's blood—
"

"Means nothing. She is not yours to take." His voice was cold and hard in warning. "You will not touch her."

"She is mine," Theseus replied in frustration.

"You were willingly released from your vow," Dionysus dismissed his claim.

"She rescinded her vow. I did not relinquish my claim."

"Ariadne carries her husband's son. She has found her peace. To appease me, you will stay far from her. If you do approach her, you will anger myself, my siblings and father, Poseidon and Aeolus. Such anger is not wise to bring down on yourself."

Theseus stood transfixed for a moment. When he spoke, his voice was weak and resigned. "Why the interest, mighty one? What stake have you in this matter?"

Dionysus's smile spread, and he pushed his cloak back over his shoulders, baring the sash to his nemesis. Theseus's eyes widened in shock. He looked at Dionysus in undisguised fear.

Dionysus nodded. "A gift from my wife," he confirmed. "She is dead to you, Theseus. Make me a vow, one you dare not ever break."

"Ariadne is no more. You have my word," he choked.

"Then you should collect your serving girl, while I return to my home and wife." Dionysus stepped through the doorway and into his home with a smile of triumph on his face.

* * * *

Ariadne woke to the feeling of Baccs laying kisses on her face. She opened her eyes to the rising sun and listened to the restless birds. It was morning? She lost the whole evening and night?

She stretched into her husband's arms. "I am sorry, Baccs. I do not know what came over me."

"Your time is close. You must let me do more while you rest."

"I love you, husband."

"Do you love me enough to live forever with me on our lovely island?"

"Until I die," she promised.

"No. Do you love me enough to promise me forever? Do you want me forever?" His face was abruptly serious, as if Baccs feared losing her love.

"Forever," she agreed, laying a kiss on his chest. "Would that we could have forever, I would give you that long."

He laughed, a sound of ultimate happiness. Baccs kissed her, a slow kiss that heated her blood for him. "Forever starts this moment, love. Celebrate with me."

Ariadne shook her head in wonder. "I will always revel in your arms." She stilled in his embrace. "Did you hear that? Was that laughter?"

Baccs laughed as he kissed her. "Birds, Ariadne. They are but love birds singing for our happiness."

Dedication

Lisa, who's always ready to be a sounding board when I'm stuck and always ready to test new stories to see if they punch the reader solidly and for all its worth.

Fran, my Radiant mother, who has traveled to the Sun's far side.

Author's Note

Gluttony:

Excess in eating or drinking; the quality of being intemperate; an excessive desire; never satiated; never satisfied; wanting more pleasure from something than it was made for.

The misconception about gluttony is thinking that it only pertains to overeating. It is about an excess of any given thing: food and drink, sex, or possessions.

There are several types of gluttons in this book. Jedean is a glutton for power and position. Even as he prevails and ensures no one will wrest him loose, there is no denying his thirst for more. In fact, it is his gluttony for power alone that causes this story to unfold. Senna is driven by what she is, and what she lacks, to a more classic gluttony, insatiable hunger. Then there is Jaysen...

Foreword: The History of Semiterr

Welcome, dear reader, to Semiterr, a world inhabited by humans and two types of mages: Radiants and Blood Mages. Radiants are children of the day, feeding their magic on radiant energy, the auras that surround every living thing. Blood Mages are children of the night, unable to withstand the intense radiance of sunlight, feeding their magic on blood taken from willing hosts, a largely peaceful race.

Mistrust, as usually will, has always run rampant between the two. Only one solid truth has kept the Radiants from eradicating the Blood Mages completely; on a rare occasion, a Radiant and a Blood Mage are destined as mates. In such a union, their magic merged, there is none on the planet more powerful than the blood mated pair.

For the last century, a war has waged, not between Radiant and Blood Mage but Radiant against Radiant for the seat of power. A Blood Mage mate would ensure victory and strengthen the bloodline of the possessor.

Thus, Blood Mages fell prey to the Radiants, forced to test and killed if not mate to the Radiant in question to avoid an enemy finding a match. Always, a few were left alive to continue their kind.

Blood Mage and Radiant have each been forced to their keeps, hidden behind shields and wards, trusting no one.

A new game is afoot. Jedean might have taken the seat of power by magic alone, but he would have had to hold it by force. How much better and more expedient to keep his place by trades for loyalty oaths, sealed in magic, for something only he possesses...

Chapter One

"Watch, Jaysen," his father instructed, pointing to the corridor furthest below their balcony perch. Jedean whispered, though the pulse of magic around them made it painfully clear to Jaysen that the shields between them and the floors below would protect them not only from attack but also from being observed or overheard.

He stared at Jedean a moment longer, taking in his father's ice-blue eyes and the light-brown curls cropped only a finger-width down his neck. Jedean's tanned chest was uncovered in his typical form of dress for inside the keep, nude save his white trousers.

Jaysen's resemblance to his father ended with the tanned skin and mode of dress; he was undeniably his dead mother's son, possessing her midnight blue eyes and black curls that he kept longer than was fashionable for a man under his father's protest.

Even his sensibilities ran more to his mother's tastes, something Jedean assured him would change as he became a man and learned more of the cares a man had. Jaysen hoped he was wrong, though he dared not speak that thought aloud.

Jaysen's mind worked at the powerful mage's great glee. It was unbecoming, something Jaysen himself had been counseled about by his teachers many times.

"This is how a man grows powerful. Watch now."

Jaysen sighed. He was ten and six winters, a moon from his manhood ceremony, and his father still treated him like a child. Still, he looked where his father directed. There was a lesson to be learned here, a lesson that might make him a mage as powerful in radiant light as his father was.

He gasped in surprise at the sight of their greatest rival, stripped to his ceremony wrap and standing in the lowest corridor of the keep, tanned skin in stark contrast to the rosestone walls, feet uncovered on the bare floors. Jaysen would have thought him a prisoner had he been restrained in any way, but he was clearly a penitent, fresh from some rite or about to engage in one.

Within our keep? Such a thing defied reason.

"What is Delek Tro doing here?" he asked in amazement.

Jedean chuckled darkly, urging Jaysen along the upper corridor ahead of him. For a moment, the only sound was that of their feet against the thick carpets of the family core, brick red to offset the rosestone and golden accent pieces along the walls.

"I possess something Delek desires...something many strong in the radiant light desire, something they will pay in loyalty oaths and riches to obtain."

Jaysen looked back, watching the house steward leading Delek the same direction they traveled. "It must be a precious possession," he mused.

"*The* most precious," Jedean agreed. "What could be—"

"She." His father stopped at another balcony and motioned to the room below.

"A woman?" Jaysen questioned in disbelief. No woman was worth the risk of entering an enemy's keep unshielded, even one as lush as the one stretched out nude on the bed below.

Though, she is a striking woman. He took a moment to consider her before stating his disbelief more firmly, certain that he was missing something that would encompass the whole of his father's intended 'lesson.'

She was young, no more than a year or two his senior, an adult but barely so. She was unadorned by jewels, her beauty speaking for itself. Her skin was unnaturally pale, a sign that she spent much of her time inside the keep...or inside some keep. It only added to her allure, setting her apart from the dark tans of the nobility. And yet, something about her spoke of a noble background, the cut of her face, perhaps. Her hair was long and straight, as black as his own, well-kept and untangled, an invitation to touch her unspoken. Yes, she was stunning.

Still, entering an enemy's keep in such a fashion was madness. Tempting flesh could only tempt a man so far. "What could—"

She opened her eyes, and the breath caught in Jaysen's lungs. *Green-gold eyes.* They fairly glowed in the candlelight.

"A Blood Mage," his father confirmed. "One of the last and of bastard lineage, but powerful and eligible stock."

But, Jaysen heard him through the haze of sexual longing. A spike of jealousy sliced through him as her gaze locked on Jedean. Jaysen wanted her to look at him, to invite him in.

"She always knows when I am near, despite the wards and shields, even if I am out of her line of sight," Jedean mused. "This is our greatest treasure, Jaysen. Every mage with aspirations of the seat of power desires her."

I desire her. I need her. But, he was incapable of forming the words to state it.

"But I have her, Jaysen. I own her."

He shuddered at the thought of the woman below being a slave of the house. *A slave to anyone.*

"Those who wish to test her passion become indebted to me."

"You let them use her?" Jaysen could hardly force the words past his dry mouth. He needed to drink of her body. It was as essential as breathing to him.

"She has no hope of better," Jedean dismissed his concern. "Her magic led her here in search of her mate."

What desperation would force her to abandon her keep and go to those who slaughtered her kind? Even if her mate was a Radiant, even if she trusted that he wouldn't turn on her as so many would...

His father kept speaking, oblivious to his contemplation. "She was young, barely ten and six winters gone, naïve, quick to test."

Jaysen stiffened. His father had used her inexperience against her. He didn't question it. In his pursuit for the seat of power, no foul trick was beyond Jedean.

"Binding her was a simple matter, once I had her trust and her arousal proved a detriment to her attention. I wasn't the mate she sought, of course, but I played the part well, I think...until I had her snared. I knew I wouldn't be." His voice showed his contempt at the thought of such a match, as advantageous as it would be. "She'd undoubtedly been one with my brother, Tason, and our close blood confused her."

"He is dead," Jaysen offered numbly. He wasn't certain whether he should feel anger at Jedean's deception or pity for the poor girl thus ensnared. She was barely a woman and a slave to the mage she'd hoped would save her from some dire predicament.

"Yes, and so there is nothing better in her future than feeding on a line of men she can never accept fully." Jedean leaned on the balcony rail, staring at her. "Though eventually, she will choose to birth a bastard. Most without mates do, as her mother did after Gavin tested her and let her live to produce a new generation."

The image of the woman below, tied down while old Gavin tested her lust and hunger, had his fury burning. Her mother would have been much like her, much like all Blood Mages were.

"She took a human, I hear," Jedean spat. "It would have been better if she'd chosen a Blood Mage to sire her bastard, but I imagine finding one was difficult. Still, this one is a strong one, considering she is a half-blood."

Jaysen's retort was cut off as the door opened. Delek stepped into the room below, and Jaysen's blood ran cold. He was here to force her to test.

Her eyes turned gold, and she moved them from Jedean to Delek. Her hunger assaulted Jaysen, making him lightheaded. She spread her legs in invitation, and his cock rose.

Delek went to her bed, kneeling between her parted ankles, his oiled skin reflecting points of candlelight. "I come to test you, Blood Mage."

Jaysen wanted to throw the older mage out, to go to her himself, to allow her to test *him* in the manner she should be allowed. And yet, he longed to watch her feed and be fed upon.

Her voice was like silk. "You and many others, Radiant. Continue, if it pleases you."

Delek darkened, his jaw tightening in fury that spoke of violence to come. "It will please you," he challenged.

Her golden eyes flicked to Jedean, then away, a wry smile curving her lips. "No doubt, it will. You know my price."

Jedean laughed harshly. "Her idea, her addition to what I require of her...and require of them. They are bound to give their lifeblood to her willingly in payment for the right to test her. They leave here exhausted from their efforts to drive her to test and a little weaker in fluids, but they leave indebted."

Delek nodded and spoke in a low voice that was lost in the rushing in Jaysen's ears.

She smiled indulgently, saying something that made Delek go shades darker.

Jaysen didn't hear it; he didn't want to hear it. He fisted his hand. Though she affected amusement well, her sadness and pain ate at him.

Jedean chuckled. "She thinks she punishes me with the knowledge that she enjoys their attention."

The force of an energy blast to the chest left Jaysen gasping for breath. It tortured him *to know it.*

"Jaysen?"

Delek lowered himself, tasting her, growing more avid as she bowed up. Her eyes closed, and her lips parted, her fangs lengthening as her cries became louder and more frantic. Her hips cycled, guiding Delek's ministrations.

Jaysen's muscles tightened in preparation for battle and his cock ached. His breathing regressed to gasps. He stepped toward her, intent on killing the one who dared touch her, who dared make her feel such dark emotions in what should be a beautiful sharing.

"Jaysen!"

Hands dragged him away. Jaysen fought them, grumbling curses, searching frantically in a mind that fought clear thinking for the battle spells he'd had driven into him since toddlerhood.

Two hands became four, then six. A heavy door closed, then a second. He roared in protest as her emotions disappeared from his mind. He had no sense of direction, no idea where she was, but he had to reach her. The voices around him made no more sense than the hum of night insects.

A sharp incantation brought his head around. His father's face was abruptly clear before him. Then all went black.

* * * *

Jaysen groaned, his head tender in a post-spell reaction. It took a moment for the scattered memories to knit into a sketch that he understood. It was no enemy who had done this to him; his own father had struck him down.

"Jaysen?" Jedean grumbled in a voice that sounded of near exhaustion.

He forced his eyes open, identifying the light beige linens, whitewood and silver accents that indicated they were in his rooms at their summer keep in confusion. The rooms were decorated, as everything in the summer keep was, to his mother's specifications. There were no rooms like this in his father's bastion.

How long had he been incapacitated? *At least, half a day to have reached the summer keep. Most probably, a full day, when one considered the time to arrange such a move on short notice.*

"Jaysen? Do you remember what happened?"

"You cast against me," he stated. How could Jedean do such a thing?

"You were crazed, a danger to yourself and others."

Was I? Jaysen vaguely recalled fighting. His knuckles ached, a living testament to the fact that he'd struck physical blows instead of magical ones. "To others," he admitted.

"To yourself, boy! You nearly threw yourself off the balcony and—"

"The Blood Mage!" Jaysen launched to his feet, intent on reaching her, then crumpled into his father's arms. He groaned weakly, his breathing labored. Visions of her green-gold eyes danced behind his closed lids.

Jedean settled him into bed again, tucking the quilts as if he were a babe.

"I must see her," Jaysen murmured. *I must touch her. I must taste her. I must protect her.*

There was silence, an unsettling stillness, a chasm that hadn't existed between them moments before.

"I want her, Father. My manhood ceremony approaches—"

"No. You will not be permitted to see Senna again."

"Senna..." A smile pulled up at his lips. The name fit her.

"You are forbidden, Jaysen." His father's voice was cold and hard in decision. "The wards and shields have already been set."

His head throbbed, and a sick swirl settled in his stomach. "But a man is permitted any boon when he reaches—"

"This is not a boon. It is suicide. You will never see Senna Ravensky again. Not while I live to prevent it."

Jaysen's protest was drowned out by his father's casting. He sank into a magic-induced sleep, welcomed by dreams of Senna, eaten up by his hunger for her.

Chapter Two

Ten Years Later

Senna lay on the bed, staring into nothingness as she did most days.

It wasn't that there was nothing to look at or nothing to do. In truth, her room was comfortable. Deep red carpet offset the rosestone walls that were hung with paintings of night scenes that soothed her and golden candle sconces that Jedean's magic kept bright and clean. There were cushioned chairs and a reading desk stocked with books, a small fire nook that was cold at the moment, and even a smaller version of his mineral pool that had been added some eight years prior.

And yet, she would give nearly anything to leave the place, but that was impossible for many reasons.

She had no concept of day or night; that most basic magic had deserted her long ago, lingering only weeks longer than the rest. Even if Senna left the lower corridors and found her way to the upper reaches once more, she could be walking into agony unknowing.

But what did it matter? She'd been bound by her stupidity and Jedean Magal's magic for the last twelve years. The locked iron doors between her and the outside world hardly mattered. It was something of an insult that Jedean bothered with them.

He hadn't always kept her behind locked doors. For the first two years Senna had been enslaved, she'd been free to wander the lower reaches of his keep. In those days, she'd had use of the main library, the steam room, mineral pool, and even the smaller fire den. She'd simply been denied use of the family core of the house. Senna hadn't used her privileges often, so angry at her enslavement that she'd sulked most of the night hours away like the child she'd been at the time.

And, you have grown so much, she chided herself. *You act like the eight and twenty you profess to be?*

No. This wasn't sulking. This was despondency, boredom, apathy.

Now, even that shadow of true freedom was lost to her. In truth, she could request books from the library, and they would be brought to her room, but her frequent depression made that an empty joy, at best.

It wasn't just her movement that Jedean had restricted. He'd not allowed her to feed on lifeblood from the day he'd locked the doors until today. Though the mundane food she was provided with was copious and well-presented, it wasn't what she craved most.

Gone were the days when she'd been free to feed from willing servants, when Jedean might deign to share her bed himself for the pleasure her nectar gave him. Gone were the days when she might trade the right to "test" her for a powerful mouthful or two of lifeblood from the Radiants' most high. Gone were her powers with it. No longer truly a Blood Mage, she simply...existed.

Jedean hadn't passed through the doors in those ten years. He had rarely peered at her from the high balcony. There had been no reason given for the change in her imprisonment, not that a slave expected one.

Thus, a decade had passed, Senna alone save the few servants granted access to her, most notably the slight, serious house steward. She typically saw the man four times a day: bringing each of her meals and picking up the final tray, always asking if she required anything more of him. Since he could not give her the one thing she wished for, the answer was typically in the negative, and she would see him no more.

Senna had often wondered if his aim was to keep her weak, to steal her magic in retribution for some offense against him. His reasons for such a thing were impossible to guess, though. She was bound, incapable of doing Jedean harm in any way: physically, politically or emotionally. That a given, it made little sense to keep her weakened and trapped behind iron doors.

The door opened, and the house steward entered, a pewter goblet in his hands instead of a tray of food. The scent of blood assaulted her first, the essence of a powerful man, one of the higher Radiants, dizzying in its potency. Her fangs lengthened, and her mouth watered to taste it.

The question of whose blood the cup contained was dismissed almost as quickly as it appeared in her mind. It wasn't Jedean's blood. As hungry as she was, she might have refused his blood, offered in such a manner.

It isn't Jedean's. For that reason alone, it was a welcome gift.

"Lady Senna," the steward greeted her. It had been years since he'd addressed her so formally, but she didn't question it.

Not while he holds the goblet of liquid life in his hands.

At times, she'd wished she could address the man by name to ease her loneliness, but a mage's servants were never addressed by name. If the steward had a name, and she assumed that he did, Senna doubted that Jedean even knew it. He had servants to keep abreast of such things for him.

She nodded, rising slowly, her eyes locked on the offered treat. Senna didn't typically like to drink in so mundane a manner, but the magic surrounding the goblet spoke of a freshening spell. The contents would be as warm and vital as if taken direct from the Radiant himself.

In confirmation of her belief, the goblet was heated; it seemed to pulse beneath her fingertips. Surely, it was a trick of the magic, but she was strangely touched by the effort. Jedean had never gone to such lengths to please her, yet more proof that the gift had not been commissioned by her 'owner.'

Senna didn't consider refusing the gift...or even asking who had sent it before she accepted it. She'd be a fool to do it. She raised the goblet to her lips and drank deeply, feeling her magic as she hadn't in nearly a decade, since just before Jedean locked her away completely from the world.

It was night. Mother Night called to Senna, welcomed Her daughter home.

Her body reacted fiercely to the stimulus, her sex dampening and begging for a lover's touch. She licked her lips, lips plumped as if already well-kissed.

The steward took the goblet from her hand. "The gift is to your liking, Lady Senna?"

"It is," she whispered, lost in pleasure, drunk in the need for more.

"If it pleases you..." He hesitated, seemingly disconcerted.

"Yes?"

"My master requests an audience of you."

Senna stared at him in confusion. To her knowledge, Jedean had never *requested* anything, of her or of anyone in his employ. And when did the steward start referring to Jedean as "my master?"

"Jedean has never asked permission to enter here before," she noted cautiously.

"Alas, Lady Senna," he began with a weak smile. "Lord Jedean is no longer master here. He has passed to the Sun's far side."

Her heart pounded in a mixture of hope and terror. "Who is master of the keep?"

Who holds my chains now that Jedean is no more?

"With Lord Jedean's death, all he owned passed to his son and heir, Lord Jaysen."

All he owned. A spark of anger ignited in her. *He owned me. And now,* Jaysen *owns me.*

"Will you come to him, Lady Senna?"

"Come? Come where?"

"To his fire den."

She considered that. Why would the young Radiant return her magic to her and treat her as an equal? The cost was certain to be a high one.

A length of black silk appeared on the bed before her, and Senna touched it, hardly daring to believe her eyes. It was the traditional dress of a Blood Mage, possibly the same one Jedean had taken from her after he bound her.

No. This one is new, without the taste of old magic mine would carry, even after a dozen years, without the protective spells my mother wove in before her death.

"A gift from Lord Jaysen," the steward informed her with a slight bow of his head.

"As was the goblet of living life?" she asked.

"Indeed, it was."

"Tell him..." She lifted the sleeve of the dress and stroked her cheek with it, sighing. "Tell him I will come to him."

* * * *

Jaysen reclined on the mattress and cushions laid before the fire nook, his skin still tingling from the mineral bath, unclothed in her honor. He'd chosen the room purposefully. It was one of the few he'd been able to redecorate so far, changing the dark carpets to light much as the summer keep was decorated. It was Jedean who had favored the deep red furnishings; as in most matters, Jaysen was more like his mother had been.

He trailed his gaze over the painted day-scapes on the wall, hoping Senna would like them as much as he did. The room was light, warm, nothing like the darkness of her cell. Of course, there was no way to learn if she liked it but to watch her reactions to it.

It was time. He'd restrained himself only three days after Jedean's death, preparing for her in what he hoped was the appropriate manner. Senna would arrive soon, and with her agreement, a decade of waiting would come to an end.

Those years had been long and frustrating. Many a sleepless night had found Jaysen wandering the keep, stopped again and again by the many shields and wards that separated him from her.

He'd known the truth within days of his father's decree, but no amount of reasoning, pleading, or threats had swayed Jedean in the slightest. Jedean had been wrong about Senna's intended mate, though he'd been right about the fact that his blood had confused her. Tason's blood hadn't been that which she sought; it was Jaysen's. His father had dismissed that idea, since Jaysen had not yet been a man when Senna appeared at the door.

Had she come to the keep two years later, how much different their lives might have been. But, Senna had no doubt assumed that her mate would be an adult, as she was at the time.

There was no question that Jedean knew what Senna was to Jaysen after his reaction to Delek's 'test.' Nor was there any question that it scared the old mage to death to know it. Hence, he would not relent while he lived, just as he'd vowed.

Perhaps he feared Senna had gone mad in her enslavement and would harm Jaysen rather than accept him.

Perhaps Jedean feared losing position. Though Jaysen cared little for the tales of the shared magic, it was undeniable that, with Senna as his mate, there would be no higher Radiant than Jaysen. He would win and hold the seat of power without effort, and Jedean had never backed down from a contender to his place, even if it were his own son.

Or perhaps Jedean simply feared Senna's wrath, were she free to vent it.

Jaysen never learned which it was. His father had died without comment on the matter.

He straightened as the doors opened and the steward announced her. His heart pounded, and his mouth watered in anticipation of her taste. Her power washed over him before she appeared, a glorious blaze of her full strength unleashed.

Then she was there, in the doorway, making her way to him. Her smooth, black hair fell to her hips, shimmering in the firelight, looking like a short cape against her equally-black gown. Her skin was pale and unblemished, her lips red as blood and eyes wide and bright.

The door closed behind her, granting them privacy.

Senna walked across the room, her head held high, a proud woman who owned the very air around her.

He smiled. Of course, she owned it. As her mate, all that was his was hers, though she didn't know it yet.

She stopped at the edge of the mattress, panning her eyes down the length of his body, regarding his rising cock in the same boredom she'd shown Delek years earlier. "You called for me?" she asked, the bite of ice in her voice. She kept her mind shielded, a sure sign that she didn't trust him.

"I *invited* you to join me. Would you rather I come to that foul cell?" He'd determined not to go to her there long ago. In addition to the fact that she'd been imprisoned there for so long, which was sure to make her uncomfortable, the memories of Delek drinking of her would drive Jaysen mad if he attempted it.

"A slave is a slave, wherever she lays."

Jaysen ground his teeth in impotent rage. "I cannot deny it," he admitted.

"I suppose you wish to test me, Radiant?"

"One does not test a Blood Mage," he countered. "The Blood Mage tests him...if she wishes."

She hesitated, her eyes narrowing, seemingly wary. "You do not require that I submit to you?"

Finally, she was asking the right questions. "I do not demand that you submit to anything."

She stared at him, her mouth working as if to question him further. Senna looked into the fire.

"That confuses you." He'd expected that it would. He knew he'd probably have to lead her into the concept that she controlled her own destiny this way.

"I cannot deny it," she taunted him.

"What do you want, Senna?"

She didn't seem to know how to answer that. After so long as a slave, he'd expected as much from her.

"Sit down," he invited.

Senna sank to the mattress beside him, seemingly lost in thought. She looked down then winced, no doubt in the realization that she'd obeyed him. She refused to meet his eyes. That was unacceptable.

Jaysen slid the tiny sacrament blade out of the sheath beside the mattress and sliced a shallow track in his index finger, letting the blood well up. He tossed the knife away.

She looked up, her eyes golden, her fangs lengthening, intent on the sluggish flow. "You tease me," she whispered.

"Is this not the way a hopeful entices a Blood Mage, Senna?"

He *was* teasing her. There was no denying it. Jaysen was playing on her hunger after his father's cruelty. He'd considered this moment long and hard, nights of planning how best to approach her. This was how she should have been approached, the traditional way a hopeful mate appeased a Blood Mage. Senna deserved no less from him.

She shifted toward him, her breath heating his fingertips, the sharp movements of air making his head spin in response.

"Do you want this, Senna? Do you...need it?" *I need it. What will I do if she refuses me?*

He'd let her go, even if it killed him to do it. Jaysen just prayed she'd choose to stay. Her eyes closed, and she leaned toward him, stopping just short of his offered gift. Jaysen knew the dance well. He'd studied ancient texts tirelessly, researching the proper ceremony, a ceremony that reportedly hadn't been used in nearly a century.

He caressed his fingertip across her lower lip, painting his blood on her, the first sign that she was his.

* * * *

Senna sucked his fingertip into her mouth, smiling at his groan of pleasure, at the plea she'd seen in his midnight blue eyes even before she'd accepted his gift. His heartbeat quickened, and his arousal flavored his blood.

His magic was strong, nectar even more potent than his father's had been. She wondered at that, the mad realization that Jaysen might be lord by virtue of murder; his potency proved him more than a match for any other Radiant she'd met. Then again, if it was Jedean Magal he'd murdered, she wasn't certain she'd consider it much of a crime against society at large.

She pushed that thought out of her mind with a silent plea for forbearance from Mother Night. It wasn't a Blood Mage's way to be... Well, that was the worst pun she'd considered in a decade.

Senna released his finger and licked her lips, unwilling to waste a drop of him. The dance of enticement was something she'd lost hope of experiencing long ago. Perhaps, if she hadn't been so young and awed at the concept that a Radiant as strong as Jedean was bound for her, she might have insisted that he...

He wasn't mine. He'd never been destined for me. I should have known it was wrong when he treated me like a human lover, when he wouldn't...

Jaysen's fingertip glided along her upper lip, seducing her with the promise of sating her hungers properly for the first time in her life. She sucked it in again, drinking of him, feeling her powers swell.

Mother Night, I never realized how powerful I'd become in my full maturity.

That cleared her mind. Of course, she hadn't! Jedean had kept her leashed and on the edges of starvation, even before he stole her magic entirely. Senna had never been permitted to taste her full strength.

She sucked him more urgently, greedily using him to strengthen herself.

"Moon and stars, yes," he whispered.

Senna released his fingertip and surged toward him, sealing her mouth to his. His lips parted further, and their tongues danced. Jaysen buried his hands in her hair, fisting them as she cupped him.

He was more than adequate in size, already hard. With a few delicate flicks of her tongue, he'd pour out his seed for her as Jedean had, in the early days, before he'd locked her away. Jaysen pressed his hips up, begging for more.

Use his hunger.

The thought appeared in her mind from nowhere. Senna tried to argue her way out of it, but it proved impossible.

Jedean had used her passion and her hunger to trap her. What better irony than using his son's to free herself?

I would be no better than Jedean!

But did not a prisoner wrongly held deserve freedom at any cost? She conceded that it was so.

Jaysen sank to his back, drawing her over him.

Memories of the long line of lusting Radiants turned her stomach. A single certainty rose in her. This was the last one who would touch her. When she was free, she'd kill Jaysen and take her leave from this place for all time.

Their lips parted, and Jaysen rolled her beneath him. She opened her eyes, gauging his involvement in the affair and finding him fully immersed. It was time to make her move.

"Is this what you want, Jaysen?" She forced herself not to show her distaste at speaking his name aloud.

She hadn't addressed a Radiant directly by name since Jedean betrayed her. It had been her defiance. They'd stripped her of her name, called her 'Blood Mage' as if they were addressing the cook or house steward. She'd done the same to them to show her contempt for them. They were less than human to her.

His voice was graveled in arousal. "You know it is."

"Sex with the slave," she sighed. Senna thanked Mother Night that he was so different in appearance than Jedean had been. Though she'd like to claim the resemblance wouldn't have unnerved her and caused her to tip her hand, it might well have.

He winced. "Never."

"Unless you free me, that is all there can ever be between us." Her heart pounded in near-terror that she masked carefully.

Jaysen opened his startling blue eyes, seemingly assessing her.

If he saw through her ploy, what would he do? Take what he wanted, despite her wishes, master and slave? Lock her in that damned cell and starve her into compliance? Whatever he chose, she would be bound to all but verbal agreement to his course.

He will never make it past the first trial. She'd been too quick with Jedean...and confused. No Radiant save him had mounted her since; none had earned the right to. Since her mate was dead, none ever would. Even if Jaysen tried her, he'd leave as unsatisfied as the others had, drunk on her nectar and loss of blood, aching for her, for that one thing she would never grant them.

Jaysen owns me. Like Jedean, he could demand more of her. His protestations that he would not aside, he was his father's son. When her nectar enflamed him, and his body cried out for her, he would take what he wished. His father certainly had, in the early days.

Time slipped away in silence, setting her nerves on edge. "You are right," he stated. "You will not come to me a slave."

I will not come to you at all. I will not come for you and your male ego, either. She held her tongue, unwilling to risk her promised freedom in so foolhardy a manner.

She shivered as the words of binding rolled off his tongue, an ancient verse that she'd heard last in the midst of sensual bliss, Jedean's cock buried inside her and her fangs in him. By the time her muddled mind had identified the spell, it had been too late to stop it. This time, she welcomed the words, the spell spoken then unspoken to break the chain.

Memories of Jedean's smug smile fueled her rage. He'd laughed at her scream of outrage and horror, taunted her as he spilled his seed inside her, seed that thankfully had found no purchase. It was, perhaps, a blessing that he'd never thought to order her to forsake the spells that kept his seed from planting, that he hadn't forced a bastard of his loins upon her. Then again, Jedean probably found the thought of engendering such a child more distasteful than she did.

He would pay for her pain a thousand-fold. *His son will, when I am free.*

The final syllable died away, and Jaysen smiled his father's smile.

Senna grasped his head between her hands, intent on snapping his neck. She trembled, and her arms seemed to bleed strength away. She stared into his questioning eyes, the urge to harm him lessening, confusion setting in.

A sob escaped her lips in realization. "You lied to me." To the end, he would be Jedean's son.

* * * *

Jaysen stared at her, confusion cutting through his arousal. "Never," he assured her. "I would never lie to you." Why would she think he had?

"You...must have," she hitched out. Tears rolled down her cheeks, pinking her fair skin. "I am still bound."

"You are not. I assure you, the words were spoken." *Is she mad that she believes the ties still bind her?*

She looked to her shaking hands in apparent misery, and her meaning became clear to him.

"You mean to harm me but cannot." Jaysen didn't question it.

Senna drew her hands back to her chest, swallowing unevenly, grimacing. He laid his forehead to hers. "Why do you seek to harm me, Senna?"

"You are... You..."

"*I* am not my father. *I* would have freed you ten years ago, when he...admitted to me that you were a slave to him. Do you not know yet that I speak the truth to you? That I never wanted this for you?" She had to know it, or Jaysen would be tossed aside.

Her body quaked against his. "If... If you speak the truth, why can I not harm you?"

His heart ached at her blindness. Did she truly not feel the attraction between them?

Or did she not trust her feelings after judging Jedean so poorly?

"Why?" she insisted.

"Do you feel anything for me?" he asked bluntly.

Senna hesitated.

"Tell me truthfully. There will be no punishment. You have my vow."

"What should I feel for a warring Radiant lord?"

Jaysen bit back a scream of frustration. His father had done it; he'd stolen Senna from Jaysen as he'd always vowed he would, only he'd done a more effective job of it than Jaysen had ever anticipated.

He moved off her, not daring to meet her eyes. "Leave me."

She lay there, stunned, seemingly terrified. "Where—"

"You are free now. Go where you wish. To your home, if that pleases you. To your kin, if you have any left. The steward will...pay you for your service as you leave."

Her eyes narrowed, and she pushed to her feet. "I want nothing from you."

Hence, the problem. "As you wish, Lady Senna."

Senna stared at him, shifting from foot to foot nervously. She nodded. "Good evening, Radiant."

Jaysen didn't answer. He wasn't certain his voice would issue forth if he attempted it, and he had no clue what he'd say if he managed it.

She turned and strode from the room, her back straight and head high. He closed his eyes, abruptly cold. Surely, he would never be warm again, even in the full radiance of the midday sun.

* * * *

Senna forced her breathing to even, reasoning that she feared some trick but that the only hope of besting the trap when it came was a cool disposition and a plan of action. She was powerful and she was determined. She would leave Jaysen's keep.

No trap came.

At the door, the steward offered her a heavy cloak. She started to refuse it, then reminded herself that she'd need it. Jedean had taken all she'd carried into his keep from her, including her mother's cloak. It was the least he owed her.

The planetary elements wouldn't affect her as long as she had her strength, but the skyborne ones were another matter. Blood Mages were children of the night, sisters to the stars. Their skin was pale and without natural protection from the sun. Without shelter or their cloaks, they burned and peeled within moments.

She pulled the heavy material around her shoulders—the finest quality, she noted—fastened it at the neck, and turned to the doors, shuddering at the realities of her existence outside the protection of these walls.

Protection? she berated herself. *Iron doors and binding spells are no favor.*

The steward opened the great doors, and she took a calming breath. It was there in her grasp...freedom in the form of the packed-clay path, lined with flowering fruit trees. And yet she tarried with no possible excuse to. Any sane Blood Mage would be halfway down the path by now.

Move, coward!

Senna took two shaky steps forward, held her breath and stepped through the shield that protected Jaysen's keep from attack. For one horrifying moment, she swore the damned thing held to her, restraining her.

Then her feet touched the path outside, and the night wind welcomed her. *The caress of Mother Night's hand.* The half-moon, peeked through a break in the clouds, lighting her way, revealing the rolling hills and the river between. Without conscious thought, she picked out the hill that hid her keep from view, a four-hour walk distant.

She sobbed in what she would like to proclaim was joy, but she'd have been lying to do so. Sadness tore at her. Loss. Confusion. The urge to flee to Jaysen in his fire den was strong. *Too strong.* It had to be a trick of some sort, the trap she'd believed would come.

There is no magic here, no taint of bending a will.

But it was a feeling that fought shaking off, despite the solid facts. Returning to Jaysen made no sense, and still she ached to, with no idea why she would.

"Do you need anything, Lady Senna?" the steward offered.

Jaysen. She shook her head, forcing one foot in front of the other. The sooner she left, the sooner she would reach her own keep.

The door closed behind her with a finality that chilled her. Senna swallowed hard, blinking back tears.

She was free. That was all that mattered.

Chapter Three

Senna pushed the servant away, annoyed with herself more than him. True, he was frustrated with her, considering the possibility of leaving her service. She couldn't blame him for it. Had she ever been so demanding?

In her youth, she'd indulged her hungers often. There was no denying it, but she'd known limits then. She'd been fulfilled once she'd fed, sated in all ways for a week or more.

In the six days since she'd left Jaysen's keep, she'd known no peace. She fed constantly and without relief from it. Even when her magic wore on her in its intensity, she felt the need for more. The hunger assaulted her even as she took in the nectar of life, until she used her servants sorely, taking more than was prudent from them, more than they were comfortable giving, which was a grievous offense for beings that only took what was willingly offered.

Senna would have liked to claim it was a reaction to the years of starvation, of want and longing, but it wasn't so. She'd lived lean times before; a few solid feedings had always set her straight again.

She'd have liked to argue that she simply craved the lifeblood of a Radiant, but she didn't. Though she'd determined not to indulge a Radiant sexually again, she had coin enough to buy her fill from one of lesser family without the promise of testing. The thought killed her appetite as nothing else did, but not for long.

She was insatiable, glutting herself on blood that brought no solace from her maddening needs.

"Lady Senna?" her servant questioned, reminding her that he still waited her pleasure.

Pleasure? There is no pleasure for me. The bitter truth stung her. Whether she fed or not would make no difference. "Leave me."

He did, and she winced at the memory of another dismissal, just as cold and callous as hers had been. The memory of it still pained her, though she couldn't state why it did. He'd freed her. Why could she find no solace in it?

Senna had felt no pleasure from that day to this. Finding her wards in place and her keep unmolested hadn't moved her one way or the other. Rebuilding her world had brought her no joy.

The fact that she was rebuilding it as she last saw Jaysen's keep was more than a little disconcerting. Thankfully, she wasn't recreating the dark room where she'd been imprisoned. Senna would have considered her sanity more closely if she were. She was recreating it based on Jaysen's fire den. Several times, she'd consoled herself that the light feel of the room was what she sought, that it was coincidence that she chose paintings by the same artists and of similar scenes to the ones in that room.

The change was intended to comfort her, to bring her peace. It failed.

I feel nothing but unrequited hunger.

Even as she thought it, Senna admitted that it was a lie. She felt much more in her dreams, dreams of Jaysen in his fire den, feeding her on his blood, his midnight eyes reflecting the flames, arousing her, claiming her as not even his father had been able to.

She shook away the image, noting her slick channel, lengthened fangs, and beaded nipples in misery. If she went to the mirror, her eyes would stare back gold at her.

Senna grumbled curses in the ancient language. Jaysen was a Radiant, just another greedy day-walking mage who'd wanted her power, no better than his father was. She'd been his slave.

But he freed me. He returned what was mine to me...or as closely as he could with Jedean involved. He even offered compensation for my time in service to his father.

Why had he? That was the burning question that seemed to have no answer. Why would Jaysen give up the many advantages of having her as his slave?

For the faint hope that she'd agree to let him test her? That she might be mate to him? It hardly seemed likely that Jaysen would pin his hopes on that, when no Radiant had made it past *her* pleasure in a dozen years.

Perhaps, he'd been sincere in his seeming disgust at the thought of her life as a slave. Such men existed...or so she'd heard. True, she'd never met one, and as such, she'd assumed it was a children's fable of sorts....or tales of a long-ago past, before the Radiant wars had set the world on edge. It was an unusual trait to find in a Radiant, but she supposed it wasn't impossible that Jaysen held to such leanings.

No. If that were the case, why would he press himself on her before he released her from her enslavement?

He didn't press himself. Jaysen had enticed her, attempted to seduce her, had undeniably treated her as a Blood Mage should have been treated.

"But why?" she whispered.

Chapter Four

Senna stood at the threshold, Jaysen's wards an arm's-length away. She edged a foot forward, then hesitated.

It was madness to come here, to walk back into the hands of a slave master.

He isn't! Jedean was, but Jaysen treated me with respect.

Mother Night, but she'd chased this bit of logic round for days. She'd lost sleep over it, suffered in inattention, felt she'd go stark raving mad in the cyclic argument. Of course, the hunger had nearly driven her that far, in and of itself.

She was here, acknowledging the insanity of her actions, and still she ached to go to him.

I am a Blood Mage. My mother was Lady Settaya. I have been raised a leader. I have been trained to be decisive, to maintain control.

Senna groaned. Lack of that precious control had made her a slave.

I am in control this time. Slavery has taught me well.

But she wasn't in control. The hunger was. Even here, outside Jaysen's domain, her body responded as if he offered his lifeblood to her. Her fangs would not retract more than halfway.

I must end this. I must know. That was the only point she'd never truly argued.

There seemed only one plausible reason for her reaction, if it were an honest response to stimuli. Perhaps Jedean had been wrong, and Tason had never been her destined mate. Jaysen had been an adolescent when she'd been tricked and enslaved. His father wouldn't have considered the possibility that he was the mate she sought.

Or...perhaps I have simply gone insane over the years within these walls.

Senna cursed herself as a fool and stepped through the net of his shields and wards. The gusting wind ceased to buffet her; the air moved gently within the shield, the fruit trees beside her ceasing their rustling from one footstep to the next. She marveled that the shields still allowed her to pass inward when they stopped even a bitter wind, when they were designed to stop anyone who might be a threat to Jaysen.

She raised her hand to knock on the war-wood doors, then pulled it back on a gasp.

A ceremonial foot-washing trough appeared before her, sending swirls of steam into the cool night air. Senna raised her dress, stepping into it. It was the perfect temperature, a touching gesture of respect.

She laughed, tears stinging her eyes. "Thank you, Jaysen."

Senna didn't question that he could hear her. His power wrapped around her like a second cloak.

* * * *

Jaysen felt the presence lurking at the edges of his domain. It was a dim spot in his vision, possibly friend, possibly foe. It was more likely an enemy than a friend; an ally wouldn't hesitate at the edges of his wards.

He considered leaving his mineral bath, but there was no need to unless attack came or this teasing of his shields continued. Even if that happened, he could cast from here as well as anywhere else in the keep.

The room had been redecorated much as his fire den had been, much as all the rooms he'd changed had been. It was one of the few comforts in his life since Senna had left him, and he wasn't going to leave it for the dark shadow of his father's tastes unless it was necessary to do so. Jedean had cost him more than he cared to consider; it was one of the reasons he was so adamant about eradicating that influence in the keep.

The shock of her passing through the shields sent a bolt of pleasure through him. Jaysen checked his senses again, certain he was hallucinating.

"Senna." It was a prayer, a giving of thanks, a wish breathed into the steam rising from the mineral pool.

His mind worked fast. A Blood Mage guest was at his door...and most heartily welcomed. He gathered his power, rushed through the incantation and sent a trough of his own water to her to ease and bathe her road-worn feet.

Her laughter warmed him, light and pleasant. "Thank you, Jaysen." She was silent for a moment. "Your gift is most welcome and appreciated."

He smiled in spite of his nervousness, as giddy as a boy at his manhood ceremony, acting the part of a man, though all knew him to be inept.

He sobered abruptly. *No. I cannot make assumptions about why she's come here.* Senna might have come to finalize their monetary settlement for her service. She might have come to bargain her magic for his.

Jaysen climbed from the pool, willing himself dry with a spell, then pulling his white trousers on with a heavy heart. The minimum of dress was required for such a meeting. He could not presume to meet her as he had the last time, a man intent on enticing her to test him. He went to the table, settling in a cushioned chair. It was the right way to greet her, the only way not to offend her, considering her refusal of him.

He shifted, trying to get comfortable in a chair he'd never had such a difficulty with before.

Comfortable? That was the most ridiculous thought he'd indulged in for quite some time. How could he be comfortable when he already ached to see her, when his nerves were on edge in the need to claim her as his mate?

The door opened, and the steward announced her, as if Jaysen needed an announcement to note her presence. Senna's magic was a near-blinding aura around her. Even he hadn't realized the depth of her power, a magic that was his to share in, if she accepted him fully.

"Lord Jaysen?" The steward shot Jaysen a look that labeled him perplexed. He'd never had to wait orders before.

"Refreshments, steward."

Jaysen didn't take his eyes off of Senna. She shed her cloak, handing it off to the steward, seemingly oblivious to Jaysen's presence in the room with her. Then she looked around, her eyes flickering between green-gold and pure gold.

She feels it. At least subconsciously, she feels the attraction between us.

"Already prepared," the steward interrupted his musing.

The tray slid onto the table between them, unheeded by both. Several heartbeats passed in silence.

"Leave us, steward," Jaysen ordered.

The doors closed behind him. Still, Senna didn't move.

"Would you like to sit, Lady Senna?" he offered, conscious that every choice must be her own.

"I would." She slid into the chair beside him, most of the length of her left leg uncovered in the split of her skirt. They were the two halves of a whole being: she dressed in black in deference to Mother Night and he in white in deference to the radiant light of auras. It was what made the mating of a Blood Mage to a Radiant so wonderful, the acceptance of the duality of existence, the melding of their beings until neither was what they once were.

Jaysen reached for the sacrament knife on the tray, the same one he'd used at her last visit with him, preparing to offer the traditional taste of his blood. Her hand closed over his, urging his fingers away from the hilt. She switched her grip from one hand to the other, raising the fingers of his dominant hand to her mouth.

His breathing hitched as her fangs lengthened. She played the tip of one over the pad of his index finger, taunting him.

"You are most welcome to it," he rasped. It was typically an invitation she would issue and not one he would, but the ceremonies he'd researched had never mentioned this possibility. He had to improvise.

The razor edge followed closely the line his knife had left at their last meeting, a sublime mix of pleasure and pain. Her tongue circled him, stroked him in mimic of orally pleasing him in other ways, encouraging his blood to flow.

Jaysen closed his eyes, cursing the trousers he'd donned. They were crafted to mold to his body...his body when he wasn't erect. It was no wonder the other Radiants had gone to her in ceremony wraps. This was, without a doubt, one of the most uncomfortable moments of his life. In fact, his convalescence after his father attacked him was probably the only thing that bested it.

And yet, he wouldn't have traded it for anything. As long as Senna was touching him, any discomfort was a minor annoyance.

"By the gods," he pleaded. He'd thank the God of Light and Mother Night equally for more of this.

She shifted, settling into his lap, and a prism effect of energy washed over him, making the throbbing in his cock all the more pronounced. Was it happening already? Was the merging of their aspects that advanced?

"By the lights of the night," he grumbled. It was an old prayer, one that most Radiants had forgotten in the long years since they'd started abusing the Blood Mages' trust.

Her mouth left his hand and settled lips to lips with him. The next few moments were a blur to Jaysen. Her hair cascaded over his hands and chest. Her mouth meshed with his, a hard, hot kiss.

He had to get closer. The need was elemental; following the commands of his body was essential to his survival.

The crash of stoneware brought him back to his senses. Senna was laid out over the table, her arms wrapped over his shoulders, the contents of the tray shoved out of their way.

For a moment, they stared at each other, their breaths coming fast and heavy. Senna drew his hand to the slit of her skirt, arching up as he slid his fingers beneath.

Her center was weeping and ready, and Senna responded to his touch with wild abandon, her hips cycling to his stroking fingers, moaning in delight, her fangs lengthening fully, her golden eyes pleading for more.

Jaysen thrust two fingers inside her, and her entire body tightened and drew up. The contractions of her sheath around him let him know that he'd done what few had before. He'd driven her to release. No one, not even his father, had driven her to more than two.

He slid his hand out of her, and she whimpered at the loss, shivering. It was time. He would go no further without her verbal agreement to test her passion.

"Jaysen," she pleaded, reaching for him.

He raised his fingers to his mouth, licking them clean. Gods, but she tasted better than he'd dreamed she would.

Senna moved toward the edge of the table in a sensual slide, baring more of her body to him. He stared at her, licking his lips, his mouth watering for more, but he would not go further until she invited him to. Senna had to want him to test her, and she had to invite him properly. She was the Blood Mage; he was the Radiant. It was the dance they danced.

"You are most welcome to it," she breathed the traditional words.

"Am I?"

"You know you are. Surely, you feel it."

He nodded, sinking to his knees. She was hot against his tongue, as pungent as sweet wine. Jaysen forced himself to attend to her and not lose himself in the dizzying effects of her nectar.

He spread her wide, sucking in at her engorged nub. Senna cried out harshly, her hands fisting in his hair. He paid unwavering attention to it, suckling gently, nipping, stroking his lips and tongue over it.

Senna screamed in a second release, whispering pleas for him to claim her.

"You are not sated," he whispered. Jaysen moved lower, nibbling at her outer lips, stealing the nectar she'd poured out for him.

She thrust against him, murmuring his name, reaching for another climax already.

Senna was coming to them faster now. Soon, she would be ready for more.

She gifted him with a full-throated scream and a fresh wave of her elixir. His vision blurred, drugged, and yet he craved more. With every climax, she became more potent, and the final gift she'd give him was reportedly better than the rest combined, the proof that he was her mate, the tie that would make them one.

He drank her down then buried his tongue in her, driving her over again. Senna screamed his name, her hands fisting in his hair, tugging, urging him up in words and action.

Jaysen refused her, returning his attention to her pleasure. At the moment, her womanly urges were speaking for her, the same ones that had allowed his father to trap her in the first place. *Quick to test*, but only because Jedean's blood had confused her.

Her womanly needs were not enough. It was the Blood Mage who had to demand more, who had to test *his* worth. Jaysen wasn't Jedean. He wouldn't take her at the words that it was time; it would be a proper test or none at all.

He forced her to still another climax in a few strokes of his tongue then sucked gently at her nub again.

The growl from above was his only warning that the tables had turned. In a heartbeat, Jaysen was on his back on the thick rug, Senna astride him, both nude thanks to her magic.

She was beautiful, her golden eyes glittering in the candlelight, her black hair a curtain around them, her magic a fog, clinging to her skin and teasing his. Her fangs dimpled her lower lip.

"You think yourself worthy of me?" she challenged.

It was not a question that was typically asked. Jaysen considered how best to reply to something so unusual. What did she need of him? "Only the gods know for certain. Only you may decide to test it, but I believe..."

She waited for his answer.

"I believe no man is worthy of you who has not your love."

She stared at him, seemingly disconcerted.

* * * *

Senna's mind reeled. No man had said such wonderful things to her in her lifetime.

Not even Jedean, who had flattered her out of her common sense.

Jedean hadn't pushed her to test as Jaysen had. He hadn't forced her to an instinctual response. At her first pleas for more, the old Radiant had mounted her. *Mounted me!* She'd always known that had been wrong, but she'd wanted a mate's touch too much. His seeming madness for her had warmed her, and she'd ignored her niggling of unease.

"Have I offended you?" Jaysen asked, his voice slow, drugged in her aphrodisiac nectar.

"If I left you?" she whispered. She had no doubts that he'd *allow* her to leave without interference, even now, but would he pay with more than his uncomfortable cock?

Pain twisted his features, what seemed to be a crushing blow to him. "Do you intend to?"

His reaction told Senna all she needed to know. He hungered, and not just for her nectar. She lowered herself onto him, forcing her eyes open when she wanted to close them in delight, lost in the wonder that came over him.

Jaysen grasped her hips, thrusting into her, a groan rumbling from deep in his chest. His eyes pleaded with her.

Senna nodded, and he turned his head, offering his throat. She stared at the pulsing artery beneath his skin, the blood rushing in her own matching it.

The hunger ate at her, a maddening need to know if Jaysen was her true mate. Fear stayed her; if he was not, Jedean had been right that her mate was dead, and she would be alone forever.

Jaysen's voice cut through her indecision. "We must know, Senna. We both must."

She leaned over him and sank her teeth deep in the join of his neck and shoulder, moaning in a combination of his flavor and his reflexive thrust into her. Jaysen went wild beneath her, his hands fisting in her hair.

Senna pulled back, barely breathing. It was the moment of truth. She prayed to Mother Night as she hadn't prayed since she'd been a hopeful young Blood Mage of ten and six at Jedean's door.

Jaysen ground his teeth, teeth that lengthened into fangs before her eyes. Senna fought for breath, her climax nearing in the knowledge that her mate lived.

"Not yet," Jaysen ordered, his speech garbled, unaccustomed to the dentia he now possessed. One fang cut into his lower lip, and the blood welled up.

He didn't give her a chance to take advantage of it. Jaysen grasped the back of her neck and pulled Senna's throat to his mouth. His newly-developed fangs broke skin, and she screamed in pleasure, the first whispers of climax stealing what remained of her sanity.

Jaysen flipped her beneath him, rearing back, her lifeblood mixing with his on his lips. He surged into her, sealing his mouth to hers, their blood mingling, the power binding them. She closed her eyes to the soft brush of his aura against hers.

The moment was sweet agony, her body contracting, his heat flooding her, their hearts beating in unison. Jaysen held her as the waves of pleasure receded, as they explored each other, mouths meshing, fingers tangling...and finally, darkness descending.

Chapter Five

Senna came to consciousness slowly, disoriented. Her senses told her it was day.

The sun was low but still aloft. Why would she wake now?

As if in answer, a hard cock slid between her thighs and fangs scraped at the back of her shoulder. The marks at her throat warmed, just as the ones on Jaysen's shoulder would be warming.

She smiled, brushing her bottom against him. "Hungry?" she purred. She knew he was. She could feel it from him, enflaming her own hunger.

"After a decade of wanting you and being forbidden a single touch? A single..." His teeth fired her nerves again. "Taste," he breathed.

Senna turned abruptly, her mind working fast. Jaysen had wanted her all that time. That would indicate he'd not only known about her but had been close enough to experience the call. "A decade?"

Jaysen didn't seem to notice her upset. He nipped at her chin. Her body responded despite her better judgment.

"Jaysen!"

"Anything," he vowed.

Senna pushed him away, meeting his startled gaze steadily. She took his confusion to heart. Jaysen wasn't his father; he wasn't trying to deceive her. She was certain of it. And yet, she had to know when he'd come into the radius of her power. She had to know how she could miss so momentous an occasion.

"A decade," she repeated.

He nodded, sobering somewhat, his fangs retracting.

"You were forbidden to...Jedean knew." *Dear Mother, this was why Jedean locked me away, why he starved my magic out of me. He was afraid of our union.* Knowing Jedean, he'd probably been appalled by it...perhaps threatened with the loss of his precious seat of power.

Which still left her the question of when and how Jaysen experienced her, in the first place. "You...if you ached for me..."

Jaysen's face darkened, and his muscles tightened in apparent fury. "He wanted to gloat. He hadn't considered the possibility that I was the one, until... When Delek came to you, he meant me to watch it."

She gasped at the idea of him learning what he was that way.

"I went mad. I tried to reach you, and when they stopped me, I fought them. Jedean cast against me to still my fight. I asked for you when I woke from my father's attack, the right to approach you at my manhood—"

"And you never came for me?" Her heart ached. Had he tried to reach her at all once he'd been refused?

"The wards and shields were set before I woke. It took a fortnight for me to heal, a fortnight during which Jedean made them impenetrable. I tested them constantly, until he set painful spells on them...and then still until he threatened to send me away from you entirely. Until he died and—"

"All that was his passed to you," she finished for him.

"Yes. With it came the power to undo the walls between us, and I did."

"And now that you are no threat to Jedean..." Her mind locked on another fact, one that might have influenced him. "You will hold the seat of power now that—"

Jaysen pulled her to his body. "And that frightens you. Do you wish me to hide our union? I can—"

"You wouldn't," she gasped. It was too close to the deception of her own birth. There was one thing Senna was adamant about; no one would call her children 'bastard' and live.

"I want to love you openly, Senna, but the choice is yours." He wound his fingers through hers. "Just as the choice to test me was yours. I can wear a Radiant's white, hide the signs with a glamour—"

Senna kissed him, silencing her laugh in the process. He was sweet to offer it, but it wasn't what she wanted. "You will do nothing of the sort, Jaysen."

He smiled, lifting her from the bed and striding into the corridor.

"Jaysen, we are unclothed," she protested. Though several of the servants had seen her unclothed in her years within the walls, and likely seen Jaysen as well, it didn't seem proper to walk the corridors thus.

His fangs peeked past his upper lip. "You wish to celebrate our union in the traditional manner. Do you not?"

Her heart skipped at that. "Oh, yes." How long had she dreamed of it? Probably since she'd dared peek at the sun as a child, flirting with the gods' wrath in the vain hope that her human father's lineage would protect her.

"Have you ever seen the sun?" he asked.

"Once. It was very painful." And her mother had refused to heal it with her magic, a punishment for risking herself.

The doors before them swung wide in the push of Jaysen's magic, and a glorious sky filled her vision, a rainbow of color from the yellow-white crescent of the sun over the hillside, orange and pink, lavender, blue darkening to the color of Jaysen's eyes far above her head.

He set her at the rail, facing outward to the glory he brought to her world. The view took her breath away. While she would never be able to walk the midday sun, the ability to tolerate the muted radiance of the dawn and dusk, like the ability for her to sense auras and the melding of her magic with Jaysen's, were gifts of the mating.

Jaysen's breath warmed her shoulder, and she spread her legs, closing her hands around the rail, knowing intimately what he intended. He covered her hands with his own, pulling her earlobe into his mouth and nipping at it. Nectar overflowed her sheath, teasing her as it caught tendrils of the cooling air.

"I hunger," he grumbled.

"As do I." It was said a blood mated pair hungered for each other endlessly. "Feed."

His cock slid home, laying claim to her in the dying rays of daylight. "I will feed from you. Then I will feed you." He thrust slowly, drawing out her pleasure painfully. "Is it true that my essence will now be the elixir to you that yours is to me?"

Her head spun at the thought of it. "So they say. I would like to know."

"And so we shall." His teeth sank into her, forcing her to a blinding climax that he followed with a groan.

He held to her in the aftermath, his lips pressed to her throat, panting hard. "Jaysen?" she questioned him.

"I hunger."

Aftershocks wracked her. "Take me to the mineral pool and feed me your nectar. Hunger should never be wasted."

Glossary

Wul male—buck

Wul female—bitch

Wul mother—dam

Wul father—sire

Wul young—cubs

Wul pack leaders—alpha buck and alpha bitch

Lyx male—tom

Lyx female—fem

Lyx pregnant/nursing female or the mother of a particular Lyx, no matter how old he may be—queen

Lyx father—sire

Lyx young—kit

Lyx nest leader—the queen's-queen (the eldest able-bodied female in the nest)

Chapter One

Anha arched her back, thwarting Thoman's move to bite her neck even as she drove her bottom toward the pillar of his cock. Some fems let toms mark them indiscriminately; Anha was not such a fem. Though it was unlikely that she'd find a true mate, Anha wanted to go to him unmarked if she did.

Thoman hissed lightly in his displeasure. "Little tease."

On some level, he was correct. Still... "All unmated toms want is the *pussy*." She purposely used the human term for it as both a pun and a further tease. "It is pride that makes you seek more."

As if I am not seeking more? She pushed away that thought. It was for another time and place.

Thoman drew in Anha's scent noisily, stroking her hood with two rough fingers. Her pupils widened, sharpening the contrast of the lush forest around them in the half-light of the moon. She rasped the tip of her tongue over her lengthened fangs, her mouth watering in need of an end to this maddening heat.

Thoman played his cock at her entrance, growling out his thoughts aloud. Her heat had her slick and ready...more than ready to be stuffed full of randy tom cock.

Anha nodded, her breathing hitching as he pinched at her hood. She drew in the scents of her heated core and his pungent musk, soil, growth and decay...and Wul.

The shock of the final in their vicinity sent her into motion, knocking Thoman's hand away and scrambling from beneath him. His hand grasped at her hip, then released her. He turned and stood, placing himself between Anha and the enemy, as any tom was expected to.

Anha came to her feet, her enhanced vision picking out three of the curs. She let her vocal chords shift slightly to rumble the information to Thoman, uncertain that his lesser abilities could provide it for him. His nod was curt, and she let her throat revert to a human shape again, lest she tire herself unnecessarily when the need to fight might arise.

The Wul were clothed, and they stood between the two Lyx and their clothing. As Anha watched, one of them lifted her jeans from the ground, scenting them. The threat wasn't spoken, and yet she shivered in understanding.

"What do you want, Wul?" Thoman's voice was coarse, a sure sign that his fangs were extended.

Anha swallowed hard. Unless one was exceptionally old or strong, that was the most either Lyx or Wul could do without a powerful moon. She could do more, but she'd only prove it if she had to.

The one holding her jeans settled a look of warning on them. "I want, little cats, to know what two Lyx are doing on Wul land. Surely, you scented our mark."

They hadn't, which probably meant the Wul had laid the marks after they'd passed. It was an old trick that the Wul used to justify ambush. Since the precious old growth was in dispute, one never knew who would scent and claim it next, but it was good luck to conceive broods in the sacred wood.

Thoman scanned over the line of Wul, apparently deciding that it was not his night to fight them. "Then we will take our leave...with apologies to your alpha for this trespass."

Anha held her breath, looking for some sign of acceptance from them. It would be an embarrassment to walk back to the nest in the nude, but it would be a welcome exchange for death.

"I think not," their leader stated, scenting her jeans again, leering at her.

She shook her head in disbelief. They'd rutted on Lyx fems before, but never one in heat as Anha was. Her heart pounded in terror, and her mouth went dry. The copper taste of blood rose up strong in preparation to fight or run.

There were tales, old stories of half-breed abominations. Were they true? Would she catch a half-Wul brood instead of one from the deposit Thoman had made the night before?

The Wul started to circle. Thoman tensed, hissing and growling, his fine, black hair standing on end. The lead Wul closed on him, growling deep in his throat, and Anha shivered in response, her gaze darting between the alpha of this small group and his betas.

Whatever the sound the Wul made meant to a male, Thoman seemed to lose his composure. He pounced on the larger male, his mouth opening to bare his fangs.

The Wul dropped her jeans and dealt a staggering punch to Thoman's head. His pack brothers held their places, shifting back and forth as if preparing to stop her if she attempted escape.

Thoman came at him again, and the Wul administered another blow; this one took the tom to his back. Before Thoman could react, the alpha was on him, sinking his fangs into the tom's exposed throat.

Anha leapt toward them, though she knew there was little she could do. The other two Wul were suddenly upon her, not engaging Anha but keeping her from the fight.

She showed her claws...literally. Anha shuddered in pleasure as sleek fur appeared on her fisted hands, bones shifted, and her claws extended.

One Wul pulled back; the other bared his fangs and took a step toward her. Anha lashed out, gouging tracks in the closer beta's face to drive him back.

He recovered quickly and howled out his intent to hunt, to kill. She braced herself for a fight. Though the howl meant the older toms and fems would be on their way to defend the territory, they still had time to kill her...or commit other offenses against her.

A growl brought the closer two to a halt. The abrupt change startled Anha so much that she didn't note the third moving until he had her by the wrists, pinning her to the nearest tree. He extended her arms above her head, his legs between hers, forcing hers out.

He surveyed what he could see of her body, finally meeting her eyes. The deep brown was disconcerting, so different than the green-gold or ice blue of a Lyx. For a moment, they stared at each other, neither moving.

"Bind her wrists." The slightest edge of his fangs peeked past his lips.

Self-preservation reared up, and Anha hissed at him, fighting the strength of his grip. It was of no use, of course. Like most males, Lyx or Wul, he was larger than a fem, and Wul were larger than Lyx. In moments, they had the belt looped around her wrists and cinched tight, cross-threaded to secure the woven strands.

Anha stilled, abruptly aware of her position. She was full-out against him, her legs hooked around him, his erect cock nestled to her still-heated core.

Hotter!

No. It was a trick. It had to be.

The Wul cycled his hips against her, and her body's answering call named her a liar. Admit it or not, she wanted him more than she'd wanted Thoman...more than she'd wanted any tom of her species.

It's the heat. My body is confused.

But that was a lie, too. Anha had been through heats before. She knew well enough that the heat didn't make an unacceptable male acceptable or a loathsome one appealing.

Then why do I want him? She rejected the idea that she found the Wul buck appealing, in some way. That was a stomach-churning idea.

He backed off a step, then a few more, dropping to his knees with Anha wrapped around him, following her down to the soft forest floor she'd thought to share with Thoman. It was all she could do not to press up to him in an unspoken plea for more.

"Hold her arms down."

The grip on her forearms was rough. The hands exploring her body were anything but. Anha swallowed down a moan of pleasure.

The Wul's weight left her, and he wrenched her legs from his waist. His hips thrust forward, forcing her as wide as she would go, pressing the evidence of his arousal to her.

It was too much sensation, too potent. Anha closed her eyes and rode the ridge of his body, needing the joining as she never had before.

"Such a good little *pussy*," one of the others taunted.

She froze, her heart sick. *What am I doing?*

"Silence, Seten." The promise of death was in the alpha's order.

Noises broke the silence, and Anha opened her eyes to investigate them. The Wul leader was patiently disrobing, his lightly-furred chest appearing from behind the blood-stained shirt. His chest fur was the same red-brown of the thick pelt on his head. The sound it made was crisp, not the silken slide of a Lyx tom's fur.

Anha dimly noted that the blood on his shirt was Thoman's. She should be appalled, sickened, enraged...

Then the shirt was gone, and the Wul started working at his jeans. Her thoughts scattered, and Anha stared, watching his length appear, her body weeping in welcome. Her muscles felt warm and weak.

He was over her again, his face buried in her throat, growling but not in pleasure. It was a sound of warning that sent shivers down Anha's spine.

The strokes of his face against her were universal. He was a tom scenting a fem, drowning the scent of a rival tom...or whatever the Wul called their males.

He worked his way down her body, stroking his musk-laden hair and skin over her, nipping at her breasts and stomach. By the time he started lapping at her nether lips, Anha was writhing beneath him, her breathing ragged, her body stoked to a steady burn.

One of the other Wul tweaked a nipple, and she stilled, tensing. The growl from below sent the other tom into retreat. Then he was working his way up her body again, washing away that scent with the rest.

He settled over her, his cock poised to take her. The joining came a few finger-widths at a time, a torturous stretching. He was wider than any tom she'd taken before him, making her feel deliciously full.

He was longer, too. Anha cried out softly when he surpassed her normal range. Still, he eased in, coming to rest against the gates of her womb...and held there, teasing her.

Anha trembled, awash in an unfamiliar sensation.

"You've never had this large," he guessed.

One of the others chuckled, then sobered at a sharp motion from the one impaling her.

"Have you?" There was a challenge in that.

Anha considered lying to him, but she found she couldn't. She shook her head silently, blinking back tears at the expected taunting.

None came. He nodded then eased back, thrusting up into her again.

She whimpered in a mixture of pleasure and discomfort. A few thrusts later, those whimpers turned to sighs of satisfaction. As if her body gave him some signal, his thrusts quickened, deepened, and he grumbled something she couldn't comprehend.

Anha felt her climax rising and fought down the sounds she wished to vent. No matter how good it felt, this was a Wul...the enemy.

Of course, she couldn't stop the physical responses of climax. Nor could she hide them. He groaned as her body milked him toward release, lifting her hips to thrust harder into her.

His cum was hot, an insistent drumming in counterpoint to his continuing thrusts. His cock swelled within her, a gentle caress of stimulation rather than the barbs of a Lyx tom. Anha cried out harshly in response, dizzy in pleasure, tears she didn't remember shedding cooling on her cheeks.

His mouth covered hers, forcing her lips open beneath his. Anha met him in a fierce kiss, entrusting her vulnerable tongue to the mercy of his teeth as he did with hers.

Lyx seldom kissed. It was typically something reserved for mates. Still, she wanted this Wul's kiss as she'd wanted the rest of him.

"Mattayas," one of the others growled. "This is foolhardy."

Mattayas. She committed it to memory.

He released her lips, locking gazes with her, his cock subsiding slowly. Something feral burned in his expression.

"If you waste much more time," the third stated, "no one else will get a taste."

Her heart sank. Of course, he was going to let the others play at her. She was a prisoner and meant nothing to him.

Chapter Two

Mattayas felt a sick twisting in his stomach at her look of hurt...at the disappointment in her ice blue eyes.

What was wrong with him that he was acting so out of character? Screwing a Lyx bitch that was fertile, heedless of the old tales? Risking her kiss?

His mind had taken leave at the first scent of her, and the scent of another male on her was maddening.

His cousin Seten lowered his head, taking one of the Lyx's pert little nipples into his mouth. She closed her eyes and turned her head away, clenching her teeth. There was no sensual show now. Her body cooled around his still-raging cock. To his shock, fresh tears glistened on her dark lashes. She sobbed.

His next coherent moment was the realization that he had his hand wrapped around Seten's throat. He didn't question why he'd do such a thing. She'd sobbed, and Seten had scented the Lyx. Either was reason enough.

"Do not touch her," he growled.

The young bitch stared at him, seemingly as stunned by his actions as he was himself.

Mine. Mattayas shoved Seten further away, then slid from the bitch's body, smiling at her shiver and mew of protest.

"Turn over," he ordered her.

It was madness. He was ordering her into the submissive, demanding that she take him as she would a mate...or at least one she wanted a brood from.

She nodded her agreement. His cock released a stream of cum that simply.

"Mattayas," Seten grumbled, an unspoken rebuke for his folly.

He didn't answer. Instead, he hooked two fingers inside her heat. The little bitch pressed her hips up, thrusting against them. She bit her lower lip at his withdrawal, drawing a bead of blood with her half-extended fangs.

Mattayas stared at her, hungry for her body again. "Release her, Tragan. Let her turn."

The buck released her arm, though he grasped the length of belt dangling from her wrists to keep her from attacking Mattayas with her clawed paws. Though she'd laid Tragan's face open in four lines, it seemed she had no urge to harm any of them.

Confirming that impression, she pulled her legs back and rolled, pillowing her head on her bound hands and settling high on her knees to spread for him.

Oh, Luna, yes! Would that he had the night to feast on her. But, he didn't. Tragan's war howl would bring the Lyx all too soon.

Mattayas thrust into her, his heart pounding at her gasp of delight. He eased his hand from her waist to her clit, and she circled her hips against him, taking all he had to give.

The need was pressing, and Mattayas pounded into her, thanking Luna as the bitch met him, push for push. She half-swallowed a cry of pleasure as climax took her, and her body urged him on.

Mark her. Luna, but he had to.

Mattayas grasped her shoulder, dragging her throat up to his mouth, his fangs extending fully. He expected her to shy as she had from the Lyx buck.

If she does, I will hold her down to do it. She must carry my mark. He didn't question that it was so.

She didn't move to avoid him. The bitch swung her black hair to the side, tilting her head to invite him.

"Mattayas."

He bit down, growling at her scream, releasing into her at her shudder. His cock thickened, stimulating her again...if it did so with a Lyx bitch.

Her blood coursed into his mouth, salty and pungent, imprinting her scent into his hardwired memory. She could never hide from him now—he could track her, wherever she went.

His cock had just started to ease when Seten pulled at his shoulder. Mattayas growled at him, his shoulders tensing, unwilling to leave her.

"They're coming, Mattayas. We are outnumbered."

His mind warred with his instincts. Normally, they would tell him to run, but it was his mind telling him that now. They had to leave, but his stubborn Wul instincts roared a protest at the idea. What was it about the bitch that did this to him?

Mattayas thrust his wrist in front of her mouth. "Mark it," he ordered.

She hesitated, though she had no reason to. He was offering her the same advantage he had over her. He wanted her to have it.

"Now!"

"Mattayas." Tragan's hands joined Seten's, pulling back at his shoulders without success.

She nuzzled then bit down, her short, sharp teeth drawing his blood then retreating. Her rough tongue teased at the wound, drinking him down. His body was on fire, pulsing, leaking more cum into the liquid heat between her thighs.

"Mattayas!"

He nodded. Their escape would be a close thing. Mattayas swept his hand away from her mouth and left her body, his heart aching at her soft protest.

She curled to her side, shaking, her thighs pressed together, her bound hands drawn up beneath her bloodied mouth.

Mattayas pulled his shirt over her and rose, shifting form and leading his pack mates away. His sensitive hearing picked up sounds of the Lyx pursuit, the sound of his name from her lips...and the bitch's name.

Anha.

* * * *

Everything happened at once. Mattayas and the other Wul toms were gone, and she laid there, abruptly cold and aching.

"By Luna," Eva—the queen's-queen of their nest—proclaimed, appearing at Anha's side.

She stripped Mattayas's shirt off with a disgusted grimace, and Anha shivered convulsively, her fingertips and lips numb. Anha sucked in her lower lip in an effort to warm it, groaning at his taste flooding her mouth again.

"Your shirt, Ronel. Then catch those beasts," Eva ordered.

A shirt covered her. Anha thanked Luna for its warmth even as she acknowledged that she missed Mattayas's scent. She whispered his name, letting her eyes slide shut.

"All is well, Anha. The fems and queens protect our own."

But Anha didn't want protection. She wanted Mattayas, his cock working her, his mouth teasing her. Her inner muscles clenched in aftershocks, and she sobbed in the intensity of it.

The toms departed at a run, leaving her in the company of only the older fems. Anha kept her eyes shut, exhausted.

There was little discussion among the others. Two went to work at the belt around her wrists, increasing blood flow to her hands. Others searched for injuries. Anha kept her legs clenched together when they sought to spread them. They moved on without forcing the issue.

Eva cupped her cheek and prodded at the bite, prompting a hiss of pain from Anha. Her neck and shoulder throbbed in early healing.

"The cursed Wul," Eva spat. She lowered Anha's head with a caress along her jawline. "Still now, young one. We will bathe and care for you."

"She injured two of the three, by the signs," Zuma whispered. As Anha's eldest sister, Zuma took pride in the fighting prowess of another fem of her sister-bed.

Anha didn't answer that. She'd injured one. The other...

Why did Mattayas insist I mark him? What reason could he have for it?

The fems eased Ronel's shirt around her body and lifted her between them. Her head spinning, Anha let sleep drag her down.

* * * *

Mattayas shifted back to human form, passing into the inner den buck naked—to employ a sad human pun—since he'd abandoned his jeans and boots at the shift. As if an answer, Seten handed the former over silently. He must have scooped them up as he ran, guarding Mattayas's back.

He pulled them on, leaving them unbuttoned. It was a safe bet he'd be washing up shortly, and fastening the denim over his semi-erect cock sounded less than appealing.

Not that clothing was strictly necessary. He could walk around the den or outside nude, and no one would think anything but that he was comfortable that way. The lack wouldn't be a problem until the autumn rains and winter snows fell again.

Seten and Tragan rested, their breathing slowing. They'd run the whole way in human form, and they weren't happy about it.

Finally, the demand came...from Seten. "What in the sun's fire was that, cousin?"

Mattayas warned him off with a growl and started moving again. In truth, he wasn't certain what lunacy had gripped him, and he didn't want to discuss it while he was in such turmoil. The most disconcerting thing was that he wanted more of it. Mattayas licked his lips, savoring Anha's flavor...her mixed flavors: blood, female musk, and saliva. It had been a feast, and he felt he would starve without it.

Other pack members approached, then pulled back from him, some with sneers or comments that he should wash the Lyx stench from his body. Were the only scent that of the buck, he'd have agreed, but Anha's scent was neither unappealing nor unwelcome.

Still, he headed for the underground river at the edges of their tunnels and waded in to his waist with his jeans on. The current buffeted his sensitized cock, urging him up again. He plunged his hands in, wincing at the sharp pain of Anha's bite, healing over though it was.

Mattayas let his eyes drift shut, laying his head back. Visions of Anha taunted him. Mad thoughts of tracking her and stealing her back plagued him.

What is wrong with me?

His sire's voice added to his inner turmoil. "Mattay... Dear Luna, Tragan! Have a healer see to your face."

"It will heal," the young buck countered, probably envisioning honorable battle scar stories, though he'd be lying to claim it.

"Now," Dievan growled, putting the full weight of alpha buck behind his command.

One set of footsteps moved away. Seten obviously stayed.

"What happened, Mattayas?"

He sighed. "Two were in our territory."

"And?"

"I killed the buck." *And experienced something I've never dreamed of with the bitch. With Anha.*

"You were injured."

It wasn't a question. Still, Mattayas had no clue how to answer it.

Seten saved him the trouble. "He gave the bitch his blood, after he took hers."

"Anha," Mattayas informed him, bristling at anyone else calling her a bitch, though it was the proper form of address for a female and not a slur. "Her name is Anha."

"What difference does that make?" his cousin snapped.

"I... I don't know," Mattayas admitted. It shouldn't make a difference, so why did it?

His sire's voice was strained calm. "Leave us, Seten."

Mattayas immersed himself in the river, then rose and strode toward his sire, buttoning his jeans.

Dievan sat atop a boulder, assessing every move Mattayas made. Mattayas hoisted himself next to his sire, bracing one bare foot on the rock before him, in case an attack was in the making.

"You *gave* her your blood? You gifted a Lyx that power over you?"

It was a matter of honor that he not lie to his pack mates. Mattayas prepared himself for punishment. "I did. Luna help me, it was madness, and yet...it felt right."

There was a moment of tense silence between them. "You must never see her again."

His breathing hitched, though Mattayas had expected that and worse.

"Find a bitch in the den, son. Forget this Lyx bitch. If she tracks you here, we will kill her...and you will lead the hunting party that accomplishes it."

Mattayas couldn't respond to that. It was probably better that he didn't; doing so would have prolonged the discussion and might have led to an order to track and kill her immediately. Something told Mattayas he couldn't risk that.

As it was, Dievan left with that little instruction.

* * * *

Anha pushed away the quilts piled over her, wincing as her muscles protested her bid to rise from the sister-bed. She relieved herself in the dirt-corner, feeling raw and empty, then staggered toward the common nest in search of food and water.

Her head was fuzzy, and she was uncoordinated. Overall, it was a disconcerting state for a Lyx to find herself in.

Her musing of how long she'd been unconscious was answered by a wail in the common nest just ahead. Anha knew before she'd breached the tunnel mouth that it was Thoman's queen.

The sight of the old fem holding her son's bloodied shirt shook Anha to the chilled core of her being. Meera screeched her agony, and the sound of shredding material overlapped with it.

Memories cleared Anha's senses with a rush of ice down her spine. Thoman was dead, and Anha was the one who'd bid him come out for a romp. Thoman was dead, and Anha had reveled in the cock of his murderer before the tom's body had even gone cold. She'd accepted his mark. She'd obeyed him and taken him like a submissive little mate.

Mattayas.

Anha weaved on her feet, grasping at the smooth wall as if it would provide purchase. It didn't, and she found herself on the floor, holding weakly to consciousness.

The room went silent, and she forced her eyes to focus. As she met Meera's eyes, Anha wished she hadn't succeeded.

Thoman's queen stood, surrounded by her fems and Anha's, tears streaming down her face. Anha slumped against the wall, waiting for blows, harsh words...banishment.

Meera crossed the room, squatting before Anha, the bloodied shirt fisted in her hand. Anha stared at it, choking on a sob.

"You drew blood on them?" she asked.

Anha nodded, not trusting that words would issue forth if she attempted speech.

"Did you scar them?"

She hesitated then nodded again. Mattayas might carry her mark...or not. His beta would.

The fem took a calming breath. "Then I can find them. I can kill them."

"Meera," Eva began.

She ignored the queen's-queen of their nest and focused on Anha, her gaze panning to the meat of the younger fem's abdomen. "Is there a chance?" she whispered. "Did my son deposit to you?"

"Yes."

"I hope to Luna his seed catches in you."

Anha's lips trembled in mixed emotions. "I hope so, as well." *Then why does it feel as if I am betraying Mattayas to say so?* He was a Wul, and she owed him nothing.

Anha's sisters moved toward her as Meera turned toward her sister-bed. They lifted her and took her back to the privacy of their nest, promising food and water she wasn't certain she'd be awake long enough to sample.

Chapter Three

Mattayas snuffled at the Lyx marks, his head aching in the strong afternoon light. He'd waited half a moon to attempt tracking her. He'd been at this insanity for nearly a moon, and he hadn't caught more than a faint whiff of her yet.

What am I doing here?

But he knew that well enough. He was searching for her scent, for whatever news of Anha it would provide for him. What he didn't know was why he was doing it.

He caught scent of a bitch hunting party and abandoned the question to follow the faint trail of what might be Anha...or a sibling or dam of hers. He had to catch a stronger whiff to know for certain.

Their hunt had been successful, a young deer. The bitches had trampled each other's scents in the preparation to move the kill. Mattayas was about to give up the track when he caught scent of what could only be Anha.

He followed it away from the others, finding the spot she'd chosen to relieve her full bladder. It was what he'd been waiting for, what he'd hoped to find.

The scent was strong in female musk...and bitch's warning. His heart stuttered. By Luna, she carried young. But who was the sire? Her weak Lyx buck...or himself?

His parenting instincts rose up strong and fast, demanding Anha and whatever brood she carried. Even if they weren't his get, Wul raised the young of others, though they'd never raised a Lyx cub that he knew of. He'd heard tales of human babies raised by the pack...even young wolves taken in, but never Lyx.

His mind cleared enough to reason the problem fully. If he took Anha to his pack, his sire would order her killed by Mattayas's hand. Her pack would never accept him. What did that leave them? Even if he stole her away, they would be without the pack, and their strength was in their communities.

Still, his instincts raged at him to claim her. Anha was his. She'd accepted him as her mate.

The battle between his reason and his instincts was driving him mad. Mattayas growled and ripped at the ground, marking half-over Anha's with vicious precision and purpose. That accomplished, he threw his head back and howled out ownership, then turned tail and ran for his own territory, secure in the knowledge that he'd made his meaning clear.

* * * *

Anha rolled off the sister-bed and into a crouch at the sound of the Wul howl so close to the nest. Her heart pounded, and she'd shifted halfway into her Lyx form before she reasoned that Mattayas and his betas would have to fight through a full third of the nest length to get to her current position.

Her fems surrounded her, offering their comfort and assurances that they would defend the nest and her against any marauding force. In moments, the younger fems were in a group on the bed while the eldest of their number went in search of news.

It seemed to take forever, and sounds of debate rose in the common nest. Finally, Zuma returned with

Eva. There was a tension about them, as if they'd come to some decision they didn't like...or Eva had forced a decision on Zuma that Anha's sister didn't agree with but had to accept.

Anha stared at them, waiting for whatever was coming.

"The Wul have violated our territory. Our toms cover his rancid stench, even now," Eva offered.

There was more. There had to be. Anha couldn't force the words to question what it was.

Zuma offered the next bit of information. "He tracked your scent, Anha. The one..." She motioned sharply, showing her unwillingness to state what Mattayas had done. "He marked over your scent and—"

"Why?" The inquiry was out before she could leash her tongue.

Eva's jaws snapped shut in aggravation. "We can only assume it was a sign that he means to harm you."

Again silence fell, heavy and suffocating.

"You are not to hunt, Anha."

Her heart stuttered. Anha was a good hunter, and it was a matter of pride that she provided for the nest, as all able-bodied fems should. She opened her mouth to protest, but Zuma cut her off.

"Eva has decreed it is so, Anha. If the Wul tom returns, we will do our best to kill him. Until then...and as long as we scent him on our lands, you are to remain nested."

Chapter Four

Anha stared at the three babies curled to her chest on the bed, piled together and sated from their first meal. They were born, all three toms, and she still had no indication of who their sire was.

They'd gestated for six moons, a half-moon longer than most Lyx did, but not out of the realms of possibility for a Lyx brood. It was a full moon shorter than the average Wul brood gestated, which gave her hope that the young were of Thoman's seed and not Mattayas's.

Young always smelled of their queen alone for a moon or more. Then their sire's scent would out. It was to hide the new young from predatory males who might harm them but didn't dare attack with a queen protecting them.

Further, they all had black pelts, just as she and Thoman had. Had the young been born with red-brown pelts, their sire would have been clear. Black told her nothing, since her own black pelt might have won out in the mix.

Not even their eyes would give a clue to their sire for ten nights or more. Until their sealed lids opened, the color was a mystery.

Anha sighed, stroking her fingertips through the silken fur of the largest of her sons, smiling as he purred in contentment. Surely, purring was a noise a young Wul wouldn't make.

She sobered. If they were Mattayas's young, they weren't fully Wul, which meant she couldn't anticipate what attributes they might display.

She pulled her hand back, torn. What would she do if the young were Mattayas's and not Thoman's? If she bonded with them, and they were of Mattayas, how would she hand them over to death?

I must. If Mattayas sired them, I must hand them over.

Then why did her heart ache at the thought of it? Why did tears burn her eyes and throat at losing them, even now?

Because they are my *sons!*

Even if they are monsters?

Visions of Meera gutting her sons or tearing out their throats in retribution for the wrong done Thoman left her cold and quaking. She'd do that. Eva would sanction it.

Her youngest yawned widely, then pushed off the elder babies. He wiggled over them and rooted his way to a nipple, latched on, and snuggled his feet to her chest.

Anha's heart softened, and she placed an unsteady hand on his back. "You're no monster. Are you?"

* * * *

Anha laughed, nuzzling her rolling sons. They were much more active than they'd been the first week or so. Now they cooed as well as purred, grunted and grumbled, cried and screamed. And they laughed.

Missayan wriggled toward her and stroked his face against a primary breast. He didn't suckle, as Anha thought he would. Instead, he tipped his head back and opened one eye a slit.

Her heart stuttered, and her blood ran cold. Her son's eyes were brown. Anha forced her pupils wider, drawing in light in the dim cave. She fingered the pelts on their tiny heads. Was their fur black...or deep red? Were they all sired by Mattayas? Or just Missayan? Or two of the three?

They would kill her sons...whichever ones showed signs of Wul parentage. Anha tried to come to terms with that concept, but it was impossible to. They were *her* young, no matter what else they were. They were innocent of their parentage. They were beautiful, loving...

"Mine," she promised.

But to keep them all alive, she had to find a way to leave unobserved. It would have to be in the harsh light of day, when few would be stirring and fewer would want to stop her.

Where will I go? It will be hard enough surviving without a nest, but both the Lyx and Wul will kill us on sight. Where can we hide?

It would have to be the cursed lands. No one would follow them there. They would be assumed dead. Only the dead lived in the cursed lands, and it was said that no one who entered ever returned.

Is it true? Will we escape death here only to be killed there?

It didn't matter. If they stayed here, her sons would be killed, and Anha would no doubt choose to follow them.

Maybe it's only Missayan. Maybe the other two will live. Many babies died in the first year. It wouldn't be unusual to lose one. If she stayed, she and the other two could live on in the comfort and safety of the nest.

Maybe it's not! Should she stay here, let them kill Missayan, then Mittayan, then Thomayan, as each showed signs of being Mattayas's sons, dying a little at a time herself?

That was unacceptable. She had to leave.

* * * *

Anha crept along the tunnels, passing through the common nest without incident. It was high-day, and her body protested her activity level at this Luna-forsaken hour. Still, leaving now would nearly ensure her success.

The sunlight filtering into the tunnel entrance was nearly blinding in its intensity. Lyx were nocturnal hunters. Their eyes were light-gathering, and her pupils narrowed to thorn-points to cut out as much of the glare as possible.

Her heart had eased and her spirits lightened when the sound came behind her. Anha whirled, prepared to fight for her freedom and the life of her sons...and came face-to-face with Zuma.

Her sister trailed a hard look from Anha to the babies and back again. The question of what she intended wasn't posed.

Still, answers warred in Anha's mind and fought for escape from her suddenly-raw throat. This solved every problem save her own survival. Her sons wouldn't be killed by her nest mates. Mattayas would leave the Lyx lands. Even if he followed her scent to the cursed lands, it was unlikely he'd follow her in, and if he did... She and her young faced death from the elements or starvation, so it was little added risk.

"Go." Zuma's voice was rough in emotion, and she seemed to have trouble controlling her expression.

"I must," Anha assured her.

"I know. You've suffered too much. Just...go."

Anha swallowed down a sob and turned, loping into the dense growth a few body-lengths from the nest. She turned back for one last look at Zuma, but her sister was gone. That alone almost sent Anha back, but the warmth of her sons against her chest reminded her what was at stake. With a heavy heart, she headed for the scentless boundary that marked the cursed lands.

Chapter Five

Anha paused, chewing slowly, training her ears to the forest. There was something wrong, an unnatural stillness about it. The birds didn't call. The frogs were silent. There was even a lack of scent...more than usual for the cursed lands, as if even the lesser animals had ceased to exist.

She swallowed, placing the meat on the stone beside her, making a show of settling her sons further into their sling. Anha eased her dagger out, noting a telltale skitter of leaves to her left rear. A rustle came from the right rear. Someone was closing on her...a group of unknown enemies.

Was it her own nest mates? Mattayas? Whoever it was, Anha would fight to the death. She sobered in the realization that she'd likely have to; whoever it was wasn't going to welcome her with open arms.

Ducking down to use the boulders as shelter and cover, Anha moved toward the heavy brush at her right.

"Very good," a strange fem noted.

Anha sank deeper between two stones, bringing out her left claws to supplement the dagger clenched in her right hand.

"Better," the voice continued. "You would protect your young to the death against known and unknown."

Anha eased further away from the voice silently, certain that they wanted a reply to get a fix on her location.

"A sister spirit," a second fem stated, this one from the direction Anha was traveling...and close.

Anha swallowed down a growl of frustration.

A third...closer and to her back. "Bring your cubs and come, fem."

Her breathing hitched.

"Enough," the first ordered. "Reason it, sister. There is only one thing that drives fems here."

The stories coursed through her mind. The elders said this place was cursed, that the dead lived here. She and her sons were dead to her nest, and they would curse her for saving the cross-bred babies.

The voice drew closer. "We can scent our own, and you are upwind."

"What do you want?" Anha asked. If they meant to kill her sons, they'd have to kill Anha first.

"You are our fem now. Your young cubs are of our nest."

Cubs. Not kits. They know what my sons are. "Why?" Why would anyone accept them now?

"You are a strong hunter and a strong fighter, sister. We can always use another."

"And?" Was earning their keep upon her full recovery that precious to them, or was there a trick to the having?

"As cursed, should we do to you what was done to us? Should we cast you out? Try to kill you? Take the cubs you've come to love from you?"

Anha's heart raced faster as she sighted movement. "You were also a fem mounted by a Wul tom?" she asked.

Laughter seemed to come from every direction, making Anha sick in realization. She'd already lost, if it came to a battle.

"Will you come?" the leader asked.

"It seems I have no choice."

The face of a kindly fem elder appeared above her. "Of course, you do. You could continue to live feral, but winter comes hard and fast in the cursed lands. We have food. We have shelter. You could recover...then hunt."

Anha hesitated, certain it was too good to be true. "I will...consider your offer."

A hand extended down to her, bringing the distinct scent of both Wul and Lyx. "Consider it within the warmth of our walls?"

She nodded, forced to the decision by the promise of warmth for her sons.

* * * *

Anha was overwhelmed by the comforts Siya's nest afforded. The rock walls seemed to radiate warmth, and a stream ran just beneath the caverns, alternately hiding behind the rock and pooling in corners of individual nests. It offered cool, sweet water in the common areas and cleansing water in the sister-nests. Everywhere she looked, there was stored food from successful hunts, and there was an excess of clothing and blankets.

"How do you live so comfortably?" Anha asked. "Is it the peace? The lack of competition for prey?"

Siya laughed heartily. "The humans."

Anha's heart pounded in the memory of the human tales she'd been raised on. They were weak in many ways, but they were dangerous animals. They killed for sport and took prizes of live young to cage and pelts.

She shied, seeking the shadows, her arm wrapping around the sling protectively.

"They don't come here," Siya assured her. "On the rare occasion that they do, they signal and come in to right their...*equipment* while we are gone from the nest."

"E...equip... What is that?"

Siya motioned uncertainly. "The...the things that make the walls warm when the weather is cold and cool when the weather is hot. The things that make our water clean and plentiful. The glass bits that let them see how we live."

Anha growled, her fur standing on end and growing thick over her fisted hands. "Why would you let them stalk you?" she hissed out a sibilant s.

"In exchange, they provide well for us...much better than they provide for the Wul and Lyx who do not accommodate their interest in our ways."

"Provide?" she challenged. "Humans do not—"

"Have you found the packs? The ones abandoned in the forest or washed downstream?"

Anha hesitated to answer that, unease stealing over her. "I assumed the humans lost them. They've lost them before." But, her stomach squirmed in the surety that it wasn't so.

"What humans?" Siya asked calmly. "Have you seen them? Have you ever scented a human, save on their packs?"

Anha shook her head, at a loss to explain it.

Siya nodded. "We are on protected lands...the Wul, the Lyx, and our people. No human is allowed to set foot here, save the ones that learn from watching us.

They haven't been permitted here for three generations."

"Why did the humans leave? Why would they?"

Siya shook her head, seemingly considering her answer. "Humans are complicated creatures. I've never fully understood their reasons, but the stories passed down from the queen's-queen three before me, the one who made the agreement with the humans, say the humans were *changing* us, changing how we live, harming *us* in the process."

"But...giving us the packs is interfering in how we live. Isn't it?" None of this made sense.

"That damage was done before they withdrew. We'd come to depend on the comforts stolen from human interlopers into our territory. Not even the oldest stories I know can tell me what we wore before we wore human clothing. Perhaps the pelts of prey? I cannot say with confidence."

"Perhaps we spent more of our time in animal form," Anha suggested. "The tales speak of a time when we could all change at will."

Siya seemed to consider that. "And there are tales of human cubs and kits conceived much as your own cubs were conceived with a Wul sire."

"Do you believe that may have made us unable to shift at will?"

"Who but Luna can say?" Siya smiled then turned and led the way down the corridor.

Anha spied a dark glass circle in the wall, hissed at it in warning, and moved on. Siya may trust the humans, but Anha didn't.

Siya continued as if Anha hadn't made a sound. "For now, I will show you to the nest that will be yours."

Anha considered that. "A private nest?" Was she unwelcome, after all? She'd had a private nest when her sons were born, mainly because she had no proof that they were Lyx. The older queens were hesitant to let the other young bond with what might ultimately prove to be half-Wul young.

"Most choose sisters or mates eventually, and this nest becomes empty, in wait for a new outcast to find us. Until you forge such a bond..." She pulled back the cloth door and waved Anha inside. "There is food and water, for your comfort. I know you won't want to leave your cubs to seek it soon."

Anha stepped inside, her heart pounding, but it was a simple nest, with a wide family bed and the promised supplies. "My thanks," she forced out, but Siya was already gone, the cloth swinging in her wake.

* * * *

"Anha?" Siya called out from the other side of the door.

"Come in," she grumbled in return, rubbing a hand over her eyes.

She'd slept poorly, almost worse than she had in the forest. It was no fault of Siya's. It was a new place with new sounds, new scents...a disconcerting mix of Lyx, Wul, and cross-breed, until Anha was no longer certain which she found most threatening.

The cloth slid aside, and the queen entered, setting something heavy next to the bed.

Anha forced her eyes open a slit, staring at the deep green canvas bag without comprehension. "What is it?"

"The humans know we have new young among us."

Her heart rate sped, pounding hard in her ears. Humans took young in cages. She slid to her hands and knees, shielding her sons, her fangs extending...then her claws. Her nose flattened, her face reshaped, fur sprouted and spiked in warning.

"They mean no harm, Anha." Siya kept her distance, showing respect and caution in the face of a queen protecting her young.

Anha hissed at the dark circle in the wall. If the humans could see her, they would be suitably warned.

"It seems to be a pack ritual for humans. When new young are born here or arrive from outside the cursed lands, a bag arrives. They do not approach but rather leave the bag at the boundaries of our sentries."

She growled, arching her back, her fur bristling on end.

"The humans don't interfere, Anha...even when our young die, and they have the ability to save them."

That made no sense, which seemed to be typical of humans. Anha slid back into human form, exhausted by her efforts. It was difficult to force herself so close to full Lyx form at mid-moon, but her sons were worth the effort.

"What is it?" Anha's voice was still rough, and she maintained her crouch over her young.

Siya shrugged. "Most likely clothing for you and your sons, blankets...perhaps bowls and a basin for washing. I will leave you to your investigation." She left without further comment.

Anha held her ground for a few moments, her muscles tensed. Finally, she scrambled to the bag and dragged it back to the bed. The clasp at the top stuck...then slid free. She pulled out item after item, her heart pounding in disbelief. It was just as Siya had foretold...and it was more than she'd ever owned in her life.

* * * *

Anha let her eyes drift shut but kept her senses primed, not quite sleeping but close enough to settle her mind. On some level, she wished she could sleep in this new nest. On another, she didn't dare dream of such a thing. Not now. Not while she was still without insight into their motives and means.

Siya and the others had shown no sign of aggression, and the scent of Wul and Lyx mixed should have put her at ease, but it didn't. She'd promised herself to wander out into the common nest the following day, with her sons in their sling. The only way she'd assure herself that there wasn't a threat was to expose herself to the possibility of it.

She'd been something of a coward so far. The two nights beneath warm blankets and with plentiful food she didn't have to run herself ragged to catch had made her shamefully cautious when she should be assessing dangers and making the decisions that would rule the rest of their lives.

Cowardice could only stretch so far. No matter what Anha chose to do, it would have to be soon. If she and her sons were to leave this nest, she would need adequate time to provide a nest of her own for them, as daunting as that sounded.

One of her sons latching on snapped her awake, and Anha grimaced at the fact that she'd fallen asleep. True, she was a nursing queen with new young. By Luna's design, she should be sleeping ten times what she was allowing herself. Still, it seemed she was neglecting her duty as sole protector to her sons when she indulged in her need to do so.

Torn, Anha focused on the young tom, startled to see that Thomayan had opened his eyes and joined his elder brothers in the world of the sighted. Her heart stuttered then soared at the sight of green irises.

He was Thoman's son. She had one kit that was pure Lyx, praise Luna.

Her smile disappeared, a laugh dying in her throat. Her gaze strayed to the other two young, Mattayas's young.

A single pure Lyx kit didn't change her situation. She'd left her nest to save one, two, or all of her young from being killed. What was she thinking? That she could choose to lose Missayan and Mittayan? That she could leave them for this nest to raise and return to her own without them? It was as inconceivable as letting them die.

"Never. We all stay, Thomayan," she managed. If her nest couldn't accept them all, returning there wasn't an option.

She looked at the cloth that separated her, by her wish, from the rest of this new nest. They would accept Thomayan as a pure Lyx kit, as they'd accepted Anha as a pure Lyx mother of mixed-breed young. In the morning, she would test their responses.

Exhaustion weighed on her. *For now, I have to sleep.* Without sleep, she wouldn't be capable of fighting off any threat. Like it or not, drifting rest wasn't enough.

Chapter Six

Mattayas stopped abruptly, burying his nose in the pine needles and leaves, his heart racing at the scent he'd missed for so long. He wasn't certain why he still came here, why he still searched for her. It wasn't as if she was his mate. This attraction should have faded long ago.

Of course, he knew why he was coming more often. If her young were Lyx, they would have been born long ago. If they were Wul, she would whelp them soon.

It was a useless endeavor, he was sure. He hadn't scented more than a waft of her essence since the day he'd marked over her scent in claim.

Worse, if she was denning with new young, she wouldn't risk emerging for half a moon or more after the young had whelped.

But that will answer my question, he argued silently. *If she emerges now, scented of young and milk, I will know the young cannot possibly be mine, because she should be denning in earnest.*

To his chagrin, Mattayas admitted that he'd want her, no matter whose young she'd carried. Would this madness never end?

As if in answer, he caught scent of her...a strong scent...new...not more than a quarter sun-journey old. He growled at the sweet odor of milk. She'd carried for the Lyx buck, after all.

Another scent drew his mind away from that odious thought. He inhaled deeply, letting his mind work at what he was scenting, pulling his head back with a snort of disbelief. His hackles rose, and

Mattayas forced them back and buried his snout for a better source scent.

It was young... She'd brought the young from her den? That made no sense. This scent wasn't of a toddling young. It was infant smells. No bitch brought out cubs so young. Not Wul and not Lyx, either.

What reason could a bitch have for doing so? The reason was slow coming but powerful in its surety. The young were his, newly-born no doubt. If Anha brought them out, she meant to run...to save them from her pack mates.

Where would she run?

His heart stuttered in the possibility that she'd come to him. He wanted to dismiss it, but it stuck. If Anha went to the den in track of him, she'd be killed. *My young will be.*

That quickly, he was in motion. There was no sign of her in Wul lands, and Mattayas relaxed, taking human form, then dragging on his clothing and boots.

She hadn't done something as foolish as coming here. Where else could she go?

The great metal fences were to the south. No intelligent animal wanted to pass them. Humans were said to be plentiful beyond them.

He shifted uneasily at the final possibility. She could have gone to the cursed lands. There was no other choice for a bitch in her situation.

But the cursed lands... It was said that those who went there never returned. Was there some foe there? One that didn't range but guarded its territory jealously? Just the thought of Anha and his young being hunted by such a creature brought his hackles up and ripped a growl from his throat.

Mattayas took off for the scentless border at a run, pausing only moments at the unnatural barrier before he crashed through in search of what was his.

* * * *

Mattayas wasn't certain why he felt he was traveling the right direction. The cursed lands were unnatural in their lack of intelligent mark. There was no scent of Wul, nor was there scent of Lyx. One moment, he would be absolute in his belief that he'd scented one or the other. The next, there was nothing but lower creatures. It was driving him mad.

A howl sounded deep in the wood to his right...to the east, and the fur at his hackles rose in response. A cat's growl came from the opposite quarter, and he turned that way...just in time to catch a rattle from the south and a birdcall from the north.

What was once an absence was now a cacophony. Sounds overlapped sounds, too many to be counted. Mattayas couldn't track one sound for the multitude.

He turned toward the west, prepared to bolt toward the sound of Lyx he'd first heard. Hopefully, that trail would lead him to Anha and their young.

The blade tips at his chest and throat stopped him. More pressed to his ribs and spine, the soft tissue of his abdomen...and one between his thighs.

The sensation, coupled with the abrupt cessation of all noise, made him dizzy. Faces and scents cleared slowly, bitches and bucks of both Lyx and Wul of a den together...or perhaps of mixed breed. Mattayas couldn't tell which was the truth.

"What do you seek, Wul buck?" an elder bitch that he believed was Lyx asked.

"I seek a female who passed through not long ago...a bitch with cubs."

Angry growls of both types rose around him.

The bitch waved them to silence, her expression fierce and unforgiving. "*Bitches* with cubs do not come to the cursed lands, buck. *Fems* with cubs or bitches with *kits* do. Which is it you seek?"

His mouth went dry. It was a serious insult he'd offered, apparently.

"Buck?"

"A...a fem. I didn't know the proper form of address," he admitted.

"Send him away or kill him, Siya," another bitch— *or is she fem?*—interjected. "He will never find peace here."

"Wait," Mattayas begged. "I meant no offense by—"

"You do not even address the one you seek with respect."

"I didn't know—"

"Silence," the elder ordered. She seemed to consider Mattayas carefully.

The tension was too much for him. "Please...I seek Anha."

"We *know* who you seek," the younger snapped.

"Silence!" She turned her gaze to Mattayas again. "So, you know the fem's name. You deign to use it, buck. Perhaps there is hope for you yet."

Mattayas's heart skittered. He nodded silently, hoping not to anger her again.

"Siya, you cannot—"

The elder ignored her. "Why did you come here, buck?"

How could he answer that? There was no rational answer he could make to it. "For Anha," he breathed.

"To take her from here?"

He shook his head, his face burning. "My people would kill her. Hers would kill me. Both would kill the cubs."

"Then why come for her?"

His frustration welled. "Because I see and smell and taste her, awake and asleep. I cannot forget her, mad as it is."

"It's more important to you than your den and sire? More important than your dam and brothers?"

"Would I be in this cursed place if it wasn't?"

Silence fell, absolute silence.

"Present your arms to those behind you for binding."

"Siya!"

"The choice is Anha's. Either the buck will take his place among us, at her side...or he will die."

She waited for Mattayas's reaction to that.

He hesitated only a moment. "They'll have to move a few of the blades. Otherwise, I cannot move my arms."

Siya smiled and motioned; half the blades at his back disappeared. Mattayas offered his arms, wincing as the bindings pulled tight around his wrists.

"Should we cover his eyes?" a buck asked.

"No. As one of us or dead... Either way, the knowledge of where we sleep won't matter."

Mattayas forced his muscles looser. If he didn't have Anha, he'd be mad, and death would be a blessing.

Siya cocked her head. "No rethoughts, buck?"

He shook his head. "None."

* * * *

Anha raised her head, frowning at the ruckus from the tunnels. There was laughter, but it was dark and cruel. Shouts went up, but she couldn't make out the words.

She reached for her sons. Something horrible was happening, and Anha wasn't certain they were safe here.

"Anha?" Siya called. "May I enter?"

She swallowed hard, looking back at her sons one last time, then standing to place herself in a protective stance between them and whatever was behind the cloth door. "Enter, Siya," she replied.

The older fem pushed through the door. She scanned Anha's position, then smiled. "You still don't trust us."

"Did you? The first days after you were cast out, did you trust? Or did you run, as I did?"

"I ran. Two of my four cubs survived it."

Anha winced. "I am sorry for your loss."

"It was decades ago."

A silence fell between them, and Anha shifted uncomfortably.

"Tell me about the sire," Siya invited.

"Mattayas," she breathed. Her heart beat a little faster, and Anha tried to shake off the arousal that thoughts of him ignited. She swore she could smell him, even now.

"You knew him, then."

"Only long enough." She shook her head. "No. His lesser toms...I mean bucks, pardon the lapse. They called him by name."   '

"If you could see him again? What would you do, Anha?"

She shrugged. "He is Wul, Siya. He has no feelings for me." Her heart ached at the truth of it.

"You came to love half-Wul cubs," she pressed.

"They are mine, no matter what else they are. Surely, you know that."

"Then you feel nothing for this Wul buck...Mattayas?"

Anha couldn't meet her eyes. Why would Siya ask such a thing? "Does it matter?" There were Wul and Lyx who had mated in the cursed lands. Would such a thing damn her in their eyes?

"Yes. I'm afraid it does."

Siya pulled back the cloth, and a tom staggered through, seemingly pushed from behind. He landed hard on his knees, jerking himself back just in time to save himself from a sprawl on his face. His hands were tied behind him, but he appeared uninjured.

Just when Anha was about to question this move, he raised his head and stared at Anha.

Her knees deserted her, and Anha landed on her backside on the edge of the bed, by the grace of Luna alone missing her sons. "Mattayas." It came out a gasp, and her body forgot how to breathe.

"It matters, Anha. It matters to Mattayas. His life is in your hands."

* * * *

Mattayas watched the color drain from her face with a tightening in his gut.

Siya droned on, but he didn't hear her. He supposed she was explaining the power Anha held over Mattayas to the young fem.

Silence fell, and Anha nodded to something.

"Well, Anha?" Siya offered silkily.

"I can't," she gasped.

Mattayas closed his eyes and bowed his head. He'd been a fool to think she felt anything for him but hatred.

"You cannot accept him, and you wish me to kill the buck?" Siya asked.

"I cannot do that," Anha replied.

Mattayas snapped his head up, opening his eyes to lock her in his gaze. Anha bit at her lower lip, seemingly torn.

"You cannot watch him die, and you will accept him?"

Anha's eyes widened, and the scent of panic tainted the air.

Siya sighed. "Or perhaps...you feel unequal to such a choice while you're so confused about his drive to come here? You barely know each other, after all. There are answers you must have that may sway your choice?"

"Yes." Anha's shoulders relaxed, and she suddenly appeared weary.

She would be weary. She's had no buck to aid her in raising the cubs.

Siya nodded curtly. "Such discussions are private. We will not be far...if you need us, Anha."

"She won't," Mattayas vowed.

Anha gaped at him, but she didn't question his comment. She was still staring long after Siya withdrew.

Mattayas let his gaze wander to the tangle of miniature limbs and fur, half-covered by blankets. He ached to see the young closer.

These are my cubs. Yet, he had no idea how many there were, how old they were, what sexes they were. The slight scent of male musk attested that at least one of them was a buck. Beyond that, he knew nothing.

"Why did you come here?" she whispered.

"Why did you take me as you did?" he countered.

That question had plagued him for more than half a year. Were Lyx fems really so different that their heat made them receptive to any male? Or did she feel something for Mattayas in particular? Could he trust his memories of that night? Those memories spoke of a preference for Mattayas that she hadn't extended to even the Lyx buck.

Anha didn't reply. A glance at her showed her confusion and misery.

If she was going to accept him, there had to be truth between them. "I cannot explain why I had to have you, either," he admitted. "But I had to."

She winced, blinking back what were probably tears.

"I've wanted you every hour since."

"You...you have? You did?"

"Every minute. I risked my life to invade Lyx land for scent of you as often as I dared. I dreamed of finding you alone and about and taking you again...especially once I scented that you carried."

She took a calming breath. "And...and you came here because..."

"Come to me," he requested.

Anha hesitated.

"I am at your mercy, Anha." *In more ways than one.*

She moved slowly, sliding to the floor, then easing toward him. Mattayas held his ground though every instinct called him to get her beneath him, every curve pressed to him, bound hands or not.

Anha reached his side, and Mattayas buried his face in her hair, breathing in her scent. She stiffened, her breathing ragged.

"You are so beautiful," he whispered.

The tension in her muscles eased. Mattayas pressed his lips to her neck, tracing the raised ridges of his mating bite. His arms tensed in the need to embrace her, and he bit back a growl in frustration.

She trembled against him, leaning into him so that her milk-swollen breasts teased him through their clothing. Anha turned her head, and Mattayas pulled back, his lips skimming her chin...then her lips.

They parted, inviting him in. Mattayas obliged her with a growl of arousal. The kiss rivaled their first: hot, hard, full of sexual promise.

He broke away, nipping at her skin, then her shirt, hinting that she should remove it. When she didn't, he trailed his mouth down to the peak of a primary nipple, sucking gently, growling again at her cry of pleasure, muted as it was behind clenched lips.

"Do you feel it?" he asked. "Do you burn?"

Her hands threaded through his hair and drew his face back up, as if she meant to kiss him again. "I burn," she confirmed.

She trembled much as she had that night, but he found himself arguing again what he'd argued all these months: was she trembling in a fierce need or in fear of him?

"I am at your mercy, Anha. You can do *anything* with me you wish."

She went still, her breath warming his cheek. Was she considering his offer or considering ripping his throat out as he'd ripped her buck's throat out? If she chose to kill him, could he blame her for it? He'd cost her everything she'd held dear—her male, her family, her den...

Her hand settled over his cock, stroking up and down. Mattayas thrust his hips up, urging her on.

Anha pushed down on his shoulders, guiding him to his heels so that she was higher than he was. She straddled him, bringing the heat of her core to his cock. Mattayas thrust up reflexively, his mind spinning. Luna, but he wanted her to mount him, still bound for her as she'd been for him.

Her mouth merged with his, hungry, seeking more. She worked at the buttons down his chest, one small hand delving inside and tracing rigid muscle...and a peal of laughter filled the air.

Anha broke off the kiss, snapping her head around. She vaulted off his lap, turning to the low bed, her cheeks glowing crimson.

Mattayas took a moment to compose his wits, wondering at the change in her. "Do Lyx kits not see their dam in heat with a buck?" he inquired. He knew little of their customs.

She paused. "They do."

"Then we moved too fast. You're uncomfortable."

"We were supposed to *talk*, Mattayas."

"Then we will."

Anha turned to him, a young buck on her hip. His eyes were a brown that closely matched Mattayas's, and his hair was red-black. The cub looked at him curiously.

"What is his name?" he managed.

"This is Missayan."

He glanced toward the sleeping cubs. "And the others?"

"Mittayan and Thomayan."

Mattayas nodded. "There are three then?"

Anha stiffened.

His heart sank. "There were more?" Were they born dead? Killed by her pack mates? Killed in her bid for escape? Of illness? Or perhaps while she was unprotected in the cursed lands?

It's my fault. However it happened, it's my fault that it did.

"No. Only the three." She shifted from foot to foot as if preparing to duck an attack.

Revelation came in a flash, not unlike lightning outlining a foe in the pitch of a moonless night. "How many did I sire, Anha? How many are of your buck?"

Anha eased further to the side, taking a protective stance before the still-sleeping young.

"Anha...please..." Was he begging now? Begging for the tiniest details about the brood she'd birthed?

"You should leave," she whispered, in apparent misery.

"I can't." Even if Siya wouldn't kill him, he couldn't leave now.

She sank to the bed, drawing the cub to her chest as if she took comfort from their son. "Oh...yes. Acceptance or death. I forgot."

"Why won't you tell me?"

Anha stared at him.

Working his way to the answer took him longer that time. "Your bucks kill the young of others?" he asked, aghast at the concept.

"If they feel they have a claim on the fem who bore them. Your bucks don't?" It seemed to surprise her.

"We rear those who aren't our own," he informed her. "Orphaned young...bitches who have no buck to help them care for their young." Surely, he could raise the slain buck's young out of Anha.

"Our fems do likewise, but the toms are another matter."

Mattayas waited, barely breathing.

"Two are yours," she offered. "The last... I believe I always knew it. *Thomayan* was the only one I named..." She darkened, her eyes widening.

"You named the other two for me?" His heart leapt at that.

She cleared her throat, averting her eyes. "Think nothing of it."

He bit back a smile. "May I?"

Confusion creased her brow.

"May I see them?"

"All of them?" He seemed to surprise her at every turn of the conversation.

Mattayas sighed. "I am not one of your Lyx bucks—"

"Toms," she corrected him.

Mattayas forced his voice to emerge calmly. "Toms. I don't *like* that you bore his kit and my cubs together. For that matter, I don't like that I killed your tom, in the first place, but—"

"You don't?" Her voice rose an octave at that.

"No," he admitted. "There was no glory in killing him. He'd surrendered to protect you. We had the advantage. We had numbers and—"

"Which you didn't use," she interrupted.

"He was *nude*, Anha. I shouldn't have done it."

"Then why did you?"

* * * *

Nothing he was saying made sense, but Anha had to hear it all. When he didn't answer, she asked the question again.

"Because your scent was driving me mad. Because his scent on you was intolerable."

Memories of him scenting her assaulted her. "And when your pack mates touched me?"

"I wanted to rip their throats out, too." It was blunt, cold, the promise of a hunter, a predator who was accustomed to taking what he wanted. Mattayas met her gaze solidly. "You didn't want their touch."

She shook her head.

"But you wanted mine, even when I left you." He didn't question it, though his eyes pleaded for assurances.

"Yes. Asleep and awake."

He nodded. "Let me see the kit, Anha. I took his sire's life wrongfully. I won't do the same to Thomayan."

As if in answer, a body snuggled to Anha's back. Then a second. She drew her sons onto her lap, watching Mattayas for signs of aggression.

Mittayan sighted his sire and leaned forward on his chubby hands to look closer. He made questioning noises that Missayan answered with gurgles and babble. It seemed to satisfy the younger cub, though he cocked his head to one side.

Mattayas smiled. "Do you know me, cub?" he teased.

Thomayan let go of his foot and turned toward Mattayas's voice. The buck's smile faltered, but he didn't tense, didn't growl, and didn't bare his fangs.

"I am sorry, little one," he offered.

Thomayan looked up at Anha, then started to work his way down to the floor. She turned him and planted him firmly next to his brothers with a rumble of a queen's concern.

Mattayas shot her a look of hurt.

She found it hard to form a response. "I should..."

"Let them, Anha." There was something of a plea in that.

She lowered Missayan and Mittayan to the floor, certain that they were safe with Mattayas. His jaw tightened in anger, but he nodded.

The cubs took to hands and knees, clamoring off in investigation of the new buck in their midst. They pulled up on their knees by their grips on his jeans, burying their faces in his thighs and waist.

Mattayas murmured to their sons...

My sons!

But they weren't hers alone, and if she accepted Mattayas...

"How do Wul rear their young?" she inquired.

He didn't look up at her. "What are you asking, Anha?"

Could she say it without offending him? "Lyx toms have little to do with kits until they are half-grown, unless they are mated to the queen. Then they are intolerably pushy about their young. Still, the fems care for the kits, day to day."

"What do the bucks do here?" he countered, his voice clipped.

"They are cross-bred bucks...or mated to a fem already. And they don't dare approach and...offer as you say bucks offer to aid a queen without a mate, because..." She shrugged.

His head came up, his eyes hard. "Wul bucks help rear their young...or any young they take into their care." He looked at Thomayan pointedly. "We do this from the first scent of the young, at the bitch's permission to approach, unless they are a mated couple. We care for young in all ways but nursing."

Anha nodded. Then he would expect to take the place of a mated tom and more. That would likely cause tension between them, since she was unaccustomed to the idea of a tom interfering in child rearing.

"Did you know?" he asked.

She stared at him, trying desperately to follow the conversation. "Know what?"

"When you left your pack—"

"Nest," she corrected. If she had to learn his words, he had to learn hers. If for no other reason, he'd offend someone in the mixed nest if he didn't learn them.

He took a calming breath and shifted his weight on his knees. "Nest. Did you know when you left your nest that you had a kit they wouldn't kill? Or did you believe you'd lose them all?"

Anha stiffened at the possible implications of that. "Meaning what? What are you asking, Mattayas?" *And why is he asking it?*

"Perhaps I simply want to understand you, as you claim to want to understand me."

As if she would believe that. "And who are you to question me? Where were you the moons I carried? Or the half a moon since?"

He didn't reply in kind; his voice was calm, measured, nearly cold. "You didn't know then. You left because you were afraid you'd lose them all. You were desperate to—"

"How dare you. You know—"

"You didn't know," he pushed.

"I didn't know, but I still chose to leave...without knowing. I love them all, Mattayas. It wouldn't have mattered if they'd killed all three or only Missayan."

Mattayas nodded, his expression softening. "Missayan was the first...the first to show signs of being my get?"

Anha stared at the cubs, smiling weakly at the sight of Mittayan leaving wet spots on the denim that signaled he'd soon seek a nipple. "First born and first to open his lovely brown eyes."

His chuckle brought her gaze back to his face. Anha replayed her words, her cheeks hot in the realization that the cubs had his eyes, and she'd just called them 'lovely.' "Think nothing of it," she managed.

"I wouldn't dare," he teased in return.

Thomayan made another bid for escape, and Anha slid to the floor, easing her youngest son between Mattayas's knees.

The buck stopped laughing and stared at the exploring kit as if in wonder. Thomayan raised his head, green eyes meeting brown.

Mattayas's throat bobbed, and he took several slow, deep breaths. "Thank you, Anha."

She relaxed hands she hadn't realized were fisted. Perhaps, Mattayas was sincere.

Chapter Seven

Mattayas sat on the bed, his now-bare feet stretched out toward Anha and the young, his still-bound hands pillowing his back against the cavern wall. Anha had removed his boots. She'd fed him from her own hand, then fed the cubs and kit.

What she hadn't done was fastened his shirt again, and the landscape of his chest and abdomen drew her eyes often. It gave him hope that she intended more when the young were settled.

They were all but asleep now, nuzzling at three of her four breasts. Mattayas hardened more forcefully at the sight of the exposed secondary breasts that would shrink to dark thumb-print-sized circles when the young were weaned, the layer of fat redistributing and the nipples flattening.

He closed his eyes, forcing his breathing to even. Luna, but he had to touch her soon. Seeing and scenting her were not enough for him.

The bed shifted, announcing Anha's approach. Mattayas didn't look at her. Convincing himself not to shift to affect his release from the binding was fast becoming difficult. If tempted again, he might follow his instincts and do it, and Luna only knew if he could gain her trust then.

"Why did you come here?" she whispered.

"Do you wish I hadn't?"

"I..." Her breath bathed his neck. "I don't know how to answer that." But her lips trailed up his throat to his jawline, her tongue darting out to take a taste.

Mattayas fisted his hands. "Are you ever going to release my arms?"

She nipped at his earlobe, sending shivers of delight down his spine. "Perhaps I like you tied up and in my bed."

Breathing was abruptly difficult. "I could come to like it, I suppose." Already, visions of her mounting him tied this way had returned in force.

She worked his jeans open. "You could come," she agreed.

Her scent surrounded him, making Mattayas dizzy in arousal. No bitch compared to her. He was certain none ever could.

Anha sank to his half-freed cock, her rough tongue bathing the swollen head. It was torture; it was ecstasy. She took him in, and Mattayas moaned, lifting his hips to her. Luna, but she could emasculate him with one snap of her jaws, but she was giving him mind-altering pleasure instead.

Mattayas writhed beneath her, working his way to a more comfortable position, watching her suckle at him through half-lidded eyes. Her mouth rose and fell, coating him in hot saliva, exploring his cock as he'd explored her their first night together.

"Oh, Luna, yes," he panted out. "More, Anha. I—"

He cried out harshly at the edge of pain slicing at him, pressing back to the wall as if he could escape her. What had she done to him? He smelled his own blood, blood she was sucking at as his cubs would suck at her milk-full breasts. The pleasure and pain mixed unbearably.

Her tongue snaked through the cut she'd made in his foreskin, and he bowed up under the brutal assault of sensation. Mattayas had never known a buck could feel so much.

The next slice was less painful, probably because he was lost in bliss. By the third, so much of the deliciously-sensitive under-flesh was exposed he would have begged for more.

Mattayas might well have literally begged for it in is delirium. Anha was eating him alive, and he'd never dreamed it could feel so good.

She released him, kneeling up and meeting his gaze. A smear of his blood colored her lower lip, and he hungered to lick it off.

His jeans slid to his thighs, and his cock bobbed in the cool air, seeking more. Her roughened tongue returned, pulling away the last tattered scraps of his foreskin while he moaned and writhed under her.

Anha retreated, leaving him gasping and dry-mouthed, shaking at the edges of climax. Sounds pulled at his muddled mind, and he forced his eyes open.

Her jeans were open, and she was shimmying out of them, her hips swaying in invitation as the material lowered. Her fragrant black curls appeared, and he moaned in need. A trickle of his fluids stung at the raw tears on his cockhead, and he hissed in discomfort.

She chuckled, drawing one leg from her jeans. "Now you're making the correct sounds," Anha teased.

Mattayas glared at her. "If it will get you to me faster, I'll learn to hiss for you."

Her second leg appeared, leaving her naked and, by her glorious scent, ready. She smiled a knowing smile. "It might."

He forced the foreign noise out, and Anha crawled up his body, straddling his hips. Her heated core stroked over him, setting off those mixed touches of pleasure and pain he was coming to love. It was almost too bad the damage would heal in a few days.

His fangs extended halfway, and a more realistic hiss escaped him...followed by a growl of warning.

"Better," she crooned.

Before Mattayas could retort, she'd guided his cock to her and impaled herself on him.

He let his head drop back, baring his throat fully. "Oh, Luna," he breathed. "Oh, Dam."

"It feels like nothing you've felt before." She didn't question it.

"Yes."

With that assurance, she started moving, raising and lowering her body around him. Mattayas felt every ridge of muscle, every whisper of movement.

He thrust up against her, and her eyes widened, a gasp escaping her.

"You haven't forgotten how good we are together, have you?" he teased.

"Never."

That one word shattered his thinking mind. The next few moments passed in bodies working furiously against each other, sounds rising and melding into a mating song.

In the end, Mattayas lasted only as long as she did. They climaxed together, sweat-soaked bodies scenting each other, his engorged cock wedged tight in her little body.

Just as his heart started to slow, Anha slid off his length and started stroking her tongue over the cuts.

They opened again, feeding her on his cum and blood. He hissed, biting at his lower lip hard enough to cut two furrows that welled up blood.

As if that was too much enticement for her, Anha covered him with her body, drinking down that blood, as well. Dimly, Mattayas reasoned that his blood was rebuilding her lost reserves and strengthening the milk that would feed their young. If she had need, he would provide.

"Don't you want to know?" she asked.

He stared at her, confused.

"I'm not going to let the wounds close, Mattayas. Not for at least three days."

He shivered in delight at the idea. She'd have to tongue him at least twice a day to keep them open.

"If you please me for those three days, I will accept you as my mate."

Mattayas nodded. "This is how Lyx take a mate?" If so, their toms were lucky animals.

"Yes. The mating will be often and fierce. If you perform well, I accept you."

"And toms that don't perform well?" Not that he was worried about it. Mattayas wasn't going to fail this test of his virility.

She licked at the blood welling up on his lip. "They never mate, because the other fems consider them unworthy."

He nodded, an idea taking shape. "Do I have to be bound for this?"

Her head came back, and she stared at him, seemingly considering untying him.

"Give me leave, and I will show you how a Wul buck proves his...stamina to one he wishes as mate."

"Do you?" Her voice was so low, he almost didn't hear her, even with his sensitive hearing.

"Do I...what, Anha?"

"Wish to have me as your mate?"

He smiled, well aware that she could see his fangs extending for another mark. "Why do you think I marked you and ordered you to mark me?" He hadn't believed it could actually bind. Even if it could, he hadn't believed it would work when the fem was a Lyx and not a Wul bitch, but he'd done it.

"You... You've already made me your mate? Was that why you stalked me on Lyx lands?"

He forced back his anger at that question. "It was the correct ceremony, though I'd want to do it again, now that you know what it means.

"And I never stalked you. I came for what was mine, and when I was denied it, I claimed you in the only way I could...you and whatever young you carried."

Anha's breathing went ragged, but there was no smell of fear from her.

"Give me leave, Anha. Let me please you."

She hesitated, then reached a hand around to grab hold of the restraining cords. Taking that as permission, Mattayas transformed his hands to paws, slipped the ropes, and transformed back, grasping her head between his hands and bringing his mouth down on hers.

* * * *

Anha opened her mouth to protest but found herself immersed in a heated kiss. In a dizzying motion, Mattayas rolled her beneath him on the bed.

It should have frightened her, but he hadn't...not since his first touch. Instead of fighting him, Anha met him avidly, arching up to facilitate his first thrust.

His mouth retreated, as he started cycling his hips, driving deep inside her, his entire body flexing and tightening in concert.

"You could have..." She gasped.

"I could have been free any time I wished," he grumbled. "But I agreed to let you decide, Anha."

And I chose him...again. "What will you do, Mattayas?"

"You'll have your three days. Then I bind you to me again."

"If I'm pleased," she managed. Luna, but was there any question that she would be?

As if he took that as a challenge, Mattayas doubled his already-formidable efforts, driving her to climax and following her over a few thrusts later. She licked her lips, mired in the release of endorphins and the sweet bite of his smooth cock.

Moments later, he was kneeling beside her, offering his cock for another go. "Unless our young need you or you require food or sleep, you are mine, Anha. I will please you until you beg me to stop."

She didn't doubt that he would.

"Anha," he hinted.

She took Mattayas into her mouth, opening the new tissue again, closing her eyes to his groan of pleasure.

* * * *

"Anha," Siya greeted her.

Anha shifted Missayan on her hip, offering a slight tip of her head. Beside her, Mattayas balanced Mittayan and Thomayan on one muscular arm. It was a gift that Anha trusted him to care for the kit, and Mattayas resolved himself to earn that trust fully.

"You've accepted your buck, I see."

She touched the fresh bite on her neck, darkening. "Yes. I have."

Mattayas's matching mark throbbed pleasantly in reminder of the silent vows to protect his mate and young.

Anha straightened. "It was my choice," she challenged.

"It was indeed." The fem ranged an assessing gaze up and down Mattayas's body. "I assume your mate will join the hunts?"

Mattayas stared down at her, offended at the merest hint that he wouldn't. "If you don't fear my sire and pack tracking me, I'd be honored to join the hunt. A buck supports his young and mate. Would you prefer me to hunt in human form or Wul?"

Siya raised an eyebrow. "You can take Wul form now?"

He scowled, working at his buttons with his free hand.

"I believe you." The old fem chuckled. "Well, I'm overjoyed Anha chose to save your life then."

"You may not be if my pack tracks me here," he grumbled, tensing.

His sire was certainly not amused by recent events. For the loss of his prized first son, who knew what retribution Dievan would seek?

"Your *pack* has already been turned back, young buck. This is your nest now."

Mattayas was silent for a long moment, his tension increasing. "Are they dead? Are any of them?" And what would he do if she said they were?

Siya smiled. "We don't kill when we can...deter by other means. Now, do you accept this nest as your home?"

Mattayas drew Anha to his side, and she snuggled beneath his offered arm. "My nest is wherever Anha and our young are. She chose this nest, thank Luna. That makes it mine, as well."

The fem waved the way to the inner den, where curious pack mates...nest mates waited to greet the new additions. "The hunt begins at dusk, Mattayas. Good hunting."

She glided away with warm words for other members of their community. Mattayas settled his small pack within the larger pack that had taken them in. It took only moments of ease to realize that he'd truly found home.

Foundling

Vahlrae raced from tree to tree, drinking the night air. The evening hunt was over, so she wouldn't be sanctioned for scaring prey with her romp. It wasn't often that she had so much of the night to run and play, and she intended to enjoy every moment of it.

The change on the air was so subtle she almost missed it. There was a taint of something dark and dangerous. Not for the first time, Vahlrae wished she could taste the air like her pack could.

She didn't see danger, didn't hear it, but all of her senses were weaker than those of the others. True, she was a lost one, but her birth den must have been inferior to Dievan's stock. Perhaps it was better that she'd found her way to this place.

The sense of violence was stronger now. It wasn't the energy that rode the wind before a hunt. Not that there were any predators large and strong enough to hunt the Wul.

The Lyx are. Vahlrae shivered at that thought, scanning the wood for some sign of the curs. Panic rising, she looked for snakes, scampering back a few steps in anticipation of a strike that never came.

Her mind worked fast. Lyx were a possibility, but it was dark and cool. Snakes would be curled up on themselves asleep now.

The tingle down her neck that announced she was being watched persisted, and Vahlrae took a step toward the den...then a second and third. In moments, she was running the opposite direction of the way she'd come.

Crashing behind her told her that she was being chased. Whatever the interloper into their territory, it was big...and it was fast. She used the rush of adrenaline to push herself to the limits of endurance, hoping to outrun it.

Hope came forcibly to ground as she did, buried under the near-crushing weight of a growling mass with a decidedly male scent. Vahlrae clawed at her attacker, her heart stuttering at clothing bunching against her fingertips.

Lyx!

Her scream died in her throat at the sound of her name being growled in a familiar voice. "Mannias?" she gasped, praying it wasn't a trick of her weakened senses.

The next growl was fiercer, more guttural, and her heart stuttered at the sound. It was a rumble she'd heard before, one she'd thought she'd never hear directed at her.

And this is Dievan's son. His second son, but with Mattayas lost to the scentless lands, Mannias would lead, in his time.

Hands pulled at her shirt in the dim light beneath the trees, and Vahlrae moved to aid him. Bucks enflamed to mating had no patience, and though Mannias would give her his own shirt after they were one, it would leave him prey to the elements. She couldn't live with that.

The rip of material announced that she'd moved too slowly, and she hastened to unfasten her jeans to save them a similar fate, her mind spinning wildly at his fervor.

The chase. He'd chased her down, and that would make his need all the stronger.

As if in confirmation, her shirt shredded, and his rough hands explored the heated flesh beneath. Vahlrae arched into his hands, using the move to push her jeans away.

His long, silken hair glowed snow white in the muted light, and his scent intensified. Their gazes met for a moment; then he was rubbing his hair and cheek down her body, sensitizing her.

Scenting me. Before he was through, she'd be marked as his, inside and out. That thought was enough to dampen her thighs. Of course, what he was doing could accomplish that alone.

Mannias's mouth joined in the play, his extended fangs scraping at her erect nipples, his tongue washing away the sharp little pains in waves of pleasure that had her wiggling against him in search of the next touch.

Vahlrae traced her short, blunt fangs with her tongue, wishing that she could extend her own and join in the play. Her heart ached at that. Her stock was so weak, it was amazing that Mannias wanted to make her his bitch.

The nip at the soft meat of her belly wrenched a soft cry of surprise from her throat and dragged her mind back to what he was doing. Weak or not, Mannias intended to bind them, and she intended to enjoy every minute of it.

The challenge growl came without warning, and Mannias tensed over her, his hot breath stirring the fur at the apex of her thighs. Vahlrae grasped at his shoulder with a shaking hand, unsure of what she was asking for.

She wasn't asking him not to fight for her. He'd been challenged; the bucks never turned from a challenge.

She might be telling him to come back to her unscathed. As Dievan's son, he was of the strongest stock. He could even shift at a lesser moon, when he needed to. The chances that he would lose this battle were slim.

Was she asking for reassurances that he would prevail? Whichever of them won the challenge would claim her as prize. Vahlrae wasn't certain which buck was challenging for her, but she knew she wanted Mannias. Would she want the other, as well? She'd been told bitches sometimes rejected bucks, but was she strong enough to fight off a buck she didn't want to accept? Vahlrae wasn't sure.

Mannias ducked his head to brush his soft hair against her throat again, rumbling a calming sound for her. Then he turned to the challenger and placed her at his back.

She was spellbound on the sight. His broad back and arms were strung tight as if to pounce, his knees bent to give him a solid fighting stance. Though the ground was cool, Mannias was barefoot, which meant he could shift all the quicker, though it was unlikely he'd need to shift to best the interloper.

The low rumbling from both bucks gained volume and depth. Mannias's claws extended, scraping hard at the thick loam, marking his intent to stop the other buck there.

The challenger stepped into a shaft of light, and Vahlrae let out a low whine of distress at the sight of Tragan. The wicked slashes the Lyx bitch had left on his face had always frightened her, and his cold eyes and colder manner had made her seek her dam's protection on more than one occasion. Now he was trying to claim her as his mate. If he bested Mannias, she would have to do her best to fight him off.

At her sound of distress, Mannias tensed again, but he didn't pounce. He was a patient hunter, and bucks knew that the one who attacked in anger usually lost.

Tragan moved left, attempting to outflank Mannias. Not to be fooled by such a move, Mannias stepped directly to that side, not backing to Vahlrae, letting the challenger close the distance between the two bucks rather than abandoning the line he'd set. Mannias let out a complicated series of growls she couldn't follow. In the next moment, they were rolling together, barking, hair standing on end. The flash of teeth in the moonlight made her heart pound sickly in her ears.

Vahlrae's instincts said to run, but Mannias had placed her with a purpose. The rock face at her back made her position defensible. No buck could come at her from behind. If she ran—

There may be others. One could catch and claim me before Mannias can. She shivered at that thought.

The ruckus was growing more intense with every passing heartbeat. She started to ease her jeans up; if she had to fight Tragan, she couldn't do so with her jeans around her thighs.

Vahlrae paused, considering that. Whoever triumphed would want to claim her immediately, on the rush of adrenaline. She could fight as well unclothed as clothed, and it would save her clothing further damage if she didn't manage to fight him off. Self-conscious, she started stripping her boots and jeans away.

As if the move had some bearing on the fight, it stepped up another notch. Clothes tore, and the sound of snapping jaws was chilling.

Vahlrae's breath caught in her throat at the sound of a yelp of pain. Which buck was injured and how badly?

As if in answer, Mannias rose and took a step back, growling fiercely. Tragan staggered to his feet, blood coursing from a ragged tear in his shoulder. His gaze strayed from Mannias to Vahlrae, and Mannias lunged for him with a bark of order.

Tragan skittered back several steps, then turned and loped away, most likely to seek a healer for his wounds. His sounds tapered off, but Mannias held his ground a few moments, probably still tracking his retreat with his stronger hearing.

Then he turned to her, assessing her state of undress, his head cocked to one side, seemingly amused. Vahlrae half- expected to see his tongue loll out in silent laughter.

Instead, he drew his shirt off over his shoulders and dropped it to the forest floor beneath him. His muscles rippled at his approach, and she stared at them, transfixed at the beauty and power, numbly noting his jeans opening in a single pull.

Mannias dropped to his knees, his legs fencing in hers, his breathing harsh. She buried her face in his sweat-coated chest, closing her eyes to the sweet pounding of his heart.

His hand fisted in her hair, and he guided her face up, his mouth closing on hers. Vahlrae moaned, opening for him. It was a sign of trust that he kissed her. As a rule, Wul didn't kiss. She'd only seen it a few times that she could remember.

His tongue was hard and thick, and the taste of copper in his mouth fired her senses. In moments, they were meshed together, their tongues circling and stroking, Vahlrae on the ground beneath him.

Mannias started scenting her again, as if the scent he'd left scant moments ago had faded. There was no stopping at her belly this time. His hungry mouth explored her furred mound, then the sensitive nub hidden beneath, prompting a cry of pleasure from her.

He dragged her legs from between his own, forcing them up and out to bare her pussy to him. Then his mouth was buried between her legs, his tongue rasping over her, drinking her musk as if starved for it.

His hair stroked at her inner thighs, sending shivers of delight down her spine. She'd heard such wonderful stories about a buck's claiming, but Vahlrae had never dared hope she'd find a male intent on her.

Intent certainly described Mannias. Little growls sent shards of sensation rumbling through her empty and aching body, and she gasped pleas for more. He suckled hard at her nub, then nipped, and she bowed upward in pleasure, her breathing ragged and her body rioting in need.

That only spurred him on to more play. He nipped at her nether lips, suckling away the pain and replacing it with indescribable pleasure. Her body went rigid, and her hands clawed at the dirt beneath them.

Fire licked up her body, and colors exploded before her eyes. A scream burst from her throat, raw and rough. Vahlrae didn't know what he'd done to her, but she wanted it to go on... and she wanted it to end. It was too intense to bear, too—

Mannias rose over her and thrust inside, ending her debate about the rest. Pleasure-mixed pain blurred her vision, and she screamed a second time, clawing at his chest, her breaths coming in disjointed hitches.

He growled at that, his back arching, driving him further inside. Heat rushed into her, and his cock expanded, stretching her already-tight muscles further to accommodate him.

There wasn't enough air for her to scream again. She whimpered, her hands shaking against his chest, her pussy twitching in continuing protest-plea against his cock.

"Oh, yes." It was the first coherent words he'd managed.

His cock lessened, and Vahlrae sucked a startled breath, too overwhelmed to answer in kind.

He didn't waste a moment. Mannias eased her legs from around his waist, leading her muddled mind to the question of when she'd wrapped them around him.

She didn't have long to wonder. He was moving her, turning her. Vahlrae reached out, planting a hand on the body-warmed ground unsteadily, seeking for elusive balance.

She didn't find it. Her breathing hitched at the feeling of his renewed cockhead prodding at her swollen nether lips. She'd known he'd want her more than once. Mannias would likely mount her countless times in the next few days, but she hadn't expected this whirlwind the first time.

He thrust inside with a grunt of satisfaction, and she let out low cry at the brush of pain against the raw, torn tissue inside. That seemed to bring the buck under some semblance of control. His hand skated from her hip to her mound, and he dipped two fingers to her nub, rubbing in soothing circles. His cock bucked inside her, but he held his ground much as he had during the fight, patiently waiting for his moment to move.

Vahlrae wasn't as restrained. His stroking fingers soon had her shifting her hips, riding them. She threw her head back, turning her face to feel his chest fur against her cheek.

"My little bitch," he grumbled.

She was. There was no denying that she wanted to be. Vahlrae moaned at his speeding fingers, trying to keep time with her hips.

Mannias's move was sudden and unexpected. He planted a hand at her shoulder and forced her further down onto him, grinding up into her hungry pussy hard.

At her scream of climax, he brought his mouth to her opposite shoulder, nuzzling, then biting down hard. Her next scream was one of pain, though her contracting body quickened in response to the added stimulus, pain or no.

His mouth retreated and his tongue bathed the wound clean. Vahlrae let her head drop forward, panting in a confusing mix of sensation.

Mannias pressed his wrist to her lips. "Mark me," he ordered.

She stared at it blearily, her mind working to the truth that he wanted her to bite him in return.

"Now, Vahlrae. Do not refuse me. Mark me, and accept me."

She had to bite him to seal the union? No one had warned her about that. Her stomach rebelled, but she argued it was no worse than eating the meat of prey.

Resolved, Vahlrae bit down hard, trying to make her ineffectual fangs do the job his had. She tasted blood. Not a lot of it but enough to let her know she'd broken skin.

Mannias groaned in what sounded like excitement, his hips sliding back and forth smoothly, his cock pounding into her. "That's right. Take my blood, as I took yours."

She wasn't taking much. He couldn't be losing more than a trickle, but apparently it was enough to satisfy Mannias.

His shout of climax preceded the second wash of seed into her. His howl of triumph followed close behind, and Vahlrae turned her head, letting her cheek rest against his forearm, exhausted, her eyes slipping closed to the feeling of his cock swelling and locking his seed inside.

A strange sound sent her eyes fluttering open again...then a second. A pinch of sensation like an insect bite to her thigh made her heart pound in apprehension.

Mannias tensed as if for attack, and fur sprouted on his hand, then retreated. His weight forced her to the ground beneath him.

Her move to protest ended mid-growl, her eyes slipping shut.

Darkness closed on her, and sleep won their short battle.

* * * *

Sounds that she was sure were words played at her mind.

Only a few made sense: asleep, hurt...

There were two voices. One was female and lyrical. The other had her tensing to fight; it was a strange buck.

Her eyes flew open. Vahlrae squeezed them shut against the glare around her. Wherever she was, she'd somehow lost the night and found herself trapped in bright daylight without her pack to protect her.

She wasn't in the forest. The surface beneath her was soft but cool. Her lip curled at the strange smells and the lack of intelligent mark. It was like the scentless lands.

Have I been captured by the creature there? She was certain she hadn't strayed toward the border. Had the creature left his territory to snatch her from Mannias?

Mannias! He wouldn't let another male take her from him willingly. Had he been injured trying to stop it? Had he been killed?

Vahlrae forced her eyes open again, growling in warning. She tried to turn and scratch at the strange buck's face, but something stopped her movement. Her hands were held tight by something hard and lined in cloth.

Without hesitation, she tried to bite at it. Hands grabbed at her shoulders and dragged her away. She turned her head and bit down hard at the closest hand, noting the male scream of pain in satisfaction.

Shouts followed, and the hand was whipped away, leaving Vahlrae free to attack the thing restraining her wrists. She yipped at the insect sting to her buttocks then returned to her gnawing.

Her heart seemed to beat too loudly, and her muscles went warm and heavy. Vahlrae couldn't hold up her head any longer. A moment later, she was staring at unknown faces. Then darkness swallowed the light...and her with it.

* * * *

The nuzzling at her face brought Mannias's scent. Vahlrae sighed in contentment. It had been a dream. There were no strangers, no bright lights and strange smells. There was no creature stealing her from her mate.

"Another male has touched you."

The words chilled her, and she opened her eyes to the sight of Mannias's tense jaw. A lump lodged in her throat. It was unheard of for another buck to touch what wasn't his. What would Mannias do?

He answered with a rumbling growl of displeasure and the stroke of his silky head over her, drowning the offensive scent on her skin with his own. When he reached her mound, he sniffed...then tasted, the tension draining from his muscles.

Vahlrae nearly sobbed in relief. Whatever the interloper had done, he hadn't tried to stake a claim on her.

As if in confirmation or renewal of his own claim, Mannias started licking in earnest, waking her body to arousal. When she was frothing in her own musk and his saliva, he came to his knees and drew her onto his lap, lifting Vahlrae and easing her down his length.

Her body tightened around him, and he groaned. His hands closed on her hips, positioning her for his pistoning cock. They started off slowly, but that didn't last long. No doubt Mannias was intent on making his claim again, filling her with his musk and cum so that no one would dare touch her, washing the memory of any other buck from her mind and body.

They came together fiercely, their sounds rising in the waning night. His climax came a few heartbeats after hers, and Vahlrae smiled at the thought that he'd waited for her...or that her climax had called to his.

His cock nestled inside her and swollen there snug to aid in the conception of his young, Mannias's hands mapped her body.

The pull at her shoulder was so unexpected, she recoiled with a yelp of pain and surprise. Mannias went still, then eased his hand to the spot he'd found...his bite and something more. He gifted her a soothing rumble in response to her whimper of fear.

His cock subsided, and he set Vahlrae off of him, turning around her to examine it better.

* * * *

On the ridge, Dr. Emma Starling bumped up the magnification on the cameras, watching the screens with bated breath, praying the male wouldn't rip out the stitches she'd set.

If he did that, she'd have to tranq them both again and keep the young woman sedated at the lab for the week until the tears healed sufficiently. Then would come the tricky evolution of releasing the young foundling into the wild with her mate again. That wasn't the preferred course of action. As it was, tranqing them to offer her medical aid was interfering with the experiment, but Valerie Norton wasn't a were. Though she would likely have lived after the mating bite, she would have suffered for the group's inattention to her care.

"I still say we shouldn't have done this," Dr. Tim Webber repeated.

She sighed. "We've been through this, Tim. She would have scarred without their advanced healing. She would have had problems moving her arm for the rest of her life. She would have been in constant pain. It would have been inhuman to let her suffer that."

"I don't mean that. You've convinced me that offering her aid was the right thing to do, even if I got bitten in the process."

Emma sighed in relief at the sight of the male bathing the stitches with his tongue. He wasn't attacking them as Valerie had attacked the soft shackles. That meant he'd leave them in place to dissolve.

She reminded herself of Tim's cryptic comment. "What do you think we shouldn't have done?"

"Returned her to them. She's human, Emma. The team leaders a decade and a half ago never should have left her with them."

She'd like to argue that, but she couldn't. The idea of leaving an orphaned preschooler, swept downstream and into the preserve, in the care of the weres who'd found and adopted her had never seemed right to her. Valerie's grandparents had reportedly joined search parties for weeks in the hopes of finding her alive. They'd have rejoiced in having her back. Though the group would have had to tranq the entire were pack of weres to get the child back, it should have been done.

But then they'd start attacking other human foundlings, the team leaders had told her when she'd offered her opinions on the subject.

It might be true; it might not, but by that time, Valerie had been with the weres five years. She had hardly been recognizable as a human child anymore. She growled and whined...and spoke in the half-barking sound that the weres used in human form.

"Emma?"

Valerie nuzzled her face into her mate's shoulder, nipping at him playfully, smiling at his growl.

"She's acclimated now. You saw her in the lab. Do you think she'd ever accept returning to human society? She's more wolf than human."

"Emma..." He sighed.

On the screens, the male started dressing Valerie in his shirt. He took great care not to disturb the stitches, as if he knew instinctively that they were helpful.

"Emma, this isn't right," he pleaded.

Valerie brushed her lips over her mate's. The big male stopped, his gaze lingering on her lips. He licked his own, then sealed their mouths together, laying back and drawing her after him, so her stitches didn't rub the ground.

"It's right enough for her, Tim. Clearly, she loves him."

Mama's Tales

Dedication:

To the stories we're raised on. It's the love of hearing them, of reading them and reading them to our children that make us want to write them.

To Sissy and Dad, for reading to me and making me what I am today in the process.

Note from the author:

Why should fairy tales and nursery rhymes be only for children? I don't think they should be. Like myths, these stories often tell the stories that almost are. I'm pleased for the opportunity to tell the whole story. I hope you enjoy this look behind the pages as much as I do.

Happy reading!

Brenna

A Perfect Record

Georgie Porgy, Puddin' and Pie
Kissed the girls and made them cry.
When the boys came out to play,
Georgie Porgy ran away.

George Beauregard Bradford spied on the group on the porch below. In a moment, the boys would go in and Becca would be alone.

She'd signal him today. He felt sure she would. Becca hadn't motioned to him in five long days, though she knew Georgie was watching every night. If he didn't know better, he'd swear she was punishing him for something, though he had no idea what Becca would want to punish him for.

He held his breath as the boys filed inside: Abe, Billy, Danny, Joel, Lewis, and Nathan. Becca's six older brothers were stricter than her parents had ever been, and they were Georgie's adversaries. They were a rough bunch that few messed with, and most people in town simply called them the Shuster boys.

For a moment, Becca didn't move, and his heart sank. She was going to make him wait another day? Was she heartless?

She stirred, rising from the porch swing and ambling across the yard to the fence. Her dark hair was bound into a tight braid. He wished it was loose and blowing around her face in the wind. He wished he was close enough to see her eyes.

His breathing was harsh in his own ears. *Please. Just give me the signal.* Georgie gripped the tree bark beside his cheek until his fingers ached.

Becca smiled, but her hands remained still.

He cursed under his breath. She knew she was driving him insane. She was doing it on purpose.

Her hand crept up, a languid slide over her bare leg, then the front of her shorts.

He bit back a laugh. She wasn't going to make him wait.

She continued up her abdomen to the hollow between her breasts, teasing him now with what he'd have to wait hours to have, for the body he'd picture vividly until he could touch it.

His cock ached—but it wouldn't have to for long. A wicked smile curved his lips. So, she wanted to tease him? Two could play that game. Maybe she'd forgotten how he'd earned his nickname, but he hadn't.

Georgie charged at her, and she gaped in surprise. He grasped her cheeks and sealed his mouth to hers, taking advantage of her parted lips to make the quick kiss he'd steal count. For one glorious moment, she responded favorably.

Then common sense kicked in, and she pushed him away, her eyes wild. Georgie grinned at her and blew a kiss, turning and sprinting toward the woods as the back door burst open and the boys stumbled out after him.

"Georgie Porgy," Becca shouted, "you'll pay for that!"

He laughed heartily. The thrill of the chase and pure joy fueled his burners. Whatever 'payment' Becca had in mind was worth it. He sobered. Unless she changed her mind about tonight.

"No. She wouldn't do that," he argued miserably. She couldn't possibly make him wait another night—or five.

He'd wanted to be above board. He'd tried to ask permission to date Becca in a respectable fashion. He still wanted to; but Abe, Billy, and Nathan had threatened Georgie's early departure from life if he dared darken their doorway again—all for one stolen kiss when he and Becca were twelve that had earned him his nickname of Georgie Porgy.

Georgie had been miserable when they'd refused. He'd moped around at the old cabin for days—until Becca had sauntered up and informed him that he'd been asking the wrong person for permission. Thus had started their game.

He hadn't slept with her for the first few months, but eventually their touching led to more. Dishonorable or not, he couldn't regret a minute of it—even if the boys caught and killed him for it.

* * * *

"I can't believe that bastard—"

Abe cuffed Nathan in the head, stilling his explosion. "Not in front of a lady," he growled.

Becca rolled her eyes. She'd never been a lady; and until Mama and Daddy died, Abe couldn't have cared less what language he and her other brothers introduced her to, despite Mama's complaints.

Lewis placed a hand on her shoulder, and she shook it off in annoyance.

"Aw, come on, Becca. I just want to make sure you're all right."

"I'm just fine, no thanks to you," she grumbled.

"We did our best—"

She turned on him. "If you'd let me date like a normal woman, men wouldn't feel compelled to steal kisses."

Abe stepped between them. "No respectable man steals kisses. Why can't you date a normal man like Jack or John?"

She swallowed a wave of bile, sneering at the idea. "Only you would suggest that a complete klutz and a narcoleptic are normal."

"Daddy wouldn't have approved of Georgie Porgy, and you know it."

"Why not? George Bradford is one of the most wealthy young men in the county and—"

"And one of the most randy," Danny spat. "Mary said she saw a love bite on his shoulder last week, and Tom Piper and Tommy Lin said he had claw marks on his back a month ago." He scowled. "You really want a man like that?"

She felt her cheeks heat. Giving Georgie that love bite and those scratches had been damned fun, as she recalled. "Yes," she asserted. "I do. And since when do you take the word of a contrary prude and a couple of trouble makers as Gospel?"

Billy grumbled a curse that earned him a scathing look from Abe. "We promised Mama that we'd take care of you."

"By locking me up for the last seven years?" she exploded. "You know, you push a woman too far and you won't like the results."

"Planning to put starch in our shorts again?" Danny asked.

Becca met Joel's eyes. The only one of her brothers who had a clue what she was up to, he offered a strained smile of encouragement. While he'd given up arguing her case directly three years ago, he'd supported what he termed her 'mad scheme', and she owed him for that.

She nodded. "Never you mind, Danny Boy. Just rest assured, you won't like it." She turned on her heel and stormed to her room, locking herself in.

When their parents died, Abe had insisted on giving Becca their room, so she'd have a private bath that she didn't have to share with the boys. That allowed her to take leisurely baths, primp, and dress without alerting them that she had plans. She set about it, determined to finish this maddening game tonight.

She smiled at her reflection in the mirror, then placed her challenge on the dresser, unlocked the hall door silently and slipped out the ground-floor window on the opposite side of the room. There was no sense in making Abe break the door down when Joel did his part.

Becca hurried along the trail to George's cabin, giggling to herself. Georgie didn't know it yet, but he was in for a night he'd never forget.

She smiled at the lights shining through the cabin windows, slowing her step. She still owed him for the stunt that afternoon, but with the surprise she had planned, he'd pay his dues.

Georgie turned as she opened the door, a slow smile spreading his sensuous lips. His green eyes glittered in mischief, and locks of his chestnut hair curled over his forehead. He wore only his jeans, and he was already erect.

She closed the door behind her, clucking her tongue. "Is that for me?" she teased.

"After the show you put on for me?" he countered.

* * * *

Georgie felt it hard to breathe or think, let alone talk. Becca was fantastic. Her deep blue eyes cut through him. Her sleek, black hair was unbound, and the matching skimpy dress she wore was little more than a heavy slip. How she made it here on those CFM heels was a mystery even Sherlock Holmes wasn't man enough to solve.

Becca sauntered across the room to the bed, leaning over as she poured herself a glass of the wine on the table. Her bottom pressed to the black sheath, smooth and unlined.

He groaned. "Are you wearing underwear?" he asked.

She turned to him, sipping the wine, her cheeks a pretty pink. "Why don't you come find out?" she invited.

"Is this my punishment for that kiss?"

"No. That is still to come."

His patience worn thin, Georgie crossed the room, took the wine glass from her hand, gulped it down, and set it on the table. He kissed her, a fierce unrestrained possession that he prayed would convince her not to torture him with waiting this long again.

Even as he did it, Georgie realized how ridiculous that wish was. Knowing how crazy she could make him would likely convince Becca to do it again. She loved to make him crazy.

He ran his hands up the backs of her thighs, cupping the globes of her ass and groaning into her mouth as he encountered the straps above her nude backside. She'd bought a thong.

"Do your brothers know you own this?" he managed, flicking the elastic.

Becca laughed heartily. "*My* brothers? Can you imagine my brothers following me into a lingerie department? What I wear under my jeans is definitely something they don't want to know."

"What if Ms. Swann says something? She is the biggest gossip in the county, you know." And it wouldn't do to have her brothers find out about their love affair that way.

Georgie wanted to marry her. He'd have gone to Abe long ago if Becca hadn't talked him out of it. Still, he intended to do at least that part in a respectable fashion.

She smiled, snuggling her body closer to his. "I didn't buy them at Ms. Swann's store. All she's seen are my cotton dailies and lacy fancy wear."

"She owns the only shop in the county where you could buy something like this." He wondered how far she'd ranged to get these. Of course, it made sense that she'd done it. It would keep her brothers in the dark, but when would she have had the time to arrange it?

As if she read his thoughts, Becca answered them. "I went to London, where no one knows and no one cares."

"London?"

She nodded, offering him a sly smile.

That was a full night's trip in Tinker's company. Georgie couldn't imagine Becca willingly submitting herself to hours with the selfish sprite, and Ms. Bell's price for the trip would have been steep. Not to mention, there was always the chance that Tinker would pull a prank and leave her stranded in that far-flung place for a few weeks.

"Why would you go to London?" Why would she chance it?

Becca pulled at his jeans, opening the buttons one after another. "I just wanted to buy a few things," she answered evasively, wrapping her fingers around him.

"Hmm. Like those shoes?" he asked.

She smiled widely. "You like those?" she replied a little too innocently.

"Oh, yeah." He was a visual man, and she knew it. Becca had devised countless tortures for him based on it.

Georgie grasped the edge of her dress and dragged it up and off, tossing it over the foot of the bed. He scanned her body slowly. "Torture," he whispered.

All she wore beneath the dress was the scrap of blue fabric over her shaved mound and those shoes. He shivered in anticipation, tracing the edges of the thong and trying to regain speech.

"Your favorite color," she purred. "Should I leave them here to remind you? Maybe hung over the headboard?"

The mental picture coupled with the thought of her going home nude beneath the dress was almost his undoing. "What if my father comes up here to hunt?" He raised an eyebrow, hoping for a blush that he knew wasn't forthcoming.

She tugged his jeans down. "Maybe he'll make you marry me," she suggested.

Georgie growled at that. He lived to marry her, but she kept talking him out of it. "Maybe your brothers would if they knew what we're doing." He held out little hope of that, but it sounded good.

She offered a noncommittal sound that spoke her doubts better than a full soliloquy would have. Becca eased his jeans down his hips, reminding him that their time together was limited.

He sighed and stripped his jeans off. "Aren't you ever going to marry me?" he demanded.

"Of course, I am."

"When?"

She walked her fingertips up his abdomen. "Soon."

"*This* is my punishment for the kiss," he grumbled.

"Now why would I punish you for a kiss?" she asked in a coy little voice.

"Hmm. I seem to remember a bowl of porridge drying in my hair," he noted.

"I was twelve, and you didn't have permission. Besides, Abe's punch had to be worse than a little bowl of porridge."

He pulled her to his body. "Nothing was more painful than you rejecting me," he admitted.

"Then you should have asked. Remember, my brothers are refusing you because of that impetuous moment."

"You'd think they'd never made a mistake," he complained.

"Kissing me was a mistake?"

Georgie sputtered for a moment, then picked up the challenge. "Maybe I shouldn't have kissed you senseless that day. It doesn't seem to have worn off."

Before she could form an answer to that, he had lowered her onto the bed and pulled off the little blue thong. He hung it over the headboard with a smile.

Becca reached for the heels, but he guided her hand away. He lifted her feet to the edge of the mattress, spreading her knees up and far out. He took a moment to admire the view, then sank to his knees. Before he was done, Becca really would be senseless. Maybe then she'd agree to marry him.

At the first circle of his tongue over her clit, she closed her blue eyes and arched up for more. Georgie was more than happy to comply; he loved to watch her come.

She threw her head side to side and panted out pleas for him to stop playing around and make love to her. He bit back a laugh at that, anticipating his next move. Her hands fisted in his hair, alternately tugging gently as if to draw him over her and pulling him closer as if to urge him to continue.

"George, please," she all but screamed.

With one last concerted effort, she shattered. Georgie pushed to his feet, thrusting deep inside her, then gritting his teeth to stave off his own release.

Becca screamed in pleasure, wriggling beneath him, her nails raking fresh tracks on his back. He groaned. She was so physically expressive when he pleased her, he found himself planning how best to accomplish it before every meeting.

She calmed slowly, her breath coming in rapid gasps.

Georgie smiled. "Enjoy yourself?" he taunted.

"Ohhh...You...you..."

"Georgie Porgy?" he suggested.

She flushed a deep crimson.

"That's why you love me, isn't it? You love the bad boy who steals what he wants."

Becca smacked his arm, not bothering to deny that she loved him or any of the things she loved about their relationship.

He chuckled, sliding free of her body, pulling her shoes off and tossing them to the center of the floor.

"And just what do you think you're doing?" she demanded. "I'm not through with you yet."

"You're right," he agreed, lifting her to the center of the bed in his arms and pulling a quilt to their hips. He wasn't nearly through with her. Before he was through, she'd beg him to ask Abe to marry her.

A ruckus from outside made his heart stutter. "What is that?" he asked.

"Most probably my brothers," she noted calmly.

Georgie chuckled. "You wouldn't—"

The door crashed open, and his gaze locked on the double barrel of Abe's shotgun swinging toward him. His mind rebelled; even his lungs seemed to freeze in disbelief. *Dear Mother! She did.*

* * * *

Becca fought to keep from laughing at the shock on Georgie's face—or on Abe's. She didn't bother to cover herself, determined to make her meddling brothers squirm as much as possible.

"Why, you—"

"Don't, Abe," Joel ordered, grasping the barrel of the shotgun and swinging it toward an empty stretch of wall.

"Are you nuts?" he thundered.

"Are you? If you shoot, you'll hit Becca."

She raised an eyebrow. "If you miss me and hit George, you'll leave me an unwed mother," she pointed out.

Georgie winced. "Egging him on is a bad idea, Becca. He'll kill me," he grumbled. "You—" He looked at her abruptly, his eyes wide. "You're serious, aren't you?"

Becca smiled. "Of course. It was your idea, you know."

"My...idea?" His voice squeaked.

"As I recall, you said a shotgun wedding would solve all our problems."

He groaned, risking a pained look at Abe. He *had* said that—in joking; he'd simply never expected Becca to latch onto a mad comment like that and run with it. He'd probably thought she was still using the preventatives she'd been using in the beginning...until now.

"You know," Joel mused. "It's really not a bad plan."

"Can't we take it out of his hide first?" Billy grumbled.

Danny scowled at them from around Abe's shoulder. "Maybe a kick in the balls to remind him—"

"Don't even think it," Becca snapped.

"You really want to marry this creep?" Lewis asked.

"Yep. I certainly do."

Nathan snorted and rolled his eyes. He pointed at Georgie with a look that promised death. "If you ever hurt her—"

"I would never," Georgie protested, obviously highly offended that her brothers would think such a thing.

"Who said I agreed to this?" Abe interrupted him.

Becca turned toward her brothers, nestling her back to Georgie's chest. "Who said you had a choice? It's my life. Last time I checked, I was an adult."

"We promised Mama and Daddy—"

"So, marry me off, and your job is done," she reasoned.

"Don't forget the baby," Joel cautioned.

"How could I forget?" Abe thundered, slipping the EPT from his pocket. "Where would you get something like this?"

"London," Georgie guessed.

"You took her to London?" He pulled at Joel's hold on the shotgun.

"Of course not! I'd never take her to someplace so dangerous!"

Becca chuckled. "Tinker took me."

"You trusted that pixie?" Abe growled.

"I wouldn't have to, if you'd stop meddling and let me marry George."

"You're going to keep doing things like this until I give in, aren't you?"

"Would I do that?" She raised an eyebrow in challenge.

Her oldest brother scowled, and the others mirrored it—all except Joel, who was busy trying to keep from laughing.

Abe lowered the barrel of his shotgun. "Yes, you would."

"Well then, since the justice of the peace isn't open, I suggest you come back in the morning when it is."

Joel smiled. "We'll be here with shotguns in hand," he promised. He clapped Abe on the shoulder. "Just imagine marching Georgie Porgy through town at gunpoint," he sighed.

"Now just a damn minute," Georgie began.

Abe laughed harshly. "I do believe I'm going to enjoy this," he decided. "In the morning, then. I do suggest you meet us dressed—unless you *want* to get marched through town as the Mother made you."

"I don't believe this," he breathed.

Her brothers filed out, closing the door behind them.

Georgie muttered a few choice curses.

"You wanted to marry me," she reminded him.

"Yes, but—"

"And you did suggest this alternative."

"Not seriously."

She turned to him, tracing the line of curls down his chest. "You don't want children?"

"You know I do!"

"Then what's the problem?" she asked innocently.

"I wanted to do this in some respectable manner," he complained.

"Oh, why break a perfect record?"

He stuttered over an answer for several long moments. "Being marched through town at gunpoint?"

Becca laid a kiss on his lips. "*That* is your punishment for the stunt this afternoon," she assured him. "I would have convinced my brothers to just let us find our way to the JP on our own if you hadn't given me reason to make you regret doing that to me again."

Georgie smiled a mischievous smile.

"What are you thinking?" she asked suspiciously.

"Only that I have the next fifty years of keeping a perfect record. You may regret being Mrs. Georgie Porgy before long."

She chuckled. "I doubt it."

"Even if I arrange to have us marched through town as the Mother made us?" he hinted.

She traced her fingertips over the scratches she'd left earlier. "I think I might enjoy the attempt."

Sweeter Than Honey

Goldie and Sammy, sittin' in a tree
K-I-S-S-I-N-G.
First comes love. Then comes marriage.
Then comes Sammy with a baby carriage.

"One more branch," Sammy called out, hoisting Goldie up to the tree house. He looked down at the three rampaging bears nervously, but they were still growling and circling the tree trunk.

He hefted himself onto the platform and followed her into the ramshackle clubhouse they'd abandoned more than a decade earlier. It was still sturdy, much to his amazement.

Goldie grumbled a curse, fussing at her torn dress, then abandoning it in annoyance. She met his eyes sheepishly. "I guess I should thank you."

"You're welcome. What did you do to piss them off, anyway?"

Her face, neck, and all he could see of her chest through the torn bodice turned a vivid red. "Well, I... Sort of... It was like this..."

He groaned, sinking to the floor across from her. "Not porridge," he begged.

Goldie was notorious for her sweet tooth. More than once, she'd dipped her finger in the wrong baker's cake or little boy's pie.

She was a stunning beauty, a woman who'd have men flocking around her—if she weren't constantly in trouble. You never knew what Goldie would do or say next. Sammy had had his own fantasies about her in those early pubescent years, even from time to time in recent years. Then she'd show her true colors, and he'd come to his senses and remember why no sane man would get into a relationship with her.

"It was just sitting there, slathered in honey, the door wide open—"

"Who would... Scratch that! Who in her right *mind* steals from bears?"

Goldie stared at him in guilty misery, twisting one of her namesake curls around her fingertip.

Sammy pushed to his feet and peeked over the edge of the platform again.

"They can't climb up," she assured him.

"Oh, really? Last I heard, bears climb trees nicely, thank you." Coming up here was probably a huge mistake, but there was nowhere else to go, and he hadn't been thinking. Maybe spending time with Goldie was having a detrimental effect on him.

"Mama Bear insists on a well-groomed and manicured family. They can't climb trees with clipped claws."

He turned to her with a raised eyebrow. "How could you know that?"

Her blush darkened by several shades, but she didn't answer.

"You've done this before?" he demanded. Was she insane?

"Not—precisely. You see..."

"I don't want to know," he announced. Trouble! Goldie had been trouble when they were kids, and she was double trouble now.

He went to the doorway and peeked down at the bears again.

"I told you they can't come up!" She had the nerve to sound offended at that.

"Neither can we go down while they are there," he countered patiently, calling on the last of what he thought were his endless reserves of calm.

"They won't stay long," she offered brightly.

He sighed in relief. He wouldn't be forced to endure this madness for hours. "Good."

"They should be gone by morning."

Sammy spun around to stare at her. "Morning?" he shouted.

She winced, then nodded, her gray eyes stormy with near tearfall.

"Morning." He raised his hands in frustrated entreaty to the Mother. "Someone should find us before then," he assured himself. "Your parents will miss you at dinn..."

He realized he was shaking his head in time with hers and shook himself mentally.

"My...um... My parents don't seem to notice when I've gone missing," she admitted.

More likely, they revel in the reprieve! "This can't be happening," he complained to the cosmos at large.

"Oh, be a sport! One night of roughing it in a tree house won't kill you. You could look on it as an adventure."

"And have the whole town saying I spent the night with you?" he qualified. Ms. Swann would gleefully spread this story from Goose Neck to Seaside to Never Land.

She furrowed her brow. "Would that be so bad?"

Sammy stared at her in disbelief. Considering the other stories circulating about her on a weekly basis, he would think she wouldn't want to invite more. *I don't want to invite it!*

"I mean, we *will* be sleeping together, right?" she continued.

He panned his gaze over her, barely breathing. Goldie was frustrating, but she possessed an excellent body.

If you're going to pay the time, why not do the crime? his mind argued. What was the harm in it, really? His voice broke on his question. "Are you offering?"

* * * *

Goldie rolled her eyes. How dense was the man? Where else did he expect to sleep? Outside on a limb? "Of course."

He sat down beside her, touching her curls as if in a daze. Then he leaned toward her, his lips brushing hers, then exploring more purposefully.

Her eyes fluttered shut. She had no idea what brought this on, but she wasn't complaining about it. Most men found her irritating; she'd only been kissed by a precious few men in her years, and she hadn't formally dated any. She'd always known Sammy was different, and this difference was one she liked quite a bit.

His mouth left hers and trailed down her throat and shoulder. He pulled at the tear in her bodice, easing it to one side until her nipple was uncovered. Before she could reach to cover it, his mouth closed around it.

Sammy sucked gently at her, and she groaned at the heat and wetness between her legs. His tongue stroked lightly over the hardening tip, and a low pulse of desire overlaid that heat.

She fumbled at the row of pearl buttons down the bodice, popping off two in her haste, determined to see what his attention to the other nipple would feel like. He raised an eyebrow at her fumbling, and she felt her cheeks heat.

"It was already torn," she defended herself. "It's not like anyone is going to know I tore it further."

He smiled the smile that had always made her go weak-kneed and stuttering. "Very true," he conceded, his blue eyes glittering playfully.

Sammy unbuttoned the last three buttons smoothly then peeled the bodice off her shoulders, his eyes not unlike Jack Horner's when his mother was baking. He brushed his thumb over the opposite nipple as if testing how firm it had become. He sucked at it, growling as she arched her back.

Goldie pulled at his shirt, desperate to touch him as he touched her. This clarity was disconcerting. Her thoughts had always been as scattered as ranging bees in the spring. There were no tumbling thoughts now. Her mind was focused as it had never been before.

"Calm," Sammy whispered. "We have all night." A smile curved his lips.

"If you do this all night, I'll be *Jell-O.*" She winced at her frank speech. It never caused her anything but trouble, but she couldn't seem to keep her mouth shut, even when she knew logically that she shouldn't say what was on her mind.

He chuckled, stripping her dress down to her hips. "Then I'll just have to lick you up," he replied. "After all, we'll be so hot, you'll melt."

She bit her lip at that image. With Sammy's hands on her, it wasn't hard to envision herself melting into a puddle. Goldie groaned at the thought of him licking her entire body.

"Oh, yeah," he rasped. "I definitely have to lick you up."

Before she could question that comment, her skirts were tossed into her lap. She furrowed her brow; watching him remove her shoes, stockings, and panties with rising interest.

Sammy grasped her legs and settled her knees over his shoulders. She floundered, landing on her elbows, staring up at him. Then he buried his face between her legs. She cried out in surprise as his tongue tickled at the lips of her sex. His growled comment was muffled in her body. Then his tongue returned, dancing over her body and then inside.

Blinding pleasure blocked the rest of the world. Goldie was only vaguely aware that she was laid back on the floor, making breathless little sounds while her mind was absolutely still. His mouth retreated, leaving her a shivering mass, aching for him. He placed her legs back on the floor.

"Hmmm. And what is this?" he teased.

Goldie forced her eyes open, focusing with some difficulty on the plastic bottle of honey in his hand.

She vaguely noted that he must have removed it from the deep pocket in her skirt.

"I think we need to test this," he continued.

"But if you put that on me..." She felt her cheeks heat. Honey took a long, concerted effort to clean off. She really would melt.

Sammy's hungry look made her mouth go dry. "You're the one with the sweet tooth," he said. "I think it's time for us to take our clothes off."

She nodded numbly, barely achieving the last of her own undressing, rapt on the tan skin and wiry curls appearing from beneath his clothes.

Goldie stared at his cock longest of all, the throbbing intensifying at the sight. She had no doubts that Sammy meant to take this experimentation to the ultimate conclusion, nor did she question that he'd leave her aching like this for him for the rest of her life.

He sat with his back against the wall, opening the honey. "Would you care to do the honors?" he offered.

She shook her head. "I'd end up spilling it all over you," she admitted.

"Well, that would be a shame." His tone indicated that it wouldn't be.

She bit back a sigh of frustration. Why couldn't people say what they meant? She did, not that it did her any good. When no one else around you did, saying what you meant was nearly useless.

"I would just hate to have your mouth all over me."

"You're joking," she guessed. She prayed he was joking. Otherwise, why were they doing this?

As his answer, Sammy drizzled the sticky liquid down his chest and abdomen, and over his cock.

Goldie shivered in anticipation, licking her lips as she dropped to her knees. "Both of my favorites in one place," she breathed.

He cocked an eyebrow in seeming amusement but made no comment about her choice of words.

She leaned over him, licking a drop off his nipple. He sucked in his breath, and his abdomen tightened.

Encouraged, she traced the lines criss-crossing his body, drinking in his panted entreaties to The Mother.

Goldie paused, looking at the final trail of honey in a hunger unrelated to her sweet tooth. Sammy thrust his hips upward as if begging for her, and she smiled. In all her life, there was very little she'd done right. This, it seemed, was her strong suit.

She took the head in her mouth, and he groaned. A hint of flavor mixed with the honey; a wild, heavy, slightly-salty taste. Goldie trailed her tongue along the channel, collecting more of it.

Sammy's hands fisted in her hair. She glanced up at him, then stopped in surprise. His eyes were closed, and his face was a mask of what looked like pain. His eyes flew open, pleading with her. He raised his hips, a fine sweat coating his body and his muscles taut.

Goldie captured him in her mouth again, and a strangled groan escaped his lips. She took him deeper, no longer concerned with the honey coating him. The other flavor was a thousand times more appealing, and she instinctively knew she could make him release more.

He urged her up, sealing her mouth to his and releasing her hair to guide her astride him. His cock pressed to her core, and she settled him inside, forcing down as he thrust up.

A minute pain announced that a bit of her hymen remained, despite riding and a myriad of accidents she felt sure had taken it years earlier. It was quickly forgotten as Sammy propelled her into pleasure by way of deep thrusts inside her.

She grasped at his arms, memorizing the ripples of muscle and moaning at the feeling. Her sheath seemed to constrict until she felt every ridge of his length sliding in and out of her.

The explosion of sensation took her by surprise. For one glorious moment, everything in her mind was ordered and sensible. Of course, the only thing that mattered was Sammy and the way they moved together.

He shouted harshly, a sound she'd identify as triumph. Minutes earlier, she would have sworn under oath that she couldn't feel better. Then he released wave after wave of his heat into her, and she stared into his eyes in the fading light, the entire world seemingly existing from heartbeat to heartbeat and thrust to thrust.

Sammy collapsed, his sweat-soaked body supporting hers as they panted in the aftermath of their passion.

* * * *

A smile struggled to break free. Sammy wound one of her curls around his fingertip, wondering at how enjoyable that had been. It was an experience he was eager to repeat—often.

Goldie shifted off him, offering a shy smile that belied the vixen she'd been only moments earlier. She started collecting up her clothing. He hesitated to tell her it was a waste of time; he wasn't nearly done with her. If she believed he was going to let her walk away without more, she was insane.

He looked to his flaccid member, stilling in disbelief, his heart pounding. Even in the fading daylight, the streaks of blood were unmistakable.

"You were a virgin?" he demanded.

She stopped and stared at him, straightening her panties as she seemed to consider him. "That was important." Her voice made it seem that she hadn't realized it was.

"Of course," he replied in exasperation.

"But..." Her eyes darted about, and her fingers twisted at the stockings laid over her thighs. "I don't understand why," she admitted.

"If you're a virgin, it's unlikely that you're on some form of birth control," he explained patiently. *Mother!*

Did she ever consider that? She steals from bears! Of course, she didn't. Why did I believe there was no harm in this?

"I'm not accustomed to doing this," she protested. "What's your excuse?"

Sammy growled a curse, and she flinched. "When you offered to have sex with me, I assumed you were protected. I can't believe I assumed it, but..."

For a moment, she didn't respond. He wished he could see her face clearly in the gathering darkness, but she was too deep in the shadows.

"I didn't offer to have sex with you." She sounded confused.

"You did so," he snapped. Was she scatterbrained?

"I didn't. I only offered..." She groaned, and he vaguely made out her pressing a hand to her forehead.

"Goldie?" he questioned. Surely, she remembered saying it.

"Sleep! Mother lives! I said we'd sleep— I never said sex. I didn't."

Sammy felt the blood drain from his face. It had been an honest mistake, but still... "You don't offer to *sleep* with a man unless you mean it," he growled. "Don't you know that?"

"I did mean it," she shouted. Goldie started collecting up her clothing again. "I said what I meant," she grumbled.

"What are you doing?" he asked. "You can't leave with the bears down there."

"I haven't heard them. I think they left." She pushed to her feet and strode to the doorway.

Sammy scrambled after her. "You can't take that chance," he protested.

"I can't stay here either."

He grasped her arm. "Why are you doing this?"

She pulled away and stepped toward the edge. The roar from below seemed to shake the floorboards, and Goldie lost her footing. Sammy grasped her arms and dragged her back. Her clothes slipped from her hands, and she lunged after them, shouting a protest as he held her back and they slipped over the edge of the platform.

Goldie crumpled to the floor with a sob. He sighed, easing down beside her, cradling her to his chest. Her entire body convulsed in sobs, and tears splashed onto his chest.

Sammy smoothed her hair, feeling abruptly awkward. Why had he yelled at her in the first place? It *was* an understandable error, and it had been *his* error, not hers. "It's all right," he soothed her.

"No," she choked. "It's not. It's never okay."

He didn't know how to answer that. It had never occurred to him that Goldie's incompetence bothered her. She always seemed unaffected by the chaos she created with her mad antics.

"Now look at me," she complained miserably. "Nearly naked in a tree with a man, trapped by bears and blocks from home. I don't even want to consider what new jokes will come of this one. What do you think they'll say? Three bears chased Goldie up a tree. Isn't she a spaz? Her sweet tooth got her in this mess, screwing out what little brains she has."

He had to admit it wasn't a bad rhyme, though he winced at the fact that it probably wasn't far from the truth of what someone would come up with. "It could be worse," he offered, realizing it was a lame line even as he uttered it.

"How? And don't say I could be dead. I'll probably wish I was before this is over with."

He winced at that.

"Do you have any idea...? No, of course you don't. How could you possibly understand what it's like to never do *anything* right in your entire life?"

"I'm sure you do some things right," he argued. "Actually, I know you do at least one thing very right." His cock rose, seconding the motion with gusto.

"Nothing! I make bad choices. I don't think before I act—or speak. Even when I fall in love with a man, I botch it." She groaned. "See! I shouldn't have said that, either."

"Yes. Yes, you should." If she loved him, she should definitely say it.

"What's the point?" she grumbled. "You don't even like me."

"Maybe you're right. Maybe you *are* always wrong."

She sniffed back more tears. "Gee, thanks."

"You're not thinking again."

"I get the point," she shouted, pulling at his grip.

"No. I don't think you do." He captured her hand and guided it to his aching length, hissing out a breath as she touched him. "I don't make a habit of *sleeping* with women I don't like, Goldie."

She swallowed hard. Sammy sought her mouth blindly, and she responded with fervor. He followed her down to the floor, dragging her panties off and tossing them after the rest of her clothes.

Goldie trembled. "You—really don't hate me, do you?" she whispered uncertainly.

"Whom do you love?" he countered.

"You."

Sammy surged into her, smiling at her choked cry. "Then you won't balk at marrying me."

"Because..." She faltered as he thrust again.

"If you're asking if I love you..." He set a slow, comfortable pace, reliving all the time they'd spent together and his current situation. "Yes. I think it's safe to say I do."

"But I'm..."

He stilled inside her. "Infuriating and klutzy?" Sammy slid to the hilt, groaning with her. "You're also honest, caring..." He started punctuating his words with rolls of his hips. "Unassuming, giving, and hot—in—bed."

"We haven't been in bed together," she replied automatically.

He chuckled. Why had he never noticed how literally she spoke and interpreted before? It was charming, once you realized what she was doing. "You'll be hot there, too," he assured her. "I still have to turn you into that puddle of *Jell-O.*"

Goldie groaned.

"Tomorrow morning, you'll wear my shirt..." He shivered in the memory of tossing her panties over the edge. "*Just* my shirt. We'll go to Ms. Swann's shop and—"

"Ms. Swann's? Are you insane?" she squeaked.

"Not at all. We'll be buying you a wedding dress, underclothes, and new shoes."

"In your shirt?"

"Goldie, think—"

"Think? While you're—"

He kissed her. "Making love to you? Try."

"About..." She arched up to him, her fingertips digging into his hips. "Sammy, I don't—"

"To get home—or to my house..." He trailed off, hoping she'd pick up the hint. Some corner of his mind hoped she'd react to the offer of going to his place instead of home.

She groaned. "I'd have to pass Ms. Swann's. There's no way she'd miss me. She'll be outside knitting at sunup, without fail."

"Now you're thinking," he complimented her.

"I always think better when you... Oh, dear Mother! What am I saying?"

Sammy laughed heartily. "Keep talking."

"You don't mind?"

"I'm starting to appreciate your honesty. It certainly makes it easy on a man to know where he stands." He closed his eyes, trying to stave off his release. "Now. Ms. Swann—"

"I'm doomed," she grumbled.

"No. I am—if you want to look at it that way. I prefer to think of it as being immortalized in rhyme."

"What?" Her voice was thick and breathless. Her hands tightened, and her fingernails bit into his back.

Good. A few scratches will lend credence to the story. "I intend to do a little bragging," he informed her. *The whole town will know before I'm done.*

"About?" she inquired, though it was hard to tell if she really wanted an answer with her hips meeting his smoothly, seemingly completely immersed in the experience.

"How I threw your clothing out of the tree house and made love to you until you agreed to marry me."

She gasped. "You're going to lie like that?"

"No. I did throw the last of your clothing over, and it was my fault that you lost the rest. So... Who's going to know that I didn't throw it all?"

"But—But—"

He kissed her again, groaning as she responded in wild abandon. Sammy broke off the kiss, smiling at her sharply in-drawn breath.

"Don't argue," he ordered.

"But the rest," she reasoned.

"It won't be a lie. We're buying a wedding dress, remember? And the JP opens at nine."

"Ohhh. Oh!"

He groaned as she climaxed around him, following her over in just a few more deep thrusts. The silence was broken only by their ragged breathing.

"Goldie?"

"Yes?" her voice was hesitant.

"I asked you to marry me," he reminded her.

Her chest heaved once then again. Sammy's stomach rebelled. She was crying? He brushed his fingertips over her cheek then stopped when he found no tears.

"You're laughing?" he demanded.

Goldie choked out laughter, her cheek heating under his hand.

"What is so damned funny?"

"If I said I wasn't convinced yet, you'd have to convince me," she managed.

Sammy found himself laughing with her. "I wouldn't want to be called a liar," he agreed. "And, I would hate to have to piss those bears off to get you up here for another night. I don't suggest you make me do that."

"You wouldn't!"

"I never bluff." He did, but he wasn't about to admit it.

She hesitated. "You would really do that?"

"Yes. I will stock the cabinets with honey and—"

Goldie purred. "Forget the honey."

"What? You're turning down sweets?"

"I've found something better," she protested. "How come no one ever tells you how good..." She groaned. "There I go again."

He smiled. "Looks like there are a lot of things I have to teach you. So, are you going to marry me?"

"Well, I certainly don't want to get stuck up here another night. We'd get hungry and..."

"And?"

"Well, I think I have a splinter."

"I'll take it out. Is that a yes?"

"Yes, but I wonder..."

"Wonder what?" he asked honestly.

"With the story you intend to tell, what rhyme do you think people are going to make up?"

"Why don't we beat them to it and make our own?"

"Like what?"

"Goldie and Sammy, sittin' in a tree...K-I-S-S-I-N-G..."

"We're doing more than kissing," she pointed out.

"Yes, we are." He remembered her lack of protection. "You do want kids, right?"

"Yes. I do."

He smiled.

"First comes love," she ventured, obviously still trying to complete their rhyme. "Then comes marriage. Then comes Sammy with a baby carriage?"

"You know what that means, don't you?" he teased.

"Uh... I'm sure you're about to tell me."
"I think I'd rather show you."

When She Was Good

There was a little girl
Who had a little curl
Right in the middle of her forehead.
When she was good,
She was very, very good,
And when she was bad,
She was horrid.

Davey watched Lady Thereasa hungrily, reminding himself not to be caught at it and looking away only when she or one of her family turned his direction. Though the woman was sex personified and definitely the girl in town he'd most like to find adventure with, she was a lady and the heir to the Gosling fortune.

It was a shame that she was such a good girl, but what else would one expect from the jewel of her social-conscious family. For years, she'd been taught nothing but proper etiquette and ladylike manners, and she was an adept student, the best her masters had ever encountered. It was never questioned that she would be the one her aunt named as heir. Of all her sisters, Thereasa was undeniably the finest example of nobility in the land.

And now, he was charged with carrying her to her dowager Great Aunt Goosie's home to take her place as lady of the manor. She was twenty now, the age when such things occurred in Goose Neck.

In preparation for the trip, her father and elder brother had drilled the laws of the faraway realm into Davey, fairly threatening his life if he dared stray from them in the slightest. The laws of Goose Neck were many and rigid, especially the ones dealing with relations between a man and woman. It was no wonder Lady Thereasa had been chosen to lead. None of her sisters could ever hope to live up to the laws that would bind them.

The trip would be arduous, a three-day journey by carriage from Seaside to Goose Neck, but the length of the journey was only half the battle to be fought. They hadn't even left her home, and already the strain of her company wore on Davey, tempted him almost to his endurance. How he would survive the trip was beyond him.

Thereasa leaned into the carriage, her smile warm. "Ready?" she asked.

"As you wish, Lady Thereasa." Davey bowed his head slowly, noting her father's wary attention to every move he made.

She scowled at him then took her place on the seat beside him.

Davey whistled the horses up to a trot and nodded to her parents as they were away. There had been no warnings this morning. Even her father must have realized that none were necessary.

For leagues, they rode in an uncomfortable silence. He glanced at Lady Thereasa, unable to take his eyes off of her for long. She didn't seem to notice, and for that he was grateful. It wouldn't do to have a fine lady like her catch him ogling her.

She sighed and loosened the ties on her cape, letting it fall to the seat at her back. Davey glanced her direction again then stared, his mouth going dry.

Her dress was a form-fitting creation that barely held to the join of her shoulder and arm, shelved her breasts so the ample globes mounded neatly in soft cups, and her back was nude to a man's hand width below the center line of her breasts, announcing her lack of typical underclothes definitively.

"You like my dress," she noted.

Davey snapped his eyes back to the road, grinding his teeth at the weight of his erect member. He nodded, gasping out his answer. "It's—striking, Lady Thereasa."

"Yes. It is, at that."

He ventured a look at her face, studiously avoiding the deep cleavage so close to his arm. She didn't appear angered by his reaction. In fact, her dark eyes glittered under a corkscrew curl that escaped the pins in her hair.

"A step in the right direction," she purred.

Davey shook his head in confusion. "What is?"

"You're looking at my face instead of my feet."

He took a calming breath. If he looked at her feet, a much more arousing sight would capture his attention. "Does your father know you own that dress?" he inquired. The lord was hardly known for his patience with impropriety.

Thereasa stretched her arms over her head. "It was a gift from my Aunt Goosie," she confided.

"Really?" he managed, confining himself to a single peek at her chest.

"She sent me a half dozen of them. Not all like this, but close enough." She lowered her arms, leaning toward him so as to maximize the effect of the dress. "You might as well enjoy yourself."

"Enjoy?" What in the Mother's name was she talking about?

"You want to look," she stated calmly.

He did, but hearing her say it didn't put him any more at ease. "You want me to look?" he asked, searching for solid ground.

Lady Thereasa smiled. "For a start."

Davey flicked his eyes to the pale skin of her chest then away, returning to stare hungrily. Had she just invited him to touch her? No. That wasn't possible. Was it?

Her hand settled on his leg, and he swallowed a groan. "Did you know that I requested you as my escort?" she asked.

"No." He hadn't known it. Davey had assumed her father had chosen him, trusting him not to do what he ached to do.

"What have you heard about my Aunt Goosie?" Thankfully, she changed the subject.

Her palm slipped up his leg a hand length, and he cleared his throat, thinking coherent thoughts and forming speech abruptly tedious.

"That she is very wealthy." Little was publicly known about the dowager. She was a very reclusive person.

"Did you know that I am her chosen heir?" Her fingertips traced circles on his inner thigh, scattering his thoughts.

"Yes. Your father mentioned it." *A few hundred times.* He met her eyes, forcing himself not to lean in for a kiss.

"I thought I should tell you that."

"What—what difference would your fortune make to me?" He was no fortune hunter.

"My fortune isn't the important factor, Davey."

"What is?"

She stroked his erection through his trousers, her eyes wide in what appeared to be wonder. "The rules I live by," she whispered. "I am not in my father's house now."

Davey pulled the horses to a halt, panting back the urge to do something insanely stupid. Her aunt's rules or not, the laws of Goose Neck had something to say in the matter. True, they didn't forbid her to take a lover, but they did forbid her marrying without her aunt's permission. They also frowned upon lovers without that permission.

"You want to," she teased him.

He didn't answer—wasn't capable of answering.

Her hand cupped him, her thumb stroking over the sensitive head. "Do you want me to stop?"

Yes. He couldn't say it. "We shouldn't," he grumbled. *If your father ever found out, I would be beaten within a fingerwidth of my life!*

"You're right. Not here. Bargain with me." Her fingers continued their exploration, and she gasped as his sac tightened.

"Bargain?" He couldn't even think, and she wanted him to bargain?

"Kiss me, and I'll stop—until a more appropriate time."

He looked to her lips, shivering in anticipation.

"A real kiss," she qualified. "Kiss me as you would a maid or washwoman."

Mother, but she had him ready to fall on her as if she were a common streetwalker. Davey nodded, lowering his face to hers and groaning as she met him with parted lips. There was an awkward moment before they found a comfortable rhythm.

He took her mouth in a ravenous haze, dropping the reins and turning to her, tracing the neckline of her dress, her bosom like silk. Thereasa moaned, arching to him and shaking him out of the trance he seemed trapped in.

Davey opened his eyes, guiltily taking in their positions. Lady Thereasa was reclined into the corner of the cushioned seat; he was over her, his cock pressed to her thigh. Her hair was mussed, her lips plumped with passion, and her dress rumpled. He released her breast, grimacing that he'd gone so far.

She arched her back with a lazy smile, nearly sending the tops of her breasts into close contact with his chin. "You see? That wasn't so difficult, was it?"

"No," he admitted. "It wasn't difficult." He could have done much more with very little enticement.

"Well, then...I must live to my end of the bargain. I will not press for more from you until we are at a more suitable location."

He nearly groaned at that. Half of him wanted to take her here and now. The other half prayed they wouldn't reach their first stop until she was too exhausted to continue her seduction.

Davey sat back as she straightened, grasping for the reins with numb fingers. She put the cape back on, and he winced at the sense of loss that plagued him.

He should not want what he did. Her father trusted him to deliver her unmolested.

He whistled the horses up to a trot again, then slowed them, determined to reach Pumpkin Corners as late as possible.

"It won't matter," she informed him, chuckling openly at some secret joke.

His stomach crawled in apprehension. "What won't?"

"We'll be stopping at Piper's Glen for the night."

Davey stared at her. "What? Why?" It would only take four hours to reach Piper's Glen. "We can make Pumpkin Corners easily."

She smiled. "And we will...tomorrow. Aunt Goosie made the arrangements."

* * * *

Terri smiled at Davey across the table, easing her foot out of the low slippers Aunt Goosie had provided. He was trying to avoid her eyes, but he wouldn't be able to avoid this.

He stiffened as she trailed her stockinged foot up his inner thigh, rattling his bowl of soup. His blue eyes were hot, but she couldn't decide if they were hot in passion or anger. His face flushed as she traced his rock-hard member, and her core heated in the knowledge that he enjoyed her touch.

"Is there a problem, sir?" the matron asked brightly.

Terri smiled, raising an eyebrow at his hesitation.

"No," he grumbled. "All is well."

"Very well. Call if you need anything." She ambled away, speaking to other patrons.

"An appropriate time," he whispered in a voice edged in the promise of violence.

"The tablecloth hides us," she reasoned.

Despite his reservations, he thickened at that. He pushed a hand through his honey-colored hair, creating more spikes than he smoothed with the motion.

"I could make your meal very enjoyable," she offered, stroking him. Terri wondered if she could make him climax. She wondered what he would look like if he did.

"Not here," he pleaded.

"A more appropriate place?" she suggested. "Bargain with me."

"No. No more bargains."

She pulled at the ties on her bodice, loosening them and baring more of her cleavage. His eyes went wide at the unspoken threat; he shook his head.

"Bargain with me," she repeated in a voice so low he would practically have to read the movements of her lips.

Davey closed his eyes, though his member strained against her toes. "What bargain?" he managed in a rough voice.

"I will come to you tonight, and we will touch. Just touch, nothing more. You do want to touch my breasts. Do you not?"

He looked to the cleavage this style of dress exposed, then away. "Yes," he admitted. "You know I do."

"Then you agree?" If Davey agreed, he wouldn't renege.

"Yes. I agree." He met her eyes, seemingly tortured by his hunger.

Terri pulled her foot back, sliding her slipper on. "Until tonight, then."

She forced down food, though she hardly felt like eating. Her stomach roiled in excitement. If she succeeded in her quest, she'd have everything she'd ever wanted: a home away from her father's endless rules, her fortune...and Davey.

* * * *

Davey paced his room, his heart pounding. He'd agreed to touch her? He ached to touch her, but this bargain was madness. It might mean madness!

He pulled at his tunic as if to remove it, then thought better of it. The more clothes he wore, the better. That way, he was less likely to end up screwing her.

He looked to the door miserably, wondering what he'd do if someone saw her enter his rooms and told her father the tale. Whether Lady Thereasa was her Aunt's heir or not, the lord would make Davey pay for this.

A sound behind him made him jump and whirl about in surprise. He gaped at the open door and the room beyond. The rooms connected, and he never realized it. He'd assumed it was the door to a closet, and since they'd only be here for the night, he'd never opened it. If he had, what delights would he have seen?

Davey looked at Thereasa, his mouth watering. She wore a knee-length gown of translucent peach-colored material with matching panties beneath. Her nipples were clearly visible, as was the fact that her feminine curls had been shorn off.

Nude, yet not. His body responded to it, demanding what he staunchly argued he could not indulge in.

Thereasa glided toward him, shamelessly offering herself. She didn't speak. She took his hand and led him further into the room. He went without question, not daring to examine his actions for fear that he'd realize he'd lost control.

She laid back on the bed, pulling gently at his hand to urge him down beside her.

Davey sank to the soft surface, rapt on the dark circles that capped her breasts. He touched them, watching them come to points as if he'd never seen a woman's bosom before. He licked at the tips, closing his eyes to her moan of pleasure. It was madness, and he was lost. He sucked at her, needing more.

Her hand pressed to his aching length, and he went still. Madness or not, he couldn't go that far.

"Not yet," she whispered in what sounded like a promise. "Kiss me. Please, Davey."

He straightened, pressing his lips to hers, then parting them, tasting her mouth slowly, then more urgently as she started to explore his own.

Her hands were everywhere over his clothes, then beneath his tunic. She enflamed him and he joined in the dance, his fingers tracing the damp expanse of her inner thighs to the wet fire at her apex.

Thereasa arched against him, begging him to touch her in a gasping voice.

Davey took stock of their situation, forcing his mind to function when it wanted to stay submerged in the pool of his arousal. If he didn't stop now, he wouldn't be able to. "No more," he managed, his voice strained. "We've touched." *More than enough. Not nearly enough!* "You should go."

For a moment, she seemed hurt by his proclamation. Then Thereasa smiled. "You kept your word," she agreed. "Until tomorrow, then." She straightened the gown that was pooled around her hips and pushed to her feet, heading to the door to her room, her head high and her back stiff.

He swallowed a groan at the scent of arousal on his sheets. "Lady Thereasa?" he called out.

"Yes?" she inquired sweetly.

"There will be no more bargains between us."

She turned back to him, raising an eyebrow, looking much as her father did when he was about to offer correction. "Indeed," she offered cryptically. Then she disappeared through the door.

* * * *

Davey nodded curtly as Lady Thereasa took her seat beside him in the carriage. He ground his teeth at the errant thought that she certainly hadn't acted the noble lady the night before. She'd acted more the maid or washwoman she'd wanted him to pretend she was in the carriage, despite her fine sleeping gown, a gown designed to make certain no man lying next to her could sleep—as he hadn't slept more than two hours of the preceding night, lying instead in aching discomfort and sorely tempted to bring her back to his bed.

He tried not to look at her, then gave up and examined her from head to toe.

I'm just making certain she shows no signs of use. He called himself a liar before the thought was fully formed.

She wore a double-skirted dress with a cape about her shoulders. He bit back another groan at what surely lay beneath the cape, what she would undoubtedly reveal to him when they were out of the village.

Davey returned to his assessment. Thereasa's skin fairly glowed, and her lips were lush and dark, but her hair... Ringlets of deep coal-colored hair hugged her cheeks and cascaded over her shoulders and down her back.

The sassy curl over her forehead drew his eyes. He wondered if she styled it there or it fell there naturally. Her hair had always been tightly restrained at home, so he'd never seen the enchanting curl before. *Much as she'd been restrained, and I'd never seen the wanton in her.* He pushed that thought away, well aware that he'd left propriety behind.

"Comfortable?" he asked.

"Very, thank you. Shall we be on our way?"

"Of course." He whistled the horses to a trot and watched the village fall away.

Thereasa made no move toward her cape; her hands rested primly in her lap. Davey found himself glancing at her more and more often, anticipating seeing what she'd hidden from him, longing for it.

Damn it! Why can't I find relief in this reprieve?

"Is there a problem?" Thereasa asked in what he'd lay high odds was mock innocence.

"Not at all," he lied.

"Then you aren't waiting for me to continue my seduction?"

He cleared his throat, feeling his cheeks heat. "No. Of course not." His voice cracked, and he winced.

She smiled. "Well, you aren't a good liar," she noted. "I'm glad of it. A woman always prefers a man who can't lie to her."

Davey ground his teeth. There was no safe answer to that. If he admitted he was lying, it meant he wanted her to seduce him. *Dear Mother!* If he tried to insist he wasn't... She was correct. He'd never been a good liar.

Which meant he wanted to be seduced. He glanced at her and away again. Of course, he wanted her. He'd always wanted her.

"Well, since you've waited so patiently—"

"No!" He grimaced at how desperate he sounded. "I mean..."

"I know what you mean. You could bargain—"

"No!" That was out of the question. He lost ground every time he bargained with her.

Her tinkling laughter warmed places that needed cooled. She untied the cape and dropped it to the seat.

Davey shook his head, cursing under his breath as he looked at her, needing to look at her. He pulled the horses to a halt, gasping for breath, searching for signs of other travelers frantically.

"Is there a problem, Davey?" she purred.

"Problem?" he shouted. "You're..." He motioned at her dress hopelessly.

Half a dress! At least, the dress the day before had covered the essentials. This one had panels of the translucent material in place of a proper bodice. No one passing could miss seeing her perfect breasts.

She stroked her fingertips over one nipple, making it harden—and him with it. "I quite like it," she announced.

Davey tried to pull her cape around her shoulders, but she shrugged it off with a look of warning.

"Please, Thereasa," he begged, ignoring the nagging voice chiding him for not addressing her by her title.

"Terri," she said calmly.

"What?"

"My name. Aunt Goosie calls me Terri. I rather like that, too."

The sound of a horse made his heart stutter. "Please, Terri. Cover yourself," he whispered, praying the rider was further away than it sounded.

"Bargain with me."

"I can't!" But, it was close, a horse-drawn buggy or carriage.

She crossed her arms under her breasts, shelving them and making her nipples more prominent.

"I won't take your barrier," he blurted out. Anything else was worth her covering herself before the approaching traveler could see her this way.

Terri seemed uncertain. She nodded, sweeping her hair forward, covering her chest effectively.

Davey breathed a sigh of relief as another carriage rounded the corner toward them. The gentleman inside tipped his hat to them. Terri waved with a bright smile, and the carriage continued on, disappearing from view.

He squeezed his eyes shut. What had he done? He hadn't even set terms to their agreement. The Mother only knew what she'd ask of him, and he was honor bound to bend to anything but taking her barrier. His cock throbbed at the idea of going to his knees before her, licking his way up her thighs...

"Don't worry, Davey," she assured him. "You'll enjoy yourself."

He nodded. That was the problem. He'd enjoy it far too much for his own good.

* * * *

Terri smiled, noting Davey's stiff posture. "This isn't a punishment," she chided him.

He managed a weak smile, though he still looked as if he faced the Reaper's blade.

She ambled to him, reaching for his trousers.

"No." Davey moved away, shaking his head.

"It's not what you think," she soothed him. "If you refuse to remove your clothing, I suppose I'll have to remove mine."

His eyes widened and he pulled at his clothes frantically, peeling off layer after layer until he stood naked before her.

Mother! She wanted him, and he obviously wanted her. Terri stroked a finger along his length, her heart hammering as it bobbed its appreciation of her touch.

Davey stiffened. "I won't—"

She kissed him. "I won't ask." *Yet.* "But, I will touch."

He nipped at her lips, his breathing deep but erratic. "Yes. Touch."

"Come to the bed," she whispered. Whether his legs would hold him through what she planned or not, her own would surely fail her.

He didn't question her, didn't argue. Davey took her hand and led her to the bed as she had him the night before. He flopped down, pulling her over him and seeking her mouth. She pulled back slightly, licking her lips, her whole body tingling.

"You want," he managed in a strangled voice.

She collected up the folds of her sheer sleeping gown, wrapping them around his erect length. He stilled, meeting her eyes as she started working the blue silk that nearly matched his darkened eyes up and down him with her fist.

Davey turned, leaning half-over her, his mouth closing on hers, a slow mating of lips and tongue that became more heated as he neared release. Gasps and groans passed between them. His hands traced her back then squeezed her ass.

"Don't stop," he pleaded, his eyes closed.

"Come," she begged, watching his expression avidly.

He dropped to his back, panted, licked his lip, groaned. Sweat beaded on his forehead. She could almost taste how close he was.

Then it happened. His length pulsed between her fingers. His hands tightened on her, and a strangled cry escaped his lips. Rivulets of milky semen spurted from him, and his entire body tensed.

"Oh, yes," he whispered, his muscles relaxing and the pulsing slowing.

Terri kissed his chest.

He groaned deeply, jerking again in her hand. "Please. No more." His eyes remained closed, and his breathing took up a deep, measured cadence.

She eased away from him, brushing a kiss over his lips. "Until tomorrow," she promised.

"I cannot take your barrier," he grumbled. "You cannot ask it of me."

Terri winced, retreating to her room and the bath she'd ordered before she went to Davey. She soaked in the warm water, wishing she could take heart in her successes so far.

She couldn't. Not while he so doggedly refused to take that final step.

I cannot take your barrier.

She gasped. Of course! It wasn't hopeless after all.

* * * *

Davey opened his eyes, running a hand over his morning stubble. Something was wrong, but he couldn't put a name to it—until he moved to get up.

Nude! "Oh, Mother! It wasn't a dream." How could he let it go so far?

He pushed from the bed, wincing at the sticky proof of his misdeeds. *How could I? Worse, how far would she 'bargain' to take it tonight?* He moaned.

It couldn't be allowed. There had to be limits, a line they couldn't cross. *Her barrier.* It was a physical line, one that had so far been easy to keep in mind. He could play at love with her, but he could not consummate with her.

Not unless we married.

He stood at the washstand, the cloth in one hand. Would her aunt permit that? If she wouldn't, he couldn't live with just a taste of Terri, and he refused to be her kept man. If he couldn't have her permanently and openly...

There was no way to know if her aunt would permit her to marry a servant until they reached Goose Neck. Terri would have to go to Lady Goosie virginal. It was the only way.

Yes. That was it. He would have to bargain with her again. He'd promise her any pleasure—any play, if she'd agree not to cross that line with him. Now, he just had to figure out a way to convince himself to stop in the heat of the moment.

Davey considered that as he washed and dressed. Terri had kept her word so far. If he made the bargain, she'd keep her word. He knew she would.

* * * *

Terri looked up from the remnants of her plate of pancakes and eggs as Davey came to the table. To her surprise, he met her eyes directly. There was no hesitation, no evasive tactics or embarrassment.

He leaned across to her. "Are you finished?" he asked.

"I am. You don't want to eat?"

His hungry look made her full stomach flutter uncomfortably. She was abruptly uncertain. This was wrong. She was supposed to seduce Davey. He wasn't supposed to be in charge.

"If you've finished, we'll be on our way," he informed her.

She forced a superior look to her face. One thing her father taught her well was the poker face he used in negotiations. "Of course. The sooner we leave, the sooner we'll reach Banbury Cross."

Davey smiled and pushed back to his feet. "The carriage is ready," he reported. "At your leisure." He turned and left the inn.

Terri smoothed her dress and stood, striding to the door, feigning much more confidence than she felt. She took her place in the carriage, watching the leagues pass in silence.

Something had changed. She'd lost control of this situation somehow, and she had to get it back. But, how did she go about that?

"Aren't you going to bargain with me?" he asked suddenly.

"You said you wouldn't bargain," she noted uneasily.

"Then I did. Surely, you remember our bargain for last night."

The memory of his face as he climaxed made her breathing hitch. "I do." What was his game? Why did he want to bargain with her?

"Then bargain with me."

Terri affected a coy smile. "No. I don't think I will."

He stared at her, his eyes narrowed. "Why not?"

"It doesn't please me to," she informed him. "From time to time, a woman changes her mind."

Davey pulled the horses to a stop and turned to her, bringing his mouth down on hers. His kiss was hot and hard, and his hands traveled beneath her cape to cup the breasts shelved with no covering in the half-bodice. He pulled away, panting an entreaty to the Mother, stroking the nipple slowly.

"You want more of this?" he inquired.

"You know I do."

He smiled, turning from her and taking up the reins. "Then you'll damned well bargain with me for it."

Terri gasped.

"What is it?" he taunted. "The bad girl has never heard coarse language before?" He whistled a signal to the horses, and they set out promptly.

She felt her cheeks heat. She hadn't; not even from her father and brother, and she knew *they* used such language often. "Not at all," she lied. "I was only surprised that you used it. You seem so concerned with my *other* purities."

It was his turn to blush. "Will you at least hear my bargain?" he asked.

"I will consider it," she replied carefully. That promised nothing.

"I will not take your barrier," he began.

Terri bit the inside of her cheek to keep from smiling. She raised an eyebrow as if she intended to fight that.

"I will not," he insisted. "In return..." He ranged his eyes over her hungrily, stopping them on the covered bodice of her gown. "I will show you every other pleasure. We will touch, taste...I will teach you."

"You will do anything *but* take my barrier?" she repeated. "Any other pleasure either of us desires, you will agree to? I have your vow?"

"You do, but I will have your vow that you will use no trickery or coercion to make me take the barrier."

"You have it," she promised.

He smiled, scooping the edge of the cape back long enough to latch his mouth around her nipple, sucking hard as if in seal of their bargain. Just as she moved to wind her fingers in his thick hair, he pulled back, smoothing the cape over her sensitive flesh and looking back to the road. He whistled a new tone, speeding the horses.

Terri grasped the edge of the seat, looking at the passing scenery wildly. "What are you doing?" she shrieked.

Davey chuckled. "Reaching Banbury Cross as quickly as I can."

"Why?"

"Do you have that sheer gown in green, Terri?"

"What? Why? Davey!" She tensed as he barreled around a tight turn like a young, racing rake.

"Do you?" he insisted.

"Yes! Why? Davey, please slow down," she begged. Many a rake had died or been maimed in this foolishness.

"Bargain with me."

"What? Are you insane?" Had she driven him too far?

"Convince me to slow. Convince me to—wait." A smile curved his lips.

"Anything that doesn't violate our previous bargain." She wouldn't do that.

Davey dragged back on the reins, slowing the carriage to a rocking gait. He grasped her head, laying a kiss on her lips, then smiled smugly.

"You will wear the green gown for me, and I..." He trailed his fingertips over her mound through her skirt. "I will taste you to my heart's content. I am not the only one who can be brought to climax."

Terri fought for a decent breath. "Until tonight, then."

"No, Terri. Until we reach our destination. We will claim fatigue and have our meals sent to our rooms." He pushed her cape back, his eyes feasting on her breasts and his tongue wetting his lips slowly. "Or I could take you here," he offered.

She shook her head, numb in disbelief. "The inn will be fine."

He pulled the cape shut again, turning from her. "Quickly," he managed.

* * * *

Terri startled at the knock on the door, reminding herself that this was what she wanted. She squared her shoulders, strode to the door and opened it. She trailed her eyes down his body, memorizing every fingerwidth of his naked flesh, considering his erect length. The man was more than prepared for her. Her body responded as if he was already touching her.

"Your bed or mine?" he quipped.

"Yours." Her voice was rough. Terri cleared her throat and repeated herself.

Davey took her hand and kissed it gently. "Don't worry, Terri. I'm simply showing you how good it can feel to be a bad girl."

She brushed the curls off of her forehead, looking at the one stubborn holdout in exasperation. How could a woman seduce a man when she looked like a little girl?

He turned her into his arms, pinching her already tightened nipples lightly, as if proving her arousal to her. "You do want to be a bad girl for me, don't you?"

"Yes." *More than anything.*

"Then lay on the bed."

She eased down, careful not to trap too much of her gown beneath her, watching every breath he took avidly.

Davey clicked his tongue at her with a shake of his head. "I said you were to wear the gown, not the panties. Remove them."

Terri felt her skin flush all over her body. Standing before him in this outfit hadn't made her self-conscious. Stripping herself nude for him as she'd threatened wouldn't have. But now, he was directing her, and as stimulating as she found it, it made her awareness of her near nudity more acute.

She eased the gown up slowly, smiling as his gaze locked onto the movement and his cock surged upward in readiness. The panties slid down under that hot stare, warm even against her heated body.

His breathing was harsh and his voice gravelly. "You shaved for this?" he asked.

"My aunt... She arranged a treatment of wax," she admitted. And what an adventure that had been! Thankfully, her aunt had hinted to her father that a young lady about to become lady of a manor should have certain privacies, including rooms that men were not welcome to enter.

Aunt Goosie had been most helpful in planning this seduction. She'd visited seasonally for the last year on the pretense of schooling her heir in the expectations to be placed upon her at Goose Neck. She'd brought books about the act of love, discussed schedules for their journey, imparted memories and information that Terri might find useful, taken measurements for the dresses and gowns she used in her quest...any number of things that were invaluable in this venture.

He nodded as she slipped off the panties and laid her legs down again, spreading them for him. Terri hesitated then presented the panties to him.

Davey took them with a smile. "I believe I'll keep these," he murmured.

Her head spun at the idea of him carrying her panties in his pocket while they traveled. "Perhaps I should wear none beneath my dress tomorrow," she offered.

He sank to the bed between her ankles, tossing the panties to the bedside table. "If you do that, you will learn how stealthily I can make you climax while we drive."

"Then I will."

Terri swallowed hard as he lowered his body and laid a kiss over her clit.

"You intrigue me," he breathed, kissing it again.

"How so?" she managed.

"You are so intent on this course." His tongue stroked a slow circle around the nub, then over it, and she moaned. "And your aunt obviously supports it. That is more surprising."

"Aunt—" She gasped as he traced her seam with the tip of his tongue. "Goosie is unconventional," she reminded him.

And she wanted her heir to have her heart's desire. She insisted on it. Before Terri could claim her estate, she had to marry for love, and Davey was the only man she'd ever wanted to marry.

He drew her knees over his shoulders, his hot breath making her shiver in anticipation. "Why?"

Terri tipped her hips, begging silently for him to continue.

"Later," he growled. "We will discuss this later."

Her body exploded in pleasure as he traced every corner of her most intimate center. He licked, sucked, stroked and nibbled, murmuring endearments into her body as he took her higher.

Her breath caught as he sucked one of her outer lips into his mouth. His tongue slid just inside, and she cried out harshly. Her body pulsed in heat, and waves of delight coursed through her veins and over her nerves.

Then Davey was over her, his mouth parting hers, his cock pressed hard to her mound while his tongue delved inside. She wrapped her legs around his hips and her hands around his head, rubbing against him in invitation, offering herself fully.

She needed him. Even in climax, her body ached for him to fill it. It would never be enough until he did.

He laid a gentle kiss on her lips and eased her hands down. His eyes were half-mad in what she assumed was need, but he smiled. "You have to return to your room now," he stated calmly.

"But—"

"No arguments. In an hour, I'll call for you again— once our bodies have cooled. I'll taste the rest of you, and then..."

"Then?" she asked.

Davey ran a fingertip along her lower lip, looking as if he wished to devour her. "Any pleasure either of us wishes... Tell me you're willing to use your sweet mouth as you did your hand last night," he requested.

"Oh, yes." Her aunt told her that a man thus motivated would do nearly anything for his lady.

* * * *

Aunt Goosie was wrong. Either her lover had been a most biddable man or Davey possessed an iron will. He'd brought her to bliss a second time, then came in her mouth, his seed a potent elixir that made her want him all the more—and still he sent her away, aching and needing. They never had resumed their discussion.

She'd worn no panties that morning as she'd promised, and he'd tortured her nearly the whole way from Banbury Cross to the Dove and Wren Inn at Plum Pasture. His hands had been glorious, stroking her core with her skirts folded neatly in her lap, uncovered to the sun and wind save when another carriage neared and she'd cover up with a lap quilt.

He knew how to please a woman and how to leave one wanting. In the long hours—*the beast tarried horribly!*—until they reached their stop, he'd only allowed her release once, capturing her scream in a kiss and smiling his victory. He'd stilled every other time she'd neared climax, his hand laid on her thigh, fending off her attempts to please herself until her body unwound.

Now the knock came again. She rushed to it, determined to convince him to consummate with her tonight. She'd go insane if they didn't. Worse, they were running out of time. Even with their slowed pace, they had only their stops at Reigate and Dawson of Dover Inn left before they reached her aunt's home. After that, things became much more complex, her aunt needing to find reasons for him to stay on for a few days, explaining his presence in the main house...

She couldn't trick him into the deed. Not only had she promised not to use subterfuge, but what sort of relationship would they have if she resorted to that?

No. She had to offer herself and allow him to follow through on his needs.

Terri pulled the door wide, throwing herself into Davey's arms and enticing him into a passionate kiss. They backed into his room, heading for the bed in a haze of touching. He lay down and reached to pull her over him. She hesitated, dragging off the red gown and dropping it to the floor.

Davey stared at her, his eyes wide, nodding stiffly. She sank to the bed over him, pressing her hips to his. He hissed out a breath, his muscles going taut beneath her.

She pressed her lips to his chest. He loved that, and she loved to hear him moan. He didn't disappoint her.

In moments, they'd resumed their frantic pace. Hands and mouths explored, mated, moved on to other pursuits, then returned again. Bodies slid against each other. Whispers teased lips and skin. Limbs and fingers entwined, and bodies turned and arched against each other.

Finally, Terri made her move. She stroked him, guiding him to her body, capturing his length between her thighs and moving against it, spreading her moisture over him and using the lubricant to its best effect.

"Mother alive," he breathed. "It's so good."

"Please, Davey." She'd promise anything, if he'd agree.

He pushed away, dragging a hand through his already-mussed honey hair, shaking his head adamantly though his cock pulsed in excitement. "We can't. Return to your room. I'll... In an hour."

"As you wish." She managed a smile that felt strained and pushed from the bed, sauntering to her room without donning the translucent gown, giving him a full view of her backside. Terri looked back at the doorway, smiling at his pained expression. "I won't ask you to take my barrier again," she vowed.

Davey let out his breath in a rush of air. "Thank you."

She closed the door behind her, looking at the vibrating dildo in misery. How many times had she come to this moment and backed away? At least after each time he'd proclaimed the hour wait. How many hours had she stared at the damnable toys her aunt had arranged and inwardly shuddered at what she was considering? At least half the night.

"Too many," she decided. Davey was what she wanted. He wanted her, as well. It screamed in every touch and every kiss. If this was the only hurdle between them, she would do what he wouldn't.

Terri stretched out on the bed, considering how best to accomplish the task. The books said it was less painful when a woman was highly aroused. That should be the first step.

In her already sensitized state, that wasn't difficult. Terri took the dildo in her hand, switching it onto the lowest setting and rubbing it along the cleft where Davey had been minutes earlier. She closed her eyes, imagining his body next to hers, his hand following the paths and doing the things her free hand did.

She could almost imagine his voice, urging her on, telling her how he'd make her come. Then she was there, awash in bliss yet aching for him. That time, there was no resistance when she eased the head into her—until the searing pain registered.

Terri pulled the toy free with a yelp of pain, pressing her thighs together and curling to her side, her eyes shut tight. The book lied! Arousal did nothing to relieve the pain; or if it did, she would wish taking a barrier without benefit of it on no woman.

She opened her eyes and stared at the bloodied toy in exhaustion, switching the vibrator off. She'd done it. She just prayed it would work.

* * * *

Davey groaned at the soft sounds coming from Terri's room. She was trying to drive him stark raving mad, and she was doing an excellent job of it. She was pleasuring herself, a good show of it by the sounds he could make out through the door.

This hour was supposed to allow me to cool the fire for her, but her antics are making that impossible. "It would serve her right if I made her wait an extra hour," he grumbled.

But he wouldn't do that. Even if he steeled himself to the wait, chances were good that Terri would do this to him again, and a two-hour erection wasn't his idea of a good time.

A wild image of him striding into her room and presenting his aching cock for her to suck dry taunted him. He rejected it. If he walked into that room and saw her pleasuring herself, he would be on her in a trice and deep inside her to boot. No. His self-control would only stand so much.

Davey considered stroking himself, letting her hear his climax. He rejected that, too. He wasn't blind to the fact that he wanted *her*. He couldn't imagine beating off when he could have Terri.

I can't have her! Damn it all! Until he knew for certain that her aunt would approve of the match, he couldn't have her. By the laws of...

She yelped, and he jumped in response, his heart pounding. That was pain. It had to be pain.

He vaulted to his feet, hesitating for just a moment. "Terri?" he called out, praying she'd answer.

She didn't. He headed for her room, cursing himself as a fool. In this state of mind, seeing her naked again would be deadly to his tenuous control. Davey opened the door between them without knocking, frustrated and wary of some trick. He stopped, staring at her in shock.

Terri was curled on her side on the bed, a blood-streaked sex toy fisted in her hand.

He darted to her side, pulling the foul thing from her fingers and tossing it toward the fire. He eased her to her back, spreading her legs gently and wincing at the trickle of blood from her sex.

"Dear Mother! What have you done?" he asked, reaching automatically for a washcloth and the pitcher of water. He wished that it was warmed, but even room-temperature water was better than none.

"I took my barrier," she replied in a meek voice, as if he needed her to tell him that.

Well, I did ask, he reminded himself. He wiped away the blood tenderly. "Why did you do this?" he asked, forcing back his anger and confusion studiously. She was in pain, and his fury would only frighten her.

A deep flush tinted her body. "You said you wouldn't. You said anything else—"

"Terri!" He reined in his upset again. "Have you no concept of what you've done?"

"You said—"

"I *said* I wouldn't take your barrier, because I will not compromise you. Unless I am certain your aunt will permit a marriage—"

"Is *that* what your objection is?" she asked in seeming amusement.

"Of course! Mother alive, woman! By the laws of Goose Neck—and by your position as heir, that law does apply—you may not enter into a union—"

"I know."

"Then, why—"

She touched his face, laughing heartily.

"Terri," he barked. "This is not amusing. I will not compromise you, and I will not live as a kept man. Without your aunt's approval—"

She laughed harder. "It is funny," she assured him. "We should have finished the discussion last night."

"I don't understand," he admitted.

"You realized my aunt supported this seduction. Aunt Goosie is unconventional, but she is not in the habit of endorsing empty relationships, Davey."

He fought for a decent breath.

Terri smiled, touching his lips. "I already have her permission to marry you."

"In writing?" he asked urgently.

"In my case." She was positively gleeful about it.

"Why? Why would she approve your marriage to a servant?"

Her smile faltered. "Do you know why Aunt Goosie has no children of her own?" she asked solemnly.

Davey shook his head. "I told you that I know almost nothing about her. No one does."

"She loved a man her father disapproved of, a simple farmer who lived outside Goose Neck. Since he would not grant her permission to marry whom she wished, she refused to wed at all. She saw her love in secret for many years. Sadly, he was lost to an accident before her father died. She never had the chance to marry him, and she loved him dearly.

"So, you see... As her heir, I am not..." She glanced at him, wringing her hands.

"Not?" he prompted her.

"In order to inherit, I must do what Aunt Goosie never did."

"Marry?" he guessed. Was he a means to an end?

She shook her head frantically, her eyes wide. "Marry for love. Only for love."

He started to speak...then hesitated, fighting back a wide grin. "You love me?"

"Why else would I do all the foolish things I've done in the last few days?" She grimaced. "Good Lady! When I threatened to expose my breasts to the passing carriage, I thought I'd die. And—" She motioned to the sex toy in misery. "I would have given anything to have you—"

Davey kissed her, a slow, solemn kiss. "I will."

"But I've already—"

"We shall see." If she pulled back from the pain early and any of her barrier remained, it was his to take. If not, he'd still gift her with the pleasure she'd not felt with that damned toy.

* * * *

Terri wound her hands in his hair as Davey settled over her. He tossed the washcloth away, then kissed her again. As in his room, they touched and kissed, rolled and held to each other.

"Davey," she pleaded. "When—"

"You will know when," he vowed.

His stamina astounded her. Long after she ached for him, he still made no move to enter her.

She gasped, closing her eyes as her body exploded in pleasure. "Please," she begged. "Davey, I'll die if—"

He thrust into her, one slow slide punctuated by a stab of pain. She jumped in response. He stilled, crooning to her. Terri moaned, the pulse beat in her sheath overwhelming the pain and washing it away.

"So full," she whispered.

Davey chuckled. "Not yet. I'll fill you, if you're ready for me."

She opened her eyes. "More?"

"As you wish."

He eased back, then returned, deeper but gently. There was no pain, no discomfort.

"Are you ready for me?" he asked, a crooked smile lighting his eyes.

"Yes."

Davey lifted her knees over his forearms, fitting her tight to his hips. "We shall see." He hesitated, seemingly stunned.

"What is it?"

"You said you love me," he breathed.

"Yes. I did." Her heart ached. What did his shock mean?

"I didn't tell you I love you in return. I won't do this until you know I do. I can't. I—"

She laughed and sobbed at the same time. "I know. Please..."

His smile returned, and he started moving again. Terri screamed in pleasure as the new position allowed him to thrust deeper.

Davey groaned, moving faster, deeper, his hands caressing her thighs. Then she felt it. His seed was hot, drugging. They cried out together.

He cradled her to his chest, pressing kisses to her forehead, stroking the curl over her eyes. "I love this curl," he murmured. "When you pin your hair up to play lady of the manor, you *will* ensure that this curl always escapes—for me."

She chuckled. "Shall we bargain for so odd a request?" she teased.

"There are other positions that will allow me to take you deeper," he offered.

"I believe we have struck a bargain."

"I believe we have."

 Fates Magic

Ondrea O'Ken stared at the invitation, her heart skipping with excitement. She'd been invited to a choosing event.

A magic user wasn't invited until the matchmaking elders saw the need, and most weren't invited until they'd reached their thirtieth years. At twenty-four, Ondrea would be one of the youngest admitted.

Her head spun with plans.

What should she wear? Since Ondrea would be meeting her destined mate, the urge to impress him beat at her. Only her finest would do.

But he was her destined mate. He would love her for herself. Ondrea shouldn't seek to put on airs.

How would she know him? There would be dozens of magic users invited.

Ondrea shook that thought free. The elders would see to that, with their fate magic and choosing tools. She'd lay wagers it would be impossible to latch onto the wrong man at such a function.

At least...she hoped that was true.

* * * *

Kieran Medici staggered from the Fates Room, pressing a hand to the wall to steady himself. He'd heard of the power of the room, but he hadn't believed it.

"You've found her, then?" one of the red elders—one of the most revered and strongest of her kind—asked, her weathered face pulled up in a smile.

"Is the room always right?" he replied. Spirits and spells, but he hoped it was...and he hoped it wasn't.

"Always," she confirmed.

"Then I've always known," he breathed. *Ondrea O'Ken.*

She chuckled, then laughed outright. "A blessing in itself."

Or a curse. He'd been so rude to her.

I was a child. But that didn't excuse him. The spirits only knew if Ondrea would forgive past offenses.

The Fates Room says she will.

But not outright and immediately, he cautioned himself. Knowing one's destiny didn't preclude working for it.

The elder's voice shook him from his internal argument. "The welcoming ceremony is about to begin. You should hurry." She turned to go as her sister elders had no doubt done while he was in the Fates Room.

"Wait," he called out.

She turned and nodded permission to question her.

"Why was I granted this? Why before the event began?"

"Anything worth having is worth fighting for," she answered cryptically.

And winning Ondrea will be an uphill battle. He winced at the term. Who knew, after all the horrid things he'd said to her, that the fighting would fall to himself?

Kieran bowed to the elder. "My thanks."

She walked one direction, at a speed surprising for one of her advanced age. Kieran set off in the other, smoothing his clothing and finger-combing his hair.

He slipped into the back of the ceremony room, joining the ranks of men waiting to be blessed by the elders. Kieran paid little heed to their descriptions of the many tools for finding a match. Instead, he sought out Ondrea in the crowd of women.

She'd developed since he'd seen her last, of course, her waist slimmer over her woman's hips and her breasts fuller and matured. Her light oak-colored hair shimmered in the candlelight, falling in loose curls to her waist, and her dark eyes reflected points of the same luminous flickers.

Ondrea's gaze strayed from the elders to the invited men often, and she fairly vibrated in anticipation.

She's been sanctioned so many times for fidgeting.

Kieran's attention snapped back to the elders as the invited moved forward for the blessings. They filed up, and the elders alternated...first a man then a woman...

His turn came and passed in a blur. If Fate blessed him with Ondrea, it was more than he'd dared hope for.

His gaze locked on Ondrea, Kieran barely noted the rest of the blessings...save one thing. They ended on a man. Beginning on a man and ending on a man meant there was one more male than female present.

That fact set his mind working. Only those invited would be admitted. Surely no one had refused the invitation. The healer in him hoped it wasn't some accident in transit.

Kieran smiled at the truth that such a thing wouldn't be fatal...or even likely serious, just a delay in arrival time. After all, were the woman in question fated to die, the elders would have seen no need to invite her mate.

His mind at ease, he headed for the meeting room to mend past hurts.

* * * *

Ondrea forced her feet to the floor, reminding herself that a lady didn't fidget. Still, her nerves jumped and her mind rioted. She had no clue how to proceed.

She replayed the tools for confirming a mate she could recall, but they required both man and woman touching them at the same time...or at least one partner with the other firmly in mind. True, simple palmistry and crystals would give a picture, but they were wildly inaccurate, and Ondrea wanted an effective tool.

"Ondrea," a deep voice greeted her.

Her smile of greeting dipped somewhat at the sight of him. That simply, her fidgeting fled, and she stiffened. A hundred unkind words paraded through her mind, all from those deceptively-lush lips.

"Kieran." She offered a slight tip of her head, just enough to be considered polite, not enough to invite his company.

As if invited, he raised her hand and pressed his lips to the back. Her heart skittered at the contact. Kieran didn't release her; he held her hand, stroking soothing paths over the lines in her palm.

"I've heard you're a healer," she managed. He knew calming touches from his training. It was nothing more.

His smile made her stomach do a little flip, and the stroking moved to her wrist. He must be a very good healer to affect her so with a touch.

"A small practice with my father and grandfather," he confirmed. "And you?"

Ondrea bristled at the fact that he hadn't cared to follow it. *He's always assumed I'm like my father.* "Life studies," she informed him. "I'm a plant healer."

"There aren't enough. You'll be in high demand." Kieran hesitated only a moment, moving from her left hand to her right. "Perhaps you'd see fit to examine my healing herbs...at the usual healer's fee, of course."

"But I've yet to qualify." Surely he knew that. She'd been two years behind him in school, after all.

Kieran raised her hand and laid another kiss. "You have always been an adept student," he complimented her.

Ondrea fought for clarity. That wasn't what he'd said ten years ago. He'd claimed her difficulty in mastering a defensive spell was due to the fact that finesse was beyond an O'Ken butcher. Even now, it stung.

She pushed away the memory, then forced her gaze from his. "If only I knew where to begin unraveling this problem."

* * * *

Kieran swallowed down his disappointment. She hadn't agreed to the work he'd offered. His compliment had gone awry somehow, and now she was looking to find a man other than himself to spend time with.

She's worth fighting for.

"There are many tools," he began.

"But they require the couple in unison," she dismissed him.

We are. We could use any of them. But she would balk at that, at laying her hand alongside his to test it. "Not all of them." *Perhaps this is why I was given the gift of the Fates Room before the event. Perhaps Ondrea will believe nothing less than that.*

"Crystals and palmistry," she complained. "Hardly worth the magic to fire them."

"There is another, a powerful tool that requires only one mate."

She turned her cool, brown eyes to him. "Which?"

"The Fates Room." His heart skipped at the possibilities. "It is never wrong, you know." But would she believe that, when it was Kieran she saw in the reflections?

Her eyes lit in excitement. "Yes. I've heard that." She looked around frantically. "An elder could direct me."

"I know where the room is." He offered his arm.

Ondrea hesitated, then took it, seemingly stunned. Kieran took a calming breath and guided her toward the corridor they needed.

"Ondrea!"

She jolted, then turned, releasing Kieran's arm to clasp both hands offered by Gabriel Sarke. "Gabriel, how nice to see you."

Jealousy ate at Kieran that quickly. Ondrea's smile was wider for Gabriel, her pleasure at seeing the other man genuine and not faked as it was for Kieran.

They were raised together, he reminded himself. *Their fathers are in business together.*

But the way Gabriel looked at her was anything but brotherly. It had never been, as far back as Kieran could remember.

"How...*telling* that we got the invitation together," Gabriel suggested.

Ondrea blushed.

Gabriel looked around, feigning a sudden awareness that Kieran was there. "Medici, I hear you are busy living up to your name."

Putting together what you tear apart. He dared not say it in front of Ondrea. Instead, he forced a smile to his face. "Trade is brisker than a healer wishes," he admitted.

"It's all coin, healer," he chuckled.

"Were it simple comfort potions, I would agree. I cannot see lives as coin, I'm afraid."

Ondrea stared at Kieran, her expression unreadable.

Gabriel drew her attention back to him. "It's been months. I hope you'll pass some time with me." His eyes shifted to Kieran in challenge. "If you don't mind, Medici?"

Though it galled Kieran, there was only one reply to give to that. "That would be Ondrea's choice, of course."

She looked from one to the other, offering a tip of her head to Kieran before she turned away and accepted Gabriel's arm.

Kieran stared after them, fisting his hand in frustration. He forced himself to calm with one fact. No matter how well they knew each other or how polished Gabriel Sarke was, he couldn't fire the tools with Ondrea, and Kieran could. In the end, Kieran knew who Fate intended for her.

* * * *

Ondrea gasped in the aftermath of Gabriel's kiss. It had been so unexpected, she hardly knew how to respond to it.

Gabriel stroked her cheek. "I hope you don't mind."

She shook her head. Stars, but the kiss had been good.

His smile was wide and heartfelt. "I always knew it would be you."

"You—you have?" How could he? True, she'd had a few daydreams of Gabriel, but not as many as she'd had about others.

"Oh, yes." He turned and ambled toward the gardens.

Ondrea hurried along with him, feeling like the tag-along she'd been when she'd been four and he a schooling six. "But how?"

His laugh was rich, vibrating his broad back. "Love is familiarity, Ondrea. We've known each other since the cradle. We share interests and sensibilities."

Some sensibilities. "But what proof do you have that we're destined for each other?" He seemed so certain, she had to know.

Not that she'd balk at the idea of life with Gabriel. Their differences aside, they'd always gotten on well.

He was a handsome man, and that kiss had been toe-curling at worst.

"We make our own destiny," he decreed.

Ondrea furrowed her brow in confusion. "That's not what we were taught."

"The love arts lobby," he teased. "May I show you?"

She nodded her agreement. Gabriel took her arm and led her further into the castle. He stopped at a brass globe. Ondrea looked at him, questioning silently.

"The Ellix Spinner," he explained.

Ondrea dried her sweating palm on her skirt and placed it on the globe. After a moment, Gabriel's hand joined hers. She held her breath, but there was no response from the tool.

Her heart sank. He'd been wrong.

She knew very well what to expect of the Ellix Spinner. Her own parents had proven matched by it. But there was no golden glow and music for herself and Gabriel. They weren't destined.

He lifted her hand to his arm. "Don't frown, Ondrea."

"But you were—"

"Fate magic doesn't work on my family," he confided. "It hasn't for three generations, at least."

Her head spun lightly. "How did they find their destined mates? If the magic works in neither direction..."

"What happens when all the matches have been made?" he countered.

Ondrea worked at that. "A woman would be unmatched, still searching for her mate."

"A woman for whom the magic does not work. Yet, the elders see a match. Thus, she is invited."

"Then I should be searching out a mate. If they all match without me—"

Gabriel sighed as if she'd disappointed him.

"The Fates Room only requires the magic of one," she continued.

His brow rose, and he nodded. "A fine suggestion. If you see nothing there, will you consider the possibility that we are destined?"

Though the thought of such a dark union chilled her, Ondrea nodded her agreement.

* * * *

Ondrea stepped inside the Fates Room, looking around at the many mirrors in awe. Each was a different size, framed in a unique way. Most were startlingly clear; a few were cloudy or cracked. Magic beat at her from all sides, not a single flow but overlapping fields emanating from each mirror.

"Your parents felt nothing here?" How could someone miss this power?

"Oh, they felt magic," Gabriel confirmed. "But the mirrors remained dark. Still, the elders confirmed they were meant for each other."

Ondrea considered it, biting back a wince at the bleak reality they'd faced. She'd always basked in magic. Finding a mate without the glory of the magic she'd hoped for was unconscionable.

"Close the door, Gabriel."

He crossed his arms over his chest, seemingly confused by the request. "What?"

"If there is no reaction, perhaps—"

"You still believe there will be?"

Ondrea took a calming breath. "We both wield magic. We shouldn't scoff at it. Your line may well not experience fate magic, but mine does...or has until this point. My mother and father tested on the Ellix Spinner."

"But it didn't—"

"For you. The Ellix Spinner requires both mates. The Fates Room requires only one."

He seemed to consider that. "Sensible. Though I still believe there will be no images, you may well see us in the mirrors, when I cannot."

And if I cannot see with him present, I will come back alone. Perhaps Gabriel himself is a damper for fate magic. But he would think such a suggestion less than sensible.

Gabriel reached for the door, and Ondrea closed her eyes. She waited, and nothing happened. She opened her eyes to the dimmed room, but it was still and silent.

His expression clearly announced that Gabriel believed himself vindicated. Ondrea looked at the far wall...and it struck.

The room went dark, save slats of light that raced overhead, front to back. Vertigo assaulted her, and she stumbled, catching herself on a gilded frame inset with roses.

The vision burst into view in the mirror, the colors blinding in the near darkness. Ondrea lay on a lush bed, her legs wrapped around the man's...

"Spirits and spells," she breathed.

He was making love to her, a vigorous pace, viewed from above. The Ondrea in the vision arched her back and opened her mouth to make some sound, pleasure or pain—it wasn't clear—etched on her face.

The living and breathing Ondrea felt her breasts come to hard peaks at the show. She wanted to turn to Gabriel to be sure he couldn't see it, but she dared not look away until she'd confirmed the man's identity.

He had shoulder-length dark hair. It could be Gabriel. It could also be at least a dozen other young men of her acquaintance...or a third or more of the magic users she'd seen blessed an hour earlier. After all, long hair was the current fashion for men.

I must know. Who is he?

The view shifted, until Ondrea stared out from her own eyes...at Kieran Medici. She pushed away on a gasp, turning at last to see if Gabriel showed any sign of awareness.

The next mirror caught her halfway, and the slats speeding past sent her careening into it. Ondrea lay on a different bed, laboring hard, holding tight to Kieran's hand while he cast a spell with the other.

She shook her head in disbelief...and the slats raced again. Ondrea reeled, landing hard against another mirror.

Kieran held a little girl on one arm and wrapped the other around a very-pregnant Ondrea. He laughed, lines crinkling the edges of his blue eyes.

Her breathing harsh in her own ears, she spun from the mirror. The slats of light were dizzying. The mirror she grasped at was a small one...a hat mirror at best.

Kieran was young again, his jaw set in fury. He shouted at Ondrea, and she did the same in return.

Is this what life will be?

Ondrea chastised herself silently. Her parents, in love as they were, destined for each other, still argued. Her mother said that being mated didn't mean an easy road, but one worth taking.

Guiltily, she searched out another scene to balance the last. The moving slats seemed more pronounced, leaving her gasping for breath.

The mirror frame cut into her fingers, sharp shards drawing blood that stained the thorn branch design darker still.

The vision drew her eyes up. Kieran lay on the floor, his blood pooling around him, his shirt plastered to his chest with the same. Ondrea knelt at his side, pressing ineffectually at the wound, her hands and forearms covered in his precious lifeblood, sobbing.

"No," she whispered. "No."

Her eyes took in details. They were young. It wasn't far in their future together. The dress she wore...

Ondrea glanced down at herself. It was the dress she had on now. There was no question that it was.

She returned to the vision, needing every clue she could gather to prevent this.

Could she prevent it? If not, she knew Kieran survived it. She'd seen him older, their children together...

Do I know it? Did the mirrors show possible futures or fated ones only? Ondrea's specialty was far from fate magic. Was paradox theoretical or factual? She couldn't remember.

How does this happen? I must know.

As before, the view shifted, moving around at sickening speed...to Gabriel. He stood over them, one of his magical daggers in hand, a half-mad smile on his face.

Ondrea staggered backward, venting a scream of horror.

Arms circled her, and Ondrea beat at her captor. It was Gabriel, and she'd just seen a side of Gabriel she hadn't known existed. He was crazy, dangerous, a murderer.

"Ondrea," he shouted. "What is it?"

Frantic, she bit at his hand, and Gabriel released her with a howl.

She turned, searching for the door. Everywhere she looked, she could see Kieran: tickling her, holding her, kissing her, touching her...and Gabriel standing over his broken body. The slats of light shifted back and forth in sickening waves.

"What is wrong with you?" he demanded.

And then she saw the door. Gabriel stood between Ondrea and the way out. Worse, if she attempted a translocation spell, he'd have time to stop her.

* * * *

Kieran wandered aimlessly, heartsick. His only hope was that Ondrea would still go to the Fates Room. If she did, she'd know the truth.

But will she accept me? Mates didn't typically turn from each other, but he'd spent years making a bad impression. Perhaps it would prove insurmountable.

His nerves jumping, Kieran headed for the Fates Room. He needed reassurance. He needed to see more of their life together.

At the turn of the corridor, a scream stopped him short. For a moment, Kieran stood frozen in shock. He was a healer, not a fighter.

"Ondrea! What is it?"

That set his feet in motion, storming toward the Fates Room. No matter what she'd seen, he knew *who* she'd seen. Obviously, the shock had been formidable. If there was one thing a healer could do, it was lessen shock and calm the body.

A male shout of pain sent Kieran from a march to a run.

"What is wrong with you?"

He yanked the door open, flooding the room with light and silencing the mirrors.

Ondrea was pressed to the far wall, staring at Gabriel in stark terror. Drops of dark blood gathered on her fingertips and fell to the polished wood floor. More than a few had dotted her fine peach-colored skirt.

Kieran pushed past Gabriel, rushing to her side. He turned her hands up, evaluated the wounds, then looked around for the blades that had made them...something of sharp spikes.

The mirror frame was grotesque, dark wood with darker spikes, stained in what Kieran was certain was human blood. Of all the magic in the room, the magic from that mirror was seething in something unpleasant, most likely fed on the blood sacrifices of generations of magic users. Kieran shuddered to consider what such a mirror would show one.

"What do you think you're doing?" Gabriel demanded.

Kieran turned to him, noting the bite on his hand in mounting concern. There was no question Ondrea had done the deed. But why would she?

"She's injured," Kieran challenged him. "I'm a healer."

Gabriel reached into an inner pocket of his jacket, and Ondrea pulled her hands from Kieran's, stepping between them.

"No." Her voice was low and wavering.

Gabriel raised an eyebrow then pulled out a cloth to press to his bleeding hand. She sighed, relaxing visibly.

"You have nothing to say to me, Ondrea?" Gabriel asked.

She shook her head, trembling hard.

"Are you all right?" Kieran asked, certain that she wasn't but at a loss to name what ailed her...beyond the cuts on her hands.

Ondrea managed a tense nod. "Yes."

Gabriel reached his unmarked hand to her, and she shied from it. Taking it as a threat, Kieran guided her to his back.

"What do you think you're doing?" Gabriel repeated.

"Are you well, Ondrea?" Kieran asked again.

Gabriel tried to round him, and Kieran shoved him away. The older man stumbled into the corridor, and Ondrea vaulted between them again.

"No," she ordered Gabriel. "I won't stand for it."

He glared at her. "You have always known your mind until now, Ondrea."

"I know it still," she countered.

"Then make it known."

She didn't hesitate. Ondrea turned into Kieran's chest, pressing her cheek to his pounding heart. He wrapped his arms around her, certain he had missed something of importance but too stunned to work it through.

Gabriel snorted and turned on his heel, muttering something about bad investments and insensible women.

In the aftermath, they stood motionless. Kieran inhaled Ondrea's scent, nearly reeling. The scent brought visions of a home the likes of which he'd suspected they'd form together since she was a budding teen he couldn't get out of his fevered adolescent mind.

"Will you allow me to heal the cuts?" he asked.

Ondrea nodded, her head tipping back so that their gazes locked. Kieran swallowed hard, the urge to kiss her riding him. A spell to stop the flow of blood and one to ward off infection later, they were in motion. It was best to wash the wound properly before administering the final spell to heal it.

Two turns away, Ondrea stopped short.

"What is it?" Kieran asked.

She raised a quaking hand to a metal sphere. Ondrea looked to him, and Kieran nodded his understanding. He placed his hand next to hers without breaking eye contact.

The sphere came to life, spinning beneath their hands as if oiled. The color lightened to gold, and a glow surrounded it. The whirring became a sweet tone.

Tears gathered in Ondrea's eyes and spilled over. Kieran raised his hand to brush them away, and the sphere slowed.

"Please, don't," she begged.

Confused, Kieran placed his hand over hers, and the sphere came to life again. Ondrea laughed and sobbed nearly in unison.

"It's beautiful," she stated. "It's just as my parents described it."

* * * *

Ondrea entered Kieran's rooms, her heart pounding at what she was doing. She was going to a man's bedroom, unchaperoned and with full knowledge of what might happen within.

Of course, he was her destined mate. Her parents knew there was an even chance she'd return from the castle bound to her mate already...or at least warming each other's beds. It wasn't uncommon.

And she knew Kieran. They were schoolmates from age ten through sixteen.

The door latched behind them, and Kieran led her to a marble sink. His hands were gentle on hers, washing the wounds. His spell warmed her cheek and puffed strands of her hair. The lingering pains disappeared, and her fingers tingled in the wake of his magic.

Kieran raised her hands, raining kisses over the newly-healed skin. "Have you other injuries?" he asked formally.

She nodded, and he led her to a velvet sofa. Ondrea removed her jacket and bared her bruised forearm to him for inspection. The spell was repeated...as was the brush of his lips over the site of her injury. Her breath caught at that.

"Will you kiss every hurt?" she asked.

"Do you mind it?"

Mind it? Was he mad? "I believe other places may have need of your attentions," she offered boldly.

His head came up, and he released her arm. His look of longing made her heart race.

In the next instant, his lips feathered over hers. They retreated, then returned more purposefully.

Ondrea had played at kissing men before, rushed encounters that only her chaperone knew of. This was nothing like it. This time, there was no chaperone. There was no need to stop at a groping hand over her gown...or beneath her skirt.

Their positions shifted, Kieran laying her back on the sofa and following her down. He parted her lips and invited her to dance, his hips pressing to hers, bringing the length of his erection to her through layers of clothing she wished to dispel with a word.

He eased back, breathing hard. "Are there still more places in need of—"

His question clipped off at her move to unbutton her bodice.

"The bed might be best," he rasped.

At her nod, Kieran pushed to his feet and lifted Ondrea after him.

He paused. "If you wish to wait—"

She unbuttoned two more of the moonstone studs. Kieran gazed at her exposed cleavage and nodded. Then he led the way to his assigned bedroom.

The sight of the bed stole her breath. Ondrea knew very well what was fated to happen here. The mirror had been explicit. In a daze, she unbuttoned the bodice and went to work on the skirt.

"Spirits and spells," Kieran choked out.

Ondrea sought him out, her cheeks burning at the sight of him stripped to the waist. She took a step toward him, stroking his exposed skin, mapping his body.

Kieran's hands closed on the open front of her bodice, easing it back and down her arms. His breath warmed her lips, and he pulled her against him, their chests touching through the insubstantial layer of her underclothing. He dragged down her skirt, releasing her outer clothes to the floor. For a moment, he didn't move.

Then he lifted her onto the high mattress, pulling up one foot after the other to ease her low party shoes away. His boots and socks went next, and his weight settled over her again.

Kieran's mouth played at hers while his hand pushed up beneath her knee-length camisole. Inch by inch, her thighs and belly met the heat of his body.

His mouth left hers, and he freed her breasts from the band, sucking one nipple into the moist delight of his mouth. His hand settled over the other, bringing it to an even harder peak.

Ondrea wiggled against him, moaning pleas for more. In answer, he switched sides. She dragged the camisole off, dropped it to the pillows, and buried her hands in his hair.

His groan rumbled against a sensitized nipple, nearly bringing her off the bed. His lips trailed downward, and his fingers hooked in her panties.

Realization that he'd have her bare and more than ready had her already-wet core weeping onto her thighs. She tipped her hips up to aid him in removing the last of her clothing.

"Yes, Kieran." Her voice came out a strained whisper.

As if that urged him on more than her words themselves, her panties were abruptly at her knees and, a heartbeat later, gone. Kieran spread her legs up and out, settling her calves to his shoulders.

He came at her, tasting and taunting her, moving with Ondrea. It was maddening—too much and not enough.

"Be done with it before I demand a taste of my own," she exploded.

Kieran faltered. His head rose and his body followed until he knelt between her thighs. His hands worked at the fasteners on his trousers.

Ondrea licked her lips, and he groaned as if in pain. The trousers and underclothes slid away, revealing the length of his rigid cock.

She glanced up at him, then eased to sitting, her legs spread wide around his. At the first stroke of her tongue over the soft, pink head, Kieran shivered in delight. At the second, he spasmed against her mouth.

Ondrea took the head inside, sucking lightly, learning his tastes. They were easily learned. Kieran pushed deeper with a breathless curse.

Several long minutes passed, his cock sliding over her lips and tongue, his muscles tensing and flexing against her hands.

His retreat came without warning, leaving her stunned, and he whipped off the last of his clothing.

"Kieran?"

His fingertips traced her lower lip. "Either we're going to finish with two busy mouths or with your sweet sheath full of me."

The vision from the mirrors danced in her mind. She wrapped her legs around his thighs. "Full of you," she managed.

His eyes closed as if in prayer, then opened again. He lowered himself into position, drawing her legs up further.

At her next breath, Kieran was lodged inside. She arched against him, awash in pleasure and pain, her body and his spasming against each other.

"By the elders," he gasped. Kieran thrust deeper, holding her tight against him.

Ondrea's body reached for something nameless, and she fought his hold, forcing him minutely back and forth. Kieran pistoned in and out, fevered, driven as he'd been in the vision.

"You will be full of me, Ondrea. So full."

She gasped at his double meaning. Soon, she'd be filled to overflowing with his seed. Just the thought of it sent whispers of power and pleasure mixed over her nerves. Ondrea tried to hold it back, afraid she'd cause some mishap with unintended magic; it was a mistake any magic user over the age of ten loathed to be caught in.

"You can't hold it in, Ondrea," he rasped. His body sped to a furious pace, and an expression of bliss softened his face. "Fate, but the magic is wonderful." His skin shimmered in magic.

Ondrea stopped fighting the rise of her own, and the sweet agony of it overwhelmed her. She grasped at his shoulders, and the feel of his muscles working beneath his skin finished her off.

She screamed, her concentration tearing into a thousand fuzzy pieces. Her muddled mind processed the sharp smell of plants in transition from immature to ready herbals.

Kieran's shout mixed with hers, his heat bathing her and spilling over. A second touch of warmth, of magic unleashed, followed the same paths. The slight pains of use disappeared in a haze of continuing climax.

Then Kieran's mouth was over hers, in hers...his body hard and manner insistent. He pulled away slightly, trailing hands over her possessively. "Thank you for that gift, Ondrea."

Her cheeks burned at his meaning. "My maiden's barrier?" He knew she was a chaperoned woman. If she came to him as less, what would he think of her? Such a thing was unacceptable.

A male smile of satisfaction curved his lips up in a crooked bow. "That as well." He shivered, and a jet of his seed caressed her. "Being your only lover is quite the gift."

"Then what?" What other gift had she presented him with?

He laid a kiss on her chin. "Your trust." One further along her jaw line. "Your passion." On her cheek. "Your magic. Spells, but I am going to have to make love to you in the greenhouse. With power like that, you could cure legions of injured and ill."

His mouth captured hers in a drugging kiss.

Injured... Kieran had to know. Ondrea drew her mouth away, loathe to interrupt such a moment for something so unpleasant. "Kieran, I must tell you—"

He thrust into her, bringing Ondrea off the bed in delight. "Later, please. For now, I want to taste your passion again."

She nodded her agreement, her breath stolen away by his renewed vigor.

Later. Before we leave this room, he must know about the threat Gabriel poses.

* * * *

"Kieran," she pleaded.

He cupped her face in his hands. "I believe you, Ondrea. I do."

"But how do we stop it from happening?"

The words fought emerging. "Perhaps we can't," he suggested. "Fate is fate."

She shook her head, seemingly horrified by the thought of it.

Kieran laid a gentle kiss on her lips. "If all the visions are true, I survive it."

Tears pooled in her eyes. "He means to kill you." She choked on the words.

"We have no proof, but we have foresight to arm us."

"The elders—"

"Even if they expel him from the castle, the attack will come. We don't know where it is meant to happen. Perhaps it was never here."

Ondrea took a shuddering a breath. "I'll burn the dress," she vowed.

She'd have to. The blood stains were likely permanent, induced by magic as much as the physical spikes.

"Ondrea," he soothed her. "The dress is a minor thing."

"Is it?"

Kieran sighed. In truth, he didn't know how fates and possible futures overlapped or entwined. "Would it make you feel better to leave the castle?"

She looked at the bed, seemingly torn between fear and longing. "Yes. As soon as possible."

He pulled Ondrea to his chest, rocking her back and forth. "I'll pack and send my belongings ahead. Then we'll retrieve your belongings. We'll be gone before lunch."

* * * *

What caught Ondrea's attention first was an uncertain thing. The image coalesced into a heart-stopping whole in a few beats of her racing heart.

She grasped at Kieran's hand, yanking him to a stop, staring at the carpet then the decorations on the walls of the sitting nook. Her mouth went dry, saliva replaced with copper fear.

Why didn't we translocate? It would have been rude, but it would have been safe.

"Ondrea?"

"No," she protested. "We must leave." She pulled him back the way they came, prepared to drag him from harm's way, if needs be. "Wait. We can translocate to—"

But 'harm' stared them down. Gabriel stood in the doorway, clothed in the same suit he'd worn the day before, his hair in disarray and his eyes red-shot.

He performed a similar inventory on her, then glared an accusation at Kieran. The fact that she hadn't changed clothing but Kieran had wouldn't escape Gabriel's notice.

Ondrea backed off a step, running aground on Kieran's chest. Under any other circumstances, she'd find his touch comforting. At the moment, it was a glaring reminder that she could lose him to death within the hour.

Kieran guided her around him, stilling her fight to shield him with a bark of order that stunned her to silence and compliance. He faced down Gabriel, calm though he knew what was coming as well as she did.

Gabriel scowled at them, a look not unlike the one he used when his morning juice was soured. "Was he talented, Ondrea?"

Her face burned at the audacity of such a question.

"Do you always address ladies so rudely, Sarke?" Kieran inquired, neither confirming nor denying the accusation.

"Was she a lady in your bed, Medici? Not an hour earlier, she accepted my kiss, you know. How ladylike of her."

Kieran stiffened, but he didn't take the offered bait. Ondrea touched his shoulder, both wanting to deny it to give Kieran ease and wanting no lies between them.

"She's chosen me," Kieran replied shortly. "Nothing Ondrea did before she knew our destiny together is of any consequence."

Of course, he knew well enough that a kiss or two was nearly the extent of the liberties she'd allowed anyone.

Gabriel's jaw tightened, and his eyes hardened. "Destiny? It is an abomination, a fool's game...a sham at best."

"No. It is not," Ondrea insisted.

"Isn't it? A day ago, you loathed Medici."

She shook her head. "I didn't." Hadn't she considered how different he was than her memories of him? Hadn't she rationalized her attraction to him away?

"You didn't trust him," Gabriel insisted.

"I didn't know Kieran then."

"You don't know him now!"

Ondrea recoiled from his vehemence, and Gabriel pressed onward.

"You know me. You've always trusted me. Then the mirrors wove their illusions, and what did you do? Bed a man you have no reason to trust and rebuff one you always have."

"The destinies—"

"Are self-fulfilling," he thundered. "Don't you see that? We make our own destinies, when we choose to."

Ondrea shook her head. The magic wasn't wrong. It couldn't be.

Gabriel advanced a pace, and she retreated. Kieran did the same, keeping her at his shoulder.

"Not all magic users are invited here, Ondrea. Some of those with no destinies marry happily. How? Why do they? Reason that." He took another step.

"Keep your distance, Sarke," Kieran ordered.

Gabriel moved his eyes from Ondrea to Kieran, an expression that promised pain twisting his features. "Fate magic is for the weak mind, the easily led...the easily corrupted. I thought Ondrea too sensible for it, but I see now that she's another sentimental fool."

A cold smile pulled up at his lips, and Ondrea shuddered, grasping a handful of Kieran's jacket. It was coming. The attack was closing fast.

"That's too bad, really. I was hoping she'd be reasoned enough to avoid the trap." His gaze panned Kieran's body. "Of course, there is a way to prove I'm right."

"No," Ondrea pleaded. "Don't do this, Gabriel."

The dagger materialized in his hand, gleaming silver inset with rubies catching the light. It had a kris-shaped blade, snaking in graceful arcs that Ondrea would once have described as "a work of art" or "a singularly elegant display of master craftsmanship." No doubt, it was his father's work; even Gabriel wasn't gifted enough to craft such a blade yet.

She wrapped her arm around Kieran, intent on evading the blow, if they could. The kris was, first and foremost, a stabbing weapon, though its shape increased effectiveness in a slice. If Gabriel meant to kill Kieran, he'd be aiming a thrust for the ribs.

He sliced instead, cutting the air and sending the wake of magic to do the work for the blade. The magical strike took her forearm along with Kieran's chest. Ondrea screamed in pain of both the body and soul.

Kieran collapsed to his knees, a hand pressed to the wound. Ondrea urged him to his back, rattled, trying to apply pressure though her hands didn't cover the length of the damage. Her blood mixed with his. She sobbed in the impossibility of stemming the flow.

"Help! Someone please—we need a healer." Only the elders lived within the walls, but there might be another healer about...or someone who could translocate them to a healer.

Gabriel laughed. "There'll be no time for that." He raised the dagger for another blow.

Her mind spun then locked on her early O'Ken training. Her family's strength was in offensive fight spells, not magical weapons like the Sarkes but spell work.

Ondrea had never been able to work them correctly, worse even than she worked defensive spells. Though neither was likely to save them when pitted against Gabriel's prowess and weapon, the only spell she could call to mind was from her weaker spell set.

Fate does love irony. How often had her father said that? Too many.

There wasn't time to analyze why it was happening this way or to complain about it to the gods. The words rolled from her lips, and her hands left Kieran's chest to flow through the motions. The power swelled in her, and Gabriel's smile faltered.

All around them, glass shattered, hurtling at Gabriel. He lowered the blade, gaping at the efficiency of her attack. His free hand came up to initiate a defensive shield...a moment too late.

The glass pierced his body from all angles, and the dagger fell to the carpet. Gabriel's roar of pain dug at her ears. Then he fell—writhing, panting...an obscene, moving pincushion.

Kieran moaned, and Ondrea dragged her gaze back to him, restoring pressure to his wounds, sickened by what she'd done.

As if he knew her mind, Kieran offered assurances. "Anything...worth having...is worth fighting for."

She wanted to argue it, but it was precisely the choice she'd made.

His eyes slid shut, and her heart stuttered. She was losing him.

"Kieran! Fight, Kieran. Life is worth having; fight for it." Her further reasoning that their future was worth fighting for was cut short by a most unexpected sight.

The elder Medicis rushed into the room, averting their eyes as they passed Gabriel's still form. Kieran's father reached him first. He pushed Ondrea's hands away with a growled order for her retreat.

"I might have known a Sarke and an O'Ken would be involved in this butchery," he accused.

"He would have killed Kieran. I had no choice," she protested.

Markus Medici ignored her, putting his attention to his son's injuries. His power beat at Ondrea's nerves, a raw brush against the remnants of the O'Ken spell she'd used to kill. It was no wonder he'd pushed her away. This magic wasn't nurturing, as her plant healing was. She'd dampen his efforts until the effects faded.

Malcolm dropped down next to his son and grandson, casting a different spell over Kieran than his son did. The lacerations knitted loosely, and the blood around him disappeared, most likely into his body or a cleaning spell that would prepare it for safe transfer back into Kieran, at a later time.

"Good enough to move," Markus stated.

"There was no hope for the other," Malcolm reported. "I sent the remains to the elders. They'll handle the...removal."

"I agree. Kieran is our only concern."

Ondrea scrambled to her feet to accompany them. Two pairs of deep blue eyes regarded her stonily.

Markus forced his voice first. "Clean the blood from your hands, O'Ken. You are an affront to the senses."

His dismissal laid a deeper furrow than Gabriel's bespelled blade had. "But Kieran is—"

"None of your concern, butcher," Malcolm growled. "I cannot even heal you, what with the stink of death on you as it is. You won't be fouling my grandson's healing."

It was only then that she realized Markus was casting a translocation spell.

"Wait," she cried. "Where are you taking him?"

They were gone in a blink. Ondrea looked around, a sob catching in her throat. They were gone, and she had no clue where to. Tracking had never been a talent she possessed. Even had she, she was too weary to cast such a complex spell.

Silently, the blood evaporated from walls and carpets, forming a red mist, a pale smoke...then nothing but the scent of lilacs on the air. The glass fragments glittered in the late morning sunlight, rising from surfaces all over the room. In a tinkling, the windows, mirrors, and sconces reformed.

There was no sign of what happened, save her own bloodstained hands and clothes. The sensation of a soiled soul persisted, and Ondrea rushed to her rooms.

With a quick spell, the fire was roaring. She fed the dress to it...then the rest of her clothing.

The tub saw three consecutive scrubbings of her body, emptied between, with the addition of salt, sage and lavender at the final washing. It was a futile attempt at purification, she knew, but the need to purge herself of the pall of death ate at her. In the end, she wasn't certain she'd done more than burn at the still-open wound.

At a loss for direction, Ondrea dressed and sat on the sofa, stitching her wound with only her medicinal plants to dull the pain. That accomplished, she stared at the door.

Kieran was her mate; surely, someone would send word to her about his condition. Or he'd return to her.

* * * *

Her head snapped up at a light knocking. Ondrea moved stiffly, noting the fire burning low in the hearth. She opened the door, blinking in the much-brighter light from the corridor.

The form of an elder coalesced. Ondrea bit back a sigh and waved her in, clearing the way to the sitting area. She closed the door and lingered at it, wondering at the visit. It was unlikely that news would be delivered to her by an elder, but she held out hope that was the case.

The elder tsked her loudly. "You should not hide yourself, young one." She lit the lamps and sparked the fire with a wave of her hand.

"I'm not hiding. I'm waiting." There was no need of light for that.

The elder settled in an overstuffed chair. "Waiting? Whatever for?"

Ondrea found she couldn't meet the old woman's gaze. "For word on Kieran."

"His family is too angry and upset to consider sending it," she imparted.

Ondrea nodded, swallowing down a sob. They didn't approve then.

They'll never approve. She should have reasoned that. Kieran's bias against her at school had stemmed from his family. He'd been too young to form such hatred from personal experience.

"He is whole and resting," the elder continued. "The young Medici will carry scars, but he'd expected that, I'm certain."

She sagged against the door, tension easing from her muscles. "Good. As long as he's well."

"But you're not."

Ondrea cleared her throat, for once not attempting to still her fidgeting. "I'm well," she lied. It wasn't quite a lie. Physically, she wasn't badly marked, though she wore the bandage and would always wear the scar. O'Ken only sought out healers for life-threatening or debilitating injury or illness; all were trained to treat minor injuries themselves.

"A person who is well eats," the elder countered.

Just the thought of food turned her stomach. And... "I can't do it yet."

"Do? Whatever must you do?"

"I can't see them together. I hear them in the corridors...laughing. It's too much to ask."

Ondrea saw the sad shake of the elder's head out of the corner of her eye. Words passed too low for her to hear, and a steaming plate of food appeared on the table next to Ondrea. She stared at it, dismissing the idea of eating, no matter how it offended the elder.

"You must eat, Ondrea. The nutrition taken early in pregnancy and before is paramount to a babe."

Her heart stuttered, and Ondrea met her eyes fully. "From yesterday and this morn?" she managed. The odds on such a thing had to be astronomical.

The elder's smile widened. "No, but very soon. It is fated, after all."

A spike of wholly-unexpected disappointment sliced at her. Ondrea rationalized that the visions of a happy pregnancy were simply preferable to the misery she was currently experiencing.

Soon. "Only if Kieran returns to me," she reminded herself.

"You doubt he will?" There was no anger in that. The elder seemed genuinely curious.

Ondrea considered her words carefully. "What about Gabriel's mate? He was invited here." Her heart ached for an unknown woman who wouldn't find what she sought, when she'd come here full of hopes and dreams.

"He had no destined mate. There is no one seeking him."

She ambled to the sofa and sat, her mind rioting. "Then why was Gabriel invited?"

The elder didn't answer, leaving Ondrea to reason it.

"So I would kill him?" she demanded. "Because it was fated for him to attack Kieran within the castle and meet his end?"

"Fate decreed an end to the Sarke line. The entire experiment was an abomination." The elder looked affronted by nothing more than speaking about it, though Ondrea couldn't fathom why she would.

"Experiment, elder?"

She sighed, the lines on her weathered face creasing further in her misery, her over-bright eyes focusing on the flickering flames in the hearth. "Four generations ago, the elders of the time reasoned—being users of fate magic with too little respect for Chaos—that the balance of Fate and Chaos was a fallacy. That Fate was...superior."

The elder paused, her hand moving in the beginnings of a spell, then stilling. "They dabbled in futures and found a man and woman without set destinies, Chaos's children. The probable futures showed them to be a good match."

Ondrea forced a steady breath at the revelation. "So the elders invited them to the castle and pronounced them destined mates?"

She winced. "Just the pair. No others."

"They lied. They..." Spirits and spells, but the thought was horrifying. "It wasn't just the pair." Gabriel's family had sent generations of invited to the castle to find mates. "It was generations of—"

"The line created," the elder amended. "It seemed to be going so well that they brought each descendent back to be matched. None of them... None of them had destinies."

"Because they all belonged to Chaos," Ondrea stated the obvious.

"Worse," the elder croaked. "They lost the awe of magic they'd once had. You saw what a monster four generations of tampering created."

Her mind spun. "But he was right," she breathed.

"Pardon?" the elder asked.

"The Sarkes *did* make their own destinies. Their fates were lies, self-fulfilling fantasy stories."

"They didn't weave fates," the elder fumed. "I admit they were lied to. Left to me, it never would have happened."

Ondrea nodded, heartsick.

"Your destiny, on the other hand, is real. You must know that."

"Is it? Or is it real, because I choose to follow it?"

"I don't understand."

Ondrea stared at her. Had the elder never questioned? Had she never considered what would happen if one abandoned Fate? "Does anyone choose to escape Fate? Does anyone choose to take another path and not the one destiny indicates?"

"Chaos's children do not have destinies, but they forge their own paths."

"Of Fate's children?"

"Why would one wish to?"

"Do they?" Ondrea pressed, her heart racing as if she were at the precipice of some great discovery, something more than the manipulation of the Sarke line.

"No. I don't believe they have. Oh, I admit some might have tried, in a show of temper, but who can escape destiny?"

"Then how can you know they aren't all self-fulfilling?"

That seemed to confuse her.

"The users of fate magic interfered in Chaos. What would happen if Chaos did the same?"

The elder's face twisted in a look of horror. Ondrea didn't get an answer.

* * * *

Kieran shifted beneath the blankets, his senses alive to the sounds and smells of his home. He didn't recall coming home, but perhaps he'd been translocated while he lay unconscious.

He forced his eyes open, but he was alone. His heart sank, and he realized he'd been expecting to see Ondrea, hovering over him, sick with worry, or maybe asleep at his bedside. Kieran called for her, certain she was near.

Footsteps rushed toward him, and Kieran sighed. It seemed his family wasn't content to wait until he'd greeted his mate. The door burst open, and bodies crowded in. Kieran looked from one face to the next, but Ondrea wasn't among them.

He sought out his mother's eyes. "Where is Ondrea?" he demanded.

Her brow furrowed. "Kieran?"

"My mate?" Why did no one understand what he was talking about?

"The O'Ken?" his father asked.

"Yes. Ondrea." Kieran's patience was fraying fast, and it showed. "Ondrea O'Ken...but only until we marry formally," he amended.

"Fate loves a good irony," his grandfather muttered. He darkened, and his eyes shifted toward the window.

"Hardly," Kieran replied. "Ondrea isn't like her family."

"Tell that to the man she killed," his father huffed.

"In defense of me." Though Kieran was no admirer of violence, the choice of Gabriel's blood or his own had been simple enough to make. "If anything, I'm concerned for Ondrea."

"She's an O'Ken," his father scoffed. "Killing is in her blood."

"Markus," his mother admonished.

"She's a plant healer," Kieran argued. "Killing... Fighting in general is against her nature. She has problems making even defensive spells work properly. Her family's proclivities are discordant to her base nature and her natural magic."

"She overcame *that* well enough," his grandfather quipped.

"I doubt it." Just the sight of violence in the vision had unnerved her. She was surely suffering in her choice, though he'd tried to calm her. "How long has it been?"

"A day," his mother offered.

"A day! A full day?"

Tears glistened in her eyes. "I was afraid you'd never wake."

"I told you he would, Ariel," his father soothed her.

I should be soothing Ondrea. Kieran pushed to sitting, wincing at the sting of his still-healing tissues.

"What are you doing?" his grandfather inquired.

"My mate needs me." And he needed clothes before he went to her. "Mother, I'll need help to translocate to..." Spells, was she still at the castle? Had she sought a healer's aid or her family's solace?

"As your healer," his father began.

"Then bring Ondrea here," Kieran countered.

"Where the healing spells are working? Are you mad?"

"She can improve upon the herbs you're using."

"No!" His eyes flashed in fury.

Kieran started to pull the blankets back. The sharp command from his grandfather startled him. Hands caught Kieran as his eyes slid shut. His mother's shout of protest disappeared into the mental buzzing of magic-induced sleep then was swallowed up in black silence.

* * * *

Ondrea took one last look around her rooms, sighing that there was nothing left to be done. It was time to leave.

She'd given Kieran three days to come to her...then tarried two more, simply to avoid returning home to her family. She'd sent requests to join her mate to every place she knew he might be, but Gabriel had been right about one more thing; she didn't know Kieran well enough to know where to send word to him.

Kieran hadn't answered, and he hadn't come to her. That meant he'd decided to end it, no doubt. Though he'd been willing to accept Gabriel's murdering ways as fated, it seemed he wasn't willing to accept a mate who showed the slightest inherited O'Ken talents, no matter how unreliable they were.

Ondrea shifted, disoriented by how simple it had been to kill...too easy for her comfort. Why, after all these years and all the failed attempts at mastering fight spells, did killing come effortlessly?

Her hands shook, and Ondrea fisted them within her travel gloves. The pale gray leather was spotless, but the image of blood-soaked hands persisted.

"It is past time to leave this place," she decided. Most of the destined couples had already done so, and the castle was quiet, lending to internal dialog Ondrea would like to avoid. Even her father's chatter and questions would be better than this.

He'd begged her return a dozen times in the last five days, demanded answers she wasn't ready to give. He'd even offered to aid her, if she had need of him. A short note asking forbearance had been her only reply so far.

But she'd stayed too long. Obviously, Kieran had decided to escape their destiny.

A sudden certainty that the Ellix Spinner and Fates Room would have different results now occurred to her. A mad need to test the latter assaulted her, and Ondrea pushed it away, reasoning that it would be one last proof that Fate was not absolute that she couldn't stomach right now.

Ondrea bit back tears and translocated her belongings to her rooms at home. SanCee would take care of the unpacking, and her rooms would be prepared long before Ondrea reached home by conventional means. True, she could translocate herself, but she was in no hurry to explain a single hour of her time at the castle.

Resolute, she opened the door to the corridor...and came face to face with Kieran.

* * * *

"Kieran... Kieran?"

His mother's whispered voice cut through layers of confusion and exhaustion. "Mother?"

"Good. You're waking."

Kieran licked his lips, trying to force his eyes open. His limbs tested better, moving...however sluggishly.

"You must hurry. They'll know what we're doing soon." There was a note of urgency in her voice.

"Wh-what are we doing?" he grumbled. *And who are 'they'?*

"Getting you to your mate."

His heart raced, and his eyes opened. Kieran scrambled to sitting. He was stiff, but the healing spells had done their work. *How long did I sleep? Damage this deep would take days to heal.*

Kieran grasped the soft lounging shirt from his mother's hands and dragged it over his head.

"She's asking for you, Kieran."

He paused with one arm in the shirt, his already-dry mouth going parched. "Ondrea?"

His mother nodded. "She wants to join you."

Kieran stuffed his other arm in and left the bed on bare feet. "Father wouldn't let her." He didn't need to ask it.

A sound from the stairs caught his attention.

His mother grasped both of his hands. "Keep the location in mind, Kieran. I'll fuel the spell."

"But—"

"Ariel?" his grandfather called out.

"Now, Kieran," she ordered. "Think."

Of where?

The castle! They shouldn't be able to follow him there...not without permission of the elders to enter uninvited.

If Ondrea has left the grounds, I am no longer invited either.

That will place me outside the doors, and they will let me enter.

He closed his eyes, locking onto the site of Gabriel's attack. Kieran would rather translocate directly to Ondrea's rooms, but having never been there, he couldn't visualize it.

The door opened...and Kieran stumbled through emptiness and onto a thick carpet.

"Ah, you've arrived."

He looked around, spying the same elder who'd spoken to him after the Fates Room. "You knew I'd be here?"

She smiled. "It was destined."

"Of course." Kieran had never realized how annoying it was to deal with the elders before. Fate magic could make one so smug as to be irritating.

She motioned the direction he'd been traveling with Ondrea. "I assume you want to reach her before she leaves."

His heart faltered in its steady beat. *How long did I sleep?* "Assuredly."

"Then come along."

Kieran glanced down at himself, blushing at the fact that he was barefoot and dressed in bedclothes. "That might be wise."

The elder's laughter preceded him down the corridor. Two turns later, the elder waved him toward a door, then disappeared further down the hall.

He took a calming breath and placed his hand on the doorframe, wishing he had more information. How long was he away from her? She was leaving; it wasn't a matter of hours. It was time to knock and learn the answers to his questions.

The door swung open, and Ondrea halted. Her dark eyes panned from his chest to his face, her head tipping up slightly to accomplish it. Kieran held his breath, waiting for her reaction, hoping for relief, joy...anything positive.

She paled a notch, and her lips parted in a look of shock. There was no move toward him, no comment.

It's been longer than I thought. Kieran reached for her, searching for a way to open the discussion. Ondrea's move was so abrupt, he nearly pitched forward into the now-empty space in surprise.

"Why are you here?" There was a note of something fearful in that, almost panicked.

"Ondrea?" The question made no sense. Didn't she want him here?

Tears reflected the lamplight, making her expression harder to grasp upon. "Why did you come here?"

"We're fated to—"

The curse leaving her lips was so unlike her it stunned him to silence. Ondrea crossed one arm over her chest, pacing the width of the room. She played with a curl that cascaded over her shoulder, a nervous habit she'd had as long as he'd known her.

Realization that he was still standing in the corridor and barely dressed sent Kieran toward her. He closed them both into her rooms.

Ondrea stopped short, her eyes widening and breath hitching at the sight of him leaning against the door. She fidgeted from foot to foot.

"How long have I been gone, Ondrea?"

"You...don't..." She shook her head, her color rising.

"I was placed in a healing sleep." Kieran motioned to his lack of appropriate clothing. "I came as soon as I was able."

"I see that." But her tone said she wasn't mollified.

"It wasn't my idea to keep you away," he assured her.

"No. It was your family's." Again, there wasn't a hint of give in her.

"Not all of them. My mother broke the sleep spell early and fueled the spell to send me to you." But what difference did it make? They were destined mates.

She nodded but didn't comment.

His heart ached at her emotional distance. "How long?"

"Five days," she whispered.

Spirits and spells, it's no wonder she doesn't trust me. Kieran took a step toward her, and Ondrea retreated.

"Perhaps we should..." Her gaze flicked from surface to surface, optical fidgeting at its finest.

"Yes?" His heart worked hard in a fear he couldn't place a name to.

"Slow down. See if...if this will work."

"It's *destined* to work," he reminded her.

"I'm an O'Ken." Her voice held a bitter bite at the mention of her own name.

"That doesn't matter to me," he pleaded.

"It mattered to you." There was something unforgiving in that, the same accusation he'd feared after he'd seen their destiny in the Fates Room.

"I was young and stupid," he admitted. "It *didn't* really matter to me." Given the chance, he'd have bedded her in secondary.

"No." Her voice raised to a shout. "You were just repeating what your family said. *Their* poison became *your* poison...and it still flows in their veins."

He couldn't deny that. "They'll come around once they get to know you."

"How can you be so sure? I see little chance of it."

"We're destined to—"

"Stop saying that!" There was no mistaking the panic that time.

"Why?" It was true. Why would he stop saying it? Why would Ondrea be frightened by it? They'd passed the worst of what she'd seen already and survived it.

She shifted aimlessly, agitated. If he scanned her body's functions, Kieran felt sure he'd find her highly distressed, though she hid it well.

"They will never accept me, Kieran."

"They will. I saw it in the mirrors. They must."

Ondrea didn't respond to that immediately. "When? How long will they hate me?"

"They don't hate you," he protested.

"Of course, they do. They're *healers*."

The bite in that one word made his heart stutter in apprehension. "You're a healer."

"A plant healer. I have no reason to loathe fighters, unless they burn crops."

"I'm a healer!" He was shouting now, stung by her refusal.

"And you're only here, because we're destined," she accused.

"That's not true." How dare she accuse it!

Ondrea stormed to him, her expression passing from confusion to fury and back again. "Are you saying you'd have ever courted me, Kieran? Be honest."

"If I thought I was welcome," he raged.

"Whose fault was that?"

Again, he couldn't deny the truth of her words. "I've always been attracted to you. That didn't start with the Fates Room. Why do you think I was so...vehement in school? It confused me to be attracted to someone... I don't deny my family filled my head with stories, but I learned to separate reality from them...in time."

"But your willingness to pursue the attraction did start with the Fates Room. Your willingness to pursue me did," she qualified. Her lip curled in a look of disgust at the concept.

"I love you." Wasn't that enough? Couldn't she see that and forget Fate for a moment?

"You don't know me."

Kieran considered that, calming himself, forcing his voice lower. "You love strawberries, but they give you an allergic rash. You eat them anyway." *And never seek a healer for it.*

She gaped at him, a soft sound of confusion escaping her lips.

"Your favorite color is green. Not surprising for a plant healer. You love Rajicar O'Berio's paintings and the harp playing of Mahree Tabor."

"How—"

He raised a hand to silence her. "You watch mirror ball to be sociable, but you don't like the sport."

A tear spilled down her cheek. Kieran took a step toward her and brushed it away on the pad of his thumb, heartened that she didn't move to avoid him.

"You like to ride," he continued. "You're not proficient, so you avoid it."

"Why?" she whispered.

"I don't know that," he admitted. "I imagine...so you don't look foolish. I want to know the whys, Ondrea."

"No. Why did you watch me? Why did you consider it important enough... Why did you take note of all of these things about me?"

Kieran leaned toward her, feathering his lips over hers.

Ondrea hesitated, then did the same in return. "I want to know, Kieran. I want you to know."

He smiled, capturing her mouth in a more purposeful kiss.

Ondrea's hand slid beneath his shirt, tracing the scars marring his chest. She pushed up at the fabric, baring him and pulling her mouth from his. Kieran moaned out a protest, shaking his head.

"I want to know," she repeated.

He nodded, easing the shirt off for her and dropping it to the floor. Ondrea stared at the damage, visibly pained. Before he could reassure her, she pressed both hands flat to his chest and started tracing the still-sensitized tissue with her lips.

Kieran gasped, reaching up to circle her wrists with his hands, visions of making love to her on the nearest flat surface nearly masking his senses. It couldn't mask them completely, and a healer couldn't miss the feel of a bandage, even incapacitated and through clothing.

He pulled at the fasteners on her dress, peeling it down her body to the chorus of her urging, but this wasn't sexual...yet. The dress pooling around her boots, Kieran dragged her injured arm up. He started unwrapping the linen.

"Kieran?"

"You still have an open wound."

"Not open...healing well, I think."

"It's unacceptable. It should have been healed."

Her breathing hitched. "I'm an O'Ken. Unless it's life-threatening, no healer will trade with me. And...only then out of a sense of duty."

He looked from the sloppily-set stitches to her eyes, horrified. "I would have," he vowed.

A smile pulled up at her lips. "I believe you."

"Then you've come to know me."

Kieran cupped his hand over the raw wound and evaluated it. "Excellent choice of herbals." He winced inwardly at the fact that an O'Ken would need to know them, plant healer or not.

He couldn't heal her as completely as his family had healed him. Not alone, without aid in his healing. Not as young and weakened from his own healing as he was.

Still, he had to do what he could. The spell trilled off his tongue. Ondrea tried to pull her arm away, and he clamped down on it.

"You can't," she reasoned. "You're still recovering."

"I can't heal you completely, but I can speed the process of your own healing."

Her arm relaxed in his grip, and Kieran completed the spell, knitting the flesh and skin lightly and removing the stitches. He stroked at the deep red line.

"You'll always carry the scar," he apologized. "I would remove it, if I could."

She kissed at the longer of his scars. "I'd remove yours."

Kieran cupped her face up, returning to the kisses that would lead them to some close surface. Her legs shifted against him, and her low boots thumped against the wood floor. Her arms circled his neck, and Kieran lifted, fitting Ondrea to his body, kicking her clothing and boots away on the way to the sofa.

They came aground on the large table in the center of the room. It wasn't his first choice, but it would do. As if in agreement, her legs wrapped around his.

Her mouth left his and a whispered translocation spell swirled between them. Kieran expected to find himself in bed with her, but they didn't move.

He dragged one strap of her camisole off of her shoulder, intending to bare her breast. "What did you move?"

A sexy smile graced her lips. "It was more...removed."

Her camisole still being in place left only her stockings and panties. Kieran thrust a hand beneath her camisole, confirming that it was the panties.

"Stars and spells." He stroked at her ready body, dizzy in need. He had to get his sleep pants off.

Ondrea's hand slid down his chest toward the tie, and Kieran captured her mouth, his tongue dancing hard against hers.

The spell unfolding dragged his attention around to the crowd appearing in the room with them. *What in the great Fate's name is this?*

"Ondrea," a strange man shouted, clearly shocked.

"Kieran," his father warned.

"Oh my," the elder sighed but with an expression of glee that said she wasn't the least bit sorry for translocating their fathers into this scene.

"Fated, elder?" Kieran accused, irritated at her interference.

"Undoubtedly," she replied.

Ondrea pulled down at the camisole, urging Kieran's hand from beneath, her skin burning crimson against his body. "Father, remove yourself," she demanded.

"And you, Father," Kieran added.

Neither moved to do so.

O'Ken motioned to them, his mouth moving as if to protest. "This... This is unacceptable," he finally managed.

"Do I tell you and Mother how to make love?" Ondrea huffed, straightening the strap over her shoulder again. Her legs lowered, hanging down around Kieran's, a stark reminder that she was bare and opened for him.

He forced his mind from it, taking a deep breath and willing his cock down a notch or two. "I recall you and Mother telling me any mate destined for me would be a joy." In fact, his father had told him he'd never know sexual fulfillment as he would with his mate.

"Ondrea!"

"Kieran!"

The two older men glared at each other.

"I do not approve." O'Ken's voice was tense and cold.

"On this, we agree," his father stated.

Kieran's heart ached. This was what Ondrea felt those five days of being rebuffed by his family.

"You don't have to approve," the elder reminded them. "The Fates Room and the Ellix Spinner have both attested to the match."

O'Ken glared at her, then turned his attention to his daughter. "Come with me, Ondrea. We'll discuss this away from these *healers*."

Ondrea stiffened against him, then pushed toward the edge of the table. Kieran placed his hands on her hips and eased her to the floor, unsure of her intent.

She turned to her father, fairly vibrating in anger. "I-am-a-healer." Each word was enunciated and clipped, lending a military air to the response.

His expression announced he found that an unfortunate situation he wished he could remedy.

"And I am a fighter," she informed him.

"As I well saw," Markus quipped.

"Be still, Father," Kieran ordered.

"Kieran—"

"Enough!"

His father ignored the warning to cease hostilities. "Her games nearly saw you dead."

O'Ken turned on him. "Ondrea doesn't play games with life, Medici."

"No. She ends it like you, O'Ken."

"Enough," Kieran and Ondrea shouted together.

"Ondrea—"

"Enough, Father. I'm staying. You're leaving." She glanced at Kieran. "They are of a type, you realize."

"I do now." He sighed, exhaustion weighing him down.

The movements of O'Ken's hands and lips drew Kieran's attention, and he yanked Ondrea behind his body to block her father's view of her, severing the half-formed translocation spell.

"Kieran, enough is enough," his father insisted.

"Yes, it is. I'm seriously considering whether we'll be safe in either home."

"Now just a—"

His protest died as Ondrea's arm circled Kieran's body, anchoring her to him to avoid being translocated without him. Their fathers wore matching expressions of shock. O'Ken gasped, and both paled.

Kieran looked down, confused at the change. They were half-dressed, but they'd been so clothed the entire time.

It took a moment for the significance of what he was seeing to sink in. Ondrea's arm lay roughly as it had on the day of the attack, completing the unbroken line of Gabriel's single slice. To reinforce it, Kieran traced the line from his abdomen, over her forearm, and across his chest.

Markus found his voice first. "What was she doing?"

Ondrea answered, providing the bit of information Kieran wished he understood himself. "I was trying to push Kieran away from the fight." There was something meek in that, as if she anticipated either Kieran or her father to take her to task.

He reined in the urge, his heart warming that she'd tempted Fate so sorely on his behalf. "I told you to stay behind me." It came out a growl, but it was better than the rant he'd stifled.

Whatever answer she might have made was drowned out by her father's protest. "Sarke attacked *my* daughter?"

"Oh, but it was acceptable that he attacked my *son*?" Markus roared.

"What? Of course, not! I never said that."

"Perhaps they would be safer with Medici."

O'Ken glowered down at his opponent in this verbal sparring match. "Are you mad? Kieran placed himself between Ondrea and that murdering whelp. All of O'Ken would lay down our lives for him."

Markus raised an eyebrow. "Yes, but you'd need an army of healers to handle the casualties."

"So, your son *is* an instig—"

"Of a type." Kieran shook his head wearily. "Elder, if you would be so kind as to translocate our fathers to a place to discuss this..."

She nodded and cast the spell. Their fathers disappeared, protests at being forced away echoing after their physical forms were gone. The room went unnaturally still in their wake, but it didn't remain so for long.

Ondrea's hand slipped down his stomach and into the front of his sleeping pants. Kieran moaned at the first stroke of her hand up his half-erect length.

It wasn't half-erect for long. A heartbeat later, he filled...then overflowed her hand, wrenching a gasp from her. She eased around his body, looking down at the damp spot on his sleeping pants with wide-eyes.

Kieran pulled at the tie and let the pants dip, revealing the tip, nestled to her delicate fingers. "Did you miss me?" he teased.

"Intensely." She released him, planting both hands on the tabletop and levering herself up. Her legs circled his again, reeling Kieran in.

He cupped the back of her skull with one hand, and thrust the other beneath her camisole, playing at her still-wet slit. "Now, where were we?"

"Not far enough," she breathed.

His mouth covered hers, and his tongue surged inside. Kieran groaned, as she followed suit. Ondrea pushed his pants down his thighs and grasped his cock, stroking him then bringing the crown to her ready body.

Kieran surged inside, their lips parting as Ondrea arched her back. A moan rose between them then panting breaths. Kieran drove into her, anticipating her milking climax, holding off to feel her come for him.

Ondrea's magic beat at him, playing against his own. He closed his eyes, imagining years of this. What had he done to be so blessed?

"Will we really do this in the greenhouse?" she gasped.

"And the bath... The mountains... Lake Chaos..." He matched the cadence of the words, groaning at the first whispers of her release. "Every room of the house... There are so many places and positions, Ondrea."

Her short nails raked at his back, drawing a hiss from him.

"Every one you wish to experience," he offered.

Her climax sent a wave of nurturing energy over him, and plants burst into bloom all over the room. Kieran couldn't hold off longer. In the next moment, he was releasing waves of his fluids into her. Ondrea groaned, leaving new furrows on his back.

He laughed in relief of his pent-up need, a need that had been denied while he healed. Silently, he promised a less frenetic encounter for the next time, something he promised every time and had yet to deliver on, in the heat of the moment.

Ondrea's fingertips left his shoulders and gripped tight at his buttocks, forcing Kieran deeper inside her. Her hips tipped back and forth, sending sparks of arousal up his length and racing through his body.

"What do you want, Ondrea?" Spirits and spells, he'd give her whatever she asked for.

"The bath. Oh yes, the bath will be just right." Her eyes were closed, her face a mask of longing and hunger.

He eased Ondrea off his cock and to the floor, stripping the last of her clothing off then his own. Halfway to the bathing room, a spell stopped him in his tracks. The smell of roast meat teased his senses.

A platter of food and drink was settled in the center of the table they'd just vacated. Kieran stared at it in confusion, trying to work through who'd sent it or why. The idea that the elders were spying on them didn't sit well with him.

Ondrea's lips pressed to the hollow of his shoulder, drawing Kieran's attention back to her. "They are intent on me eating correctly," she explained.

Before he could question that, she ended the conversation with a massage to his sac. Whatever she knew could wait. For now, he intended to be buried inside his mate...first his tongue and then his aching cock.

* * * *

Ondrea shivered at the intent gaze Kieran raked over her, taking the offered bit of meat from his fingertips. She chewed and swallowed, disconcerted by his silence.

"Kieran?"

"Do you need to return to your studies?" he asked.

"No. My mentor has excused me from formal studies...for now."

His hand settled on her woman's curls, his thumb stroking idly at her clit. "How long?"

"I—" Ondrea gasped then forced her breathing to even. "I don't know."

"Three weeks," he requested.

"A month, if you like." A month of this would likely kill her, though the mirrors indicated it wouldn't. Oh, but what a way to die.

Kieran shifted his hand, stroking two fingers inside her. "Perfect."

"Is it?" Ondrea spread her legs, more interested in what he was doing to her than what he was saying.

"It won't take more than a month."

Her heart skipped in excitement. "Planting your seed in me?" The elders had said it would be soon, and the mirrors concurred.

Kieran turned her chair, forcing his knees between hers and urging her wider. "Considering your cycle, that will take only days...if it's not accomplished already."

Ondrea's body reacted fiercely to that. "What will take a month?" she managed in a thin voice.

"Breaking the families of their bickering." Kieran started pumping his fingers in and out of her, making her cream flow in preparation for climax.

She moaned, shaking her head. He believed that would take a month? Impossible.

Kieran's fingers disappeared, and a hastily cast translocation spell sent the tray away. In the next instant, she was on her feet and bent over the edge of the table. One more, and Kieran was inside her, not gently as he'd been in the bath but with a growl that announced his intention to master her.

The heat of the tray teased at her nipples, and Ondrea pushed back on him.

"A month, Ondrea," he vowed. "But we must work together on this."

She nodded, incapable of speech as he worked at her arousal, enflaming her body with precision.

"Until one or the other offers to work toward resolution, without us suggesting it, we stay here. We don't—" He groaned, stroking a hand through her hair then fisting it. "Leave here."

"Will the elders allow that?"

"I imagine they will. Spirits and—"

His translocation spell sent them to the bedroom. Once the mattress supported her abdomen instead of the edge of the table, he was ruthless. Ondrea licked her lips at her rising arousal. Even if Kieran was wrong, and they didn't cave in a month, a month of this would be Fate's Fields on the face of the world.

* * * *

"I'm simply stating—" Markus began.

Kieran sighed. "If you state it again, we shall take our leave for the next eight months."

"Kieran!" His mother's voice went panicked at that, and he shot her a wink behind his father's back. Ariel forced down a smile. "Really, Markus! Do stop. Kieran may decide to follow through. He has been serious about every other threat...er...warning."

Yes, he had...and so had Ondrea, which was why there was something resembling peace between the two families.

It had started with two weeks at Fate Castle. As long as the missives either demanding their presence or vying to outdo the other family in bringing them home continued, they'd begged off on leaving. The Medicis had hit on the, to employ a pun, magic combination first. They'd invited the young lovers to dinner and included a guest list...topped by the O'Kens.

The dinner had been tense but civil. Ondrea's mother, Alia, had graciously accepted Ariel into the wedding plans discussed after the meal. The men had shared whiskey in the small drawing room...and a second dinner had been arranged at the O'Ken household two weeks after.

Those two weeks had passed with Medici, but missives had flown between the two households several times daily, and Alia had made twice-weekly trips to conduct wedding planning and visit. More than once, Kieran had come upon Ondrea and both of their mothers, laughing like school girls, most likely sharing stories about their men.

The Medici family would travel to the O'Ken estate with Kieran and Ondrea and stay for dinner. After that, the two weeks until the wedding would be spent at O'Ken. Though they hadn't confirmed anything past that, it was a safe bet that they'd split their time between the two homes to keep the peace...as long as the families continued to behave themselves.

"Kieran," his father pleaded. "The earliest days of a child's development are so important." He dared not say more than that. Any outright accusation that the O'Ken estate might be counterproductive to a forming infant would go too far, and he knew it.

"Ondrea assures me that her home is very calming. The herbs sent to her were grown there. If such superior healing plants can grow, I imagine our child will do well."

"Very well," he conceded, but Kieran could tell his father was reserving final judgment until he'd established the harmony of the O'Ken household for himself.

Ariel offered a smile and followed Markus out of the room.

Ondrea pressed to Kieran's back, chuckling. "Why do you do that?"

"Do what?" he asked, perplexed.

She hesitated for a moment. "You didn't see our child's birth in the mirrors."

His heart stuttered at that. "No. You did?"

A sound of pleasure escaped her lips. "I know very well what bed she's fated to arrive in."

Kieran looked to the bed they'd shared for the last two weeks, a smile spreading on his face. "Do me a favor."

"And that would be?"

"Don't tell my father."

The laughter she vented into his shoulder choked off at Markus's call to join them for the translocation to O'Ken. Oh yes, keeping the families in line was going to be a joy.

We Shall Live Again

Chapter One

"Dr. Hastings?"

Anna swiveled her head around, and she stared at the student, lost in thought for a moment longer. His face was hidden in the shadows thanks to the sun at his back. His name filtered in, and she forced it past her lips. "Adam? You were saying?"

"We're ready, Doctor." He shifted, the outline of his fit body raising her interest and hunger.

Anna mentally shook it away. It was her exhaustion and the dreams working on her perceptions. Adam Valeri was a hot body on her crew at a time when she wanted one...desperately.

True, he was only a few years shy her thirty-two, and he was a doctoral student rather than the graduate variety Evan had provided to the dig. But he was a student and a member of her crew; that was a line Anna had never crossed before. She didn't intend to start now.

She clicked her pen shut, gathering the papers into the leather binder, her hands shaking lightly. "The burial chamber?"

"Precisely where you'd postulated it would be," he confirmed.

Great. Evan is sure to pounce on that. Anna nodded, jumping to her feet. She'd worry about her older brother later. For now, there was a dig to complete. *The sooner it's over with, the sooner I can get back to something resembling a rational existence.*

She turned and led the way without looking up at his face, completely engaged in trying to stop her hands from shaking and her knees from buckling. She paused for a moment as Adam zipped the outer door of her two-room tent shut.

Precisely where you postulated.

Of course, it was. Anna had been dreaming of this day for weeks...any sleeping moment she hadn't been dreaming of *him.* "Amun," Anna breathed.

She'd been dreaming of Amunmaruku for months, practically since the moment they'd breached the tomb entrance.

As if her voice was a spell summoning him forth, Amun's breath teased at her ear, carrying her name.

Anna...my name. Not hers.

The combination of her simmering arousal and his body heat sent her mind reeling.

Hands pulled her to a broad chest, snapping her back to a fuzzy version of reality—trembling, gasping for breath, sweat beading on her forehead, more than aware of the man behind her.

"Anna!"

She winced at her brother's voice, opening her eyes to the sight of Evan loping across the sand toward her. His hand cupped her cheek, and Anna pushed it away.

"I'm okay, Evan. I just left the shade too quickly." Anna straightened, taking several deep breaths that drew Amun's scent into her lungs.

Adam's hands retreated, but he didn't back away, setting off the internal calculator of how long it had been since she'd gotten laid.

Almost a year. At least...by a flesh and blood man, it's been that long.

Evan wrapped an arm around her as if to turn Anna toward her tent. Relieved of her care, Adam headed for the cataloguing tent where he spent most of his time.

She planted her feet, shaking her head, both in refusal and to knock loose the last of the cobwebs and clear her mind. "I'm fine, and I want to see the burial chamber."

"Anna—"

"I'll drink water on the way," she conceded.

His scowl melted with an exasperated sigh and settled on a brittle smile. "Just like Dad."

She nodded, though it was a lie. Anna had never resembled her parents, nor should she have. As a foundling left on their doorstep, it was hardly a surprise dark-haired, amber-eyed Anna was a square peg in the blond, green-eyed round hole of their family, but they'd accepted her, nonetheless.

At least being in Egypt again means Evan's skin is tanned nearly as dark as mine is.

"Okay. Water on the way down." Evan didn't release her, though he did lead her toward the tomb entrance.

Anna took a moment to appreciate the find yet again. They'd never seen anything like it. No one had, which meant it would literally *make* her career. For that matter, it would make the career of everyone on the dig.

At first glance, they thought they'd found a large mastaba, a simple rectangular tomb super-structure, the precursor to the step pyramid. But this was like no mastaba discovered before, leading the crew to the initial conclusion that it was the tomb of a second dynasty ruler...until they got inside.

Unlike the stark mastabas of the kings, this tomb was heavily decorated. Unlike the tombs of the later nobles, this one was etched and painted with images of the gods and hieroglyphs instead of scenes of daily life.

More surprising, the gods depicted were a combination never seen before, unable to be attributed to a single place and time in dynastic history. Three gods featured prominently and two others less so, some from as late as New Kingdom, though the tomb was much older than that.

It was a wild mix of influences that had scholars breathing down their necks for a determination on the validity of the find. Some were of the opinion that the mastaba must have been faked somehow, but how would someone fake such a super-structure?

Anna glanced at the largest of the murals on the way past. Sebek, Min, and Ma'at were at the forefront, Amun and Anubis secondary. She hesitated, letting the choices wash over her. Sebek...fertility. Min...fertility again...or regeneration, since she couldn't lock this collection to a single time and place in history. Ma'at...justice. Amun...air, wind...or things hidden. Anubis...death. The combination was intriguing.

"Matt has been working on the hieroglyphs," Evan interrupted her thoughts.

Her mouth went dry. "And?" *Why am I asking? I know what it's going to say.*

"Roughly the same as the others."

"My brothers and sisters favor us. Ma'at, aid us. We shall live again." There were prayers and pleas to the gods, all ending with those three lines, throughout the tomb.

"You've got it."

Anna nodded and headed for the burial chamber, passing chambers that had held crocks of food, wine, and beer, some inexplicably emptied. The passageways twisted and turned, until she felt she was going to collapse in dizziness.

One final turn, through an entryway opened in what had appeared to the naked eye to be a solid wall, brought her into the outer chamber. It was filled with weapons and tools, and the stone that blocked the entryway to the burial chamber was flanked by tarnished statues of Min and Sebek.

Her eyes strayed upwards, locking on the painting on the stone. Her knees buckled, and Anna found herself sitting on the stone floor, staring up at the stylized face of the man she knew so well.

"Amunmaruku," she breathed.

Evan paused, bent halfway to her. "What did you say?"

Anna swallowed hard. Nothing on the tomb thus far had identified its occupant. There was still the hope that something inside the burial chamber would.

Her brother drew Anna to her feet, testing her uncertain balance with a tense jaw and narrowed eyes.

"Matt, get Adam and Josh cataloguing. We'll open the burial chamber day after tomorrow. I want the hoist and rollers in place by tomorrow evening."

"You got it, boss."

Before Anna could protest either Matt's insistence on calling Evan "boss" or the delay in opening the inner sanctum, she was being whisked back through the passageways.

* * * *

"You're being silly, Evan," Anna protested.

"Eat," he ordered again.

She took a bite of the pita sandwich, wishing she had mayonnaise to make it more appealing. Late on a dig, it was the little things you tended to miss most.

But she had bigger problems at the moment, most of them centering around an overbearing older brother. It was bad enough Evan had her in bed at before sundown. Now, he was forcing food and water down her, treating her like a child.

"Now," he began. "As I said, you are just like Dad. You're not eating enough. You're working too hard and not sleeping enough."

Her face burned in embarrassment, and Anna took another bite so as not to blurt out that she slept long enough but her dreams robbed her of true rest. The dark circles under her eyes were there, whether she slept six hours in a night or ten. The problem was, she woke no less than once a night—wet, aching and disturbed in body and soul.

"You're going to bed as soon as you finish eating," Evan decreed.

Anna swallowed the mouthful of masticated sandwich, staring at him in disbelief. "But I have to—"

"I have to." It came out sounding like a curse. "Dad worked himself to death after you and Mom left. You weren't there to see it happen, Anna. I was. I won't let you do the same. I can't let you do it." His eyes pleaded for her agreement.

Anna nodded, forcing down another mouthful of the dry, bland sandwich. Behind the mask of her acceptance, she was already planning how she'd manage to catch up on the work tomorrow.

"Good. Then I'll—"

"Hey, boss," Matt called out.

Evan turned toward the tent's outer room. "Come on in."

Matt ambled in, a jeweled sword balanced in his hands. He glanced at Anna, then focused on Evan, as usual. Though she'd gotten her doctorate the year after her brother, Anna had been in the field more than Evan had, but archeology was still considered a man's world in many ways. As such, Matt still deferred to Evan. Evan's students had a reason to defer to him, but Matt didn't.

Thank goodness for Adam, Emil, and Julia. At least those three remembered who the lead archeologist on the dig was.

"What is it, Matt?" she asked, a subtle reminder that Matt answered to her, not Evan. Three years age advantage and a Y chromosome were not prerequisites of being lead archeologist.

"Down in the...ah...chamber..." He shifted uncomfortably, his eyes flicking back and forth between them again.

Evan crossed his arms over his chest, staring Matt down, demanding an answer silently.

"After Anna...fell..."

Annoyance that he was giving his report to Evan almost overwhelmed her amusement at Matt's diplomatic handling of what had happened in the tomb.

"She said something. It sounded...sounded like Amunmeruka, but it c—"

"Amunmaruku," she corrected coolly.

His eyes widened, and his face paled several shades. Matt stared at her, clearing his throat.

Evan ambled to him, taking the sword from Matt's hands. He turned it, examining it, his color rising more than the few shades Matt had lost. After a few minutes, he handed it back and murmured something that sent Matt scrambling away.

The zipper sounded far too loud in the resulting silence.

The half sandwich she'd managed sat like a clay brick in her stomach. Anna set the rest aside, missing it, though she knew she'd only make herself sick if she attempted to eat more.

He didn't look at her, though his voice carried a wealth of inferred expression. "Is this the Valley of Kings all over again, Anna?"

"No. Trust me, this is totally different." She grimaced at the lie. The sexual dreams might be new, but the rest was all too familiar.

"Good. Because, if you start shouting dead languages and rattling off stories like you did at Tamekyn's tomb—"

"What? You can't send me back to America like Dad did, Evan. I'm the lead—"

He turned on her, his eyes hard in decision. "I can have you removed."

"Only if you can prove I'm unfit."

Evan seemed to consider that. "One more dizzy spell or fainting spell and—"

"I haven't fainted." *That you know about.* The fainting spells and blackouts were definitely something Evan didn't need to know about.

"That I know of," he stated simply.

Anna bit back her natural responses to being caught in a lie. Evan stared at her, probably waiting for her to slip up. Finally, he sighed.

"One more, Anna, and I'll force you back to Cairo for a full medical work-up. Understood?"

She swallowed down her frustration. "Understood. Now, if you'll excuse me, I'll get that ordered rest."

Evan hesitated, confusion etched on his face. "Okay," he managed. He turned her lantern off and headed for the doorway. "Good night, Anna. Sleep well."

Sent to bed like a toddler. Damn this! "Night." *What night?* It wasn't even dark yet.

Chapter Two

It happened suddenly, as it always did. One moment, Anna was stretching out on her bunk, clad in a t-shirt and underwear. The next, she was in "the room."

Anna knew every inch of it, from the murals on the walls to the table laden with fruit and wine, from the personal possessions of Amunmaruku to the bed they'd soon be sharing.

She took a moment to admire herself. One of the things she could never anticipate was her clothing.

Tonight's variation wasn't the pleated linen kalasiris that reached neck to ankle, or even the silk kalasiris with the matching circular cape. This time, it was a simple linen kalasiris that cupped her breasts up, leaving them uncovered. Straps of the same material hugged the outside of her chest, pressing in slightly to accentuate her cleavage.

Anticipating Amun's appreciation, her nipples hardened in the room air, inviting him.

"Yes, they do," he agreed.

Anna whirled to him, her eyes straying from his bare, shaven head to the tented front of his shenti. It was a simple white with gold thread woven in at the edges, beneath his station she felt, though Anna would never tell Amun so.

Well, Dea-ana wouldn't. That meant Anna wouldn't, since she was hindered by the other woman's sensibilities.

His hand stroked at his cock through the material covering it. "You want to see it?" he tempted.

"Oh, yes."

Amun ambled toward her, his bare feet whispering over the stone. Without conscious plan, Anna found herself backing to the bed, slower than he was approaching, so the press from the front and the rear came simultaneously.

He drew her hands to the tie on his shenti silently, ordering Anna to remove it. She untied the linen then uncinched the girdle, pulling them away and tossing them to the bed.

Her hands stopped, millimeters from touching him. As many times as they'd shared themselves in dreams, it seemed incongruous that she'd hesitate to touch him, but she always did, until he gave her permission to do so.

No...until he gave Dea-ana permission to touch him.

When Amun remained silent, Anna panned her gaze up to meet his, unable to beg for the electric skin-to-skin contact in any way but in her expression.

The hard lines of his face softened, and one hand came up, cupping her breast, his thumb feathering back and forth over her beaded nipple, sending waves of delight through her. Anna eased her hands away from his body, taking his move as an order not to touch him.

"I should have dressed you like this long ago," he murmured, his eyes hot in promise.

"But I am..." What was she? Beneath him? Any woman was beneath him; he could have any woman he wished.

Something niggled at her consciousness, something disturbing she couldn't name. It was more than that. Anna was even further beneath Amun than other women were.

Beneath him? Good gods, I'm a twenty-first century woman having dream sex with an Egyptian prince from an indeterminate time period, most probably 2500 BCE or so. I'm more than beneath him; I'm either insane or in some anachronistic hallucination brought on by my psychometry, half-immersed in the mind of a woman dead for three or more thousand years.

"Enough," Amun ordered. His hand left her breast and fisted in her shoulder-length, unbound hair, pulling her to her toes as his mouth covered hers.

The kiss was hard and demanding, driving the doubts and arguments from her mind. Dream or psychometry, Anna didn't care.

No woman refuses the prince.

His mouth left hers, his ragged breathing mixing his air with hers. "You wish to refuse me?" It wasn't a challenge. It seemed an honest question.

A shaft of fear shot through their shared heart. "No, Amun. I would never—"

"I didn't ask if you would. I asked if you wanted to."

Memories of the first dream coursed through her mind, followed by the second...the third... "No." The fact that the one she inhabited—the body and soul she shared in the dreams—wanted Amun aside, the part that was undeniably Anna wanted him.

His smile was devastating, and his fingers stroked along her cheek. "Tamekyn never counted on you."

The vertigo his American euphemisms and accent typically caused her was overpowered by a spike of fear...of panic. Her heart raced, and her head spun.

"Tamekyn," she breathed. Why did everything come back to Tamekyn?

"Dea-ana, no!" Amun crushed her to his ready body, his expression one of stark terror. "Do not take us there again."

In the next instant, he was gone, and Anna was stumbling forward, righting a tray that was tipping precariously.

"Clumsy," a voice she vaguely recognized chided her.

Anna turned, stunned, to face an older woman dressed in a sleeveless knee-length kalasiris and collar that announced her station in life, the head servant in charge of the kitchens. Her hair was long and dyed a rich burgundy to hide the strands of gray.

A moment later, Anna's own nudity struck her solidly. A hundred small braids stroked her bare shoulders, tangling with heavy earrings. Other than the earrings, the only thing she wore was a light chain at her waist.

She stared at it for a long moment, a pleasant shiver working down her spine at the memories of the hanging jewel Amunmaruku sometimes placed on it, the jewel that would tease at her body while he played with her.

"Move on," the head ordered. "I cannot see why the prince tolerates you."

Heat rose in her cheeks. Amunmaruku's seductions and games were no secret from the head, but dare she believe it stayed his hand? He was a god with hungers, and she amused him...for a time. She rushed down the corridor, reminding herself that she would cease to amuse him someday. It was one of the unpleasant facts she secretly hoped never to face.

A few male servants and guards shot appreciative glances at her that she pretended not to notice. It was her state of undress, she knew. They all knew why she was clothed in such a manner.

The prince could afford to dress his personal servants in finery, and he usually did. Her lack of clothing had nothing to do with his ability to clothe her, or her willingness to be clothed, and everything to do with his interest in seeing her unclothed...and to take advantage of that state.

Had Dea-ana not known Amunmaruku was entertaining, she might have believed he meant to play with her again. Knowing he had a guest, she straightened and hurried along, smoothing her hair with one hand so as to reflect well on her master.

In his rooms, she worked quickly and efficiently, laying out the food and wine with hardly a sound. From beyond the drape, she heard the deep rumble of Amunmaruku's voice.

"A gift for me? How intriguing."

The answering laugh was feminine and all too knowing. Just the sound of it made Dea-ana's stomach flutter uncomfortably.

"A willing gift, I assure you," she purred.

"Hmmm...I would be rude to refuse my brother's gift to me."

Dea-ana hesitated, the serving tray held to her breasts. She'd been summoned to serve Amunmaruku and his guest. Whether she cared to hear their passion or not, she was bound to serve them.

As if motioned to being by her thoughts, the unmistakable sounds of their foreplay pierced the curtain between the rooms. Dea-ana fisted one hand, pressing it to her belly, forcing her breathing to a more natural rhythm.

He was a prince, a god among mortals, someday to be Pharaoh. Amunmaruku had to take a queen and consorts worthy of his station. So far, he'd refused; that could not continue forever. A low consort or two would hardly be refused him; a low queen was inexcusable.

She'd always known that, of course. Dea-ana had simply...foolishly never believed she'd be forced to witness his duty fulfilled.

And so enjoyably, she thought bitterly.

What? You believed he only made those sounds for you? With you?

Dea-ana would happily have gone to the ibu thinking that was true.

She set the platter down and started straightening the room, miserably trying to ignore their love play. The mussed cushions beckoned, and she knelt to them, grasping one at random.

The snap of power coursing from her fingertips inward rocked her head back. Dea-ana had felt it before but never this powerfully. Her eyes slid shut, and the vision took her.

She was lounging on the cushions, playing at the circular cape over her shoulders, providing tempting glances of her bare breasts to Amunmaruku. The man in question moved closer, and her eyes strayed to his rising cock.

Good. Just as we'd hoped.

He reached out and flipped the cape up, uncovering them, his hand cupping one heavy globe, bringing the nipple up. She moaned, but it was a fake moan.

Not as talented as Tamekyn, but all the better that I retain my balance.

"If you intend seduction," Amunmaruku stated, "you are wasting your time."

A slice of unwelcome fear played at her senses. Confusion followed. What could he mean by that? Surely, he had no idea why she was here or who had sent her.

"Seduction is for the untouched or unattainable. You have only to make your wishes known. Why play at possibilities when we could seize the known?"

An honest smile broke out on her face. *It is simply too easy.* "Very well then. I want you."

Amunmaruku chuckled darkly. "Say it again, and we will move to my bed..." His head cocked to one side. "Where you can tell me what has brought you to me so boldly."

"I want you."

He rose and offered his hand to help her to her feet.

I want you dead, and at the height of your pleasure, Tamekyn and I will be ripened for the throne.

Dea-ana tossed the cushion aside, staggering to her feet, dazed as she always was when she came out of a vision.

The sounds from Amunmaruku's bed shook her mind right. Dea-ana knew his sounds intimately. He was close, which meant the other woman would soon strike.

She half-tripped to the drape, her heart pounding, prayers that she wouldn't fail him spinning sickly in her mind. Halfway through, Amunmaruku's climax crested. The sight of the slim dagger arcing down sent a scream of Amunmaruku's name from Dea-ana's lips.

The rest passed in something of a blur. Amunmaruku's eyes flew open and he jerked toward sitting beneath his attacker. The assassin's head snapped around. The two combined sent her blade into his shoulder rather than the center of his chest.

Amunmaruku fell back with a cry of pain that wrenched at Dea-ana's heart. The assassin raised the dagger again, and Dea-ana was in motion without another thought.

She grasped up a short sword, crossing the room with a battle cry. The other woman turned on her, still impaled on Amunmaruku's length, hampered in movement by his body between her thighs.

They struck together, Dea-ana's blow, poorly-executed as it was, slicing a line along the side of the assassin's throat, sending her sprawling toward the floor. The counter-strike landed a heartbeat later, the full length of the shorter blade into the soft meat of Dea-ana's belly.

Dea-ana crumpled, the sword falling from her fingers. She groaned at the jarring stop and yank of hands, landing on the bed beside Amunmaruku. The last image of the assassin to pass by her was the blood pulsing from her neck, while she jerked and spasmed on the floor.

Then Amunmaruku was over her, his expression pained. "Why?" he breathed. "Why did you risk yourself?"

Tears misted her eyes, half in pain and half in misery of the heart. She loved him, but such a love was beneath him...beneath his notice.

His hand cupped her jaw and his thumb played along her lower lip. "Do not lie to me, Dea-ana. You do not lie well."

She tried to avert her eyes, but that brought her gaze to his blood-covered chest. Dea-ana tried to staunch the flow with her hands, crying out in dismay when it seeped around.

"I never knew you returned the feeling," he mused.

Tears of joy rolled down her cheeks, and a sob brought new pains to her body and soul. He knew. He loved her, as well, and now it was too late for her...but perhaps not for him. If they worked quickly—

"You knew," he pressed her. "You came here to save me."

"I failed you," she hitched out. "The vision came too late."

"Vision? Of the future?" His eyes lit in interest.

"The past. Her diseased mind. Her plot with—" Her breathing hitched.

"Tamekyn," he growled. Amunmaruku seemed far away for a moment then focused on her. "He will pay a traitor's penalty," he vowed.

His blood coating Dea-ana's hands reminded her that she could not lose sight of the near future, as she sometimes did. It was connected to her ability to see the past, she was certain. They were wasting time. "We must call for a—"

"The blood canal leaks. I have seen it. Nothing can be done for me."

Dea-ana choked on sobs. It was bad enough that he'd been injured. He would not survive the day, if—

"Say it," he demanded.

She stared at him, lost for his meaning. Say what words? What could he possibly mean?

"Speak the words. Tell me you love me now, and there is still hope for us both."

"What hope?" she stammered. Did he mean to take her to the afterlife with him?

"We can live again, Dea-ana. But to speak the spells and make the proper alliances with my brother and sister gods in time, I must have your words now."

She nodded. "I love you, Amunmaruku. I will love you always."

"And I love you. I have loved you since the moment I saw you first. I will love only you, for all eternity."

What followed was a rush of words and incantations Dea-ana's exhausted mind couldn't hope to unravel. Darkness took her, Amunmaruku's body the warmth she clung to when all else went cold.

* * * *

Anna woke on the floor of one of the shower stalls, curled in a ball, her hands pressed to the diminishing pains in her abdomen. She shivered, uncharacteristically chilled. She'd swear her lips were blue with cold, and her teeth chattered.

Levering herself up took every ounce of her remaining strength, and Anna grasped at the wall, seeking balance. She scrubbed her skin dry with a rough towel, trying to banish the image of being covered in the blood of three people, bathed in death.

The clothing on the bench wasn't what she'd been wearing in bed. Anna stared at them, trying to right the fractured realities. How did she get here? When did she change clothes?

She sank to the bench, her stomach in knots. This was too much to attribute to sleepwalking.

"I'm losing my mind," she whispered. "I don't know how I got here."

Other incidences played at the edges of her consciousness: sand in her boots at odd times, bruises she couldn't remember earning, an extra set of dirty clothing, a wet towel when she hadn't showered...

"What is happening to me?"

There was no answer for that. Numb in body and soul, she pulled her clothes and boots on.

The blue-gray line of coming dawn met her aching, gritty eyes. Anna stared at it, weary to the point of collapse, certain that she hadn't slept at all.

The hair at the nape of her neck rose in warning, and her heart took up a choppy rhythm. Someone was watching her...back, to the left...there.

Anna whirled, noting the rising wind and the sound of canvas. Were it not for the gentle sway and crack of a loose tent flap, she might have believed she'd imagined it.

Fresh tracks led from the cataloguing tent toward the bunk tents, boots as they all wore. Tracking them would be a waste; already, the wind and shifting sand had all but eradicated the trail.

Chapter Three

"Have you ever seen anything more beautiful?" Evan asked.

Yes. Anna shook her head, forcing back memories of Amun's face at climax to focus on the stone easing the final distance that would allow them entrance to the burial chamber.

The thought of entering the room had her both squirming in excitement and queasy. Were it not for the certainty that Amun was not resting in peace, she'd feign illness to escape rather than disturb his tomb.

But he was most certainly not at peace. Amun needed her, and perhaps Anna would know what he needed once they breached the burial chamber.

A cheer startled her back to the present, and Anna placed a hand on Evan's arm, stopping his step forward. He shot her a questioning look.

"Lead archeologist's perk," she teased. "I get to go first."

Her brother's smile widened. "How you ever got lead over me..."

"That's simple. I'm smarter than you." *And he was teaching, which meant I was on site to make the find, taking a long weekend from my studies of Tamekyn.*

Everything comes back to Tamekyn.

Evan's smile faded. "You be careful in there."

Anna managed a brittle smile and a nod that made her rioting stomach more vocal.

"We're ready, Anna," Matt offered, his hand extended, a large flashlight gripped in it.

Evan is 'boss,' and I'm 'Anna.' She pushed that annoyance away, taking the light, hoping no one noticed her shaking hands as she made her way to the opening.

This was a ceremony of sorts, the one time they broke with protocol. Typically, lights were set up and exhaustive photographs taken. Items were tagged with what they were and their respective locations in the room before being moved.

This one time, Anna would enter alone and revel in the moment. For the next few minutes, she would be the only living soul to see what they'd uncovered. Then the others would do the same, and the work would begin.

Her light beam played over the bed first. It hardly seemed possible to miss it, between the massive structure and what lay upon it. Dreamed memories pulled at her, comparisons that made her head pound.

It can't be the same bed.

"Anna?" Evan called out.

She shifted, her light swinging to the left...to a painting she knew as well as she did the bed. "It's impossible," she whispered. Anna turned, focusing up and down, anticipating everything she'd see, in advance of their appearances in the circle of LED glow.

When the bed loomed before her again, she stopped, lightheaded. "They recreated it perfectly."

"Anna?" Evan's voice was closer, inside the chamber.

She ambled closer to the bed, shining her light down on the two mummies, laid out side-by-side. Amun's was to the right, his gold death mask and larger form making his identity clear. The mummy to the left was undoubtedly Dea-ana, preserved as carefully as her lover was, but with a death mask of linen.

"He's royal," Evan half-laughed. He repeated it on a shout for the rest of the crew outside.

Cat calls and clapping filtered back into the burial chamber.

"He's Tamekyn's brother," Anna imparted. "And she..." *Is me...or someone I am tied to.* "is Dea-ana, his chosen consort." She turned and walked away before he could question her, giving the nod to enter to the crew on her way past. Anna was in the corridor, before the first took her seriously.

* * * *

Anna tossed and turned on her bunk, for the first time in months, unable to sleep and dream.

She supposed it could be the stress affecting her. The discussion with Evan, after he'd realized she'd left the tomb and had followed her out, hadn't been the most pleasant they'd shared.

Anna had told more lies in an hour than she'd told in the rest of her young life combined. She'd claimed she'd come across mention of Amunmaruku in her studies of Tamekyn. She'd feigned exasperation that she couldn't remember which of the countless sources had contained it. She'd delivered an abbreviated recap of Tamekyn's plot to murder his older brother, the subsequent uprising within the royal household that had taken Tamekyn's life, and the unusual orders Amunmaruku had made before his death. Then she'd capped it all off with faking enthusiasm for dinner.

Even now, Anna had to constantly remind herself that, with the volume of ancient writings in existence, it would be impossible for Evan to prove she was lying to him. His suspicions aside, Evan was Evan. He wouldn't force her hand without proof that she was relying on her psychometry and not book knowledge.

One would think the ability to see the history of objects and who'd held them would be a useful skill for an archeologist to possess...and it would, if she could control it and it worked more reliably. But Anna's abilities came and went of their own accord, though they were strongest around the trio of Amunmaruku, Dea-ana, and Tamekyn.

Visions of the bed in the tomb danced behind her closed eyelids. It couldn't be the real bed, she assured herself. They had to have recreated it. If it were the one from Amun's chamber...

How much pain would it contain? Both of their deaths, at least. And how much pleasure? How many times had Amunmaruku and Dea-ana shared that bed?

I have to know.

Anna pushed from the bunk, pulling a pair of jersey cotton pants over her panties. She decided her t-shirt would suffice, passed on her boots, and padded barefoot across the still-warm sand to the entrance, a flashlight in hand.

"Evening, Dr. Hastings," Mo, one of the night guards, intoned.

She nodded a greeting and stepped between him and his counterpart, a young man from Evan's class named Louis.

The corridors were lit by electric lights, powered by the two large generators outside 24/7, but those lights hadn't been extended into the burial chamber yet. That chore had been left for the morning.

Anna hesitated in the doorway to the chamber, wiping her sweating palms on the knit. Could she do this? Could she watch Amun die again, just to satisfy her curiosity?

"It's not curiosity. I have to know."

Anna switched on the flashlight and padded inside. The bed dominated the room, more so than it had in the dreams...or maybe that was her mind playing tricks on her. Placing one foot in front of the other in something of a daze, she made her way to it.

"Anna, no."

Her shuffling feet went still at the order, and her hand retreated a few inches. Anna stared at the bed, so close she could touch it without moving another step.

"No." His voice was closer, stirring the short wisps of hair that escaped her ponytail.

She closed her eyes at the press of his body to hers, swallowing down a moan. "I'm crazy." The dreams were bad enough; the phantom sounds and scents in her waking moments were worse. Now she was feeling him in the present...awake. "Am I awake?" How could she be sure?

Amun's hand closed around her slightly-outstretched hand, drawing it back to her thigh. "Thankfully, yes," he replied simply.

"I don't understand," she admitted.

His lips pressed to the back of her neck and he inhaled deeply, shuddering against her back. "I've waited so long to feel you in my arms...conscious..."

His lips brushed up the line of her vertebrae. "Aware... Dreams of you are not enough."

"Why are you here?" It came out rasping, the verbal equivalent of the raw need eating at her.

In answer, he straightened, his face brushing up the side of her head, tugging lightly at her bound hair. His hand plucked at the waistline of her pants. At her moan of acceptance, it slid beneath, then inside her panties.

The first touch of his fingers on her clit had her gasping for breath, tipping her head back onto his shoulder. The flashlight slipped from her boneless fingers, clattering to the floor, then rolling.

"Are you going to send me away?" It was whispered against her ear, more than an invitation, less than a demand.

"Never." She'd always had a problem with refusing Amun, but this was even more pressing than usual. It was rare to see this side of the ancient prince. This was the side she'd never been able to resist.

His hand retreated, and he turned her toward him, capturing Anna's mouth in a searing kiss. Her hands flattened against the heated flesh of his chest, and she stroked downward, freed to be bold by the lack of Deaana's mind muddling her own.

Amun grasped her by the wrists, nestling her hands to her back, dragging her closer to his body. The kiss was fevered, drugging... She wanted him inside her.

His mouth parted from hers, and Amun took a step back, releasing her wrists. "Get these damned clothes off," he growled.

Anna opened her eyes, locking on the indistinct shadow that was Amun, her mouth going dry at the faint movements that were probably signs of him untying his shenti. The blood coursing in her ears, coupled with her pounding heart, drowned out all other sound.

"Anna," he grumbled.

She nodded. Though she was certain Amun could see no more of her than she could of him, Anna made a show of disrobing, peeling off each piece of clothing slowly, heated nearly to discomfort by the idea of him watching.

When she'd kicked away her panties, Anna took a step toward him. Amun met her halfway, his slightly-roughened hands exploring her, his mouth meshing with and parting from hers, again and again.

Anna couldn't have recounted how they made it to the floor. One moment, they were grasping at each other. The next, her head was pillowed on her pants, Amun's weight pressing her down into the smooth, sand-dusted stone.

The cum-wet crown of his cock brushed at her inner thigh, and she pressed up, seeking more. The first thrust wrenched a sob of delight from her. He'd been right; dreams were not enough.

Amun paused, a guttural sound escaping his lips. "So long," he breathed.

Anna nodded, her air processing too unsettled to make a verbal response.

"Say you're mine." It wasn't a demand.

"Yours... Always...just yours."

His thrusts came hard and fast, a palpable demonstration that it was so. Amun possessed her, body and soul, cementing the bonds already forged between them in the dreams.

He collected her hands from his back, one at a time, threading his fingers through hers, pinning her hands to the floor, driving into her.

A vague recollection of Amun doing the same to Dea-ana when he learned she was virginal flitted in her mind, and Anna shook it away, greedy for this experience as her own, untainted by the mind of the mummified servant that lay a scarce body-length from her own.

Entrenched firmly in her own mind, Anna's senses scattered; her body burned in the precursors of climax. Their sweat-soaked bodies moved together. Their breath mingled.

And then it crashed over her, sweet waves of bliss. Anna fisted her hands in his, little more than half-aware of Amun's climax, of his heat flooding her.

His weight settled over her more fully, his lips exploring her forehead. "I love you, Anna. I have loved you since the moment I first saw you."

Any answer she might have formulated was lost in a gasp of surprise.

* * * *

Her back sank into the mattress, and the abrupt light was blinding. Anna squeezed her eyes shut, searching for balance in her shifting perceptions.

Amun was still inside her, but they weren't in the burial chamber anymore. Why were they in the dream space? Had she passed out again? Touched the bed accidentally and launched herself into a vision of Dea-ana?

"Only you, small one," he replied in that disconcerting manner he had of answering her thoughts...or those of Dea-ana.

Anna opened her eyes, blinking several times while they adjusted to the abrupt glare. He was right. She didn't sense Dea-ana's mind, mixing with her own. Why would Amun want her without Dea-ana?

"There are things my Dea-ana does not need to hear. There are places and...realities that would frighten her, were she to learn of them."

She tried to digest that. Dea-ana wasn't aware of what was happening, but Amun was?

"You have questions," he stated, a slight smile curving one side of his mouth up further than the other.

"Am I Dea-ana reincarnated?"

Amun sighed, pushing up on one elbow to look down at her. "Your understanding is somewhat limited, so it might seem so. It would be more appropriate to say that her body was reborn for you, and your souls share something of an affinity...one for the other, caused by the shared physical form."

"The gods in your mastaba—"

"Are not of a single time and place," he finished for her. "At my birth, the seers and priests knew my gift of foresight. I could see things hidden from mortal eyes. So, I was named Amunmaruku."

The pieces were starting to come together. "You saw the gods before their times."

He captured her mouth in a quick kiss. "You always were a clever one. Yes. I had to know which to bargain with, after all."

Her heart stuttered at that pronouncement. "Bargain with for what?"

"For what was stolen from me."

Anna shook her head, conflicted. "Amun... I don't know how to tell you this, but there are no more Pharaohs. There is no dynasty, though Egypt still exists."

A scowl turned his lips down and creased his brow. "There are more important things than a throne, young one. I knew I'd never be Pharaoh. I knew my dear brother wouldn't live to see it, either. That is why I lived to please myself and not others."

"Then what—" The inscriptions undulated sickly before her eyes, making her head pound in a drum beat. *We shall live again.* "You wish to be reborn."

He laughed heartily at that. "I already have that wish."

"What do you—"

"Enough questions," Amun dismissed her.

"But—"

Anna was ripped away, falling though darkness.

* * * *

"Anna! Anna, answer me, please."

Her lips moved to form her brother's name, but no sound emerged. Her entire body ached, though she couldn't say why it would. Anna felt sticky...but chilled, as if she'd broken out in a cold sweat. As if in confirmation, her clothing clung to her skin.

"How long has she been here?"

Matt's voice pierced the fog in her head. "Hours. Long enough for her flashlight to go all-but dead. Mo said she came in late last night, while I was working in chamber four, but I didn't hear her come past."

Something wrapped around her body, and Anna pushed weakly at it.

"Was anyone else in here then?" Evan pressed.

"In and out. James, Adam, Emily, Emil..."

"All at night? Why?"

"We were all restless," Matt offered. "At least, James and Emily said the same, when I asked them."

James and Emily were probably together. If she didn't hurt so badly, Anna would have giggled at that thought.

Evan lifted her, and Anna settled against his chest, looking forward to her bunk.

"What's the plan, boss?" Matt asked.

"Bring our SUV around. I'm taking her in to be checked."

"You don't think someone hurt her, do you?"

Evan hesitated for a long moment, long enough to make Anna squirm in his arms at the rising tension in him.

"No, but either way—"

Anna slipped back into sleep, lulled by his even gait.

Chapter Four

"Miss Hastings?" a lightly-accented male voice rumbled.

"*Doctor* Hastings," she half-yawned the rebuke. Anna stretched, going still in the realization that her clothes had been replaced with a shift and nothing beneath it.

She forced her eyes open, searching out a native face a few decades older than her own. Over his shoulder, she could see Evan, looking weary and stressed.

"Ahhh, much better," the doctor stated with an easy smile. "As I said, Doctor... This is rather awkward, isn't it?"

"Call me Evan," her brother grumbled.

Anna swallowed down a bit of the sour taste in her mouth. "Anna," she added simply.

The doctor nodded. "As I said, Evan, Anna simply needs rest and food. Physically, she's in good form."

"Told you," Anna quipped.

"You could have told me you were pregnant, too," Evan snapped.

The blood rushed from Anna's head so abruptly she felt certain she was going to faint again. Her heart pounded, and confusing facts warred in her mind. The previous night, if it was real, was the first time in a year she'd had sex. You couldn't get pregnant in a dream. Could you?

But had they been dreams? Anna couldn't say for certain what they were. She'd been blacking out, after all. How could she know what she'd done in those lost hours?

But still... Pregnant? "I'm what?" she managed weakly.

The doctor called a halt as simply as scooping her wrist up and taking Anna's pulse. After a moment of silence, it started to slow.

"Better." He placed her hand on the bed again. "Now... You must have missed your menses by now, Anna. At least once."

She considered that and came up with a blank. "I haven't been paying attention to anything but the dig."

"Certainly not to birth control," Evan complained.

Her face heated at that. *Who knew you could get pregnant in a dream? A dream that might not have been a dream,* she reminded herself.

Then...who was the father? Did Amun plan this? Was this what he meant? Was she carrying his...regeneration? The paintings of Sebek and Min taunted her with the possibility. And what would she do, if it were true?

"Who is the father?" Even pressed, echoing at least one of her own concerns.

That one was a mine field. If she admitted Amunmaruku had fathered her child— *Did he, somehow?* If she did, it was all over. Evan would justifiably believe she was insane. If she didn't...

What will he do when no man on the dig pans out? Evan knows I haven't left the dig site in months. I can't be that far along.

Worse, what if one of the men on site is the father and knows it, and I have no memory of it? This was enough to drive a sane person over the edge.

"Anna, if it's one of my students—"

"They aren't *my* students, and they're all adults," she defended herself blindly against the accusation. "And not all of them are your students either. Emil and Adam came in from other programs. Even if—"

"Translation, it *is* one of the students," he concluded.

Anna glared at him, caught between the urge to deny it and the urge to tell him to go to hell. She'd like to deny she'd screwed anyone on the dig crew, but what options were there?

The door opened, and someone stomped in. For a moment, Anna and Evan stayed locked in their standoff, largely ignoring the new arrival.

He looked away first, his eyes widening. "Adam? What are you do—" Evan's jaw tightened, and he turned a fresh glare on Anna.

She swiveled her head to apologize for her brother's behavior...and stopped cold, her heart skipping in surprise. Her gaze did a long, slow appraisal, confirming her first impression of him.

Had she ever looked at Adam before? Had she ever met his dark eyes directly? It seemed impossible that she had, because the likeness was unmistakable. From his height and build to his facial features and—now that she could admit it to herself—his voice, he was Amun all over again.

The baby isn't Amunmaruku. Adam is.

That brought a world of questions, but the time for answers wasn't with Evan and a medical doctor hanging on every word.

In the time it took her to progress to that conclusion, Adam was on the edge of the mattress, one hand planted over her head and the other beside her hip, holding himself just over her, while he plundered her mouth. Anna met him avidly, starved for him, though by conscious record, they'd had the hottest sex of her life in the burial chamber the night before.

His scent washed over her, bringing memories of a thousand kisses, a hundred dreams. Had the "phantom scents of Amun" been Adam, all along? Part of her sincerely hoped so.

He drew away, far enough to meet her gaze. "When I got out of the shower and heard... I shouldn't have listened to you when you said you wanted to stay a little longer. I should have stayed and made sure you were all right."

She smiled, blinking back tears. The relief that he remembered it was a new high, though no other reason for his presence here presented itself. In some way, though there were no answers for what had happened between them, the idea that she'd been meeting Adam for sex was much more appealing than sex with a dead Egyptian prince.

Adam cocked his head to one side, seemingly studying her. "Are you all right?"

Anna nodded, laughter bubbling up.

"She's pregnant," Evan inserted acidly.

Adam didn't balk at that. It didn't appear to trouble or even shock him. A smile lit his eyes, and he moved the hand next to her hip to caress her lower abdomen, setting off an arousal he couldn't sate in a room full of people.

"I know," Adam replied to the accusation. He lowered his head and pressed his lips to the shell of her ear, whispering the rest. "I've seen them. They're beautiful."

"Them?" she breathed back.

Adam retreated, nodding his agreement.

"I hate to sound old-fashioned," Evan drawled, "but what are your intentions toward my sister, Adam?"

"Evan!" Anna swallowed an entire rant about where he could shove his over-protective older brother gene.

Adam cupped her chin, drawing Anna's gaze back to him. "I believe you agreed to marry me last night," he hinted.

Words deserted her for a long moment. "I don't believe the actual word was used."

"I only do forever one way," he countered.

Anna forced her breathing to even. "Got a ring?" she managed.

Adam sighed. "Like you, I haven't taken time away from the dig site, so...sadly, regrettably no. I suggest we spring you and take care of the formalities."

"Doctor..." Anna took a calming breath. "If you're done with me, I think I'd like to leave now."

The older man's knowing smile said it all.

* * * *

The hotel room door closed behind them, and Adam swept her into his arms again, enjoying the length of her body against his. Anna panted out his name, arching against him.

My name. Gods, but sharing Amunmaruku's mind, while Anna was calling for the other man, had almost driven him completely insane.

Half the problem was his precognition, of course. Adam had been dreaming of Anna since he'd been a preteen having wet dreams. He'd known her, when he'd seen her picture on the dust jacket of her book on the second dynasty. He'd jockeyed to get a spot on her dig.

Knowing Anna would be his and being forced to let her believe— No, she had been experiencing Amun, on some level. She'd been sleeping with them both, though she hadn't known it.

Worse, she'd been so immersed in her work, in her waking hours, that there'd been no opportunity to form a relationship away from the damned interloper.

And she'd seemed so unaffected by their nocturnal activities that Adam hadn't known what to make of her. Aside from the day they'd found the burial chamber, when her arousal had taunted him, he'd believed she wasn't experiencing the dreams...or wasn't remembering them.

"I...I have questions," she managed.

"Do I get to answer them like Amun did?" Adam didn't want it to sound defensive, but he failed on that one.

Her head came back, and she stared at him, seemingly hurt. "You're jealous? Or are you angry?"

"Jealous. Angry...at him, not you."

"Should I be jealous or angry that you were with Dea-ana?"

"But I wasn't. It was always you for me. And...Amunmaruku was the jealous sort. He kept a wall between Dea-ana and me. Actually, he kept a light partition between you and Dea-ana."

"There were things he thought would upset her," she replied, seemingly lost in thought.

Adam tossed the bag containing fresh clothes for them away, considering that. "Yes. She didn't know. He didn't want her to know how he was giving them their rebirth. He knew she couldn't handle the modern world or sharing Amun with you."

"Knew?"

"You forget...or maybe you never knew that Amun and I have precog abilities."

Anna winced. "And I have psychometry. You were looking forward, and I was looking back. Evan always accused that I'm blind to the present and heedless of the future."

Adam digested that. "You were blind to me?" He knew she tended not to see anyone but her brother, but he'd never considered that she hadn't known Adam existed.

"Not entirely. You certainly affected me, but I... I didn't look. Maybe I thought it wasn't professional to get involved with another member of my dig."

"As it was unacceptable for Amunmaruku and Dea-ana to love each other?" he challenged. He knew she thought that poetic.

She darkened. "Adam, I—"

"It happens all the time," he argued. "Dig crew—"

"Not to me."

That simply, she disarmed him. Adam chuckled, then laughed. "I'm glad to hear it."

"If I'd looked, so much more would have made sense."

Adam headed for the bed, guiding her backward toward it, confused by her statement. "Like?" What would have made sense?

"When Amun said he already had been reborn. If I'd ever dared look at you, I'd have realized what he meant. As it was, I didn't know what...and then the baby and—"

He settled her on the bed. "Babies," he reminded her. They were two beautiful baby girls, this time. Adam resisted, as he always did, the urge to look further and see if he'd ever have a son. He suspected he would someday.

"Babies. I still don't understand him."

Adam settled on the edge of the mattress, looking down at her as he had in the hospital. He toed off his untied boots, then started on the sandals they'd bought her in the hospital gift shop. "What don't you understand? I spent a lot of time in his head...or with him in mine, I guess."

"What was he gaining? Not me, if I'm really with you." She pressed a hand to her eyes. "Oh, that sounds demented." Her hand retreated, and Anna levered up on her elbows. "He's gone, right? I mean, it's not going to be both of you, for the rest of our lives." She bit at her lower lip, shifting as if discomfited. "It won't, will it?"

Her discomfort at the idea warmed him. Adam tossed the second sandal away and crawled up beside her, fitting Anna to his body.

"What?" she asked, her voice wavering a bit.

"I am so glad you don't want us to share you." Glad didn't begin to cover it. Adam was ecstatic that she didn't want it.

"It's hard enough to wrap my mind around the idea that the two of you shared me before."

He raised an eyebrow at her double standard.

"I thought it was psychometry. I thought I wasn't really there, but I was there enough to argue what was happening. To tell the truth..."

"Yes?" he prompted her.

"I was confused as hell, and it wasn't like I could ask anyone." Exhaustion and misery played at her expression.

"Evan—"

"Acts like it's the unofficial eleventh plague of Egypt."

A smile pulled up at his lips at that thought. "Well, rest assured that it wasn't my idea to share you. I still want to knock the mummy's remaining teeth out." That did sound tempting, if for no other reason to take out his fury on Amun in a physical sense.

"But why share me?" Her frustration leaked out around the edges. "Either play with me in dreams or give me to you...soul or body."

Adam laid a kiss at her temple, formulating an answer to that one. "He's Egyptian. Both are necessary. Besides, he couldn't very well arrange the babies without me, could he? You need the body to—"

"Which is another question," she interrupted him.

"What is?"

Anna slid over him, laying her forehead to his throat. "How do you get pregnant in dreams?"

"You don't."

Her breathing went harsh, the only sound in the room for a moment. "I don't understand."

But she did, and that might turn out to be a problem, precog or no precog telling him she'd come to terms with it somehow. "Do you remember dressing last night? After the burial chamber?"

Her eyes unfocused, and her brow furrowed in deep thought. "No. I don't. But...I was dressed this morning. You didn't—"

"Not to my knowledge. I don't remember pulling my shorts back on either, but I've come to expect that.

"I imagine Amunmaruku would have had us perform completely unaware, if he could. Or maybe not. How would he get what he wanted, if neither of us had any memory of what was going on?

"Either way, it wasn't possible. I imagine the body has to experience the sexual stimuli to perform, and the mind cannot be completely unaware of it and still function. I had to be at least minimally aware of what we were doing, as you did."

"Amun was there last night? In the burial chamber?" The thought seemed to horrify her.

"Gods, no. The bastard had to interrupt a precious moment, though."

"Okay," she breathed. "But the other times?"

"I'd find myself places...the desert, the trucks, the tomb, a deserted tent, the showers." He shivered at the memory of the two of them in the shower, Adam thrusting up into her against the slick wall. It had been one of the times he'd been most himself and least Amun's puppet.

He hurried on to his explanation, needing to distance himself from the memories he wanted to repeat without Amunmaruku's interference. "Sometimes, you'd be there already. Sometimes, you'd be a moment behind. Sometimes, I'd have enough awareness to know I was touching you in the flesh, loving you...where we were, what I was doing to you and wanted to do to you. Sometimes, when I fought the idea of it, I'd have only the dream state until afterwards; I'd wake in the shower or my bunk, cursing myself and Amun both, knowing that it hadn't been a dream, knowing he'd been using me to do what he wanted instead of what I did...we did."

"You never cursed me?" It seemed to surprise her.

"Anna..." He hesitated to admit it. "Even when I approached you last night, I wasn't certain you remembered anything Amun was doing...anything we'd been doing together. Save the exhaustion, you seemed so unaffected by the whole thing."

"I thought I was going crazy. I thought the psychometry had finally driven me insane, that I was half-stuck in another woman's life."

The truth seared him. "You thought I was him last night. Didn't you? That's why you thought you were crazy."

She buried her face in the join of his neck and shoulder. "Do you hate me?"

"Never." But it hurt that she'd thought he was Amun.

"I hate me for it."

"No. Dea-ana didn't know what was going on. You never knew there were two men involved."

Reasoning her out of guilt wasn't an option plan. She'd been played. They'd both been played. They could wallow in guilt or move on together.

"I...I think I did, on some level. I knew there were two conflicting sides to Amun, and I think that was you and him. There were times when he was cold and commanding. Other times, he was intense, involved... I loved those times. Last night was one of them, and that was you...only you."

Adam hardened that simply. "Yes, it was." Had she felt the difference all that time?

"I wish I had known it was you," she murmured.

Adam turned her beneath him, a plan taking shape. "This time, you will."

Anna slid her hands from his shoulders to his waist, pulling up at Adam's t-shirt. He dragged it off and tossed it away, moaning at her perusal, at the press of her lips to his chest wall.

Memories of the previous night teased at his mind. "What were you doing while you removed your clothes?" he wondered aloud.

A pretty blush reddened her cheeks and nose. "You couldn't see."

Her reaction finished the job of making him rock hard. "I'm about to." She'd done something, thinking Adam was Amunmaruku, and he was damned well going to see it and know it was for him. He rolled to his back, drawing Anna over him.

She pushed to her knees, straddling him. Anna met his eyes and started peeling her shirt up. Her body swayed and circled, stroking at his already-sensitized length.

"Gods, yes," he grumbled. If she'd been straddling him the first time, he wouldn't have made it into her.

Anna eased off of him and to her feet, dropping the t-shirt to the floor, revealing her pert breasts. Her thumbs hooked in the waistband of her pajama pants, her hips started to gyrate. The material slid down, leaving little blue bikini panties behind.

Adam started working his worn jeans open. At Anna's raised eyebrow, he explained his haste. "Did you enjoy the fervor last night?"

Her pants landed around her ankles, and she stepped out of them. Anna met his eyes, her hands crossing her bare midriff then sliding out and down, until she hooked her panties. Her hips swiveled back and forth in a near hypnotizing rhythm.

He scrambled out of his jeans without taking his eyes off her. Her gaze snapped to him, panning up and down his seated form, most likely taking in the differences between Adam and Amun. Short of his hair, the banded tattoos where Amunmaruku wore gold bands, and his circumcised cock, he was sure there were few to note.

The panties slid away, and Anna glided toward him, keeling on the mattress between his parted knees. They moved at the same time, her lips parting against his, their tongues dancing in a hard, demanding kiss.

Anna pressed to him, her hot, wet slit teasing at the line of his cock. Adam turned her beneath him, maneuvering his knees between her thighs and forcing her legs further apart. Her lips parted from his on a gasp, and her body rose in mute request.

Adam plunged inside, groaning at the same sob of pleasure she'd vented the night before. "Mine," he breathed. "Only mine." *Not Amunmaruku's. I'll fight for her.* But he wasn't certain how he could fight Amun.

As if in agreement, Anna's voice overlapped his mental one. "Don't let him interrupt again," she pleaded. "Just you."

His control shattered at the fact that she'd made her decision so definitively, Adam pistoned in and out of her, staking his claim.

He considered the problem of Amunmaruku. For all Adam's attempts to shake the Egyptian prince loose, he'd been unable to. The harder Adam fought, the less of Anna Amun had left him with. Would she think he was weak for admitting it?

A new train of thought occurred to him. Dea-ana...or more precisely Amun through Dea-ana very rarely managed to overwhelm Anna completely. Maybe that was where they had to strike him. "Refuse him."

Her amber eyes opened, unfocused in her impassioned state. "What?"

"You manage to argue with him." Adam pressed deep inside her and held his position, smiling at her wriggling against him. "Tell him this is what you want, not what he's offering."

He slid back, resuming the rolls of his hips that were fast driving them both over.

"But...the blackouts—"

"You have to be aware."

"Minimally," she parroted him. "You said—"

"He doesn't puppet you directly."

"But Dea-ana..." Her breaths were coming in excited little gasps that announced how close she was.

"You've never known what was going on before." As were his. "You've never fought, because you never knew you could or should." He bit back a groan at the tremors of her inner muscles, announcing the coming end. "Fight him, Anna."

"Yes." Her eyes closed, and she arched against him. "Oh, yes."

Realization came a moment later, with the ripples of her muscles massaging his length. Adam followed her over, tensing at the expected interruption that never came.

They lay in the aftermath, trembling, their lips exploring, falling asleep in each other's arms for the first time.

Tomorrow. She'll be wearing my ring tomorrow, he promised himself.

Chapter Five

"Welcome back, Dr. Valeri," Emily called out, her smile wide. The younger woman's gaze flicked to the rings on Anna's left hand, then the one on Adam's.

Anna felt her cheeks heat. "That is going to take some getting used to," she admitted.

Adam's face nestled to the side of her throat. "At least there won't be two Dr. Hastings listed on the find," he teased.

"Yes, but soon there will be two Dr. Valeris."

"All the better when we're working together as lead."

She didn't argue it. Just the thought of them sharing lead was intoxicating.

"If you have a moment," Emily continued. "Dr. Hastings is working on something in the burial chamber."

"Of course," they answered together.

Walking the corridors, Adam at her shoulder, had Anna's mind wandering to what would happen that evening, when Adam would join her in her tent.

A niggling of unease came with it. Amunmaruku and Dea-ana hadn't troubled them at all the three days they'd spent in town, but now they were back at the tomb, perhaps back within their sphere of influence. Would they have to fight tonight? Would Anna be able to turn Amun away? If it proved impossible, how could Anna leave the dig without ruining her career...and Adam's with it?

As if the thought summoned him, Adam's hand cupped her hip. "Relax," he teased. "Your brother isn't that bad."

A smile pulled up at her lips. "You didn't have to grow up with him."

"Ah...true enough. If he gets too unbearable, I could beat him up for you."

They walked into the burial chamber, Anna trying desperately to stifle the laughter that mental image set off.

Evan had been busy, in their absence, setting up the portable imaging machinery and computer bank in a PVC tent. It wasn't quite a clean room environment, but it would minimize the sand in their equipment.

Anna praised the advance. Years ago, all this had to be done off site, forcing the archeologists to split their time between the dig and the university labs.

She stepped into the anteroom, cleaning her boots on the vacuum brushes. She pulled paper booties over her boots and pulled her hair up into a boufont, then slid a set of clean room blues over her clothing. Thus adorned, she slipped inside the tent, noting Adam doing the same behind her.

Anna peered at the screen over Evan's shoulder. "What have you got?"

He pointed to the screen, specifically at the protective plate high on the left shoulder of one mummy.

"Amunmaruku," she noted. "The assassin's blade nicked the aorta. What was the precise terminology, Adam?"

His body crowded hers, taking up the last of the available space in the tent. "Uh...the...the blood canal leaks, I think."

"That's the one," she agreed. "Dea-ana will have a similar wound in the lower abdominal region."

"Left side," Adam agreed.

"Yes. Left." Memories of Dea-ana's pain had her shaking her head in the attempt to knock them away.

Adam's hands closed on her shoulders, kneading silently.

Evan turned to look at them, one brow arched.

"What?" she challenged. If he thought her husband wasn't going to touch her, he was out of his mind.

"You know all of that from..." her brother hinted.

"The papyrus I was working on," Adam inserted. "I can show you later."

Anna hid her surprise, feigning foreknowledge as best she could.

"And you were going to share this when?" Evan questioned, seemingly peeved.

"When I was done translating it. We got sidetracked. Happily, of course," he amended. "As it was, a personal update to Anna was as far as it got."

Evan snorted at that comment.

"She is the *lead* archeologist on the dig," Adam pointed out.

That earned him a glare from Evan. Her brother turned back to the computer, pulling up another shot. "Then there's this."

It took a moment for the significance of what she was looking at to hit her. "They overstuffed her to make her pregnancy more..."

"Obvious," Adam finished for her. "Dea-ana wasn't pregnant enough to show like that. I'll bet the papyrus shows that Amunmaruku ordered it. Maybe to allow room for their spirit children to grow?"

"Maybe for the bragging rights in the afterlife," Anna grumbled. It certainly sounded like something the prince would do.

"Yes, there is that."

Evan turned to them again, troubled by something. "Does anyone but the two of you understand what you're talking about?"

Anna huffed at him. "Sex isn't all we do together, Evan. Adam and I do share other passions. Pillow talk is useful; you get a lot of good relaxed thinking done in the afterglow."

Adam saved her brother from trying to formulate an answer to that. "Amunmaruku was meticulous in the spells and blessings he had woven into their entire mummification process. He believed he could draw them beyond death...in some manner, beyond what most Egyptians believed about the afterlife."

"To a second life?" Evan questioned, sliding a look at the computer that made Anna distinctly nervous.

"To...an awareness, of sorts, I suppose."

"Did it work?"

Anna gaped at him. This was Evan? This was her straight-arrow, scientific-minded older brother? This was the one that winced at the very mention of extra-sensory, let alone paranormal happenings?

Adam recovered first. "What do you mean?"

Evan turned back to the computer, his jaw tense. The keys tapping was momentarily the only sound beside the whisper of cooling fans.

"I didn't believe what Emil's computer modeling came up with. I did it again, with Matt assisting. We did the computations on Dea-ana three times and Amunmaruku twice."

She didn't question what was about to appear on the screen. There was only one thing that could, only one thing that *would* make this impression on Evan. When the computer models of herself and Adam came up, taunting her, Anna crumpled against her husband, her breathing harsh in her own ears.

Evan turned back, his eyes pleading. "I'm listening, Anna. I really am."

Adam scooped her up, his arm muscles tense and his eyes locked on the screen. "We are not them," he managed simply. "Whatever else is going on here, we are not them."

* * * *

The lips moving up her inner thigh drew Anna from her dreams. She smiled sleepily, tipping her hips up for Adam's mouth.

He came at her, ravenous, bringing her to awareness in moments. Anna reached for him, intending to tunnel her fingers in the wealth of his thick, black hair...and came up against smooth scalp instead.

She startled, her eyes opening to Amun's bedchamber. She scrambled away from him, toward the head of the bed. Amun grasped at her calf, dragging Anna toward him again. He came up over her, his expression moving from confusion to anger and back again.

His gaze locked on her chest, and Anna pressed the bedcover to it, hoping she was hiding herself from him, in whatever state was reality. To be honest, she had no clue if Amun could see her, in reality, but she suspected he could see her through Adam's physical eyes.

Anna stared into his eyes, searching for a glimmer of Adam, knowing he was there, aware or semi-aware of what was happening. She shook her head, praying Amun wouldn't force this on her. Adam would never forgive himself for it, choice or no choice in what Amun did through him.

Amun reached for her cheek, and she shied from him.

"No," she forced out. "I don't want you. I want Adam."

Confusion played at the edges of her mind, Dea-ana's confusion with the strange words emerging from her mouth, no doubt.

A mocking smile curved his lips up. "You're refusing me, Dea-ana?"

The other half of her rebelled, horrified at the thought of doing so, needing, wanting, hurting...alone. The emotions and thoughts battered Anna's mind, and she clamped her mouth shut to trap the treasonous answers inside.

"I am not Dea-ana," she managed through clenched teeth. That gave her strength to continue. Adam called her Anna; Amun never had. Amun himself had admitted she wasn't the same soul reincarnated.

Again, the long-dead servant reacted fiercely. Anna tried to cast her off, but they were stuck as if with liquid cement.

His smile faded into a look of challenge. "You're refusing me?"

No!

"Yes. I'm refusing you." It came out a gasp.

Dea-ana's howl of fury and frustration echoed in her splintered mind.

"You said you'd never—"

"*She* said she'd never refuse you, and I let her say it. I said I didn't want to, at that time." Anna had spent days dissecting those moments, separating herself from Dea-ana, so she could be certain what actions each of them had taken, what words each of them had spoken.

"Young one," he chided gently.

"You were lying to me...using me." The words came easier, and Dea-ana seemed to retreat from the argument. "I'm refusing you, Amunmaruku. I don't want you."

"I love you."

That one was hard to form an answer to. "Adam loves me. You love Dea-ana. You don't love me." Which made this tolerable.

"I do—"

"What is my name, Amun?" He'd never once said her name. The only times she'd heard it had been waking moments, Adam's voice.

Panic settled on his face.

"What is my favorite color? What is my favorite food?" Adam knew those things.

"Ah...Annnahhh...An—"

"Say you love me, and use my name," she challenged, sure now that he couldn't do it. He'd made his vow to Dea-ana, and he was incapable of breaking it.

"I... I—I—"

"You don't. You love Dea-ana, and I love Adam. Not you. Him."

"You didn't even know he breathed," Amun roared.

"You're wrong. My confusion makes sense now. I knew there were two of you from the beginning. I just couldn't reconcile how it could be two separate men, at first."

He stared at her, misery etched on his face.

"Think of this as your children having the chance you were denied," she invited. "You've enjoyed this adventure. Let it be enough."

He moved his mouth as if to speak, then stopped, grinding his teeth.

"You were never meant to be here."

"Enough, small one."

Moments passed in silence. Amun nodded and turned away, leaving Anna in the bedchamber.

When she didn't immediately return to the dig site, fear settled in her stomach. She scrambled from the bed. "Wait! What's happening?"

The cold rushed in around her, and cloying darkness closed in. A whispered farewell rang in her ears, nearly swallowed up by the howling wind.

* * * *

Anna screamed, fighting her way up from beneath what felt like a hundred pounds of shifting metal and waterproof fabric. The howling wind pushed her back, buffeting her with a stinging rain of sand through the insubstantial barrier, tumbling her back into the maelstrom of papers and lightweight camp furniture, fiberglass rods and nylon cocooning her tight enough to steal her breath before being whipped away again.

It was gone as quickly as it came, and she slipped, landing in a heap, breathing hard, crying out again as debris rained down, her legs buried beneath enough sand to make them tingle in reduced blood flow. Anna spit a small amount of coppery blood into the void around her, wiggling her legs free of the shifting trap, her mind sluggish. The air around her heated rapidly, her moist breath trapped in the nylon tomb.

It is *a tomb. I'm going to die.*

As if in rebuke, all hell broke loose around her. Shouts and pounding, sliding footsteps filled the darkness.

"Anna! Dear gods... Anna, where are you?"

She reached toward Adam's voice, coming up against her synthetic shroud. "Adam." She wanted to shout it, but her breathing was labored, most likely in a mixture of shock, exhaustion, and the psychological effects of being trapped in an enclosed space. She repeated his name, forcing air from lungs that ached in the effort, screaming it, fighting ineffectually against the bindings around her...save her legs, which were finally working their way free.

A hand closed on hers through the fabric, and she held on tight, sobbing.

"Here," he ordered.

Adam's other hand cupped her head, massaging her scalp and neck. Or maybe he was checking for injuries. Anna didn't care which it was, as long as he was touching her.

"It's okay, Anna. It's over. We'll have you out in a minute."

Sounds moved closer, voices and footsteps.

"Careful," Adam instructed.

"Damned careful," Evan qualified.

She felt the digging before she heard it, the lightening of the pressure on her legs. One large hand closed on her ankle, and she gasped in response, her hand tightening on Adam's.

"Stop," he ordered. "Pain?"

Anna shook her head, at a loss to offer a verbal response.

"Go on," he breathed...or maybe it only sounded that way through the layer of fabric between them. "Slowly."

The rip of nylon was an assault on her nerves, and Anna pressed closer to Adam in response. The hand on her neck retreated, and the material eased away. Anna threw herself into Adam's arms, holding on tight, trembling, drawing in lungfuls of the comparatively cool air outside the tent walls.

"Is she okay?" Evan asked.

Adam stood, lifting her from the skeletal remains of the tent. "Scared, but I think...all right now. We will be getting her checked out. Not an option, in my opinion."

"Glad I don't have to beat that answer into you," Evan quipped.

"Do a head count, Matt," Adam ordered. "Make sure everyone's accounted for, and see if we have any other injuries that should be checked out."

"I'm on it." The sand crunched under his boots, as he hurried away, shouting out a role call.

Anna scanned her eyes over the camp, noting the path of destruction, a straight line that started at the cataloguing tent, ripped through where the showers once stood, through her own tent and... "The mastaba," she managed.

It was half-covered in sand, the entryway indistinguishable from the rest. Mo and Louis stood to either side of the massive pile, sand dusted but apparently unharmed.

"How much is gone?" she asked weakly.

Evan jumped right in with an answer, for once not coddling her but rather treating her like his boss. "Not much, we hope. It's going to take us weeks to siphon out the sand from the mastaba, and the computers and imaging gear are likely toast. But we transferred files this afternoon, so the data is safe."

"And the cataloguing tent?" she asked.

"We sent a truck off," Evan offered. "There was nearly nothing—"

"What was?" she interrupted.

The silence fell thick and around them, pressing down on her.

"The papyrus." She didn't question it.

Adam sighed. "It hit there first...hard. There was no warning. Just the squall. I've... I found a piece of the papyrus. Looks like it shredded when the storage case shattered. We have the scans and pictures...and the scraps for dating and analysis, but the original is gone with the wind, if you'll pardon the pun."

And the spells woven into it with it. That means we're free. She didn't doubt that the mummies would have damage to the outer spell-inked layer of linen, when they dug them out.

386

She nodded. "Good work," she answered solemnly.

"You, too," Adam returned, adding an extra squeeze.

Evan groaned. "Does anyone else understand what you two are talking about?" he complained.

"Probably not," Anna conceded. She pressed her cheek to Adam's chest, closing her eyes to the steady cadence of his heart. "I love you. Only you."

"You better," Adam grumbled. "Because, believe me, I don't share."

And it was Good

Dedication

To my friends who have had the glory of discovering what lies behind the scenes with me. All the world's a play, my friends. We are but the band of players.

And it was Good

Chapter One

GOD-Node 103 looked out at the changes they'd made that day—and it was good.

But Node 60 was aging. More and more conflicts were occurring in the code, conflicts that took time and precious resources to correct for—conflicts that could cause catastrophic loss of human life. Such a thing was inconceivable. Inexcusable. The Node would soon need replaced. It was time to begin the search in earnest.

* * * *

Julee sat at her terminal, clutching her hands in her lap to keep her trembling a secret. All the time the GODs deliberated, separating the worthy young godlings from the unworthy and mediocre based on the results of their latest testing.

So far, each testing cycle had confirmed her as worthy of their continued attention, but what if she wasn't? Would she be cast out of the temple school, a fallen godling among the human inhabitants of the planet?

Would she stay on in the temple, a humble servant to those who had proven themselves worthy? No one knew for certain where the temple servants came from, and it would be terribly rude to ask such a question.

No one knew where the unworthy godlings disappeared to so quickly after being dismissed. Again, it would be rude to ask.

Rude and beneath notice of my kind. So speaks the Benevolent Ones and the Great Book. Godlings have not the concerns of lesser beings. Or those of GODs.

The screen came to life and the message appeared.

Proceed to Masters' Class, most worthy godling. Your cubicle assignment is M-2.

Around her, other worthy got to their feet, and she rushed to join them. Neither of the godlings who'd bordered her terminal moved.

Julee tried to ignore their pallor and the tang of fear in the air. She was still worthy of the GODs' attention, and it would be frowned upon if she concerned herself with the unworthy. That was the concern of the GODs and not her own. It would be presumptuous to think of herself in terms of doing the same things the GODs did.

The classroom was eerily quiet. It was always like this when the young were tested. No one cheered. No one sobbed, worthy or not. Even the unworthy had their pride and discipline.

Julee let out a breath she hadn't realized she'd been holding as she eased through the doors that had opened into the Masters' classroom. Her heart stuttered as they closed behind her. She pasted on a look of disinterest and took the next open terminal in line, bypassing the godlings still taking time to evaluate what was undoubtedly an identical but smaller classroom to the many others they'd seen.

She tested the key function on her terminal, then the logic circuits, and finally the randomizer. Relieved that all were in working order, she glanced around to take a head count of the advancing class. Julee swallowed hard at the truth.

"It's a much smaller group," the girl to her left noted. There was a slight quiver in her voice that everyone would pretend not to notice.

I will pretend not to notice. Perhaps the others truly do not; maybe I am unworthy and hiding it.

Julee pushed that thought away and did the mental math on the test results. The group was much smaller. The early testing had only eliminated two to five percent of the group at every cycle. This last had taken a full seventy percent, leaving only a half dozen worthy godlings, three male and three female.

But it wouldn't do to show more than a mild interest in that information. "They were unworthy," Julee dismissed the comment.

It was undeniably true. She'd seen many godlings fall from grace in the eight years they'd been actively tested for ascension. The ten before that had been spent in preparation for the testing to prove their worth. If a godling had faulted in taking in the sacred learning to move forward, he or she could blame no one but the unworthy self. So said the Great Book.

A snide male voice brought her head around. "Let me guess. You want to be a GOD."

"Of course," she replied simply. "Doesn't everyone here?" It was every godling's fondest wish. *Become a GOD and return to the source of all. Leave the temple and ascend on high.*

The girl who'd spoken to her shifted as if discomfited, then went rigid. She feigned interest in her terminal, performing the same checks Julee already had. So she did pretend to be unaffected, just as Julee did. That was a relief.

The boy one seat farther left, the one who'd spoken, scowled.

"Well, don't you?" Julee asked.

"The chosen worthy don't become GODs." He said it with a conviction that confused her.

"Of course they do."

He didn't reply.

She took a calming breath and motioned a screen between them with her hands. "Very well then. I will construct a game-zone. What do *you* think happens to them?"

"Maybe they're sacrifices to the GODs and only the fastest and smartest are deemed worthy to be food of the GODs."

Julee's stomach rebelled at the thought of it. "That's revolting. Sacrifices were outlawed more than twenty thousand years ago."

"You don't think they'd tell the ones to be sacrificed, do you?" There was a glitter in his eyes and something about his smile that made Julee distinctly nervous.

"Leave her alone, Caecee," another boy ordered. "The instructors and Father have already hinted that your blasphemy is unworthy of a godling."

The first boy darkened a notch and looked toward his terminal. Julee turned to the other, meeting his bright blue gaze. At a loss to find the words to thank him without seeming concerned, she tipped her head to him silently.

He looked back to his own terminal without a word or motion in return, and Julee wondered at the sense of loss that flooded her.

"Welcome, worthy godlings," the Master instructor greeted them as all their former ones had.

Julee focused on him fully, blocking out her mind's wandering to the boy who'd spoken in defense of her. To remain worthy, she had to receive, process, and apply everything the various instructors said. There could be no distractions if she wished to insure the GODs' continued interest in her.

* * * *

Staphan rechecked his code, wincing at the error halfway through. Speed was important, but accuracy was prized.

He corrected the error, then coded the transfer to the instructor. The typical praise of his work or suggestions for improvement didn't come. Instead, a split screen appeared.

On one side was his work. On the other, there was a complementary program. Scanning them, he noted conflicts that would occur when the two were run together. He positioned the cursor to work the other program into compliance with his. Before he could begin typing, his own code started to change, bringing him to an abrupt halt.

His move to correct the changes ended, just as suddenly, with his fingers hovering over the home keys. In the moment he'd tarried, the other person working the code had corrected the first conflict, without compromising his program.

His heart hammered in excitement. Perhaps he was being offered additional instruction. Such a thing would be very useful in the next testing cycle.

He went on to the next conflict, tweaking first his own and then the other program to correct for it. The other paused for a moment, then moved on to a third conflict.

Sweat coated Staphan's brow and lip. He engrossed himself in the interaction—the give and take of this new form of programming. His mind was fully engaged in the process and he was only vaguely aware of the godlings around him.

A strange noise rose to a cacophony, cutting through the haze the instruction had put him into. Other sounds followed—sharp, disjointed sounds that had no place in the temple. His heart stammering, Staphan looked around in search of an explanation.

It is a distraction!

Something primal told him not to ignore this distraction.

Caecee was on his feet, using a broken screen to beat the keyboard before him. Shards of sacred technology flew in all directions. The instructor for this lesson shouted for order.

The girl beside Caecee dove for the floor with a scream of pain, blood coursing down her cheek. The doors through which they'd entered opened. The injured girl and one of the other female godlings in the class rushed for it, colliding with the servants heading in through the opening.

Caecee let out a howl the likes of which one might expect from a wild beast. He raised the screen over his head.

Seeing the larger boy's intent, Staphan grasped the girl still seated between them and dragged her to the floor with him. The weapon passed over their heads, shattering her screen, then Staphan's. Caecee went to work on the keyboards, and Staphan pulled the girl's face to his chest and buried his own in the wealth of her dark hair.

The crashing and splintering stopped, and voices rose. Despite the situation, the servants' voices were calming. It seemed Caecee had no intention of being calmed. His shouts and curses intensified. Staphan didn't doubt the lessening of sound marked the servants dragging Caecee away and not the godling regaining control.

As the ruckus waned, Staphan realized he was holding tightly to the girl, both of them trembling wildly. He backed away, staring at her.

Her dark eyes were wide in fear, and tears glistened on her cheeks. Staphan used the wide cuff of his tunic to dry the tracks of tears. It wouldn't do to have anyone see her engaging in un-GODlike behavior.

Why do I care? He did, though, odd as it was.

She opened her mouth as if to speak, closed it, then nodded.

The thick braid of her hair was disheveled, mussed by their dive to safety and likely his grip on her in the midst of the attack. He wondered if he looked as disreputable as she.

"Julee!" one of the female servants exclaimed.

The godling in his arms stiffened. Staphan wondered at the reason for the reaction. His move to question her was interrupted by hands cupping his face and moving as if in search of wounds.

Staphan released her and glanced around in surprise at the crowd of servants encircling them, females on Julee's side and males on his. They'd appeared while he'd been lost in thought.

Voices overlapped, making his head spin.

"No injuries, I think."

"Julee, look at me."

"Staphan? Here, Staphan!"

He focused on Father, trying to attend to what the elder was saying.

"Are you well, Staphan?"

Well? He nodded, at a loss for a more appropriate answer.

His house father sighed in seeming relief, then pulled Staphan to his feet. A group of three male servants guided him toward the far door, offering support Staphan was certain he needed, though he would never have admitted such a frailty aloud.

Staphan shot a glance back, meeting godling Julee's gaze for one heart-stopping moment. She averted her eyes, then nodded to some question her house mother asked.

"Staphan?" one of his servants prodded him.

He took another step away from her, giving himself up to the care of the servants. "Of course."

Chapter Two

GOD-Node 103 watched the recorded images on the screen, wincing at the loss of one of the young godlings. While the remaining five godlings were all worthy of ascending, there was something magical about three matched godling pairs, male and female, vying for ascension. An uneven set felt wrong to them. It was... unnatural for their kind. It was time to introduce the godlings to their birthright and hope the pair to replace GOD-Node 60 would pass the final test before the old GOD-Node needed to ascend again.

* * * *

Staphan settled in an empty chair in the newly-reconstructed classroom. He tried not to look at the conspicuously empty chair Caecee had occupied two days earlier.

No one had seen the fallen godling since his rampage. His cubicle had been stripped by the time Staphan and Jeorj had returned from the healers.

The servants hadn't moved Jeorj closer in the sleeping chamber, conserving space as they usually would. For the first day, Staphan had believed that meant Caecee might eventually return. Now, he knew the other godling could never return to them. With lessons resuming, Caecee couldn't rejoin the group. He was missing vital instruction and was not physically ill. It was set down in the Great Book, and the Great Book was the final word on the lives of the godlings.

Seeing the empty sleeping cubicle made Staphan uneasy. The Great Book spoke of balance in all things: night with day, heat with cold, and male with female. The five remaining godlings were decidedly unbalanced.

He eyed the empty terminal Caecee had manned. A shiver worked down his spine. The loss of a godling had never been so apparent before, because the spaces had always been filled in or eliminated when godlings had proven unworthy.

Staphan looked up just in time to meet Julee's gaze as she did the same. His heart beat in a manner it had no right beating in. He'd never felt such a failure in his typical heart rhythms and he didn't like it.

"Welcome, worthy godlings," the master instructor for this session intoned in a more subdued voice than they were accustomed to.

This instructor was female. They never knew whether their instructors would be male or female, whether they would see an instructor daily or monthly or only once. On some days, they had two instructors instead of one.

Staphan snapped his head around. Out of the corner of his eye, he saw Julee do the same. He prayed the instructor hadn't noticed their inattention. Distraction was punished. He sighed in relief at the instructor's focus on her own terminal.

"Please attend to the lesson of the day."

The broken code and an explanation of the function it would ultimately fulfill followed. The problem drew Staphan's attention away from lesser concerns. In moments, he was engrossed in the code.

* * * *

Julee held her breath, letting it out in a steady stream as the split screen appeared again. The conflicts stood out as if they'd been highlighted for her, and she went to work correcting for them.

Her fingers went still in shock. Unlike the last time she'd coded in tandem, the other wasn't correcting conflicts. He or she was causing them.

It is a test. It has to be a test.

Julee worked harder, fixing new conflicts and old, but for every error she corrected, the other created a new one.

I'm failing. Hated tears pricked at her eyes. It was beneath her to shed them, but her normally ordered mind had succumbed to panic.

Her screen went blank, and she swallowed a gasp of dismay. It couldn't end this way. She couldn't be deemed unworthy. Not because of someone else's incompetence.

The silence in the classroom broke through her hurt and confusion. Julee looked around, noting the other godlings doing the same. The screens were blank—every one.

"Master instructor?" the one called Staphan queried.

"Godlings attend," she replied crisply.

Julee turned to her screen, and it flicked on again. Her original program was there, but a different one was to the right, one with fewer conflicts. She went to work again, as did the other. Their efforts complemented each other, but not as well as the one the first day had.

She didn't question that the two were different godlings. Every godling had a style. Though the current 'other' was accomplished, he or she had a less appealing hand for creative code than the first 'other' she'd tested with.

By the time the programs were in perfect synchronization, it was time to break for meal. Julee stretched her back, then rose and started for the corridor.

Mother and two of the female servants stopped her as Julee took the usual right turn toward the girls' meal room. Julee shot them a questioning look, trying not to show too much concern.

"Master Class godlings will eat in a different place," the house mother informed them.

Julee nodded, though she worked at the problem. The day of the attack and the day after, they'd eaten in their cubicles, as if they were ill. Morning meal was always served to them in bed. This was the first meal they'd have in a meal room since the godling Caecee had caused such uproar.

Giving herself up to their guidance, Julee followed the servants to the left and through a different door. She stopped short, and one of the other two girls bumped into her.

The boys were at the window, picking up their food trays. A searching look around revealed the room only had one table.

The set-up was shockingly new. Aside from class, they never saw the male godlings. The girls' sleeping and bathing areas were in a separate wing than the boys'. They'd always eaten separately.

Mother urged Julee to the serving window. She turned her attention to the boys, noting their stares in unease. The two males shot each other a look she couldn't decipher, then ambled away to the far side of the table.

Julee accepted her tray of food and turned toward the table, trying to appear unaffected. The other female godlings followed her lead.

It took only a few moments to decide staring at her tray was ridiculous. Whatever their reasons for decreeing that Master Class eat together, there was a lesson embedded in it somewhere. That lesson was unlikely to be embedded in her fruit cup.

She raised her head, her gaze locking with Staphan's. There were so many new experiences this week. She'd never known a boy's name before. Now she knew the names of two of the three who'd advanced to Master Class with her.

For that matter, it was unusual for a godling to concern herself with the names of the other female godlings, unless their cubicles bordered her own. Now that there were only three left—and with Julee in the M-2 cubicle—she knew both Lainee and Tiffa's names.

Realization that she was staring at Staphan sent Julee searching for the servants instead. Her heart took up an odd rhythm at the sight of the empty room. The house servants and food servants had withdrawn—even the house mother and house father had—leaving the godlings alone at the table.

Julee looked down the line of chairs on the girls' side of the table, Lainee—then Tiffa. She continued on to the scowling male seated next to Staphan, then to Staphan himself.

He stared back at her for a moment, his light eyes shining in some unfathomable emotion. Then he snapped his head down and scooped up a spoonful of his rice, leaving her to stare at the long, golden hair pulled back in a short, male ponytail.

She hesitated then did the same. For some reason she couldn't define, Julee had lost her appetite.

Chapter Three

GOD-Node 103 conferred amongst themselves. The young godlings had spent two days in close quarters, testing together and eating together. Two clear Nodes were emerging from the possible matrix of six. Only time would tell which would ascend. It was time to administer the final tests. They sent the command, hoping for the best.

* * * *

Staphan turned over in bed, cursing his inability to sleep. Every time he closed his eyes, visions of Julee haunted him. She had long, tapered fingers that danced over the keyboard. Why her hands caught his attention was a mystery to him, but he found them appealing in a way he found hard to quantify.

Jeorj shuffled by, and Staphan pushed to sitting, guiltily wondering if he'd kept the other godling awake with his fidgeting.

"Still awake?" Jeorj asked. His yawn said he hadn't been, which eased Staphan's heart rate.

"I have to use the toilet," he lied.

Jeorj weaved a bit on his feet. "Mmmm. Me too."

Staphan pushed to standing and followed Jeorj to the bathing room. Jeorj went directly to the closest urinal, while Staphan headed for the sink. He refreshed himself by splashing handfuls of cool water on his face.

Sounds intruded on the peace, and Staphan turned the water off. He met Jeorj's gaze, but the other godling seemed as confused as Staphan was.

They turned to the bathing area together, moving cautiously and quietly. Staphan swallowed hard at the sight inside the first room.

The house father was in the large tub, thigh deep in the steaming water. One of the female servants was face-to-face with him, their arms wrapped around each other. They moved slowly, their bodies stroking up and down.

Their shared whispers gave way to sharper sounds. The house father shifted, widening his stance, forcing the female servant's legs out. The move prompted a moan from her, but it didn't sound like she was in pain.

The new position allowed Staphan to see Father's cock. It was long and hard, and it was disappearing into the servant's body and reappearing as they moved.

While he watched, they started moving faster. Their sounds grew louder—loud enough to have woken the godlings and drawn them from their beds, had they not already been in the bathing areas.

Staphan's breathing went harsh in anticipation of something he couldn't name. His cock stiffened as the house father's was. Staphan touched his own, shivering at the pulse of pleasure it gave him.

The servant screamed, and Staphan took a step back in surprise. Jeorj backed off several steps, retreated to the doorway, and stopped to watch from there.

The house father withdrew and turned the female servant so she leaned forward over the edge of the tub.

Her breasts swung with each movement, and she shuddered at Father's thrust into her body again.

He quickened his pace, forcing the servant against the side of the tub. Her shouts intensified and she grasped at the edge of the tub. Father's voice echoed off the walls, and he went still, pushed tight against her.

For a long moment, four sets of rasping breathing and the swish of water were the loudest sounds in the room. Then the female servant giggled.

Father's head came up, and he met Staphan's gaze. His eyes panned down, his attention fixating on Staphan's waist.

His face burning in embarrassment, Staphan hurried back to his bed, Jeorj leading the way. He threw himself onto the mattress and buried himself under the blankets.

Time seemed to move slowly. Staphan's breathing evened out a bit, but his cock and heart continued pounding. At the sound of footsteps on the marble floor, he forced his eyes open.

Father stood over him, smiling. He'd donned sleep pants, but he was otherwise unclothed. That was as shocking as the rest.

"You have questions," Father stated. He settled to the edge of Staphan's bed.

Constructing words seemed abruptly difficult. "You... You meant for us to see this?"

His smile was stiff. "It is a gift of the GODs, Staphan. You are a Master-Class godling and of an age to realize all of the GODs' gifts to us."

Staphan worked at that idea. "And will I...do as you did?"

Father chuckled. "In due time. For now..." He grasped Staphan's wrist through the blanket and guided the godling's hand to the still-hard cock, snug inside the younger's sleep pants.

How the house father knew Staphan was still hard was a mystery to him—one he wasn't certain he should investigate too carefully.

Father pushed the godling's hand down snug against his cock, sending new shards of pleasure through Staphan.

"Learn, Staphan," he whispered. "Learn why the GODs gave us this blessing."

Father walked away. A moment later, Staphan heard whispering, most likely Father urging Jeorj to the same discoveries.

The first strokes of Staphan's hand over his cock brought him fully erect again. The next few sent his breathing into hitching gasps.

Wanting to experiment, he thrust his hand inside the waistband of his sleep pants and grasped his cock directly. It felt a dozen times better than touching himself through his clothing.

Varying the speed and grip, he found what felt best. The pleasure was intense, nearly blinding in its power. Then more. The crest came abruptly, stealing awareness of the passage of time and coherent thought. A shout that Staphan suspected was his own echoed off the stark walls.

He licked his lips, forcing his mind to function, however tenuously. The slick of fluids disconcerted him. Was he to leave the GODs' gift as it was? Was there a proper way to clean it, to show respect and reverence for such a gift? Was avoiding this situation why Father had indulged in the bath?

As if in answer, Father appeared above him. Staphan didn't question that he was there to offer instruction. With a nod of his head in acceptance, the older man imparted what Staphan needed to know.

* * * *

Julee came awake with a start. She lay in her bed, trying to place what had disturbed her sleep.

A voice set her heart pounding. It wasn't simply a new voice. It was male.

She worked at that. There had never been a man or boy in their sleeping chambers.

As we've never eaten with them? Some petulant voice in her mind taunted.

Eating isn't the same as sleeping, changing clothing—bathing! By the GODs, there was only one set of semi-private bathing areas in the girls' living quarters.

One of the female servants laughed deeply, and the male's voice emerged again, too low for Julee to hear the words.

She hesitated, torn. It wouldn't do for a godling to seem too concerned with the dealings of the servants.

I have freedom to roam my quarters. There is no privacy within the godlings' quarters. Though the godlings wouldn't spy on one another, neither were there secrets in the temple.

On that thought, Julee swung her legs out of bed and to the floor. She pushed to her feet and padded deeper into the room, seeking out the sounds.

The couple was in the farthest cubicle, entwined on the mattress, unclothed. Their mouths were opened and pressed together, their heads cocked at angles so their noses didn't bump. Slight movements of their cheeks drew Julee's eyes.

They parted slowly, a flash of what might have been a tongue between them disappearing into the female servant's mouth. She shook her head in confusion. Why would one stick a tongue into another's mouth?

Inexplicably, her own mouth had gone dry. Julee licked her lips, rapt on the male's movements, on the way the muscles in his bare back and buttocks tightened when he moved.

He moved lower, touching his lips to her throat, and the female servant bent her neck back to facilitate the movement. Lower...suckling lightly at the darkened tips of her breasts.

Julee's breasts came to hard points and she gasped. A heavy wetness not unlike her feminine blood pooled in her.

The male turned slightly to uncover the female servant's furred core. Julee gasped at the sight of the heavy rod of flesh between his legs, her mind spinning. What was it? Did all males have one?

That was likely. Females over a certain age had varying sizes of breasts. Perhaps this was standard male...equipment.

Did that mean males had varying sizes of rods between their thighs? Was this male's to the short end or the long? Surely it was one of the larger. How large could it be and not hamper a male walking?

His fingertips raked through the female servant's curls, prodding between her spread thighs. Her hips came off the mattress with a strange little sound.

A gasp brought Julee's head around. The other two godlings were crowding behind her. Lainee pressed a hand to her mouth, going pale and wide-eyed behind it. Tiffa watched avidly. At a loss to explain herself but mollified by the fact that the other godlings hadn't shied away or averted their gazes either, Julee turned her attention back to the bed.

The male stroked little circles between the female's legs, suckling at her breasts in turn. Pleas for more left her lips—then shouts.

Julee bit her lip, wondering what would happen when the house mother came to investigate the noise. She didn't and the interaction continued.

The male came to his knees between the female's legs. He lifted her hips from the mattress, positioning the slit between her legs at the head of the rod between his.

His advance into the female's body was painfully slow. Julee's lungs started to ache and she realized she was holding her breath in anticipation. She let it out, then sucked in another as the male's rod disappeared until only his furred balls were visible.

The female trembled, fisting the sheet beneath in her hands. "Matthew, please," she begged.

He chuckled, drawing back and thrusting hard. The female arched into his hands with a scream.

A trickle of fluid wound down Julee's inner thigh, sending shivers down her spine. Her nipples came to hard peaks against her sleep shirt.

The male moved faster, and their voices rose. At last, Mother arrived. Lainee took one look at her and fled. Mother motioned Julee and Tiffa toward the couple rocking on the bed.

The female screamed again, clawing at the sheet. The male growled something unintelligible, still pounding hard against her seam. In the next instant, he was pulling out, his rod spraying milky liquid over the female's seam, thighs, and feminine curls.

More wetness trickled down Julee's inner thighs and she stared at the fluid the male emitted, her knees shaking and her breathing harsh.

The female servant smiled a smug, little smile, stroking her fingertips through the male's essence, circling the nub he'd been playing at. She moaned, lifting her hips as if offering herself to the male again.

Mother led Julee and Tiffa away with a gentle embrace that encompassed both of them. At Tiffa's cubicle, she waved them toward the bed and they sat. Julee shifted, as uncomfortable with the possibility that they had done something wrong as she was with the unfamiliar sensations assaulting her.

"You understand," Mother hedged, "that they both felt pleasure from the act they shared?"

Julee glanced at Tiffa, then to the house mother. "Yes, Mother. I understand it."

Mother looked toward the whispering and sobbing coming from the direction of Lainee's cubicle. She sighed. "The other godling does not."

"Mother?" Julee chanced addressing her. "*Why* must we understand it?"

Tiffa leaned closer to Mother, seeking comfort as they had as toddlers.

Mother smiled and enfolded her in a hug. Then she answered Julee's question. "The GODs' gift is meant to be known and shared."

"And *who* should we share it with?" Julee asked, sensing that Mother wanted her to ask it.

"That will come in time. For now, you saw what the female servant did at the end? You saw the pleasure she gave herself?"

Julee's face burned in embarrassment. "Yes, Mother. I saw."

"Touch yourselves. You have many...*sensitive* areas on your body made to give you pleasure."

Mother waited for more questions. When none came to Julee's mind, Mother helped her to her feet and guided Julee to bed.

Chapter Four

GOD-Node 103 spent the next few days sending down the orders that would lead to a final choice for the replacement of GOD-Node 60. The training regimen would have to be accelerated. The aging Node was failing more than a year earlier than when they'd hoped to retire it. There wasn't time to waste.

The calculations had been done. The choices had become all too clear. In weighing skill against personalities and further in the tentative attachments forming between the male and female godlings, there was a single clear choice for the aging GOD-Node's replacement.

Still, there had to be two. As was always the way, there would be a backup system, in case the primary failed.

Her hands trembling a bit, the goddess-half of GOD-Node 103 coded in her recommendations for primary and secondary advancements. Her god-half concurred a moment later and the message went out to the other GOD-Nodes for their consideration. For an agonizing time, there were no replies.

They are evaluating our data. *It wasn't unexpected. Given the circumstances, the other GOD-Nodes were sure to comb every line carefully, making sure the choice had been objective and to the best interests of the bulwark at large.*

Her breath escaped in a rush as the first of the others agreed to the choices. Her god-half squeezed her hand and offered a broad smile. One after another, the confirmations came in. In the end, only one rejected the proposed pairings. GOD-Node 60.

Though a single GOD-Node was not enough to change the outcome of the group decision, the goddess winced that the decision was not unanimous.

"They are aging," her god-half reminded her. "Their logic skills have been failing for some time."

"Yes. I know." Further, GOD-Node 60 would not code with the new young GODs. She'd never understood why a failing GOD-Node had a vote in their own replacement.

* * * *

Staphan pushed his lunch around his plate, his mind full of the adventures of the last few nights. He'd seen servants in all manner of celebration of the GODs' gift, until he'd stroked himself off in mounting need.

It had been all he could do to attend to the lessons, as he'd gone from two to four to eight strings of code, worked in unison. With only five in the Master Class, that meant their instructors must be working the other strings, but there was no sign of which instructors might be doing so or from where.

The only thing he could say for sure—and thank the GODs for—was that they'd paired him with the same partner he'd been paired with the first day they'd worked with two strings. Whoever the others were, at least he could count on the superb coding of that individual. For that matter, the skill of the others led him to the certainty that all of them were instructors.

Movement at the window drew his gaze up. Staphan stared at Julee's full breasts. Memories of a male servant feasting on a female servant's ample globes had his mouth watering to do the same with his fellow godling.

What sounds would Julee make when he tasted her nipples? The thought was enough to drive him crazy. How much longer would he have to wait to fully experience the GODs' gift? Would he be lucky enough to sate himself with Julee and explore his fantasies about her?

She set her tray on the table across from him, and Staphan focused on the apex of her thighs. What would she taste like if he buried his tongue in her slit?

Julee settled in the chair, shocking him back to reality. It was only the time they'd spent in each other's arms that made him think of her this way.

The points of her breasts against her tunic called him a liar. He wondered if anything but sexual arousal made them rise.

* * * *

Julee's breath caught at the intent expression on Staphan's face. Visions of him over her in bed as the male servant had been over the female the first night had her body heating in preparation for her stroking hand.

She'd been fantasizing about him for two days, wondering what he'd look like as she sucked at his cock, what it would feel like sliding home inside her. It seemed she'd been dreaming of Staphan since the first moment she'd touched herself.

He licked his lips, and her body wept fluids down her thighs. There was little question he was thinking the same thing she was.

Julee had asked questions every night. She wanted to know everything Mother could teach her. Still, all the preparation did her no good. No matter how much she knew, she wasn't permitted to receive the GODs' gift yet.

GODs, please. Soon, please.

She wanted to ask that she be allowed to experience the gift with Staphan, but that might be asking too much of the Benevolent Ones.

The other male godling whispered something to Staphan, and the latter averted his eyes. Julee wondered if Staphan's cock was as hard as her nipples were.

If he stands up and proves it is, I'll need the toilet to ease my needs before instruction.

* * * *

Staphan forced the fantasies about Julee out of his mind, focusing on the code on his screen. The changes were fast, taxing his mind until sweat broke out on his body.

Time passed quickly. His body tired at the continued work. Still, he pressed on, engrossed by the new challenges presented in the code.

His screen went blank, and Staphan's head spun. Just as he was about to turn away for meal, a message appeared on his screen. He read it twice, his heart hammering.

Proceed to Demi-GOD Class 1, worthy Demi-GOD.
Blessed be.

Staphan rose on shaking legs, noting the doors marked 1 and 2. He headed for the former silently, not looking around at the others. The house father and house mother met him in the corridor. The house mother would only appear for a female godling. Holding his breath in anticipation, Staphan looked over his shoulder—and met Julee's dark eyes.

Father drew him away, guiding Staphan down the corridor and into a wing he'd never entered before.

His voice was low and soothing. "You will learn to work with your goddess-half, Staphan. Within the week, you will be presented for further testing."

He nodded, his head spinning at the speed of events. "I'm a Demi-GOD," he breathed. "I didn't realize we were testing."

"You and your goddess-half have been coding with the GODs for the last four days."

Staphan reeled at the news, and Father steadied him.

"Everything is a test, Staphan. The GODs see all. To be a GOD, you must have the knowledge of the GODs."

"Knowledge of the GODs," he repeated. Staphan didn't know what that meant, but there was time to decode it later.

Father pushed a door open, and Staphan gaped. A hand at his back sent him stumbling into a spacious room.

The chamber was larger than the largest classroom they'd had and windows stretched, floor to ceiling, overlooking the city below. Plants hung from hooks, and the smell of rich growth permeated the area. The furniture was lush and unlike anything he'd seen before.

Staphan made his way to a large computer screen, looking down at the wide seat and two keyboards. His mind making connections, Staphan turned toward the doorway.

Julee stood there, her hands enfolded in the house mother's embrace. The older woman seemed to be instructing the young godling.

Demi-GOD, he corrected himself. Julee was a Demi-GOD, just as he was. *She is my goddess-half.*

As if that thought drew her, Julee looked his way. Father and Mother took their leave and closed the doors behind them.

Before he could find the words to address her, servants entered through another door and set trays of food and drinks at the small table. They bowed and were gone with an order to leave their trays for the servants to clear.

* * * *

Julee took several unsteady steps toward Staphan. *My god-half.* She wasn't certain what that meant yet, but she'd been assured the next few days would change her life.

Staphan didn't take a seat at the table. He watched her come to him, as intent as he'd been at lunch the day before. It wasn't until she stood beside him that he chose to sit.

Trying to hide her confusion, she did the same. Julee wasn't certain what she'd expected, but she was sure his reaction wasn't it.

The first few fresh fruits they ate passed in an uncomfortable silence. She caught Staphan staring at her several times; he averted his eyes when they met hers.

When he spoke, his voice startled her.

"What did Mother tell you? Just before she left?"

"That this was a place unlike our cubicles."

His brow furrowed. "In what way?" He looked around at the room. "Besides the obvious, I mean."

"She said that everything, save lessons, are at our whims. If we wish something...anything, we ask and it will be done."

"Anything," he mused. Staphan took a bite of a ripe plum.

"Mother said we could do anything we wished here."

His gaze sharpened into an intent look that woke her body again.

"Anything," he repeated.

Julee nodded, not trusting herself to speak.

Staphan set the fruit down and reached his hand out toward her. He stroked at one nipple, bringing it up for him. Julee took a shuddering breath. Staphan stroked it again, then squeezed it lightly between his fingertips.

He looked toward one door, then the other, as if daring someone to interrupt them. No one intruded on them, so he moved on to the other nipple. She arched her back to force them farther into his hands.

"Oh, yes," he breathed. Staphan moved closer, cupping her full breasts in his palms, stroking his thumbs back and forth across her nipples. He massaged her, and her body dampened for him.

It wasn't enough. Julee turned her head, tipping it to one side, inviting his mouth. Staphan hesitated. He captured her lower lip between his...then her upper. She stroked the tip of her tongue just inside his mouth, and he gasped in response.

His lips parted against hers, and Julee did the same. She took another tentative swipe of her tongue into his mouth, started to retreat, then returned to explore the full length of his tongue. Staphan's tongue made lazy strokes against hers, growing rougher as their breathing degraded to harsh rasping.

Julee reached into his lap, touching his cock, and Staphan went still. His mouth parted from hers.

Her heart lurched at the sight of his tightened jaw. Had she done something wrong? "Staphan?"

Something softened in his eyes. "Not here." He jerked his head in the direction of a piece of furniture set near the windows. It had a high back like a chair, but it was long enough for five people to sit side-by-side on it and deep enough that only Julee's feet and ankles would overhang the edge when seated.

His lips pressed to her cheek. "There."

She nodded, and Staphan guided her to her feet. The whole way there, he teased at her body, finding spots that increased her pleasure.

They sank to the surface together, Staphan's hand between her thighs. He rubbed delicious little circles, and Julee spread her legs, inviting him.

Staphan took advantage of it. His fingers worked at her avidly, and Julee cried out.

He smiled. "I knew you'd make that sound."

She stared at him. Any attempt she would have made at a reply was lost in another cry.

She bucked her hips up. Staphan pulled at the fasteners on her trousers, opening them. In the next heartbeat, his hand was inside the fabric, stimulating her directly.

Julee fumbled to do the same, finally releasing his cock from the confines of fabric stretched taut over his increased length and girth. She touched it, stunned that something so hard could be so silken. More stunned than that when she found he was larger than the male servants she'd seen engaged in gifting the females. Was that a good sign or bad?

How could this be bad?

Staphan grumbled something that made no sense. His hips shifted back and forth. Julee clasped her hand around the shaft as she'd seen the servants do.

Something changed in Staphan. His movements were fierce and economical. His thumb ground against her nub, and Julee shattered.

Oh GODs! Oh GODs! Julee dared not say it aloud. It was surely a sacrilege, GODs' gift or not.

Bright colors danced before her eyes. Her body exploded in waves of delight.

Staphan's cock bucked against her fingers. A guttural sound escaped his lips. His male fluids splashed over her female curls.

Julee touched it, memories of the first coupling she'd seen playing in her mind. She trailed her fingertips through his leavings, moaning.

His fingers joined hers.

Staphan. My god-half.

She slipped her hand down, massaging her nub with the fluids. He stared, a sweat breaking out on his upper lip. His tongue trailed along his lips.

He means to taste me. Julee didn't question that it was so.

As if in confirmation, Staphan started to lever his body down the length of hers.

The warning tone jangled her nerves. It was only minutes until their final lesson of the day would begin.

His mouth closed on one breast through her tunic, a sweet suckling that made promises of more to come.

A clearing throat announced they were no longer alone. Julee hastened to right her clothing. Staphan took his time, seemingly in no hurry to comply.

Chapter Five

The goddess-half of GOD-Node 103 laughed aloud, and her mate smiled at her. She knew he held the same hopes she did. While Demi-GOD Class 2 were still awkward and unsure, reports from Class 1's servants confirmed the attraction she'd suspected existed between the Prime Pair.

Had the house mother and house father not intervened, the two might have ascended the first day of their cohabitation. But that would be rash. That could put the female Demi-GOD at risk, especially with an equally inexperienced male to share the experience with her. It would be inexcusable to allow her to come to harm.

She coded in a message to the house father. It would be up to the servant to rein in the headstrong young male. The GODs' gift was not to be rushed into.

She glanced at her god-half and smiled. No matter how we rushed headlong into it. *"It seems these youngsters might best our time to ascension."*

His laughter echoed off the walls.

* * * *

Julee tarried in the bathing room, her heart hammering. The clothing left for her for the night was nothing like her usual sleeping clothes. There were no sleep pants. Had the sleep tunic been of the usual style, she might have believed they'd simply split a single outfit between them, since Staphan had emerged from his bathing wearing nothing *but* sleep pants.

Idiot! For all she knew, the male godlings always slept in sleep pants and nothing more.

But this sleep tunic was nothing like the ones she usually wore. In fact, Julee wasn't certain it could rightly be called a tunic, since it was sleeveless and without shoulders, save the two tiny straps that led from the apex of the angle of fabric above her breasts, over her shoulders, to the fabric that ended mid-back. It was also longer than a tunic, reaching mid-thigh instead of her waist in length.

It is indecent.

She corrected herself sternly. *It is indecent for a godling. I am no longer of that status. I am a Demi-GOD.*

That fact firmly established, Julee left the bathing room, her head held high—and stopped short.

And there is that. She'd nearly forgotten it.

Staphan stood at the foot of the large bed they were meant to share.

He performed a long, slow perusal of the length of her body, sending pleasant chills along her nerve pathways without even a touch. Julee gasped in response.

As if her reaction meant something to him, Staphan stalked toward her, his muscles undulating beneath his skin in a way that made her heart pound alarmingly.

Not that his approach alarmed her, in and of itself. That was curiously appealing, in some animalistic way she couldn't name. It was simply her reaction that she found alarming.

But exciting.

Staphan settled his hands on her waist and pulled Julee to his body, his cock hot and hard between them. A gasp escaped her trembling lips. She couldn't account for the tremors of her muscles or the shortness of her breath.

"Shhh," Staphan soothed her. "I know what to do."

He does? How could he know such a thing? If his comments from the midday meal were as clear as they seemed to be, he could have no more knowledge about the GODs' gift than she had. *At least in a practical sense.*

His lips closed over hers, and Julee gasped in response. In the next heartbeat, they were crushed together, tongues entwined, breath mingling.

His body enveloped hers. Julee had never realized before how much larger than her Staphan was. It ramped up her enjoyment another notch.

His mouth left hers, and Staphan guided her to the bed. He hesitated a moment before he lifted her and laid Julee out on the silken sheets, her lower legs hanging off the side closer to him.

He stood over her, and Julee's heart pounded out a pleasant beat. She fought for the breath to question him. Realization that she couldn't fathom what she would ask if she did have the breath to do so made her mouth go dry.

What about the question of what he's waiting for?

Julee opened her mouth to ask it, and Staphan moved. His big hands pushed up at the sleep tunic, baring her thighs to his hot gaze. His eyes darkened as her female curls appeared from beneath the fabric and a groan escaped his lips.

There was another potent moment of stillness. Then Staphan's voice rumbled out, setting her heart stuttering.

"The GODs' gift is meant to be discovered slowly."

Julee nodded, though she didn't understand him.

"Good. Then we will proceed slowly."

He stepped toward her, between her knees, raised his hands, and slid the straps of fabric off her shoulders and down her arms. The triangles of fabric caught on the erect tips of her nipples, then slid away, sending whispers of pleasure from her breasts to her female core.

"This is indeed a gift," he breathed.

A niggling of unease at her nudity while Staphan remained dressed—*well, half dressed*—heated her cheeks. Julee considered pulling her clothing over herself.

Before she could move toward that end, Staphan was over her, his cock pressed to the hollow between her thighs, taunting her with the many pleasures she'd seen the servants engaged in. His lips parted hers, and he ravaged her mouth, leaving her lightheaded and gasping for breath.

Julee forced her hips up, seeking closer contact between his cock and her core. Staphan's hips cycled back and forth, stimulating her nub as she would do for herself.

But it is him and not me pleasuring myself. Why did that make it all the more exciting?

The heat between them rose and Julee pulled at Staphan's shoulders, wrapped her legs around his, and lost herself in the kiss. Staphan pinned her to the mattress, his cock lodged tight against her core. Wet heat bloomed between them and Staphan pulled back with a grunt. The combination of the heat and pressure shot Julee over the edge of bliss. Her shout of completion echoed off the walls.

Julee bit lightly at her lower lip, weak in pleasure. Staphan moved and her head spun at the change. An instant later, his mouth closed on her breast—and he suckled hard. That brought her mind into abrupt focus.

"Staphan." It came out little more than a gasp.

He grumbled something unintelligible into her flesh, and Julee gasped in response. Her mind rioted. One half wanted to push him away. The other half wanted to pull him closer. She'd never been so indecisive.

Staphan moved from one breast to the other, taking his time, testing the taste and feel of her breasts as if they had days to do so. Julee arched her back, urging him on with panted pleas for more.

Instead of speeding, Staphan did the opposite. He left her breasts and nuzzled down her silk-covered abdomen. That added to the depth of sensation, making Julee gasp in response.

Then his mouth was at her core, his tongue making lazy trails that forced a shout from her body. As if something uncorked in him, Staphan started lapping and suckling avidly.

Julee reached for him, catching a handful of his hair in her fist. Words stuck in her throat, and sharp sounds came out in their place.

On one level she knew precisely what Staphan was doing to her. On another, she'd never dreamed it would feel like this. Julee had never been so out of control of her own body.

The second climax was even more powerful than the first had been and conscious thought melted away entirely. Julee came back to reality, shivering, stunned by the potency of their shared experiences.

The GODs' gift, indeed.

Staphan settled his knee on the bed beside her and trailed a hand up his cock through his sleep pants.

Julee watched him, spellbound. She licked her lips.

He groaned. "Will you taste me as well, Julee?" His voice was low and breathy.

Her answer stuck in her still-unresponsive throat and Julee nodded.

* * * *

Staphan's heart took up a disconcerting non-rhythm at her agreement. Before he could right his senses, Julee was on her knees, her sleep shirt pooled around her hips.

GODs, but he'd never seen anything quite so beautiful. She was mussed and flushed. *And I caused that reaction.* He'd never realized how sexy it would be to see his focused and adept classmate in such a state.

Her fingers fumbled a bit against the tie on his sleep pants, then loosened them.

"Lie down on the bed, Staphan." Her voice was pure invitation that not even the female servants inviting the males had matched.

He levered himself onto the mattress and stretched out, his back to the pillows so he could watch what would happen next. Julee tugged his sleep pants down to his lower thighs, then wrapped her elegant fingers around his cock. The sensation nearly brought his backside off the bed in pleasant surprise.

She stroked him, up and down, until Staphan thought he might go mad in the need to climax. He let his head fall back and his eyes slide shut, giving himself up to her ministrations.

Julee chose that moment to engulf a large portion of his cock into the heat of her mouth. The sensation was too much for him, and Staphan shouted, stiffening beneath her.

She pulled back, and he shot a look of disbelief at her. For a moment, neither of them moved. Her wary expression spoke volumes about why she'd stopped. She wasn't sure he was enjoying what she was doing.

At a loss to reassure her, Staphan tipped his hips up, asking her to gift him further in the only way his muddled mind could concoct. Julee nodded and leaned over him, her breath sending tendrils of pleasure down his still-damp cock.

In the next moment, she sucked him down again, and Staphan moaned. He'd never known this would feel so much better than touching had.

And the servants say full intercourse is better. The urge to thrust inside her rode him hard.

No. Father said it had to be slowly. A day—maybe two or three—and we will be able to progress to that. What they were doing now was so overwhelming; perhaps it was better to take it slowly.

Julee experimented, moving faster, then slower, shallower, then deeper.

"Deeper," he begged.

She complied and his vision blurred. His muscles tightened in preparation for climax.

Some kernel of his thinking mind reminded Staphan that not all the female servants swallowed the male's fluids. Some pulled away instead and let the male spray outside their mouths.

Would Julee know when he felt the need to spray? Would she want to swallow or want to pull back? He'd never thought to ask these questions of Father and the other servants.

It was only right to warn her, he supposed. "I'm going to spray," he gasped out. "Julee, I—"

His voice choked off as she buried her face close to his abdomen, his cock nearly disappearing into her sweet mouth. Climax rolled through him and his hips pressed up; he seated himself at the back of her throat with a shout.

The rippling contractions of muscles up his cock seemed to go on and on. When they subsided, he lay spent on the mattress, his hand resting on the back of Julee's head. His breathing was ragged, his senses in a spin.

At last, she pulled back and aftershocks wracked him. A sticky trail of his fluids wet the sparse mat of hair below his naval. Julee licked the spot, tightening his muscles down and firing his drives for more.

She looked at the crumpled ring of her sleep shirt and made a show of removing it and dropping it to the floor. Staphan's cock ached for another taste of her.

"Did you enjoy?" he asked her, desperate to know her mind.

Her cheeks went an appealing shade of red, and she nodded. Her nipples came to renewed points, confirming it.

"You're not tired, are you?" he continued. *Please let her say no.*

"Not particularly," she replied.

Staphan smiled, and she shivered in response, her eyes going dreamy. He started removing his pants, and her gaze devoured every move.

When they were littered on the floor, Staphan cupped his fingers under Julee's chin and raised her gaze to meet his. "Good. I believe I'd like to try something in particular."

"What?" Her breathing had already gone choppy.

He trailed a finger along her lower lip, savoring her breath along the pad of his fingertip. "Pleasuring each other at the same time."

Her breasts heaved, and her eyes sparkled her agreement before she managed to gasp out the words.

Chapter Six

The goddess-half of GOD-Node 103 reached over and squeezed her god-half's hand, her heart tripping in excitement.

The servants for Class 2 had reported the Demi-GODs had slept separately. They'd entered in the morning to find the god-half on the couch, with a sheet and pillow, while the goddess-half rested in the bed intended for them both, neither asleep but neither going about a morning routine, probably in a misguided attempt to avoid passing each other unnecessarily. When they'd risen, they chose to eat at the table, the goddess-half wrapped in a blanket, seemingly shy of having the god-half see her in the night clothes she'd been given. It was not a promising start to their association.

By comparison, the servants for Class 1 had reported they'd had to wake the Demi-GODs from a deep slumber to feed them. The two left their shared bed to attend to morning needs—after pulling on sleep clothes recovered from the floor—lacking in sleep and decidedly rumpled from sexual play. Then they'd returned to the bed to share their meal. There had been no sign of full consummation, but they were well on their way to it.

Just as we'd hoped. *The goddess-half reminded herself that they'd ordered the house father to attempt to slow the Demi-GODs.* Perhaps we should tell him to let their passion take its course. Clearly, the young male doesn't lack in restraint. The chances of him seriously injuring the female are remote.

"I know what you are thinking," her god-half informed her.

She stared at him, then looked toward his side of the screen. A message to both house parents already waited her agreement to send it.

The goddess-half gasped in surprise.

"Too much?" he asked.

"Perfect," she countered. She coded in her agreement and the message was off.

* * * *

Julee waited in the bed while Staphan went through his nightly toileting routine. She ran a hand down the length of the sleep shirt provided for her that evening and considered it.

They both knew there would be more experimentation with the GODs' gift, and the sleep clothing had been discarded so quickly the night before, there hardly seemed to be a reason to wear it at all. But did she dare make so bold a statement?

The servants know we are learning the GODs' gift. They are encouraging it. Why should it be unexpected that I should dispense with the illusion that we will be keeping to our own sides of the mattress and sleeping?

That decided, Julee stripped off the sleep shirt and tossed it across the room. The momentary sense of triumph melted into uncertainty. She was sitting on the bed, nude and waiting for Staphan to emerge, her nipples already begging for his hands and mouth, her slit already wet and throbbing in need.

She considered putting the sleep shirt back on— then rejected that idea as ridiculous. Instead, she picked up one of the glasses of red liquid the servants had left for them, along with an assortment of strange little foods.

The liquid was tangy and burned a pleasant fire trail down her throat, warming her chest and abdomen. Mother's words when she'd left the tray resonated in Julee's mind.

"This will help with your play at the GODs' gift."

Julee hadn't questioned how Mother had known they'd been experimenting. The servants in the temple seemed to know everything they did and had since they were toddling godlings, playing with their first pieces of sacred technology.

If it will help, perhaps I should drink more of it. In addition to the two glasses, there was a full cut-glass bottle of the same liquid.

She took another swallow and considered that. Last night had been amazing, more pleasurable than Julee had ever imagined the GODs' gift could be. How much better could it be? What would they need help to accomplish?

The servants had never steered them wrong before. If Mother believed this was important, Julee would trust that it was so.

With that in mind, she emptied the glass and refilled it. Julee took her time with the second glass, and by the time it was also gone, her body was lazy and warm. She'd no sooner filled the glass again than Staphan emerged from the bathing room.

He stopped short in the doorway, his gaze trailing up her body and down again, his half-erect cock going stiff in approval. Julee spread her legs, bringing her knees up, trailing the fingertips of one hand up her wet slit.

Staphan untied his sleeping pants, let them drop, stepped out of them, then strode across the room to her. As soon as he was close enough, Julee wrapped a hand around his neck and pulled him into a deep kiss.

His mouth was even more succulent than it had been the night before, and she set her glass on the table to wrap herself around him. After a moment, he pulled back and glanced toward the table.

Julee followed his line of sight. She plucked the second glass from the tray and offered it to Staphan. One of his eyebrows rose in question.

"Mother said it would help in our experimentation," she offered, letting the words drip in conspiracy.

Staphan grasped the cup and drank it down. Julee picked up her own and took down another mouthful.

He eyed the move as he reached for the bottle. "How much have you had already?"

"This is my third."

A crooked smile pulled up one side of his lips. "I have some catching up to do, it seems."

He drank down the second glass as quickly as he had the first. Then a third. Julee took up the challenge and drained her glass. Staphan took them both and set them on the tray.

Then he covered her with his body, his legs forcing hers out so she could feel the touch of his cock where she wanted him so desperately.

But Staphan didn't thrust into her as she expected. Instead, he brought his mouth down on hers in a heated kiss. One hand settled at the small of her back and anchored Julee against him. The other made a rough survey of her breast and started kneading at the nipple.

The heat between them rose, and her mind retreated into faint snips of sensation, overlapping and driving her crazy with need. Julee tipped her hips back and forth, stroking herself with the head of his cock.

Staphan pulled back from the kiss on a groan. "I want to be inside you so badly."

"Then do it." What was he waiting for?

He hesitated, and Julee doubled her efforts. She levered herself down his body, capturing his cock between her outer lips.

Staphan brought his lips down on hers, fevered, the hand on her back guiding her, helping her stroke the soft top of his cock between her slit. In moments, they were both venting moans into the kiss.

He left the kiss abruptly, seated his cock at the entrance to her body, and thrust into her. Conflicting sensations overwhelmed her, and Julee arched up from the mattress, driving him deeper in the process.

For a moment, Staphan was still, buried inside her quivering body. Then he moaned deeply and started levering himself in and out. The muscles of his arms and chest undulated with every thrust, and his neck strained. His eyes were half-lidded, and his breathing came in gasps and starts.

Julee wrapped her arms around his shoulders, enjoying the interplay of the muscles down his back. Thrust after thrust drew her closer to climax, and she ran her lips along his chest, picking up droplets of sweet sweat.

He tensed, heat erupting from his cock and spilling into her body. The added layer was too much, and Julee followed him over into climax.

They lay locked together, her legs wrapped around his waist, her calves nestled to the rock-hard muscles of his ass. Nothing had ever felt this good.

When Staphan didn't offer one of his usual comments or questions, Julee wondered at it.

"Was it what you'd hoped?" she asked, trying to break the silence.

"Better. And you?"

"There aren't words to describe it. Or if there are, my mind isn't capable of retrieving them." She offered what felt like a weak smile.

He rolled onto his back, bringing her over him, still impaled on his length. Staphan hadn't gone limp yet. The male servants she'd seen always went limp. Was it because the servants were older than they were? Or was there another reason for his continued erection?

"Perhaps we should invent some," he suggested, his voice hinting at a dark secret between them. "Then perhaps more of that drink."

"Invent words?" What in the world did he mean?

Staphan thrust his hips up, and Julee arched back with a gasp of surprise.

"Word number one?" Staphan's voice was false innocence if she'd ever heard it.

And she loved it. "Oh yes."

Chapter Seven

GOD-Node 103 oversaw the preparations being carried out. Though they'd given the young Demi-GODs privacy the two previous nights, there was little question consummation had occurred. The next few hours would tell the tale. Considering what the house parents and food-servants had witnessed so far, there would be an ascension. If not today, within a few more cycles of the bulwark standard clock.

With the grace of the assembled GOD-Nodes, all would be well.

* * * *

Julee shifted beneath the sheet, groggily working at the odd sensation of silk against her skin. It wasn't just teasing at her legs and arms. The soft material caressed her hips, belly, and breasts.

At the realization that she was nude beneath the sheet again, she snapped awake. Staphan lay on his side, facing her, still slumbering.

Visions of his face at the height of their passion ignited the pulse beat of arousal in her abdomen. On its tail came an ache deep in her belly.

Julee pressed hand to it, biting back a groan. She moved toward the edge of the bed, the silk sheet trailing off her body. Her gaze locked on the blood staining the white silk, and she stopped short.

She worked at the problem. Her moon time had ended only a week earlier. It was too soon for another, but she'd clearly bled from her slit, as she would at her time of month.

Fresher trails led from the stain to her body.

I am bleeding! Was something wrong with her? Should she call the healers?

"Julee?" Staphan's hand closed on her shoulder, and he eased her to his chest. "What is wrong?"

"B-blood," she stammered.

He moved abruptly, searching her for signs of injury. His hand pressed to her inner thigh, and his breathing went choppy. "It's dried. But where—"

"I don't know," she all but screeched.

Staphan scooped her up and carried her to the tub. He settled her on the edge, turned the water on with one hand, and collected a cloth with the other.

Julee slipped into the water, sighing in relief. As when it was her moon time, the heat soothed the discomfort of her cramping.

Staphan followed her in, rubbing gently at the streaks of blood on her skin. Julee groaned at the whispers of pain.

"Can you let me see?" Staphan requested.

She nodded and rose. Julee pressed a hand to her aching slit and pulled it away. Fresh blood coated her fingers, and she whimpered. Whatever this was, it surely wasn't good.

Staphan vaulted from the tub and crossed the bathing area in two long strides. He hit the communication button with enough force to make her wince.

"We need a healer," he demanded. "We need a healer for my goddess-half."

She sank into the tub, her knees trembling beneath her.

Before she could catch her breath, servants surrounded them.

"What is it, Julee?" Mother asked urgently.

She raised her hand, showing the house mother the blood on her fingers. The woman would know Julee's cycle as well as she did herself.

As if confirming that, Mother nodded, and the servants lifted her from the tub. Sheets of soft material wrapped around her.

Julee reached for Staphan, needing his comfort.

"Not now, Julee," Mother soothed her.

It wasn't the answer Julee needed to hear. She struggled against their hold, landing sloppily on her wet feet, calling out for Staphan.

* * * *

Father grasped Staphan around the chest, holding him back. "Calm. They only mean to prepare her."

"She's injured," he protested. *And she's calling for me.* How could they ask him to ignore that?

"No. Your goddess-half is well. She is simply adjusting... changing from her Demi-GOD form to her GOD form."

Julee's head snapped around, and she paled another notch. The female servants moved closer to her, supporting her shaking form.

Staphan managed a strained smile. He wanted to congratulate her but he couldn't force the words to do it. He bowed his head to her, forcing his muscles to relax. Julee was to ascend. It was the dream of every young godling. He would not stand in her way.

"No." Julee's voice cracked in emotion. "Staphan, please."

He winced at that. She was a GOD. He was beneath her, Demi-GOD or not. She should not concern herself with him.

She is changing, enduring an unfathomable transformation. They will overlook this breach of etiquette.

Then again, they'd been taught not to concern themselves with the distractions of others while they were godlings. They'd been taught that was a concern for GODs. Now that she was a GOD, perhaps it was expected that she would concern herself with him thus.

GODs, please let that be so. If she lost her chance to ascend now, when she was so close, how would either of them cope with it?

Mother offered soothing sounds. "You are two halves of a single GOD, Julee. As you must be prepared, so must Staphan."

He looked up at Father, shaking his head miserably. "I've felt no pain, Father. I have not bled." Lying about such a thing would be dishonorable, unworthy of even a godling, let alone a Demi-GOD. Even if Julee ascended without him, he wouldn't lie to go with her.

Father chuckled and clapped a hand on Staphan's shoulder. "You hurt, young GOD. You hurt in ways vastly different but not unlike the pains of your goddess-half."

Staphan started to deny it, but he couldn't. His heart ached at the thought of losing her. "Yes," he admitted. "I hurt."

Julee smiled, though her eyes shined in unshed tears.

Mother wrapped an arm around her, guiding Julee toward the door. His goddess-half peeked back at him and offered an excited little wave of her fingertips.

Staphan's heart lurched, and he felt his cheeks heat.

"Staphan?" Father intoned. "Does it please you to be prepared for your ascension?"

We will ascend together. "Yes. It does please me."

* * * *

Julee settled to the cushioned lounge with a sigh of relief. She'd never known there was pain involved in ascending.

As if reading her thoughts, Mother answered. "The pain will pass, young GOD. There will be other pains and illnesses to come. Being a Mother GOD is not always an easy road."

Julee listened, drinking from a chilled cup the servants offered. The liquid was odd but pleasing. "Mother GOD?" she asked.

It seemed Mother had been waiting for the question. "Where do the godlings come from?"

She indulged in several sips, forming her answer carefully. "The GODs sent their beloved godlings to—"

"Not the Great Book, young one. Think now... for yourself. Extrapolate from what the Great Book says and what you have learned in your time as a Demi-GOD."

Julee drained the cup, letting her mind wander to the Great Book's tales. As when she was coding, she let associations form.

Her heart stuttered. "They made them, made the godlings. The GODs made them, male and female, in their image," she breathed. "By sharing the GODs' gift, the GODs make the godlings?"

Mother planted a kiss on her forehead. "Some of the godlings," she corrected. "Do you remember a time before you were a godling in the temple?"

Julee worked at that but her mind seemed lax and her body uncoordinated. "Flashes, perhaps. I remember color... bright riots of color." Since godlings were raised with a minimum of it, that had to be before she'd come to the temple to begin her training on the face of the world.

"Yes. Your parents' home was very colorful."

"P-parents?" Julee tried, but she couldn't picture faces to go with the title.

"Those who gave life to you via the GODs' gift."

That didn't help. "I have no memory of parents." Should she have such a memory?

Mother motioned a screen forward, and two servants obliged. Julee stared at the vid of a young man and woman playing with a small child. Though the adults smiled, there was something sad in their eyes.

"It is the day they sent me down," she guessed.

"Up," Mother corrected. "Yes. They have seen only vids of you since that day. Vids and reports of your successes in your bid to ascend."

"Up? What? Why would I move up instead of down? The Great Book says—"

"The first few generations of godlings were all descended from the GODs, in the belief that their genetics and training would be enough."

"It wasn't," Julee guessed.

"No. Many of the godlings were not suited to becoming GODs. It is imperative that we have GODs coding the world."

"Of course." It was the most sacred pact between GODs and humans.

"Testing was implemented, testing to find any child who might be suited to the duties of a GOD. A surprising number came from human families." Mother stopped, probably to let Julee digest that.

"I came from a human family?" Why had no one told her? All this time she'd believed herself divine when she was human. How could a human ascend to be with the GODs?

"One of the strongest we've ever found," she confirmed. "A worthy young GOD, as the testing showed you would be."

Julee's mouth went dry. "And Staphan?"

"Was born of a GOD pair. He will meet his family again when you ascend together."

Disturbing thoughts rifled through her muddled mind.

"Julee? Is something wrong?"

"He is a true GOD then," she mumbled.

Mother cupped her chin and tipped Julee's head back to see her face better. Her smile held a hint of exasperation. "You are *both* true GODs. If you were not, you would not be ascending. Do you understand me, Julee?"

"I understand." But she didn't. How could anyone consider her a true GOD when she'd been born of humans?

Chapter Eight

GOD-Node 103 finished the last of the coding that would be completed that day. It was time. The ascension of a new GOD-Node was always reason for excitement among the assembled GODs and humans alike. But this ascension was also the return of a godling sent down from on high. That made it all the more special to those GODs who had known him or her as a child or given birth to him or her.

The humans wouldn't know that. They would have no knowledge of the parentage of a new ascending GOD, unless they themselves were the parents of said GOD. The ascending female's parents had already been invited to watch their daughter ascend, to witness their GOD-child's triumph with their human eyes. It was a moment few humans were ever privileged enough to see.

Then again, few GOD-Nodes were privileged enough to celebrate the return of their young godling as a GOD.

* * * *

Staphan pulled at the folds of golden silk, self-conscious to be wearing nothing but meters of cloth wrapped in intricate patterns around his body and the small jewels of a matching color at his wrists. He stood in the corridor, surrounded by temple servants garbed in silk versions of their usual daily trousers and tunics, white as they always wore.

For that matter, this was the first time in Staphan's life he could recall wearing anything but white himself.

Father moved to his side and bowed his head in a way that spoke of years of ceremony. At a loss for the proper response to it, Staphan tipped his head, indicating an invitation to speak. How did one speak to someone who had formerly been your master when the roles were reversed?

"Only a moment. The servants are bringing your goddess-half to her place for the ceremony."

"Good." He wanted to know what the ceremony was, but it seemed none of the servants were inclined to explain it. "Is there anything in particular I should do for the ceremony?" Perhaps rephrasing it would result in an answer he could quantify.

Father smiled. "Answer the questions posed to you. Drink of the GODs' nectar when invited to do so. Whatever else you and your goddess-half do will be your own choice."

That was more information than he'd been given thus far. Staphan supposed he should be grateful for being told that much.

"It is time," someone else whispered.

Staphan straightened, his heart pounding in anticipation. *Time. Time to be recognized as a GOD of Bulwark Ten. Time to ascend to on high with Julee as my goddess-half.* Could life be more perfect?

The doors before him opened, and Father waved him toward the dais where two of the Masters' Class instructors stood.

Staphan didn't know the names of the male and female. They'd never known the names of their instructors and servants. There were only Mother, Father, instructors, and various classes of servants. In retrospect, it seemed odd to him, though he'd accepted for years that trivialities such as names were beneath his notice.

The hum of conversation in the room fell off at his first step through the doorway. At the second, someone gasped. Staphan didn't bother to look for who might have done so. He focused on the two instructors—dressed in silver instead of white, he noticed.

Other anomalies became apparent as he approached.

The female had an ornate hairstyle with silver beads and ribbons threaded into the many white-blond braids. Instructors and servants always had their hair loose and natural or pulled back in a simple ponytail at the back of the head.

Moreover, she had clear jewels in a pattern on her face, one at the center of her forehead and a line of them along her cheekbones.

They were both dressed in clothing like those Staphan currently wore instead of the trousers and tunics people typically wore in the temple.

It is a ceremony. Perhaps those officiating are required to dress for ceremony as Julee and I have been prepared for it.

As if the thought drew her, the door opposite the one he'd entered from opened, revealing Julee. Her hair was a close match for the female instructor on the dais—darker, but in a similar style, with beads and ribbons of red that matched her layers of silk. Jewels of shimmering red adorned her forehead and the outer corners of her eyes, accentuating the shape of her face.

She walked to Staphan, the cadre of female servants fanning out behind her as his own had probably arranged themselves behind Staphan. She came to a stop, face-to-face with him; spellbound, neither looked away.

"Welcome young GODs," the female instructor intoned.

Julee and Staphan turned their heads politely to acknowledge her.

"Welcome witnesses and blessed parents," the male added.

Julee stiffened a notch, then scanned the crowd. Her gaze locked on something indefinable, and Staphan followed her line of sight.

The couple were clearly human, dressed in bright blues and greens, in styles completely unlike those of the other witnesses to their ascension. Silver garlands encircled their heads. Staphan had no concept what the title given to them might signify, but they were clearly valued members of society to witness a ceremony such as this.

To be permitted in the upper temple at all. As a rule, humans were not permitted entry to more than the lower few levels, unless they were servants to the godlings.

The female human pressed her hands to her mouth, and the male wrapped an arm around her as if in comfort.

Julee swallowed hard. "May I speak to them?"

Staphan furrowed his brow. She wished to speak to humans? Was it curiosity? Was it a budding awareness of the GODs' duty to the humans driving her? Or was there something more to her earnest request?

"After the ceremony, you may if you choose to do so," Mother instructed.

Julee nodded, then turned back to the instructors.

As if taking that as permission to continue, the two bowed their heads to Staphan and Julee.

"Accepting the duties of the GODs is the single most serious vow a Demi-GOD can enter into," the male informed them. "Do you understand the commitment you will promise to make this day?"

To serve the humans of the world from the day of ascension until death. "I do."

Beside him, Julee gave the same reply.

The female continued. "Do you promise to code the world faithfully and with all due diligence?"

"I do." Their voices were more sure and nearly in unison.

"Do you promise to hold the lives and safety of the humans above all else?" the male asked.

"I do."

"Do you promise to be one with your mated half from this day until you ascend again?" The female.

Staphan looked at Julee, noting the color blooming in her cheeks. "I do."

"I do," she echoed him.

Mother and Father handed ornate cups to the two instructors, and they—in turn—held them before Julee and Staphan's lips.

"Drink of the GODs' nectar in solemn agreement to your duty to all of Bulwark Ten," the female invited.

Staphan took a mouthful down. It burned a trail down his throat, not unlike the drink they'd been gifted the night before. He started to withdraw.

"All of it, Staphan," Father informed him.

He swallowed down mouthful after mouthful, finding himself pleasantly relaxed by the time the cup retreated.

Julee finished a moment after he did. The instructors raised the cups over their heads and then set them, open end down, on the small table between them.

"Welcome, young GODs," the male announced. "The ascension will take place at your leisure."

That was it? Staphan had expected more.

As if in answer, everyone else in the room—save the two instructors officiating—went to one knee and bowed their heads. The marble floors rumbled at the mass movement.

Staphan looked around at the officiates for some guidance, but they had already retreated to a small room far back on the dais.

A glance at Julee revealed the look of longing she shot the two humans in attendance.

Staphan raised her hand and kissed the knuckles. "Come. Let us meet these...blessed parents."

* * * *

Julee gaped at him for a moment. Surely, he didn't understand what the title meant, just as she hadn't understood it before Mother told her.

Or perhaps he does. Perhaps Father told Staphan of his own parents.

"Julee? Are you well? Do you require a healer?" he asked. Concern made his voice soft and more than inviting.

Not now. Now I want to meet my parents. "No. I have already seen the healers." They'd tended to her aches and pains as part of her preparations.

He smiled and led her to the crowd, his hand cradling hers. Reaching her parents wasn't difficult. They'd been given a place at the front of the crowd.

They didn't look up at Julee when she approached.

They probably don't dare to. The Great Book cautioned about the dire consequences of looking upon the face of GODs.

That left Julee in the awkward position of deciding what to do next. If she ordered them to raise their heads, she would likely frighten them.

Before she could broach the subject, the male—her *father*—spoke. Julee had no memory of having a father. Mothers were for female godlings; Fathers were for male.

"Do you know who we are, young GOD?" His voice was tentative—perhaps a bit hopeful.

"Yes. I do. Mother told me this morning. I have seen vids of you."

Very old vids. They were no longer young as she was—as they'd been in the vids—and she wondered how much of the wear on them had been caused by giving her up to be trained as a godling. Since Julee had never wondered where the godlings came from before, she'd never had reason to consider the cost of giving up something as precious as a person you cared for. Until Staphan, she'd never *cared* for anyone in such a matter.

He nodded in reply, and the female—her *Mother*—sobbed. That spoke volumes of the pain she felt.

A thousandfold what I felt when the servants took me from Staphan this morning, she guessed.

Staphan shot her a questioning look.

Julee considered what to tell him and what his reaction might be to it.

It doesn't matter. This may be the only chance I have to ask them questions. To know the people who gave me life.

She started to squat to their level, but a flurry of motion from the servants brought her up short. A chair slid into place at the backs of her knees.

Is it considered un-GODlike to present myself in such an undignified position?

As if confirming it, Mother took her arm and made a show of aiding Julee to the surface of the chair. That settled, she focused on her parents again.

"Has your life been good?" she questioned them. It was the least they deserved after such a sacrifice.

"The GODs are benevolent and their gifts bountiful," her father answered automatically. "We thank them for their diligent care."

It was an answer from the depths of catechism, a meaningless reply borne of faith. *Not at all what I'd hoped for.* "Has *your* life been good to you?"

"We were compensated," her mother replied. "But we always missed you."

"Joan!" her father exclaimed, seemingly scandalized by his mate's simple statement of fact.

"It's true, Peter. Would you have our...GOD-child believe we did not miss her presence in our lives?"

He seemed unable to form an answer to that.

Julee nodded, her head still a bit fuzzy from the healing drinks and the GODs' nectar she'd been fed. Perhaps that was why Mother had helped her to sit.

Snapping her wandering mind back to the conversation, she addressed her mother again. "I imagine it was unbearable for you."

"Sometimes," Joan agreed.

Staphan's hand closed on Julee's shoulder in something akin to comfort. *Perhaps support?* It was difficult to quantify his meaning.

Her heart ached at the idea of losing them again now that she'd found them. This was inequitable. Staphan would be permitted to see his parents, since they were GODs. Why shouldn't she—and her parents—be gifted the same? Hadn't they all made the same sacrifices thus far?

"I will find a way," she vowed.

Her father started to raise his head then snapped it down again. "Pardon, young GOD?" he asked formally.

GODs were indulged, their every whim catered to. It was one of the benefits of their lifelong sacrifice and service.

My parents have sacrificed even more. Unlike Julee, they had spent the last eighteen years fully aware of what they'd lost.

"There is no reason to be hidden from each other. I know all." *Or will once I have ascended on high and have full access to the system of governance.*

Joan sobbed. "The GODs may never walk the face of the Earth," she quoted.

"Nor those of the Earth mingle on high with the GODs," Peter finished the verse for her.

That *was* a problem.

"If I may, young GODs?" Mother hinted from her place at Julee's side.

Julee looked up at her, startled at the intrusion.

"Please do," Staphan hastened to answer. There was a curious sort of energy in his voice that spoke of excitement or avid interest.

Julee covered his hand with her own, amazed at how such a small touch affected her.

Mother continued. "What your parents say is true enough, but there is another way."

Julee nodded her on.

"If it pleases you, you may meet with your blessed parents here, on the upper reaches of the temple on Holy Days."

Holy Days. Days when only the most pressing of work is done. Days when it would be wholly appropriate for both GODs and humans to visit the temple. "It pleases me," Julee decreed.

"Yes," Staphan spoke with her.

Now that she'd said it, it would be done. As if in silent confirmation, all the attending servants bowed to her.

My first decree as a GOD. And what a worthy one to make.

A movement caught Julee's attention and she looked down at her parents again. Her mother reached out as if to touch the silk of Julee's gown, stopping only centimeters away. Julee grasped her weathered hand and drew it up to her lips.

At her kiss, Joan gasped. She trembled wildly.

Julee hesitated a moment, then cupped her mother's face up. Tear-reddened blue eyes met Julie's gaze. There was a moment of stillness. Julee pressed a kiss to her mother's forehead in blessing.

She did the same for her father, noting that she had her mother's hair and her father's eyes. That made her wonder what the godlings she and Staphan created together would look like.

Father broke the silence. "You should ascend. The GODs' nectar will begin having its effect on you very soon."

Julee didn't nod in return. The buzzing in her head was more pronounced, lending credence to his warning.

"We will meet again," she promised.

At her move to stand, Mother took one arm and Staphan the other. That was a good thing. With her head spinning lightly, Julee was abruptly uncertain of her balance.

"This way." Mother's voice seemed to come from far away.

They entered a small room not unlike the one the officiates had entered earlier. There was a wide bed to one side, and Mother eased Julee to the surface of it.

Staphan seemed to weave on his feet, and Julee wondered if the nectar had made him as unbalanced as she was. Father reached out and helped Staphan down to the mattress beside her.

Father's instructions filtered into the fog of her muddled mind.

"You will be conveyed to your personal quarters now. The trip will take more than an hour."

"So long?" she slurred.

Mother smiled. "On high is very high, young GOD."

They waited a moment as if to allow for more questions. When Julee found herself unable to form one and Staphan remained silent, they bowed their heads, coded something into the panel by the doors, and left the room.

The doors slid shut, and a most disconcerting sensation of the floor moving assaulted her senses.

* * * *

Staphan considered the blessed parents they'd met. Clearly, they were the source from whence Julee came to be. So, godlings could ascend from a human birth. He'd never known that.

There are many things we are sure to learn. The GODs' gift was only the first of many new experiences and bits of information they were to encounter.

She'd said Mother had told her about the blessed parents. Father had told Staphan nothing of the sort. Had she asked a question of Mother the servant was forced by circumstance to answer? Had Staphan's lack of questioning meant they perceived he had no interest in his own blessed parents?

If Julee had them, surely he did as well. How many ways could a godling emerge into the world? Surely female godlings did not emerge via a completely different path than males did.

Or had they not mentioned his because he had no blessed parents? Had his died in the years he'd spent in the temple, lost before he could come to know them? That would be a true tragedy.

His heart stuttered at a worse possibility. Had his blessed parents refused to attend his ascension? Had they, unlike Julee's blessed parents, not missed his absence in their lives at all?

I will learn the truth. When I have access to the governance, I will learn why I was not presented a similar chance to know my source.

Julee traced a finger along Staphan's brow. "What has you so serious?" Her words slurred slightly.

He considered how much of his musings to reveal. For some reason, his obsession with the subject felt childish. Would she regret vowing to be his goddess-half if he disappointed her?

"Staphan?" Her palm cupped his cheek.

"Mother told you about your blessed parents?"

She nodded solemnly.

"Do all... Do all godlings come from such...?" He floundered for a way to ask it and not appear too concerned.

Her cheeks darkened, and her hand retreated. "Not all are human," she offered. "Some godlings descend from on high to the temple instead of ascending from the face of the Earth."

"But all are from...mated pairs, such as your blessed parents?"

Her brow furrowed in confusion. It smoothed, and her eyes widened. "Father did not tell you."

"Tell me what?"

"Where godlings come from."

Something told Staphan he was going to feel foolish for asking. "No. Where do godlings come from?"

Her face turned a deep scarlet that matched her dress.

"Julee?"

"The...the GODs' gift results in...godlings," she supplied meekly. She wiggled on the mattress as if discomforted by the discussion.

"Always?" The question was out before he could tame his tongue.

Her wiggling became more pronounced. "I don't know. I forgot to ask it."

Staphan stared at her, the spinning in his head intensifying. Had they already created a godling? How many godlings could one create? And how would they know? If she hadn't asked for the specifics, it would be yet another thing they would have to learn by accessing the governance and questioning the information banks.

"What *did* Mother tell you?" he asked urgently.

"That I ascended to the temple from my human parents and you descended from your GOD-parents."

"I have blessed parents then." That was something of a relief.

"Of course. Everyone does."

She'd misunderstood his question. "No. I meant... Do they still live? Do they not want to know me? What reason could they have for not attending my ascension as your blessed parents did?" That snub still hurt.

Julee smiled, but it was lopsided and rather weak. "They live. You will be meeting them on high." She motioned to the ceiling of the moving room. "I don't know why they didn't attend the ascension. Perhaps GODs do not?"

He'd like to believe it, but the statements thus far did not factor that direction. "GODs are permitted to enter the upper temple. Mother said so," he reminded her.

She was silent for a moment and offered her next statement in a rather sad, little voice. "Perhaps my blessed parents were not to see the faces of yours. Perhaps... Perhaps their presences precluded the presence of yours. If so... I am so sorry, Staphan."

He wanted to laugh but restrained himself. "There is nothing for you to be sorry for." He kissed her.

The flavor of her mouth went to his swimming senses, and Staphan kissed her again—and again. Each kiss was deeper and longer. He savored every one.

They rubbed against each other, body touching body through the silk wraps. Staphan startled at her bare nipple rubbing against his bare chest. He looked down, smiling at the sight of the wraps in complete disarray. A nipple poked through here. He had a peek of her naval here and another of her women's curls there. Overall, this form of dress was quite the enticement.

He pinched at the nipple, and Julee looked up at him with slumberous eyes. Staphan lowered his head and licked it, savoring her gasp.

"I know a game," he breathed into her breast, parting the silk farther with his fingers, so he could take more of the bare breast into his mouth.

"What game?" She forced her breast deeper between his lips.

Staphan didn't answer immediately. Instead, he paid brutal attention to her uncovered breast, and Julee wiggled against him. When he pulled away, he surveyed the silk wraps again. More of her cleft was visible to him.

GODs, this is going to be good.

"The game is played thus. We cannot touch or suckle or...join until the wraps are parted enough to do so. We cannot remove the wraps. They must part in play at other—" He suckled hard at her breast again. "—accessible parts."

Julee didn't waste time. She rubbed her body up and down his, seeking to bunch the wraps. Her opposite nipple pressed out at a single layer of silk and Staphan's mouth watered to taste it.

Play by the rules.

Instead, he went back to the uncovered nipple, nipping at it, licking at it, drinking in every sound Julee made and the silk against skin interplay of the game.

She made a sound that spoke of triumph, and Staphan raised his head. The other nipple jutted into the cool air, practically begging him to move to it.

"Well done," he complimented her before he obliged her.

Julee moved this way and that—then wrapped one leg around his hip. Staphan was considering telling her she was cheating when she pushed her hips up, and his bare cockhead touched wet slit.

That stole his breath. GODs, why had none of the servants told them coupling felt so good?

Probably because they knew we'd find any way we could to experiment if we knew.

Cheating or not, he wasn't passing up this opportunity. Staphan swayed forward and back, playing his cock just inside her and retreating.

Julee's hand closed in the silk at his hip and yanked. It was both pleasure and pain. The silk released the length of his cock but pulled tight around his sac.

He eased inside her, her inner muscles gripping him tight, the silk pulling taut against his sac at every forward motion. Twice, he came close to climax, and the silk held him back.

At last Julee plunged over the edge, her inner muscles milking him. Even the silk couldn't stop his ascent and he followed her over, his senses in a flat-spin.

They lay in the aftermath, trading slow kisses. Voices whispered somewhere nearby, and Staphan tried to ignore them.

The sensation of movement changed. They were no longer rising. Instead, they were moving horizontally.

The voices persisted.

"...such good luck."

"Shhh... Don't break the spell."

Staphan broke off the kiss. "Quiet. Leave us."

The bed stopped moving and all went silent. Relieved, he returned to his exploration of his goddess-half.

Chapter Nine

They'd barely yawned and started stirring the next morning, when movement on three sides startled Staphan awake. He looked around, blearily taking count of a full dozen servants waiting patiently to serve their newest GODs.

"What is it?" Julee asked, pushing the tangled hair that had escaped the braids from her eyes.

"Will you take your meal here or at the table?" one of the servants asked. This one stood a pace closer to the bed and was farther separated from the others by a red sash tied about her waist over the plain white pants and tunic.

Staphan stretched, a lazy reach to the furthest corners of the mattress. "The table," he instructed them. "In a few moments."

Julee laughed. "A new start to our life as GODs?"

He chuckled in reply. "Perhaps."

"Very well."

"As you wish, my GODs." The reply came in unison, and all the servants, save the one with the red sash, withdrew.

That one bowed again. "Does it please you to meet with a few of the other GODs while you eat?"

"Yes." Julee's voice held an edge of urgency that startled him.

Staphan stared at her for a long moment. At last, he unglued his tongue. "Is there some meaning to this?" That was likely. It seemed Mother had given her much more information than Father had given Staphan.

Her cheeks darkened in a flush. "Perhaps. I...hope there is." She shot a glance at the remaining servant.

It seemed the servant had no more idea what she might be seeking than he had. She waited silently for their discussion to end.

Why isn't she taking Julee's word on this? Is it because I've questioned her on it?

Staphan cupped his goddess-half's cheek with his hand and brushed a kiss against her lips. "If you feel it has meaning, we will meet with the GODs."

"As you wish, my GODs," the servant acknowledged. In the next moment, she was gone.

Staphan stared after her for a moment. When the door closed behind the servant, Staphan took a calming breath.

"There is so much to learn," Julee breathed.

He enfolded her in a hug. "We have access to the governance now. We will learn whatever it is quickly."

"I hope so."

They left the bed nude. Staphan wondered about that. Had the servants undressed them? Or had they done so themselves in the haze of passion?

A glance at the floor revealed none of the silk they'd ascended in. Since the servants hadn't carried it out with them, it lent credence to the concept that the servants had undressed them. *Or they came in while we slept and removed the wraps we'd doffed ourselves.* That was an equal possibility, he had to admit.

Either way, they have likely seen us naked. Had they been the servants who'd been with them for years, Staphan decided it wouldn't have felt as much like an intrusion as it did.

Perhaps modesty is another concern for godlings but not for GODs. Until they had access to the governance, there was no way to know for certain.

Julee lifted one of the pieces of clothing laid at the foot of the mattress for them. "A robe." She lifted the second, then stared at Staphan.

He didn't have to question what she was thinking. The robes—red and gold, matching the silk wraps they'd ascended in—were the only clothes that had been provided for them. As godlings or Demi-GODs, they'd only worn robes over sleep outfits. It seemed the servants expected them to wear the robes—and nothing else.

The lump in his throat wasn't nearly as hard as the cock rising against his abdomen. The thought of Julee, nude beneath such a flimsy bit of clothing, was enough to make him want to ignore the other GODs, skip breakfast, and take his goddess-half back to bed.

Probably not the safest choice, until we know the laws governing us. Instead, he cleared his throat. "We will access the governance as soon as the GODs depart."

Her face went as dark as the jewels she still wore. In the next instant, she was pulling the red robe on and rushing for the bathing room.

* * * *

The morning meal was heavy in meats and breads, lush in the scents of syrup, hot drinks, and fruit compote. Staphan had never seen so much food at a single sitting.

For that matter, he'd never been as ravenous as he was at this moment. It seemed he couldn't get enough of the food laid out for them. That might have concerned him if Julee wasn't also eating much more than usual.

"Ah... I remember our first morning on high," a female voice rang out. "The drug does make one so hungry in the aftermath."

Staphan snapped his head around and nearly choked at the sight of the two officiates from their ceremony. *They are GODs?* The Demi-GODs had been trained by GODs? For how long? How many of the GODs had graced the godlings and Demi-GODs with their presence?

He started to rise, then stopped himself. They were no longer his betters. The GODs were now his equals.

"Very good, Staphan," the male GOD intoned.

The two came to the table and the male held the chair for what Staphan assumed was his goddess-half. Now that he considered it, he realized he'd never seen them apart.

Like Julee, the goddess-half still wore the face jewels she'd worn for ceremony. He wondered if they were permanent fixtures now that Julee was a GOD.

A pulling sensation at his wrist reminded Staphan that he still wore the golden jewels at his wrists. He watched for the flash of them on the god-half's wrists and noted that he wore a clear set.

Julee swallowed a mouthful of food. "I suppose we should welcome you."

The female smiled, then bowed her head. "I thank you for your welcome."

"Are you...?" Julee shot Staphan a look he couldn't identify.

The elder goddess-half's smile faltered a notch and she grasped her god-half's hand. "Yes. Who else would request an audience today, of all days?" Her cheeks darkened in a deep blush and she turned her attention to Staphan.

The longing in her eyes seared him, and his mouth went dry. "You are my...blessed parents?" Had they come to see his ascension, after all?

See it? If it is they, they performed the ceremony to allow me to ascend with Julee personally. His head spun at the thought of such a gift.

She smiled, though tears pooled in her eyes.

Her god-half cleared his throat and nodded. "I hope you can forgive the deception. It is always done this way. Though we have often come down to the temple to see you, we were not permitted to interfere in your training."

"Not permitted?" Julee voiced the question for him. "I thought GODs were denied nothing."

"Just this," the goddess-half replied sadly. "When a young one tests favorably to becoming a GOD, we must relinquish him to training, just as humans do. I bless fate that I had one child of three who tested poorly."

"Three?" Staphan croaked. "Then I have..." *What does one call another young one born of the same blessed parents?*

As if his thoughts had been spoken aloud, the god-half sighed and stepped to one side, taking the chair next to his goddess-half. He leaned across the table toward Staphan. "They are called siblings, Staphan. You have a brother and a sister...a male and female sibling, respectively. Both are older than you are. Your brother was deemed unworthy to be a GOD and returned to us as a favored companion. Your sister did not test favorably and was raised on high with us."

His goddess-half grasped his hand. "And now you have returned." She stared at Staphan, seemingly waiting for something he couldn't name.

Realization came slowly. She hoped he would want to visit with them as Julee's blessed parents wished the same. Staphan searched for how to phrase his agreement. His eagerness. Would it be frowned upon for him to admit eagerness? Other emotional shows had been overlooked.

Julee beat him to it. "Perhaps you would like to spend time with Staphan? When...? Oh, there is so much we do not know."

The god-half chuckled. "We asked to instruct you." He met Staphan's gaze steadily. "If that pleases you, of course."

"Yes." It was out in a rush of sound that left Staphan's lungs feeling spent. "It would please us."

"Very well. What would you like to ask first?"

There were so many questions. Where did one begin? In ordering them, Staphan realized many of the questions they wanted answers to could be answered with a single one. "How do we access the governance?"

The two elder GODs smiled broadly. At last, the female spoke. "We *are* the governance, Staphan." Her hand motion encompassed all four GODs around the table. "If there is anything you wish to know, you ask an elder GOD-pair. The time will come when you will be the elder GOD-pair, teaching another young GOD-

Node the whole of their existence and that of every living thing within the bulwark."

Her god-half took over for her, in a nearly seamless way that said they were accustomed to giving this speech. "If you wish to send an e-note, that is acceptable, of course. If you wish a face-to-face meeting like this one, send an e-note requesting it. It is not courteous to expect the other GODs to always come to you, but on occasion, it is...wise to invite other GODs into your quarters."

Staphan tried to decide what to ask next. The long ride from the temple to their quarters resonated with him. "Do you... Are your quarters far from here?" he asked. How often would he be able to see his blessed parents?

The goddess-half motioned toward the door they'd entered from. "None of the GOD-Nodes are far. This high on the bulwark, the circle closes quickly."

The old saying. The circle closes quickly when one is at the edge. But what does it mean?

She continued speaking, oblivious to his preoccupation with the saying. "We are GOD-Node one-oh-three. You are GOD-Node sixty."

"Forty-three nodes separated then," Julee calculated.

The Goddess-half laughed a tinkling laugh. "Not so simple, young one. The Nodes, like other electrical components, are arranged not in a straight line, but rather in an interlinking net."

Her god-half motioned to the door again. "Through that door is a vast network of tunnels, connecting all the GOD-Nodes. There are two hundred in total. There are trams. Your servants can arrange for all your travel, if you wish, but we are within a comfortable walking distance. Much less than you ran in early physical training. If you do not wish to take the trams, you need not."

One of the servants cleared his throat.

The god-half shot an irritated look at the servant. "Yes, I know. We are safer in the trams, in case of emergency." He looked at Staphan, seemingly exasperated. "They endlessly try to tell us what is best for ourselves. They will tell you all sorts of things are best, but remember that you are the GOD-pair."

So far, Staphan liked everything he'd heard. It sounded as if he'd be able to see his blessed parents as often as he liked.

"Of course," the god-half hedged. "Of course, courtesy dictates that one should always e-note another GOD-Node before visiting. It doesn't do to show up unannounced. The servants get so picky about being properly prepared to entertain visiting GOD-pairs."

"And *some* GOD-Nodes prefer their privacy and only admit guests at their leisure," his goddess-half inserted.

Perhaps not so often. Were his blessed parents the type that liked their privacy? Staphan's heart sank.

As if the goddess-half saw disappointment in his face, she hurried on. "You will see e-notes on your terminal, or the servants will pass messages to you when you wake." She paused for a moment. "We will always have time for you, Staphan. For you both—if you wish to spend time with us." She bowed her head as if in seal of a promise.

"Yes, we will," her god-half agreed.

In the background, Staphan saw the servants bowing and whispering. Were they committing the promise to memory? How little they knew about the servants on high.

"Which brings us to our reason for coming here today," the goddess-half offered brightly.

"Which is?" Julee inquired, edging back into the conversation.

"You will have many questions," the goddess-half continued. "After ascension, the entire bulwark enjoys three days of holiday."

"Including those on high," the god-half inserted.

"During which, the new GOD-Node learns as much as they can about their new lives."

There was a moment of silence, during which Staphan weighed what they were being told—three days to learn as much as they could about their new lives.

"What do you want to know?" the god-half asked.

A deceptively simple question.

Julee started talking, words tumbling over each other. "Why does it seem the servants sometimes listen and sometimes do not? How do we know if the GODs' gift has created a young godling? What will our daily schedule be like?" She glanced down at herself. "And... how do we get proper clothing? What we wore to ascend cannot possibly be appropriate for daily wear?" At last she took a breath.

Everyone around the table stared at her, even the servants standing in the far corners of the room. Staphan realized his mouth was gaping and he snapped it shut.

Julee's face went a remarkable shade of crimson and she pressed a hand to her lips, seemingly mortified.

Both elder GODs laughed at once. The goddess-half wiped her eyes, her breathing hitching. "An excellent list. Now, why don't you accompany me, so I can explain it all?"

Julee shot a nervous look at the door to the tunnels, then smoothed down the robe.

"Not at all. I meant to the terminal."

* * * *

Julee's head spun at the simplicity of the entire system. "So the servants never respond until we have both stated agreement?" she asked for clarification.

David, Staphan's father, nodded. "If both of you are awake and present. There can never be dissent between you, just as conflicts are never allowed in the code we write."

"I suppose that makes sense," Staphan conceded. He clicked another matched set of outfits they could choose to have added to their wardrobes.

They'd soon learned that the only reason they'd been given nothing but robes was that the GODs chose their own styles of clothing from a long set of matched pairs. Whatever they wore, they would be matched. Always.

Julee cocked her head to one side, considering it. They'd already chosen comfortable pants and tunics for work time and lounging, and they'd chosen holiday wear. So far, nothing had caught their eyes for sleepwear, and Julee secretly hoped Staphan wanted to remain nude for sleep, as she did. At the moment, they were looking at simple dresses for Julee and tailored pants and shirts for Staphan. Evelyn, Staphan's mother, had explained that GODs did not wear lounging wear outside their quarters, save in an emergency.

"Julee?" Staphan prompted her.

She focused on the long dress with fasteners down the offset break in the fabric. The sleeves came to a point at the wrist, and the waist was high and beneath the breasts. "I'm not sure I like it."

"I was thinking of the times when you visit with your blessed parents," he added.

"Perhaps. Let us see if they have something similar but with shorter sleeves?"

"Oh, they do," Evelyn offered. "Two or three screens farther down, I believe."

Julee and Staphan left the outfit they were considering, then rushed through, rejecting one outfit after another. Whether they accepted the outfits or rejected them, it was required to be a unified decision. At last, the promised outfits appeared. Nearly in unison, she and Staphan accepted them.

There were only a dozen more after it and they accepted one more set. In the end, they accepted the one they'd left for further consideration. As Staphan said, it was possible they might want something with long sleeves another time.

"Good," David complimented them. "You will have clothing to wear within a few hours. Before dinner, at the latest."

"So soon?" Julee could hardly contemplate it.

Evelyn laid a hand on her shoulder. "It is all computerized, of course. The patterns to make the clothing, your individual measurements, and the colors you will wear are all stored in the banks. When you make choices of clothing styles, the computer arranges the machinery to create what you have chosen, and the servants deliver it shortly afterward."

Amazing. Though she'd been coding all her life, Julee was in awe of such a streamlined system.

"And now, young lady, you had questions about young ones."

Julee's mouth went dry, and she nodded. Not knowing was intolerable.

Evelyn stroked her fingertips over the jewels on her face, drawing Julee's eyes to them. "Do you remember the jewels being embedded in your skin?"

Julee considered that. "Not really. I remember the healers giving me meds. After that, much of what they did was a blur. My aches and pains disappeared. The jewels were there. I was being prepared for the ceremony."

Staphan touched the jewels on the insides of his wrists, his brow furrowed. Julee guessed that he had no more memory of them than she did.

"The jewels allow the healers to directly monitor all your life signs. They can tell when you are ill, when you need to drink more water, when you need more sleep—and they can tell when you conceive—when you create a young one."

"I want them to tell us," Julee demanded. "Immediately."

"As do I." Staphan's voice overlapped with hers.

David chucked, and his goddess-half smiled. She spoke first.

"Everyone—even your servants—will know, as soon as the sensors confirm that you are bearing a young one."

"Bear?" Julee choked. What did they mean...bear?

Evelyn took her hand with a sigh. "There are medical files you can read on the subject, but the goddess-half carries the young one within her abdomen until it is ready to emerge into the bulwark."

It was atrocious. *It sounds like a parasite.* At the same time, it was intriguing.

"Why should the servants know?" Staphan asked. "It sounds like a very personal thing."

"Indeed it is," his father decreed. "But the servants are charged with your care and safety. For that reason, the jewels will change color to blue when Julee is bearing, and her clothing will change to match it. It is a warning to all that her life is to come before all else."

Julee examined the jewels on Evelyn's face and David's wrists. "The jewels change color. Blue for bearing. What do red, gold, and clear mean?"

Evelyn shook her head. "I forgot how inquisitive young GODs are. Red means you are a young goddess-half of childbearing age but not bearing at the moment. Green means you are newly delivered of the young one and not yet ready to bear another. Gold means a young god-half with a goddess-half of childbearing age. Clear means the pair is beyond childbearing."

"And in an emergency?" Staphan pressed.

David straightened. "Blue and green first—young godlings with their mothers. Red and gold next. Clear after that. Then servants."

Julee glanced toward the assembled servants. They didn't seem troubled by this arrangement; she wondered why that was.

Staphan pushed a hand through his hair. "What does the old saying mean? The circle closes quickly when one is at the edge."

His parents shared a knowing look.

At last, Evelyn stood. "This is always difficult for young GODs to learn. I was afraid to look out the windows of our quarters for days after learning it."

Julee's heart pounded at the warning.

The older goddess-half turned and headed toward the floor-to ceiling windows, David in her wake. "Come. It is time you learned why the GODs are so important to Bulwark Ten."

Julee hesitated, unsure she wanted to know after such a dire warning. Staphan pushed to his feet and offered her his hand. She took it, certain that they could face anything together.

At the windows, Evelyn paused. "Hologram off," she ordered.

The sky and plants outside the window disappeared. In their place was metal, as far as the eye could see, huge pipes as large around as the largest classrooms, circular pods at the intersections, and a slight downward curve of metal at the far end.

Julee looked up, noting that the metal arch passed just above the ceiling of the room they were in. She looked down and gasped. Below them was the sky.

"Where are we that we are above the sky?" she breathed.

Evelyn took her time answering. "The sky is another hologram, one we never turn off."

"Why is it below us?" Staphan pressed.

"Because it is not intended for us. Not for the GODs and those born on high. Not for the servants of the Temple of Sacred Technology. Not for those who truly know what Bulwark Ten is."

Julee felt faint. "What *is* Bulwark Ten?"

"The last of humanity."

David wrapped an arm around his goddess-half and Staphan did the same for Julee. For a moment, all was still and silent.

David broke the spell and started to spin the tale. "The Great Book says humans walk the surface of the Earth, but that hasn't been true since they first stepped foot on Bulwark Ten."

"We aren't on Earth?" Staphan broke in.

"No. The Earth is half the solar system away and burned to a crisp. The plan was to salvage what we could of humanity—up to a billion people each on twelve immense ships. But humans are unnaturally attached to the planet that spawned us."

"They refused to leave," Julee guessed.

David nodded solemnly. "They were told the bulwarks would rest on the surface of the world, but the scientists of the time knew that was impossible. Stealth engines were designed to take them into orbit and beyond without the inhabitants' knowledge. One bulwark refused their orders and tried to tough it out on Earth. They were gone within the year."

"And the others?" Staphan asked.

"The others." The words were little more than a wistful exhalation of air from Evelyn's lips.

David sighed. "Systems grow in scope. They become more complex over time, as populations flex and the needs change."

"Of course they do," Staphan agreed.

"It is one of the most basic teachings of the Great Book," Julee added.

There was a moment of potent stillness between the assembled GODs.

"We are the governance," Julee recalled the earlier pronouncement. The rest fell into place with excruciating slowness. Words tumbled from her numb lips. "Their code was faulty. They died—humans and GODs alike. We protect the last of humanity."

"We *are* the last of humanity," David corrected her.

"I don't understand," Staphan informed him.

A chill caused Julee to shudder hard. Realization made her sick in disbelief. "There are no GODs," she breathed. "Caecee was correct."

Her knees felt weak. Staphan's arms tightened around her, holding her close. Evelyn rushed to her side and helped to steady her on her feet.

The elder goddess-half's words warmed Julee's chilled cheek. "You must understand your importance. They were dying. Starving. Suffering from improperly shielded radiation. Bulwarks started attacking others for supplies or in the hopes of refuge. Our captain..." She swallowed hard. "The captain of that dark time shot the last attacking ship from the skies."

David took over the tale, his voice solemn. "We were the last, because we had one thing none of the others possessed."

"An intact code," Staphan guessed.

His blessed father smiled a grim little smile. "Yes. And enough gifted programmers—that is the olden term for what we do—to maintain the code and train others to do the same."

His goddess-half hurried on. "It was the only hope the captain had to give the people below. You see... Hope became religion—a sacred pact for the good of all. Technology is sacred, and those who govern the sacred technologies are GODs among men. Our kind alone brought prosperity where lesser men and women had brought death to our brethren."

Julee took a calming breath. "But being descended from GODs alone wasn't enough." Hadn't Mother said that?

David shook his head. "Genetics are a tricky thing."

"Genetics?" Staphan asked.

"The...materials a young one is built from, half from each parent," Evelyn explained. "Every child is tested, high and low. Every child who shows promise is given up to training. It is part of the sacred pact that allows Bulwark Ten to thrive."

"For the good of all," Staphan croaked.

"For the good of all," his blessed parents echoed him.

"But there are no GODs," Julee pressed. She wasn't entirely certain whether she wanted to be told there were or were not GODs. Were any of them special at all or just as human as the humans below?

Evelyn hesitated. "One in ten thousand young test worthy to train for the position you and Staphan have accepted. Of the more than one hundred in your year, only the two of you have ascended. The other Demi-

GOD pair may or may not ascend, depending on the needs of the year. Does that not mark you as something more than others?"

"In some manner, I suppose," she conceded.

Julee stared at the window. The sight of the sky below them made her dizzy, and she motioned to the glass. "Hologram on." It was the most logical command, considering how Evelyn had turned it off.

The illusion of the sky and vegetation returned, and Julee's breathing eased.

David sighed. "Some GOD-pairs never choose to turn it off again."

"I suspect we will," Staphan decreed.

Julee met his eyes and nodded in agreement. "Once we come to terms with all of this." She took a calming breath, her balance a little more sure. "There is so much to learn."

His smile was a little brittle. "And only three days to learn it all."

Evelyn held her hands in a tight ball, her knuckles pale in contrast to her pinked skin. "Would you like time alone or do you feel equal to continuing?"

"Continue." The answer came in unison.

David offered a slight bow. "As you wish."

Epilogue

GOD-Node 60 stood at their window, looking out over the ship full of humans who depended on them to keep the systems running and all within in good health. The god-half's hand stroked over the goddess-half's gravid womb—and they were content.

Below, there was talk of celebrations. The young godling the goddess-half carried would soon emerge into the world. Early testing showed great promise in the young female. The news had spread like wildfire though the human population. As such, a celebration was in order, and no GOD worth his or her title would begrudge the human populace a reason to be merry.

Knowing the young godling showed promise wasn't a sad thing for the GOD-Node either. They would still raise their young godling to the age of two, visit disguised as servants for her entire life, and eventually welcome her home to their realm, as a favored companion if she proved unequal to the task of being a GOD herself—and as a GOD should she be worthy of it.

But those were concerns for another time. For now, the code had been tamed for the day. All were safe and secure in their bulwark. Their bed and the GODs' gift awaited them.

And it was good.

About the Author

Brenna Lyons wears many hats, sometimes all on the same day: former president of EPIC, author of more than 100 published works, owner of Fireborn Publishing, columnist, special needs teacher, wife, mother...and member in good standing of more than 60 writing advocacy groups.

In her first ten years published in novel-length, she's won 3 EPIC e-Book Awards (out of 15 finalists) and finaled for 3 PEARLS (including one Honorable Mention, second to NY Times Bestseller Angela Knight), 2 CAPAS, and a Dream Realm Award. She's also taken Spinetingler's Book of the Year for 2007.

Brenna writes in 26 established worlds plus stand-alones, poetry, articles and essays. She's a bestseller in indie/e fantasy and horror, straight genre and cross-genres thereof. Brenna has been termed "one of the most deviant erotic minds in the publishing world...not for the weak." (Rachelle for Fallen Angels Reviews) Milieu-heavy dark work is practically Brenna's calling card, with or without the erotic content.

She teaches classes in everything from POV studies to advanced editing, networking to marketing. Brenna enjoys hearing from people who read her work and can be reached by e-mail.

Website: http://www.brennalyons.com/

Facebook: http://www.facebook.com/brenna.lyons

Email: brennalyons4168@live.com

Also by this Author

Available from *Fireborn Publishing*

KEIF'S DEN AND PACK
Keif's Pack
Mother of the Keif
Keif's Den (Coming Soon)

PROPHECY
Prophecy: Revelations
Prophecy: Rapture
The Prophet's Mate
Prophecy: Rampage - Meet Gavin
Prophecy: Rampage (Coming Soon)

THE FANTASY CLUB
The Consort

Beyond the Veil
Fairy Wishes (Coming Soon)
Mine for the Night
Once in a Blue Moon
Overtime Pay
Stay With Me
The Fire God's Woman
The Punishment of Phoebus Apollo
Werewolf U

Available from *Phaze Books*

ANGEL-WING SAGA
Sons of Heaven: Beldon
Daughters of Man: Prize Match
Sons of Heaven: Unexpected Mates
Daughters of Man: Claiming a Princess

BRIDE BALL
Bride Ball
Poison, Lies, and No-Win Choices

COLOR OF LOVE
The Color of Love

FIRE AND ICE
Magmon's Hunger
Magmon's Lover

INSTINCT SERIES
Animal Instincts

KEGIN SERIES
Conquest
The Last of Fion's Daughters
Last Chance for Love
Rites of Mating
In Her Ladyship's Service
Matchmaker's Misery

KIELAN SERIES
The Lady's Lowborn Lover
Time Currents
Cubed

NIGHT WARRIORS
Night Warriors
Will of the Stone
Bearing Armen
Hunter's Moon
Maher Men
Choosing a Mate/Starting a War
Raised to Be His Own
Veriel's Tales I: Crossbearer Turned
Veriel's Tales II: Losing Regana
Blutjagdfrau Lost
The Warrior's Man
Damsel in Distress

STAR MAGES
The Master's Lover

XXAN WAR
Daahan Rising
Crossbred Son
Raashh Decisions

Enslaved
All I Want for Christmas is You
Fates Magic
All's Fair...
Black Sail
Mama's Tales
Dream Walk
Unexpected Daddy
Phaze in Verse
We Shall Live Again
May the Best Man Win
Nevermore
Marked
And It Was Good

Available from **Mundania Press**

STAR MAGES
Written in the Stars

Fairy Dreams
Monsters of Myth Anthology

Available from **Under the Moon**

RENEGADES SERIES
TYGERS
Renegade's Run
Max Sec

URBAN GRIMM

Catch Me, If You Can
Three Wishes
Temptation of Eve

With Great Power
Undead in Blue
Evil Overlords Union Issue #1 Anthology
Undead Embrace
"Playing Games" in *Forbidden Love: Bad Boys*
"Marked" in *Forbidden Love: Wicked Women*
"The Master's Lover" in *Forbidden Love: Sacred Bands*

Available from **Logical Lust**

"Mine for the Night" in *The Cougar Book* Anthology

Available from **Coming Together Charity Anthologies**

INSTINCT SERIES
"Foundling" in *Coming Together: Into the Light* Anthology

"Claim Mate" (available separately and as part of the *Coming Together: Against the Odds* Anthology)
"The Fire God's Woman" in *Coming Together: Under Fire* Anthology

Available *self-published*

KEGIN SERIES
Earth-Born Lord
Graham: Training the Earth-Born Lord

NIGHT WARRIORS
Claiming a Lady
Stone Lord
Mother's Son

COLOR OF LOVE
A Safe Heart

Snapshots from a Poet's Life

Award-Winning Books

EPPIE/EPIC eBOOK AWARDS WINNERS
Coming Together: Against the Odds- 2010
Time Currents- 2010
Coming Together: Into the Light- 2011

EPPIE/EPIC eBOOK AWARDS FINALISTS
Fion's Daughter- 2004
Collected Poems: Book One- 2005 (now titled *Snapshots of a Poet's Life*)
Renegade's Run- 2005
Rites of Mating- 2006
All I Want for Christmas- 2006
Phaze in Verse- 2008
"The Fire God's Woman" in Coming Together: Under Fire- 2009
Three Wishes- 2010
Matchmaker's Misery- 2010
The Cougar Book- 2011
The Master's Lover- 2011
Bride Ball- 2011

DREAM REALM AWARDS FINALIST
Last Chance for Love- 2003

PEARL HONORABLE MENTION
Night Warriors- 2004

PEARL FINALISTS
Schente Night- 2003 (now included in *The Last of Fion's Daughters*)
König Cursebreakers- 2004 (now titled *Will of the Stone*)

JOYFULLY REVIEWED BEST BOOKS OF 2010
Written in the Stars- 2010

SPINETINGLER'S BOOK OF THE YEAR 2007

NOBODY: An Anthology of Dark Fiction- 2007 (Brenna's pieces of the anthology can be found in *Beyond the Veil*)

TRS's CAPA FINALISTS
Ultimate Warriors- 2004 (Brenna's portion is now available as *With Great Power*)
Written in the Stars

LOVE ROMANCE AND MORE CAFÉ BOOK OF THE YEAR RUNNER UP
Last Chance for Love- 2008

ROAD TO ROMANCE REVIEWERS' CHOICE AWARD
Prophecy: Revelations- 2004

LOVE ROMANCES REVIEWERS' CHOICE AWARD
Black Sail- 2003

ROMANCE JUNKIES BOOK CLUB STAFF PICK
TYGERS- 2003

FALLEN ANGELS ROMANCE RECOMMENDED READ
Devon's Price-2005 (now available in *Bearing Armen*)

JOYFULLY RECOMMENDED READ
Fairy Dreams- 2008
The Last of Fion's Daughters- 2009

TREBLE HEART FINALIST
Prophecy: Revelations- 2003

www.ingramcontent.com/pod-product-compliance
Lightning Source LLC
Chambersburg PA
CBHW021212260626
47172CB00002B/384